OF THORNS AND SHADOWS

C. F. ABBOTT

First published by Kindle Direct Publishing 2024

Copyright © 2024 by C.F. Abbott

All rights reserved. No part of this publication may be reproduced, stored or transmitted in any form or by any means, electronic, mechanical, photocopying, recording, scanning, or otherwise without written permission from the publisher. It is illegal to copy this book, post it to a website, or distribute it by any other means without permission.

This novel is entirely a work of fiction. The names, characters and incidents portrayed in it are the work of the author's imagination. Any resemblance to actual persons, living or dead, events or localities is entirely coincidental. C.F. Abbott asserts the moral right to be identified as the author of this work.

First edition
Cover art by Moonpress Design

Editing by Willow Oak Author Services

Advisor: Blurbs and Baubles.

THE OF THORNS AND SHADOWS PLAYLIST

https://open.spotify.com/playlist/7Edzscto31z8BNrILJJdbq?si=ZxUncqqpRnaYljR-3zpgIg&pi=u-85GTgkfeTm6q

To my husband, Kaiser. Without your constant persistence and unconditional love, this book would not be here today. Thank you for everything that you do!

Forever and Always,
Your Ginger

And maybe I loved you in another life and I promised you that I would find you, somewhere on the other side. Or maybe you've always been in my subconscious. nudging me this way and pulling me that way until I found you. I don't know. But I do know I've felt you more than one life should allow.

JM Storm

CHAPTER 1
A DREAM OF SNOW

"Please don't go," he begged, his warm fingers curling around my wrist, his lips sweeping pleading, heartfelt kisses down my neck.

"I'll be back," I promised, stepping forward, an inch closer toward the unknown.

I tried to sound strong…to sound certain and unafraid, but I could hear the cracks in my own voice. I was on the brink of tears.

Gently, he pulled me back against his torso, and I relaxed my rigid spine, savoring his warmth…these last few fleeting seconds before condemning myself to the blustering cold.

I pinched my eyes shut and inhaled sharply, fighting back the lump in my throat and the need to ignore my responsibilities. I didn't want to go.

I didn't ever want to leave his embrace. I knew, though, if I didn't go now, I never would, and she would never relent. She'd just keep raging until there was nothing left but dreary grayness. No sunshine. No flowers. Just cold, soulless ice.

Thousands more would perish because of me, defenseless against the elements, and I would only grow sicker. I shivered at the direction of my thoughts and forced myself onward, urging myself not to stop or look back. I knew if I did, if I saw him, I wouldn't have the strength to go on.

As I left the cavern, the wind slashed at my face, frigid and vicious. It found its way underneath my clothes, blowing back the hood of my cloak and dampening my hair with flecks of sleet. I trudged ahead up snowy hilltops and powdery vineyards. I rubbed at my arms as I waded deeper into the snow, struggling to keep consciousness. I could feel myself growing weaker, my heart slowing down to a faint, barely noticeable beat. I was getting worse by the minute.

I was so cold, so unbelievably freezing! It felt like my blood had turned to frozen slush, every inch of my body stinging with sharp, prickling pains.

I stopped ambling through the blizzard, terrified that if I tried to move any further, my very bones might shatter into a million different pieces. I cried out in pain, teeth chattering, when two loving hands caressed my face.

"Perrie?"

I twirled around, hoping to see him, but found myself face-to-face with nothing. Nobody was there, just a howling wall of icy white.

I cried out again, the warm tears rolling down my cheeks and icing immediately into crystals, when the voice returned, but much louder.

"Perrie!"

I gasped and sprung up in my bed, my heart hammering and my green eyes wide with shock. It was just another dream… *he* was just a dream. I wasn't about to freeze to death. No; in fact, my pajamas were sticky with sweat. I looked up and noticed the familiar shape of my mom. She was standing at the foot of my bed, car keys in hand. A troubled look flitted across her similar features as she stared down at me pityingly.

"You're having twice as many nightmares as usual," Mom asserted, crossing her arms across her chest in a fretful manner.

"I know," I grumbled.

"It's around that time…when *it* happened all those years ago. I'd understand if you don't feel like you're ready to open up shop all by yourself just yet," Mom reasoned, her navy eyes observing me.

I groaned and crashed against my old, squeaky bed, rubbing the sleep from my eyes before kicking my way out of my soft blue sheets.

"I'm fine, Mom," I answered shortly.

I hopped out of bed and walked across my lofty bedroom, padding through the open doorway and toward the tiny half-bathroom that occupied the far end of our hallway. Mom predictably followed behind me, making the lightest of huffs escape the back of my throat.

I knew she'd be like this. Paranoid. Hoverish. A little *too* concerned. It was the same every year, nothing new or strange. Well, at least not to me.

I should've known she'd react this way about me being alone at the Flower Patch while she was away attending the upcoming floral convention. Nevermind that I was twenty-three, and just a couple of months shy of getting my bachelors. She would carry on like this for another five more months, cautiously observing my every move, as if one wrong twist of the ankle might make me dissolve through the floorboards.

I relaxed my irritated posture in front of the sink and dropped my head, trying to find it in me to be more empathetic.

"I promise," I responded in a softer tone.

I hardly had any recollection of what had happened the night I had been abducted. I couldn't say the same for Mom. Nine years later and my disappearance still haunted her. Now and then, I could hear her from across the hall, whimpering my name in her sleep.

The thought of never seeing my mother again, of being somewhere dark and repugnant all alone, terrified me equally as much as it scared her, so understandably I tolerated her hovering and over-protectiveness. I loved her, no matter how difficult she could be.

"You deserve this," I persisted, meeting Mom's gaze in the mirror. "Besides, you'll only be gone for three days. How much trouble could I possibly get into in seventy-two hours?"

Mom smiled at me lightly and bobbed her head in the direction of downstairs as I unscrewed the toothpaste and began to slowly brush my teeth.

"I'm going to make a quick stop at the fish market for fresh fertilizer before I go. You know the drill. Make sure the sprinklers are off, count the money in the till, and don't–"

"Don't leave the house under any circumstances while you're away." I smirked. "Got it."

Mom tossed me a needled smile. "I'm serious," she said, her eyes pools of navy intentness.

I nodded in understanding, and she reluctantly kissed my forehead before strolling out of the bathroom.

I waited to spit until the sound of her footsteps softened, and the lock on the front door let out a reassuring *CLICK*.

Quickly, I wiped my mouth and hurried back into my bedroom. I plopped against my unmade bed and carefully swept my fingers underneath my pillow, searching for something secret.

A triumphant smile tugged at my lips the instant my fingers made contact with the worn jacket of my journal.

CHAPTER 2
THE FLOWER PATCH

To the naked eye, the notebook was nothing special. The cover was faded and splattered with flecks of paint on its black surface. Some of the pages were old, covered in smeared blue ink and water stains, but the composition book was priceless to me. It was my greatest prized possession.

I flipped past the countless pages of jumbled-up handwriting and the numerous sketches of dark eyes and hauntingly perfect landscapes until I was staring down at a new page.

Promptly, I scribbled the word *snow* and then tossed my journal back under the pillow, prodding myself to fall back into my daily routine now that I had added yet another odd word to my collection.

I stood and walked over to my closet, carelessly selecting an outfit without much consideration. I wiggled my way into a pair of frayed jeans, shrugged on a flouncy, white blouse, and awkwardly fastened the strings of my day-to-day, green gardening apron into a limp bow behind my back. I proceeded to braid my wavy red hair into a loose tress, glancing at myself in the mirror only briefly before averting my stare. Customers often compared me to my mother. While there was certainly some validity behind their words, I couldn't help but to notice the glaring differences between the two of us. Where Mom was all spare limbs and sinewy height, I was short and round-faced, my frame more busty and soft. She had skin like a fair, rain-washed rose, and I, while just as pale, was covered in a splattering of freckles from head to toe. Our hair was our one likeness, both mine and hers being a natural shade of ginger—she a radiant strawberry blonde, and I a light copper red. I lacked my mother's confidence, though, and spent far too much time loathing my own reflection.

Once I was as decent as I could manage to make myself look, I picked up my recent library find—an old book on *The Thoughts and Testimony of Reincarnation*—and trotted downstairs and outside toward our more-or-less shed of a flower shop.

***

Originally, The Flower Patch had been an old potting barn used to house the previous landowner's yard equipment. Mom had found the hut less than a mile away from the cottage and immediately took a liking to it. In two months, the termite-ridden barn had been renovated with new shingles and freshly painted paneled wood. It was quaint, affable, and Mom's pride and joy. It brought money to the table, and for the most part, I enjoyed helping around. At eighteen, I had had my heart set on attending Cornell. Like any young girl, the allure of being on my own in the city seemed full of promise. When I showed Mom a pamphlet of the university, with its bustling residence halls and many agricultural programs, she flipped. *The world was a cruel place*, she had said. New York was too far away, and how would she manage the store on her own? No one off the street would be able to help her as well as I could and she would feel so alone. The hurt in her voice twisted my heart, and I chose to abandon all my dreams of venturing out on my own, choosing instead to join an online college so I could always be close to Mom.

I knew business wouldn't be booming. Summer had taken over Saint Simons, bringing with it flocks of tourists and beachgoers. All the formal dances and popular holidays had come to pass, and now the only business we saw came from the grieving, looking to have us cater a funeral with orchids and carnations to adorn their loved one's casket, or the uppity-rich, eager to have us fashion elaborate centerpieces and vibrant bouquets for their over-the-top beach weddings, or posh get-togethers.

As simple as our little shop was, no one else did flowers quite like Demi Adams, and The Flower Patch was renowned for its excellence in rearing gorgeous plants.

With a sigh, I flipped the sign from *closed* to *open* and entered the small, musky-smelling shop, switching on all the lights before taking my seat on the cushioned stool behind the cash register.

Once settled, I began to read. My eyes skimmed the finely printed words, but my mind kept whisking me back to my dream and that bitter, soul-destroying cold.

It had been a harsh winter the year I went missing, the coldest on record, according to Mom. I knew very little of the morning I had been found–only fragments, tiny slivers of memories that decided to resurface here and there.

I recalled being so cold that my father, who never fretted over me, told my mother I might not make it. I remembered as far back as being carried in the arms of somebody warm and then hearing the faint buzz of my parents bickering behind me before hitting that wall of white absence.

"Reincarnation, huh?" a girly voice suddenly chirped in from out of nowhere.

Slightly startled, I jumped and peered up from my book, only to find an exceptionally gorgeous young woman standing in front of the cash register.

CHAPTER 3
AVRIL

At first glance, I couldn't help but eye her in envy. She had a curvaceous frame, with pale skin, and long, voluminous hair, the color of fiery red cinnamon. She was wearing a cornflower blue sundress with pink lace-up wedges, looking as if she had just come in from a catwalk.

Her full, rose-colored lips curled into a breath-taking smile any model in the world would die for once we locked eyes. She smirked, set a bouquet of red roses on the counter, and then removed her vintage sunglasses.

"So, which era do you find yourself leaning towards the most?" She grinned. "Personally, I believe the roaring twenties was made for me. Finger waves, flapper dresses. What a wonderful time to be alive," she continued, patting at her hair.

I smiled bashfully down at the counter.

"I'm not sure." I shrugged, grabbing for the roses. "Maybe the seventies. There's just something irresistible about bell bottoms and polaroids," I said jokingly.

"You know," the girl laughed, "I could see it. You're obviously a flower child. Although, I must admit I don't remember you being into this sort of stuff before. Your mother was never one to let me babysit either, though, so what do I know? We all change as we get older," the girl said in a cheery voice.

I eyed the girl in bewilderment. *Had we met?* She couldn't have been much older than me, in her late teens or early twenties. I combed my mind for any remembrance of forgotten cousins or out-of-touch playmates and came back empty.

The girl's dazzling smile instantly softened and changed into that of a saddened grimace the moment she noticed the doubt shrouding my face. A sudden unexplainable feeling of sadness began to gnaw at me as the girl sighed and reached for my hand.

I looked down reluctantly at her shiny French manicure and finally decided to let her lay her soft hand upon my knuckles.

"You don't remember me, do you?" she asked in a softer voice, her tone laced with sympathy.

"No," I lowly answered, feeling shockingly all the more terrible as soon as the answer flew out my mouth.

She looked like one of those girls I used to fantasize about befriending, the kind of girl who would undoubtedly have been in a sorority, and would have braided my hair and painted my nails over a Cosmopolitan magazine if I had ever known her. She had the same disposition as some of the other girls that migrated into my mother's shop around formals, chattering amongst the others of their kind about the type of dresses they had picked and who was taking them… Talking about things I had missed out on.

She had one of those faces, too—a starry-eyed, princess-like look. A face too distinguishably lovely to ever do anything more than smile. Perhaps that was why her lovely frown had such an effect on me.

"I'm Perrie," I said quickly, gathering her roses and ringing them up. "I'm sorry, but I think you have me confused with someone else," I continued, hoping the friendly girl wouldn't storm off, or, worse yet, develop an attitude.

The girl laughed musically and opened a pink billfold, taking out several bills.

"No, I know exactly who you are. I'm Avril, your older half-sister." The girl smiled, her tone as warm and jubilant as a sunbeam.

I looked up again in bafflement, wondering if she had heard me correct her, and then found my brows furrowing in surprise at the severe expression on her face. She was serious. Or, at least believed herself to be correct.

She giggled then, a shifting look of amusement splashing across her features as she read my face. Usually, the look of belittlement coming from such a bubblegum beauty would offend me, but for some reason, I stood frozen in place, watching the woman adjust her many bracelets.

Did she really *know me? Could it all be true, or was it just a vicious prank?*

Everybody on the island knew about my mother. She was the odd, reclusive, batty woman who liked to play around with flowers. They knew about me too, the friendless shut-in who rarely left her mother's side, both of us the chiseled definition of hermits.

Maybe she had been dared to come here. A cynical part of me imagined. Or, maybe she had been bribed by any of the miserable old crones in town, angry we never made it to any of their tedious barbecues or local jamborees.

"Demi isn't the only woman to be beguiled by our father. There have been countless others susceptible to his charms. You and I are but a few of his eldest children," Avril clarified, her friendly tone never wavering, her ocean-blue eyes overseeing my every move. She could obviously sense my uncertainty.

"Well, sorta. My mom sent me away to live with him while I was still just a kid," Avril softly explained. "She wasn't ever really the motherly type, and luckily for me, he took me in and gave me a place to stay."

I smiled lightly and counted her money back to her aloud before handing her the roses and her change.

Mom hadn't said much about my father over the years. I had given up asking about him ages ago. What little information I could extract, she made sure to keep it short. However, she did mention that my father was insufferably rich and that he had, at some point, married my mom's sister. Together the two shared an entirely different family apart from us, making the girl's story believable.

"You're from the other family, then?" I replied.

Avril looked at me puzzled and then sashayed over to a display of potted daffodils. She sniffed the yellow flowers daintily and then shook her head.

"The other family?" She chuckled. "No, we are one big family with a few problems here and there and evidently *a lot* of unspoken misunderstandings. You and your mother are a part of the family. Demi just took off after we found you. Daddy could've made things easier, but he doesn't always think things through. It doesn't mean we don't care about you or your mother," Avril corrected.

Intrigued to hear more, I abandoned my place behind the register. Nervously, I wandered around the counter and leaned against its refurbished front, watching the girl observe all the plants and greenery in the shop from a safe distance.

If what she said was true, I had believed that the other family–my father–hated me, hated my mom. I had been told nobody but my mother had truly searched for me, that only she cared.

No. A voice in the back of my head interjected, making all my hopeful thoughts of a caring, happy family slam to a screeching halt. *Fathers spoil their daughters. Fathers brag about their daughters. Fathers congratulate their daughters.* My thoughts drifted back to my early graduation and the ample stack of acceptance letters I had received from various colleges. *Not even so much as an email from him.*

"Then why are you the only one here? Where's our father? And don't even try to tell me that Aunt Hertha doesn't hate my mother or me," I fired back.

Avril smirked down at the display table and scrutinized a speck before brushing it off and perching herself on the edge of it. She met my serious gaze and smiled even wider, swinging her legs and stretching her arms as a mermaid might while sunning upon a rock.

"All right, *all right*. Daddy would not make the ballot for the father of the year. As I said, we aren't his only children, and the man leads a hectic life. Let's just say he's up to his neck in child support charges and... business papers. He's too busy to remember what age we all are. I know, even with his messy love life, he loves us all in his own way," Avril said with both of her hands up as if she were surrendering.

I laughed dryly at her remark and then sighed, drifting off into thoughts of my father and wondering if it were true. *Did he love me?*

Suddenly I felt ashamed. I couldn't even clearly remember what color his hair was. *Did we share the same eye color? Did a tear come to his eye when I was born? Did he have any pictures of me riding a bike or blowing out candles on a birthday cake, sitting on his desk or stashed away in his wallet?*

"What about Aunt–"

"Hertha is, well, just a spoiled bitch. She hates *everyone*! Imagine how you'd feel, though, if you were not only married to a notorious cheater but a cheater willing to fool around with your sister," Avril answered.

A dead silence occupied the room after Avril's unreserved response. The only noise to be heard was the sound of birds chirping outside and the few tiny fountains my mother kept inside the shop gurgling peacefully.

CHAPTER 4
LOVE IS LIKE A FLOWER

A barreling sense of shock jolted through me, rendering me speechless. It felt as if someone had just snatched a rug out from underneath my feet. *No. It couldn't be true.* That would mean my mom was a liar, that she had been portraying herself to me as the clueless victim when she had been the other woman this entire time. I couldn't accept that possibility. I wouldn't. My mother was a lot of things–straight-laced and self-standing, pedant and strong-willed–but never dishonest. I had always trusted her wholeheartedly and without question, but now...now, I couldn't shake the feeling that something was off and that I needed to hear more.

I looked up at Avril, the much prettier girl who did know our father well enough to call him daddy, and found myself desperately searching her face for lies, for any backbiting tic that might poke holes in her story.

The only thing I knew to be true was that both my mother and our father had claimed me. Despite his shady reputation, Avril had only him and our other siblings. He couldn't be quite the self-centered monster Mom made him out to be if he had stepped up to raise an unwanted child.

"You see, Perrie, love is a lot like a flower. It can grow to be a beautiful thing if cared for properly. Although, if planted in the wrong soil or disrupted, it can also grow into something unsightly. Love has made Hertha bitter and Demi deceptive." As Avril spoke, her voice trailed off into a tone of pity, her fingers gracefully brushing across the delicate golden petals of the daffodil. "A heart can only take so much ill treatment before it becomes something dark, something impenetrable. Sure, Hertha can be a bit vindictive, but she wasn't always that way."

A pang of something like guilt struck through me for the aunt I had never truly got the chance to meet. If what Avril was saying was true, I could only imagine how different our lives could have been had my mother never fallen victim to my father's charms. Visions of Mom laughing with another woman around her age filled my mind, as well as the thought of me enjoying Avril's company far earlier in life. Would I have had close friendships with each of my cousins in that other reality? Would Mom have ever settled down and found a husband of her own, someone I could count on being there for me as a true father should be?

"I never knew… My mom has always said that my dad had kept his marriage to Hertha secret," I mumbled.

Avril tossed me a condoling look and shook her head, a sad smile upturning her rosy lips.

"There are a lot of things you don't know, Perrie. Things you used to, things that I could help you remember if you'd let me," Avril prompted.

Flickers of every dream since my kidnapping flashed through my head. Curiosity danced along with each image, each imaginary image, or at least what I had been *told* was imaginary. Visions of him, his voice, his touch, his smell seemed to spring to life. The icy sensation of snow and the smooth feel of silk grazed my skin. A strong feeling of fright and then passion settled inside me, rattling me in a way I could never explain, in a way Avril seemed to understand.

I wanted answers. I wanted to know why these feelings dwelled inside, why nothing could detach me from these fantasies or bring me any contentment. I opened my lips in hesitated response when there was a sudden loud *THUMP* at the door.

I twirled around in surprise to find my mother with a bag of fertilizer at her feet. Her lips were a thin line, and her eyes were sharp navy seas of rage. Avril, however, remained perched upon the table, examining her shiny nails with a lovely smile on her face.

CHAPTER 5
LONG TIME, NO SEE

"Avril," my mother spat, rolling my sister's name off her tongue as if it were something bitter.

"Demi! Long-time, no see," Avril sang, jumping off the table and walking over toward my mother.

Mom's eyes darted over to me and then back to Avril. Angrily, she pushed back a springy curl and placed both of her hands on her hips. If looks could kill, Avril would've, without a doubt, been six feet under.

"How'd you find us?" Mom demanded through clenched teeth.

Avril looked my mother innocently over from head to toe and grinned at her with a strictly unapologetic look. "Did you honestly think you were the only one who could throw a tantrum, Demi?"

A look of brief, stomach-turning fear streaked across my mother's typically placid face. The expression faded quickly, and she chuckled dryly and made her way over beside me. She intertwined our fingers and glared daggers at Avril.

"*He* will not have her. He is bound to his duties, and *she* is out of his reach. That romance was born to die," Mom growled, her tone as rough as gravel.

Avril snorted and then threw her head back dramatically into a burst of tuneful laughter. My mother's nose flared with rage, and her eyes narrowed, her grip on my wrist growing painfully tight.

Avril did not stop laughing until, unexpectedly, all the sunlight spilling in through the windows vanished, and a clap of thunder shook the tiny shop.

Mom gasped at the sound, her face once again blanching at the sudden eerie appearance of storm clouds. I jumped alongside her, an irrational sense of panic rising within me. *What was going on? Why did I feel as if we were all suddenly being watched?*

"*That romance*, Demi, was not and will never be yours to control. You went against your agreement, and *he* is not too happy about that," Avril daintily stated.

"I didn't expect him to be. Zane has been aware for years. Why intervene now?" Mom nervously chuckled.

"*He* has decided his responsibilities mean nothing to him without what was promised to him. He will resign from them for good if he cannot have her. He is trying to convince the others to let him fade, Demi. Daddy can't have that," Avril flatly answered.

"No!" Mom murmured, her lip trembling. "No! I won't let him! I will take her… We will move somewhere not even Holland will be able to find us, much less the likes of *you*!" she snarled.

Avril grinned and bobbed her head yet again toward me.

"Move wherever you wish, Demi. Withhold everything she has a right to know. She will remember in time. She's starting to remember now. That is why I, above all, will always be able to find her. She remembers him!" Avril cleverly replied.

Mom shook her head, anger tinging her cheeks.

"You don't know what you're talking about," Mom scoffed. "Get out of my shop." She fumed, tearing herself away from me to march toward the front of the shop.

Furiously, she swung open the door, sending the little welcome bell atop our door into a chaotic fit of jingling.

"*Now!* I want you off of my property. Don't you or any of the others ever come back here again. If what you say is true, Zane can come here and tell us himself. Until then, stay away from my daughter," Mom demanded, motioning for Avril to leave.

Avril looked at my mother sharply, an expression of disbelief settling on her face. "Okay," she conceded, smoothing the fabric of her sundress. "But don't say I didn't warn you."

Then with a sigh she put her vintage sunglasses back on and twirled around, gathering her bouquet of roses and her pink billfold off the display table of daffodils, ignoring every evil glance my mother threw at her.

She smiled at me like any older sister, I supposed, would and flounced over toward the door, auburn curls bouncing and her wedge sandals clacking sassily on the concrete floor.

"Perrie, darling, keep in touch," she boldly said, blowing me a kiss farewell and then walking out just as stunningly gorgeous as she had walked in.

CHAPTER 6
CONFLICTION

W*ait! Avril, come back! I want to know,* I mentally screamed, but stayed silent. It was too late. The door had shut ages ago. I gulped, feeling my heart sink and my head start to throb with deeply baffling thoughts of confliction.

Everything Avril had just said, everything my own mother had suddenly confessed, had been such a complete rush. It was disorienting. None of it made any sense.

I bit my lip nervously and peeked up at my mom. She was pacing the shop, red-eyed and sniffling. I had seen her mad. I had seen her worked up. Never anything like this, though… This was something different entirely. She was infuriated, yet at the same time, frightened.

"Mom…" I softly murmured.

"Can you believe the way she waltzed in here? Saying you remembered him!" Mom screeched.

"Mom…" I continued in a softer voice, hoping she'd stop patrolling and acknowledge me.

"You don't remember him! He won't get us, sweetheart. He will never get you again!" Mom frantically promised.

"Mom," I tried again.

"I should have suspected something like this. I should have known you wouldn't be safe if I left town for a few days. It was a misstep on my part, but perhaps there is a silver lining to this mistake. Maybe it's not too late. My stuff is already partially packed. We could load up our things tonight, get on a plane, and be gone by sunrise," she muttered, more to herself than to me.

"Load up our things?!" I repeated, the confusion within me swiftly shifting into something darker, into panicked concern. "Mom, what are you talking about? What about the Flower Patch... Summer semester... We can't just leave."

Something in my voice must have rattled her from her frenzied state because she stopped pacing and instead took a few deep, anxious breaths, steadying herself.

Her entire frame was still trembling slightly as she walked behind the counter, ignoring my looks of worriment. She pretended to be concerned with the register, her fingers reaching out to grab receipts from our already organized receipt holder. Her arm brushed across the cover of my book, and I instantly felt my heart leap to my throat. *Oh no!*

Slowly, she shifted her attention away from the register. She stuck the stack of receipts she had grabbed back down on the spike and then glanced down at the book, picking it up while wiping away her tears.

"What... Perrie, what is this?!"

"Mom, why didn't you tell me the truth?" I questioned, my voice rising.

She glared up at me and pushed back a lock of her strawberry-blonde hair.

"Why are you reading this nonsense? You know how I hate these types of books!" she barked, throwing the paperback.

I watched it skid across the floor and then looked back up at her with what I knew was a look of fiery resentment. I curled my hands into fists and gulped back the golf ball-sized lump in my throat, hoping I wouldn't burst into tears right in front of her.

"What was she talking about, Mom? I know you know. Why is our father involved? Who is this *he*, my kidnapper... Who was he?" I asked, this time louder, my tone insistent.

I couldn't ignore Avril's words. I couldn't carry on pretending to be normal or hoping that with enough time these dreams would fade. It felt like something within me had shifted, like Avril had awoken a dormant volcano, and now my life was as helpless as the city of Pompeii.

If I didn't make some form of noise, I could hear a voice calling to me, beckoning, a voice more familiar than the sound of my own heart beating inside my chest. *His voice.* I knew his voice, but I didn't know who he was! I knew why I was reading that book. So did Avril, and now so did Mom. Something extraordinary was missing in my life, and I intended to find out what.

"You were having an affair, weren't you?" I lowly asked. "Weren't you?!" I demanded again when she didn't respond."You knew about your sister. Y-You lied to me!" I stuttered, the feelings of betrayal evident in my every word.

Mom rolled her eyes and huffed, crossing her arms in an almost adolescent manner.

"Your kidnapper was a close friend of your father's. He was his eldest friend, much like a brother to him, to the both of us. Yes, I did Hertha wrong. I never meant to hurt her. I had a moment of weakness. It was never my intention to stay with your father for as long as I did. You are the only good thing to come from that...indiscretion."

She sighed and pinched the bridge of her nose in frustration before meeting my wounded gaze. "We broke up before you were even born. We agreed to raise you mutually. Your father vowed to take care of you, to always provide for you, and to never undermine my right as your mother, and then he went back on his promise. He let him steal you!" She roared, raking her fingers angrily through her hair."Explain this book, Perrie!" she suddenly demanded, attempting to change the subject.

I shook my head at her, feeling the tears coming to my eyes, and started for the exit.

I snatched open the door and looked back at my mother, who seemed slightly unhinged. Her blue eyes were red from tears, yet her entire posture was stiff with rage.

"I don't know!" I shouted back, slamming the shop door behind me, and bursting into tears as soon as I was outside.

CHAPTER 7
RENDEZVOUS

By the time I had made it back into my room, the urge to continuously cry had ceased. Instead, I wandered over toward my bed and pulled out my journal. I studied over each page in question, flipping past beautifully sketched pastel flowers, to the penciled-in eyes of the man who haunted my dreams. I turned to the next page and then nearly threw the book.

The charcoal sketch of a once unfamiliar woman laying upon a cabriole sofa was now recognizable as none other than Avril. Below my drawing was a line of ten numbers, and under that in pen the words *Call me!* My heart galloped, and I slammed the cover shut, instantly pushing the notebook under my pillow and falling back on my bed. *I could get the answers!*

Somehow, Avril had insanely snuck into my house and given me her number. If Mother found it, she'd... *No, she'd never find it!* I had to keep it hidden. Guilt picked at me slightly at the idea, but I shoved it back. If she could hide years of my life from me, hide information about my father, then I could keep this from her. My body instantly turned rigid as soon as I heard Mom enter the house. I watched my door, waiting for her to enter and then jumped in shock when I heard her own door slam shut from across the hallway. I relaxed against my headboard and closed my eyes, trying my best to memorize Avril's number. I would call her as soon as I knew my mother was asleep.

***

For several hours I shifted against my pillows, an unread copy of Charlotte Bronte's *Villette* precariously balanced across my knees as I waited, listening to the sounds of the house settling and the chirring of crickets outside my bedroom window. I watched the red digits on my alarm clock, feeling my eyes growing heavier with each hour that slowly dragged by.

Determined to stay awake, I reached for my laptop, allowing my thoughts to flicker back to that dream. I dissected every possible meaning behind it, Googling the significance behind snow, ice, fire, silk, and pomegranates. Once I realized none of what I learned could help me any further, I closed my laptop and started to dance around that void of absence in my mind.

What had happened the morning I had been found? Who had been that warm body, the person who had returned me to my mother? Had it been a first responder or a total stranger? Memories of waking up in a hospital weren't even all that clear. The only thing I was sure of was that my mom had always been there. It had always been just the two of us. She had made it that way intentionally. Why, I couldn't quite figure out.

***

Finally, around two in the morning, I snuck into the living room and picked up the landline, cursing each of the squeaking floorboards, praying they wouldn't wake my mom. I dialed Avril's number and chewed on my thumbnail, nervously listening to the phone ring.

What was I going to say? I had never really had much use for our telephone, and with no friends to call or family to check in with, I rarely found myself picking up the old house handset. I didn't even really know how to have a regular conversation with Avril in front of me; how was I supposed to make hushed small talk through a cold, plastic device?

"Hello?" a male voice answered, "Who's this?"

I cleared my throat hesitantly, reassuring myself I hadn't punched in one wrong digit before stuttering into the phone, "P-Perrie."

"Perrie!" a different, more musical voice instantly boomed through the receiver.

I winced at the loud, frenzied voice and bit my lip, listening to the background sound of commotion in the room that I registered to be Avril snatching the phone away from whoever had answered.

"You called me! I wasn't sure you would, but you actually called me! I guess Demi still hasn't learned that overprotective parenting produces sneaky children." Avril giggled in a devilishly astonished tone.

I smiled to myself and pushed the phone up higher on my ear, looking both ways before responding. "I want to know everything!" I boldly whispered.

Avril sighed into the phone. Just the sound of her change in breathing was enough to twist my stomach in horrified suspension.

"I thought you would, but Perrie, sweetie, everything you need to know can't be told over the phone like this. It's just too much. We need to meet some place," Avril softly replied. I exhaled deeply in disappointment, trying to think how I could sneak out of the house without my mom putting bars over my windows.

"Got anywhere in mind?" she asked.

I pondered this for a moment, wracking my brain for a place, somewhere inconspicuous that Mom would never second guess. Thoughts of my biology class seemed to spring to the surface, reminding me that I had a project due soon that would require a few books on geoscience.

"The library," I quickly suggested.

"Perfect!" Avril clapped.

I nodded even though I knew she couldn't see me, pushing back my bangs, already feeling the apprehension inside me starting to bloom like an aggravating weed.

"What time?" I questioned.

"Lunchtime tomorrow. I'll have you home before dinner–pinkie promise," she said in a delighted sing-song voice.

"I'll be there," I promised before wishing Avril a quick goodnight and then heading back upstairs as quietly and swiftly as I could.

***

I had no clue how badly my body longed for my bed until I was safely standing inches from it. *Oh, how I wished to be cocooned underneath my sea of familiar blankets.* I yawned and kicked out of my clothes, pulled on an oversized t-shirt, and slipped into bed. I was more emotionally drained than anything else. My mind felt warped, and my conscience felt severed. I just wanted to sleep. Thankfully as soon as my head hit the pillow, my wish was granted.

CHAPTER 8
WILD CHILD

The next day I woke up earlier than usual, mulling over the best way to bring my lie into action. For a while, I stared at the white wooden planks of my ceiling, acting out scenarios in my mind before eventually rolling out of bed and getting dressed. I reminded myself not to feel so sick with guilt as I brushed through my hair, going about my day-to-day routine with butterflies in my stomach.

Rallying all the bravery I could muster, I wandered out of my bedroom, padding down our hallway and into the kitchen, looking about for Mom.

She was where she always happened to be this time of the morning, standing over the apron sink with a cup of tea steaming in her hands. It was her favorite spot to stop and watch the sunrise before heading downhill to the Flower Patch. I paused at the table, my nerves bristling.

You're twenty-three, an adult. You don't need her permission to leave the house anymore, I mentally chided.

Nevertheless, I sucked in an anxious breath and decided to messily twist my hair in a frizzy knot for good measure before walking past the island. I bolted for the door, knowing full well she had seen me march by. I pretended not to notice her.

My fingers had barely gotten a grip on the handle when Mom cleared her throat.

"Where do you think you're going?"

I looked up at her misty-eyed, hoping my look of desperate frustration looked tangible.

"The library." I sniffled. "I forgot to pick a book for my biology report.

Mom, I have to go *now*; it's due today!" I said, adding what I hoped was urgency to each of my words.

Mom scoffed into her cup and swung back her bangs to look at me accusingly.

"You should've thought about *that* when you selected your book about nonsense," she snapped. "Besides, after yesterday's little escapade I would much rather you stay right where I can see you."

I groaned and tossed her a stabbing glance of annoyance. *Of course, she wasn't going to make this easy.*

"Mom, it's me," I protested, hating every word of what I was about to say next. "When have I ever given you a reason not to trust me? I know better than to trail after some stranger."

At this, all the tenaciousness in my mother's eyes softened, and for a moment I was so disgusted with myself I thought about telling her to forget it, that I'd look for something online. I had to remind myself that she had had no qualms about lying to me, so this was in a noxious way fair.

"Let me trade it out," I pressed, preparing myself for phase two of my plan. *Bribery.* Mom had always detested spiritual books. She found them all to be nothing more than out-dated, nonsensical works of squander, written to incite division and stir up prejudice amongst peoples all around the world. If I could reassure her I wouldn't be bringing home any more books on reincarnation, perhaps she'd let me go.

"I swear I'll never drag another hocus-pocus book back into this house again," I said, using her own words to describe the yellow-paged novel I had left in the Flower Patch overnight.

Mom sighed, looking over my quickly thrown together outfit and messy bun in slight amusement, and then begrudgingly nodded her head.

"*Fine*. I expect to see you reading something science-related, or at the very least something with literary merit. You're too smart to be reading such mindless nonsense. Don't you dare be late! I'm going to need help pruning the quince."

I nodded my head in agreement and swung open the door, feeling the fresh morning breeze kiss my face.

"I promise," I said, and then walked outside, exhaling excitedly as I hurried through the wet grass.

***

Instead of climbing into the Toyota, I bypassed it entirely and entered the shop. The smell of mock oranges and roses greeted me as I walked between the display tables, enjoying the different scents of each flower.

After a few minutes of silent admiration at all of our hard work, I finally decided to gather up my book and start for town. Very few people were out and about this time of the day. The typical cawing of seagulls and the honking of boats carried on the breeze.

I strolled across the pier onto the sandy boardwalk, enjoying the ambiance of town.

I always found the noises of the harbor to be incredibly serene, despite Saint Simons' growing population. Unlike other coastal towns in the Golden Isles, made famous for their rowdy pubs and nightspots, life here was still. Most of the island consisted of privately-owned businesses and lodges made perfect for easy-going tourists looking for someplace quiet to bring the family, or celebrate an anniversary. The library was a part of a small historical resort that very few people bothered to visit.

I jogged up the stone steps and nudged open the door to the library. The comforting smell of aged paper, clean carpet, and lacquered wood instantly filled my nose. I could hear the long-winded sound of Mrs. Dacey, the cotton-haired librarian, rambling to a group of students about the early colonization of Saint Simons. She turned as I passed by, tossing me a polite wave. Sheepishly, I returned her wave and silently placed my book on the return cart. I wandered through the library, searching the stacks for a streak of cinnamon hair.

I nearly jumped out of my skin when a hand clasped itself on my shoulder. Whimsical laughter soon proceeded, and I turned around to find Avril smiling ear to ear in a fashionable blouse far too eye-grabbing for my taste and a pair of high-waisted denim shorts. Her long auburn hair was flat ironed and clipped on the sides with two pearl barrettes.

"Perrie!!" she squealed in delight.

"Hi," I responded, feeling my ears go warm with embarrassment at how far Avril's voice carried in the hushed library.

"You're such a wild child now! Look at you sneaking out of the house! Ah, I can't believe we're going to have a girls' day."

"Girls' day?" I repeated, allowing her to drag me out of the library and toward a shiny red Corvette.

"Of course, with all the serious, need-to-know stuff included, babe." Avril winked, opening my door and gesturing for me to get in. I hesitantly climbed into the car and watched her sass over to her side.

"Oh, I almost forgot! I checked these out for you. You're going to need these to understand all of this." She gave me a stack of novels and then twisted the key in the ignition. The car purred to life.

I glanced down at the horde of books in confusion. In my lap was a pile of stories from both Roman and Greek mythology; some even appeared to have been plucked straight from the children's section.

The books made my heart leap with giddy excitement. These sorts of books were forbidden. Just as Mom detested spiritual books, she found most tales of folklore and mythos to be inessential. Growing up, she had never let me read anything mythology related, making me return whatever fable I had managed to smuggle from the library or school. Just holding them was frowned upon, and that made them twice as fascinating to me.

I looked over each cover curiously, moving my fingers across the golden title letters of a picture book. I couldn't possibly imagine what a mountain of crazy stories had in common with our fractured family, but I kept my lips sealed tightly. I began to open one of the books, but Avril's fingers were curled around my wrist before I could even get a little glimpse of the colorful pages within.

"Perrie, what I'm about to tell you….it's going to sound crazy. Once you hear it, I can't promise you things will ever be the same."

I looked her over, slightly taken aback by her earnest, almost grim tone, and finally nodded in understanding. She released my hand and nodded back at me with a pretty smile.

"Then let's get this party started!"

The next thing I knew, Avril had slammed on the gas, and we were flying down the road toward the more luxurious side of town. I felt my lips twitch into a daring grin. I shook my hair out of its messy bun and smiled up at the sky, feeling free for the first time ever, despite the quiet confliction inside me.

CHAPTER 9
DELIRIUM

After some while of coasting down familiar streets and zipping through near red lights, we finally turned into what appeared to be a gated community. I stared at all the luxury houses outside my window curiously. Never had I been through this part of town. It didn't take very long to reach our destination with the help of Avril's apparent lead foot. It was a magnificent glass home, trimmed with brick and cedar. The front yard was perfect, ornamented with spruce flowerbeds and several shade giving birch trees. A spectacular view of the ocean glimmered below, adding to the exquisiteness.

Gravel crunched under the tires as Avril came to a stop and shifted the car into park. She smiled at me avidly, her eyes sparkling like rays of light on a watery surface as she plucked the keys from the ignition. She danced out of the car and opened my door. I reluctantly allowed her to tug me out of my seat, suddenly feeling as sheepish and small as a field mouse. So this was it. I was about to discover the answers to the questions my mother refused to answer.

I looked up at the three-story house and gulped, wondering exactly what sort of business it was my father did. She took my hand, lacing our fingers together, and ushered me up the steps of the spacious porch, stopping a few inches shy from the front door before glancing down at my feet. She gestured at my shoes with her free hand.

"Shoes off, darling. Hertha will go insane if we get sand on the carpet." She rolled her eyes before kicking off her white heels.

"H-hertha?" I stammered, completely caught off guard. I hadn't expected to run into my aunt so soon.

"Yes," Avril groaned. "She's been an absolute joy to travel with."

Awkwardly I pushed my sandals off before following Avril across the threshold.

The air inside the gatehouse was soothingly cool in contrast to the sticky island heat. All around us, I could smell a pleasant scent of lavender. Through an archway, a sparkle of ebony caught my eye–a shiny black grand piano, sitting unused in a corner.

I followed Avril through the open room, mesmerized by all of the natural lighting the French windows permitted. We passed by a pearl-white wrap around, endowed with multiple coastal-colored decorative pillows.

The couch sat a few inches away from the instrument, occupying the rest of the living room. In the center of the room was a whitewashed coffee table, empty of any clutter.

Ahead of it sat a gigantic fireplace with a large flat screen TV hanging above its dark mantle. I wandered further into the house, passing by a colossal bookshelf filled with all sorts of weathered books and fancy knick-knacks.

Enormous oil paintings decorated the neutral-colored walls like something out of a home design magazine.

There wasn't a single cushion out of place or tousled afghan to be seen, leaving me to wonder if anyone truly lived here at all.

"I was wondering when you'd be back!" a voice like velvet echoed throughout the space.

I glanced back at Avril fearfully and then followed the sound of the voice up to a glass staircase. A woman in a flowing white kimono gracefully descended the stairs.

She was indescribably breathtaking, with long legs and a small frame. Her eyes were a stark blue, and her hair was the color of frosted gold. She was not beautiful like Avril, nowhere near it, yet, in some older, more sophisticated manner, her beauty was unchallengeable. Where Avril reminded me of a pretty princess with a heart of gold, this woman reminded me of an empress with a heart of steel.

She held a glass in her delicate grasp and swung her thick blonde hair back in a way familiar to me… I realized the woman must be none other than my Aunt Hertha.

"This has to be the cheapest house Zane has booked for us yet! Oh, and your imp son has dirtied the pool with that thoughtless wife of his and–" She stopped rambling once she caught my gaze, her blue eyes widening in shock.

"Is that…"

"Perrie, yes. She agreed to come to visit us," Avril answered.

Hertha's icy eyes pierced into mine, and then a sly grin slid onto her pretty face.

"Certainly not by her mother's wishes," Hertha smirked.

She watched the both of us like a majestic white fox, grinning down at her prey intimidatingly from behind her drink.

Avril stood her ground quite well, showing no indication of fear or worry. I merely gulped and watched my aunt's finger rotate around the rim of her glass, waiting for her to cruelly vocalize her intense dislike for me.

Much to my surprise, she didn't utter a single hateful word. Instead, she lazily wandered over to a liquor cabinet, plunged her fingers into a well of ice, and then dropped several cubes into her drink.

"So it's true then?" Hertha asked, a hint of amusement to her voice as she leveled a look at Avril. "She's absolutely clueless?"

Avril glanced back at me before nodding, something in her eyes darkening. Hertha giggled and then downed her entire scotch glass.

"I bet my darling sister is enjoying this immensely!" Hertha smiled wickedly. "You are in for a marvelous treat, my dear. Oh, and welcome back to the family." Hertha politely called, her primadonna mirth following pursuit of her words, as she proceeded into the next room.

"You've been staying at Saint Simons?" I quietly questioned, suddenly feeling winded with outrage that my father couldn't be bothered to stop by for at least a second to see me.

"We arrived a month or so ago after I managed to pinpoint your location. You aren't the easiest girl to locate. So, I told Daddy to freshen up a place for us to stay just until I could find you," Avril explained.

Something Hertha had said suddenly clicked. "You have a son?" I asked Avril pointedly, eyeing her faultless figure in confusion.

"It's a long story…which I'll get to if we can make it to my room."

I nodded, stealing one last look at my aunt before moving forward. She watched me walk up the stairs, an odd glint in her gemstone-blue eyes.

Slowly, she tossed me an encouraging wave, and I whirled around, a sense of edginess soon encasing me after.

The air was suddenly getting harder to breathe, the lights seeming dimmer. *I didn't belong here. What was I even doing? I could still make a run for it, couldn't I? I could settle. I could live with this feeling of alienation and continue my regular old life, working at the flower shop.*

I could apologize to Avril later, then ignore her phone calls until she faded from my life entirely and then.... *Wait, no! No. I didn't want that.*

A feeling of belonging and warmth enveloped me without warning, chasing away the fear and calling me back into place. I wanted answers. I did want to stay. The longer I lingered in place, the longer it felt like I was standing out in the middle of a peaceful meadow. I could smell the flowers. I could feel the sun's heat kissing my skin, reminding me of a time when I had significance...a moment when I knew who I was.

A feeling of warmth and wetness suddenly snapped me out of my revelation, and I looked up to see I was in the arms of a very handsome boy with wet, flaxen curls.

"You're back!" the boy excitedly announced. He clutched me into a tight hug.

I tried to smile, but the fear that my ribs might crack and my lungs might burst was just too much to overcome. I blushed once I noticed a smiling young brunette rushing up to hug me in her towel as well.

"We were so worried about you!" she gushed.

She nestled her wet head against my shoulder, and I frowned at the pang of guilt coursing through me. I didn't remember their faces, yet they clearly remembered mine.

"Cam! Prilla!" Avril unexpectedly shouted.

Both leaped away from me, and Avril shook her head angrily and jabbed a finger out toward Cam.

"I'll talk to you later," she said with pursed lips.

She took me by the hand and yanked me forward. We moved up the stairs. Her grip on my wrist lessened as soon as we were out of earshot of the others. I looked down apologetically at the two young strangers and then back in front of me.

On the second floor, the walls were decorated with all types of elaborate decor. Framed photos and painted portraits went up both sides of a winding hallway, some looking vintage while others appeared more modern. Before I could question Avril about the cluster of artwork, she opened a door and pulled me inside.

Clumsily, I gathered my balance and took note of my surroundings. I was standing in an enormous, pastel-colored bedroom. A romantic canopy bed occupied most of the room, with gold lights woven into the wispy curtains. Light poured in through a bay window and fell across the bed, illuminating the pink petals of a vase of roses sitting on a white nightstand. A closet as big as my own bedroom faced a large vanity. The counter was cluttered with pretty products, everything from expensive-looking brushes to trays of luxury makeup. Several shiny jewelry boxes occupied the rest of the space. Never in my life had I seen so much pink and glitter and cosmetics in one space. This truly was the room of an up-to-date duchess.

"Now then," Avril said, shutting her bedroom door behind her with a pretty look of fatigue, "Let's get to talking."

I nodded in agreement and watched Avril patter across the room and stop in front of a dresser. She collected multiple bottles of hair products and then sat down crisscrossed on her bed. When I didn't immediately join her on the bed, she offered me a warm smile and gently patted the spot beside her. "Sit down with me, Perrie."

Hesitantly, I did as she said and watched the girl pick up a hairbrush and position herself behind me. Slowly, she combed through my wavy red curls, pulling pieces of strands here and there into loose braids. After a brief moment of silence, she sucked in a shaky breath.

"Perrie, how far back do you remember?" I could now sense a bit of uneasiness in her question.

I searched my memory. I thought as hard as I could, praying the void would ease up and urging the faintest image of even an incomplete, distorted memory to appear, like the outline of a person behind a foggy shower door. But as usual, there was nothing.

"I was fourteen. Mom and Dad were shouting at each other… Someone had picked me up and was carrying me. It was cold. Extremely cold. I woke up here at Saint Simons and had no clue who I even was. My mom told me I had been kidnapped and in an accident and that's why I can't remember anything."

Avril stopped running the brush through my hair and sighed deeply.

"Perrie, you weren't kidnapped. You ran away," she said, her voice soft, cautionary.

Taken aback by her words, I spun around and regarded Avril with a look of complete and utter confusion. *What did she mean I hadn't been kidnapped?* Eager to hear some sort of explanation, some kind of wild declaration of proof, I scooted closer to her. She took a few steadying breaths, then finally met my attentive gaze again.

"W-what? Then how did I get the memory loss? That would have to be from an injury, right?"

Avril shook her head and smiled slightly to herself, then back at me.

"It wasn't long after your birthday. Daddy threw one of the biggest parties ever in your honor. Everybody was so happy and buzzing with anticipation to meet you. Demi had kept you secluded. She never let you out of her sight–ever. Not since the day you were born. I was ecstatic to finally meet you. I wanted to be the first one to greet you," she mumbled.

Her gaze shifted down to her knees, and she dropped the brush onto the bed's surface. She began to pick at a string hanging from the sheet.

"That was when you met him… That was when he fell in love with you. The instant your eyes met, there was a connection, a spark. You were drawn to each other. Your mother disapproved. She had greater ambitions for you, and it drove her crazy to think you might sway and make your own choices. She gave you an ultimatum. You chose to follow your heart." Avril's voice was nearly a whisper, growing fainter as she went, as if she was recounting a dream.

I gasped and closed my eyes, swallowing back the golf ball-sized lump that had just lodged in my throat. I gripped Avril's soft pink sheets to ground myself and slowly let out a shaken breath I hadn't realized I'd been holding in.

"H-he?" I faltered.

"Haden," Avril answered.

Haden. The name sent chills down my spine and caused a ringing sensation to echo throughout my entire body, like when a guitar string is plucked, and the rich note reverberates off everything close enough to it.

Finally, I had the name of my kidnapper. At long last, I had the name of the mysterious young man who appeared in all my dreams. I knew who I had repeatedly been sketching for the last few years of my life…I knew the name of the one who had caused my heart so much agony.

"No," I thoughtlessly blurted. "I was fourteen when I went missing–when I was *abducted*. I was a child, far too young to know anything about love." I was trying to be logical, trying my hardest to sort out everything Avril had just said about Haden, about myself. I tried to tell my heart that it had never grieved, so there was no reason for it to be leaping right now with relief that this man–my *kidnapper* was real and had an actual name.

Avril had a look of sweeping sadness etched across her lovely features.

"You weren't fourteen," she gently interjected.

I looked up at her, even more bewildered.

"What?"

"You weren't fourteen. The age you are now, the age I am, your mother, even the age Hertha appears to be, is all an illusion." Avril spoke in a steady tone as if she was scared if she raised her voice any louder, she'd spook me. "Appearance is nothing really but a trick of the light. It's as easy to change as a pair of shoes."

"Are you implying that I'm...that you're...that my mother is immortal?"

"I know it sounds crazy, believe me, I do. Think about it, though, Perrie. Why were you reading books on reincarnation?" Avril asked, her tone suddenly serious.

I looked up at her nervously and then back down at my laced fingers, shrugging and stumbling over my words.

"I-I don't know. I've always found the topic interesting, I guess. It's not something my mom would approve of. She doesn't exactly like stuff like that...or really anything that goes against her beliefs," I replied.

"And what exactly are Demi's beliefs these days? Do you both go to church every Sunday and confess your sins to some little man sitting on the other side of a divider? Or do you praise the Buddha? Or fast during Ramadan? Recharge crystals underneath the full moon? Are you an atheist? Agnostic? Don't tell me you're Cthulhuists."

I shook my head in mystified uncertainty. *What was our religion? Was it even possible to not have one? What did I personally, honestly believe?* Avril cleared her throat, jerking me out of my thoughts.

"Come on now, Perrie," Avril said in a trivializing tone. "You obviously feel like something is missing, whether in this life or a prior one... Otherwise, you wouldn't feel the need to sneak behind your mother's back and get books she disapproves of. You wouldn't be sitting here talking about this with me. Admit it; you're hard up for some answers."

I opened my mouth to protest and then instantly shut it. I didn't have any reasonable excuse to offer. Avril had me right where she wanted me.

"Why would your mother forbid books like that if she isn't religious?" Avril questioned.

Again, I had no response. I was speechless, and that made me feel vulnerable and squirmy.

"You are gifted, Perrie. Way smarter than others your age. Why is that? Could it be you've heard the material before? You feel like a misfit. You dream about people you don't know and places you've never been to. Places that have been in ruins for decades now. Why?"

I eyed Avril in a mixed state of shock and alarm and then chuckled in disbelief.

"That doesn't make me immortal," I snorted dismissively.

Avril's blue eyes lit up and she smiled at me.

"Perhaps not. Perhaps you're just as normal as you claim to be, but you don't really believe that do you?" Avril stated with a playful grin.

"So, how old is your son?" I asked, desperate to change the topic.

"How old do you think he is?" Avril grinned.

I shrugged, struggling to maintain a genuine smile.

"Two, three?" I guessed.

"Close. Cam is teetering two thousand years old," Avril said fondly.

"Cam?" I repeated in disbelief, my mind jumping back to the muscled teen I had just met downstairs.

No, I thought furiously, blinking back tears. *No, she's joking. She has to be. This must be some sort of stupid prank. Any minute now she'll admit it and try to persuade me to laugh off my sore feelings. Any minute!* Except, she didn't. Avril was utterly silent.

There was no way anyone could be that heartless, that cruel. I should have trusted my gut. I should have trusted Mom, despite her odd and secretive behavior. *You almost believed her too...* a wounded part of me fumed.

"This is completely and utterly insane!" I shouted, unable to bear my chiding thoughts any longer. I leaped up from the bed and angrily marched towards the door.

A look of unexpected shock dashed across Avril's features. She reached out for me, but I dodged her movements.

"Perrie, wait!" Avril frantically squeaked. "I'm telling you the truth!"

I skidded to a halt, grinding my teeth to damn near dust before turning back to face her.

"You're joking, right? You don't think I see what you're doing?"

Without meaning to, a laugh ripped its way out of my throat.

"You never really wanted to help me, " I accused. "Or give me any answers. You only wanted to lure me away so you could mock me. You wanted to infuriate my mom for whatever reason, and I allowed you to do so. Congratulations," I fumed.

"No, Perrie..." Avril whimpered.

"What next?" I interrupted. "Do you want me to believe that we're vampires? *Werewolves?*"

Avril tossed me a look of unreasonable annoyance, which only incited my climbing anger. She crossed her arms defensively as if she herself believed the nonsense she was spewing.

"*Gods,*" she snapped back. "We are gods."

CHAPTER 10
MONSTER

"Gods?" I repeated, the word rolling out of my mouth in flat, lifeless disbelief.

"I know it sounds whacky..."

"*Whacky?*" I repeated. "Oh, no. This is more than whacky. This is bullshit!" I snapped, storming toward the door. I burst out into the hall and clambered downstairs, angrily shoving my hands into my pockets. Avril hurried behind me.

"Perrie, please..." she cried, her voice a softened plea.

I snorted and whirled around, curious to hear whatever other sort of ridiculous excuse she'd throw at me next.

"There's nothing else for us to discuss, Avril," I said, trying to purse my lips into that familiar scowl my mother wielded so often. Avril took my stillness as an opportunity to scurry ahead of me. She stretched her arms out to block my way and shook her head.

"We have tons more to discuss."

I scoffed and shouldered past her, hurrying down the last few steps. I held onto the banister a second longer than I should have before finally snatching the door open and tramping outside. The heat hit me in waves. I grimaced and continued down the driveway, quickening my steps. It would be a long walk from here to the cottage. I usually wouldn't like to proceed underneath the sizzling hot sun. Today, I didn't care. I wanted to be as far away from the gatehouse as possible.

I broke into a jog, shunning the heavy sensation of dejection expanding inside my chest.

Maybe I could outrun it. Maybe the drone of the cicadas could deafen my upbraiding thoughts.

How could I be so stupid…so gullible!

I slowed my steps as soon as I realized nobody was following me. To my surprise, Avril hadn't bothered chasing after me. I was back in the well-to-do cul-de-sac of brightly colored homes and luxury cars. The gentle *tsk-tsk-tsk* of sprinklers faded behind me, along with the distant caw of gulls. I slipped through the community gates, giving the place one last look over before setting foot in the opposite direction.

Town wasn't too far away. If I could make it back to the library, I could possibly be home before noon. If I grabbed a smoothie, Mom might shrug off my lateness. *Maybe,* I hoped.

I hung my head and messily twisted my hair back into a coppery bun, allowing myself a few minutes to cool down before pushing myself onward. Just as I lifted my head, I felt a presence behind me.

"Excuse me," a sweet voice chirped.

I turned around and found a dark-haired girl standing on the opposite side of the lonely crosswalk. She skipped across the street and came to a stop in front of me. A glossy smile spread across her face as she began to dig around inside a Louis Vuitton bag. She retrieved what looked like a crinkled brochure and pointed down at a map, gesturing for me to study the arrangement of tourist sites and biking trails.

"You wouldn't happen to know a place to eat around here, would you? The girls and I are from out of town, and we could totally go for a few frappés. This heat is outrageous!" she exclaimed, fanning herself with the crumpled paper.

I attempted a smile, noticing a trio of girls lurking in the shade behind her. Before I could form a single sentence, the teen grabbed my wrist.

"You know what, you can just show us! We're not the best with following directions," she exclaimed, discarding the brochure with a look of distaste. She proceeded to try and walk me across the strip of pavement, but I planted my feet firmly in place.

"Sorry. I've actually got somewhere I need to be, " I said politely, slipping out of her grasp. "There's this really nice cafe a few blocks from here. You should give it a try," I suggested.

Without warning, the girl reached out and gripped my shoulder, digging her fingers in painfully. She jerked me back with impressive strength, her youthful face twisting into a gnarled expression.

"Don't make this any harder on yourself than it has to be, pet," she hissed, her voice deepening.

I blanched, struggling with all my might to break away. Out of the corner of my eye, I spotted her friends closing in on us. Their pretty faces had taken on terrifying transformations, contorting into unrecognizable sneers. Where there had once been smooth, girlish features, there were now inhumanly sharp cheekbones and unsightly gray wrinkled skin. Their arms and legs bowed and cracked as they walked, the snapping sound growing louder with every step they took. Black, bat-like wings sprang from their backs, ripping the dainty fabric of their shirts into shreds around their taloned feet.

I screamed, grappling even harder to get away. This couldn't be happening. *Things like this... they don't exist. You're hallucinating. You've had a heat stroke, and you're seeing things.*

Sharp pricks of pain radiated up and down my wrist. Where there should have been fingers, there were jagged claws. The one closest to me now had skin as gray as ash. What was once long, dark hair had receded into inky black feathers that trailed down her boney spine. Her eyes had widened into unnatural ebony slits, like the sinister eyes of a crow.

Next to her, I felt small, like a rabbit caught in a snare. I knew I was a lower, weaker being in comparison. I knew there was very little I could do to scramble free. I had to run, to escape...but how? *What even is this thing?!*

I ransacked my brain for a solution and then finally decided to slam my foot as hard as I could down onto the scaly talons. The creature let out a bloodcurdling scream, and I managed to jerk free. Frantically, I bolted down the road.

A horrifying noise sounded behind me—the heavy sound of wings flapping. I pushed myself harder, willing my legs to move faster. I didn't dare look behind me, only ahead. I had to find somewhere to hide, somewhere out of the open.

I ran towards an avenue, weaving between trees and park benches. Sizable shadows flickered on the asphalt beneath me, causing my breath to hitch. There was no outrunning them. Something sharp pierced through my shirt, grazing the back of my shoulder. I let out a yelp and tripped, landing hard on the ground.

Fiendish laughter filled the air. One by one, each of the creatures dove down, landing around me. The dark-feathered being settled before me, it's lips spread into an atrocious smile.

"Nowhere left to hide," it snarled, reaching out to grab me.

I scrambled backward, covering my face with my hands just as a familiar Corvette came to a screeching halt beside us. Avril leaped out of the car, cinnamon hair bouncing.

"Hey, you," Avril said, flinging off her sunglasses. "Stay away from my sister."

The creature stopped, cocking its head to the side. A wicked smile spread across its face, stretching into a devilishly avian grin.

"Run along, little goddess. You have no business here," the monster hissed, flexing its dark wings. The other beings bared their teeth in agreement, crouching defensively around their leader.

"I said," Avril repeated, "stay away from her."

Suddenly, a tiny ripple of power as subtle and as sweet as a waft of perfume surged through the air. It glided through the trees and flowed on the breeze. It lingered, wrapping itself around my senses. *Was it a smell…or a sensation? Did I taste something euphoric, or did I hear something winsome?* Whatever it was, it had an overwhelming grip on persuasion, and I realized it was coming from Avril.

The head creature began to grit its teeth. I noticed each of the haunched legs trembling as if standing suddenly caused the creature great difficulty. Slowly, the group began to back away.

"This isn't over!" the monster barked. "The goddess of spring will never make it back into the land of the dead. *NEVER!*"

"We'll see about that," Avril smirked, waving the creatures on.

CHAPTER 11
PIECE BY PIECE

I remained sprawled out on the sidewalk, even after the mysterious creatures had disappeared. I stared after them, watching the horizon suspiciously. Would they be back? Were they even real?

You've lost it, I seethed to myself. *Or maybe not. Maybe all of this really had happened.*

"Perrie?"

My gaze shifted, focusing on Avril. Her expression had veered from that of fair and collected to something more troubled. She crouched down beside me and placed a comforting arm around my shoulders.

"Come on," she said softly, pulling me up on my feet.

I let her guide me back to the Corvette, all feelings of anger forgotten.

"A-am I crazy?" I asked, my voice trembling.

A slight smile tugged at the corner of Avril's lips. She gave the side of my arm a small squeeze before tucking me inside the car.

"No," she responded, shutting my door.

She climbed inside the Corvette and twisted the keys. The engine thrummed to life, and a blast of icy air blew out from the vents. I watched her scramble to adjust the settings before finally turning to face me.

"Perrie," she started, flicks of pity stroking across her features.

I shook away her words, putting a single hand up to hush her.

"If I'm not crazy…and those things were really real…what could they possibly want with me? I'm nobody."

Avril let out a little sigh and shifted the car into reverse.

"Your guess is as good as mine," she answered, her fingers tightening around the steering wheel.

"Not just anybody gets chased down by a pack of harpies," Avril continued. "I must not be the only one looking for you."

I allowed myself one last frantic look toward the sky before concentrating on the road ahead of us. More people had gathered out on the streets–kids with sticky faces, teenagers with boogie boards, a group of elderly women out to browse the local antique shops.

I realized with a start that any one of them could be the monsters. The one from before had looked so normal... so *human*. I shivered at the thought.

"Harpies?" I repeated, my brows furrowing.

Avril bobbed her head, navigating us once more through the community gates.

"Nasty, covetous creatures," she answered, a hint of repulsion in her voice. "They have no loyalty but to those who can pay them handsomely."

"Why?" I raked my fingers through my tousled hair a little too roughly.

A splitting headache had begun to throb within my skull. It felt as if everything real and logical had been cleaved from my mind, leaving behind nothing but the frightening memory of the girl and her bat-like wings.

Avril stopped the car. Her home stood before us, beams of sunlight reflecting off the French windows.

"Because," Avril asserted, "you are someone of grave importance."

I stared at her in disbelief, dumbfounded. I was nobody. *No one!* My life consisted of nothing more than dirt-stained pants and fingertips smudged with paint.

"You're going to need a new shirt," Avril said, nodding her head toward my shoulder.

I blinked and then glanced at my shoulder. The fabric of my shirt had been shredded, bits of the baby blue cotton wet through with blood.

I reached to feel the surrounding skin and then decided against it; I didn't want to know just how bad the gaping cut might be. I could already see my mom's rattled expression. I winced at the thought and then opened my door.

Avril was around the car in seconds, looping her arm through mine and tugging me forward.

I followed beside her, my heart suddenly hammering again. This time when we reached the front porch, she didn't bother instructing me to slip off my shoes.

She guided me through the foyer, up the stairs, and back inside her fairytale-like room. No one had stopped us on the way. The house was quiet, empty, almost like everyone had decided to leave the second I had. I was thankful. I didn't want to see anybody–especially not Hertha. What pleasure my troubled face would have given her.

Avril disappeared inside her closet, plundering through the rows before reemerging.

"Here." She smiled, handing me a sage-colored blouse. "It might be a bit snug in places, but I think it should fit pretty well."

I smiled weakly and took the top. "Thanks," I said flatly.

Avril turned to give me a moment, and I gripped the ends of my dirty shirt, clenching the cloth in anticipation before pulling the material over my head. *This was going to hurt.* I gritted my teeth and waited for the pain, for the sharp stinging and the smear of blood that was sure to follow.

To my surprise, there was nothing, not even a slight twinge of discomfort as the top drifted across the wound. I dropped my dirtied shirt and stumbled in front of the mirror.

Where there should have definitely been a horrific laceration, I found only smooth, fair skin. I pressed my fingers against the spot and gaped at my reflection. Nothing. Not even a scratch.

What was happening?

I met Avril's gaze. She stood behind me, hands twisted together in apprehension.

"I think the books will come to good use now," she said.

I nodded my head and stumbled backward. I grabbed for the dresser, curling my fingers underneath the wooden edge until I was certain my knuckles were a blazing white.

Ground yourself! I mentally pleaded. *Focus on the feeling of the wood!*

Avril gave me one last glance before slipping out of the bedroom. I let out a shaky breath as soon as I knew she was gone and tried to still my trembling limbs. I was slipping into shock, every inch of my mind edging into hysteria. No, not hysteria. Something else, I realized. There was no word for the emotions ravaging my body, no rational explanation.

The mechanical sound of a doorknob twisting snatched me from my thoughts. I lifted my head and saw Avril reentering the room, her cinnamon hair swaying. The same collection of books from earlier were tucked snugly in the crook of her arm.

"This is going to sound majorly crazy," she warned, taking in a nervous breath.

I couldn't help but toss her a trying smile. After all of this, what could possibly be crazier than being hunted by a pack of harpies? She smiled back at me and fixed me with a serious stare.

"Just roll with me, okay?" she said nervously as if she were afraid I might bolt back downstairs.

I nodded at her in understanding and took her outstretched hand. She guided me once again over to her bed and I plopped down quietly, watching my sister organize the stack of books between us into a colorful arch. She picked up one book and began to read.

"In the beginning…before the likes of man, there was nothing but war and darkness. From that darkness sprung Gaia, and from her came the earth. The world was not as it is now. The land was inhospitable and ruled by a host of creatures known as the Titans. These beings were ruthless, quick to cruelty and violence. The king of the Titans was called Chronos. He was the most power-hungry of them all. Some say because of his wickedness the Titans lost their ability to bear children. Only his queen, Rhea, held the power to create life. However, every time his wife created a new life, he would vanquish the baby in the hopes of escaping a prophecy that foretold the end of his reign." She pointed down to a horrid picture of a vile beast of a man, devouring what looked to be a child.

I shivered at the sight and watched Avril's tiny finger trail along with the page to each baby inside of the monster king's belly.

"Hades–nowadays we call him Haden–was Rhea's first child. She crafted him from the darkness and took the fire from a thousand burning stars to bring him into existence. He was the first to be imprisoned by Cronus. Poseidon, or Parker, was her second son. In her heartache, she created the god of the sea from her very tears. She longed for a child, but Cronus was unwavering. He desired no heirs, so her second son was also consumed. Determined to have a baby, she created several other immortal children, all daughters, two of whom she rose from clay, and one she sprung from ice. Hestia was the eldest girl, and then there was your mother Demeter…Demi. Hera–Hertha–was Rhea's last and fairest daughter. She had hoped their gender would save them, but each daughter was devoured, just like all the others."

I looked up at her in horrified amazement, trying to picture how my mother could sleep soundly at night after going through something as traumatic as that. No wonder she was so overprotective of me; her own mother did nothing at all to defend her. I shivered again at the thought and then looked down in bafflement at the next page with an illustration of a woman kneeling, offering up a stone wrapped in a cloth to the monstrous Cronus.

"Rhea was a coward. She feared her husband and for good reason, but eventually the queen began to harden. She could not live with the guilt of watching each of her children banished to some unknown hell. From the electric anger inside her, she produced one final immortal child–our father. She named him Zeus and hid him away in a cave. In his place, she sent Cronus a stone that she had glamoured to look like a swaddled infant. He instantly swallowed the stone and didn't second guess his wife's loyalty for many years to come. Our father grew up in the company of three old hags. These women are known in our world as the Fates. They groomed our father to be the perfect king, teaching him to be the prophesied hero Cronus had so dreadfully feared. He later waged war with the Titans, poisoning his father and freeing all of his other fellow Olympians." At this, a huge grin spread across her face.

"Does our family still have powers or have we lost them? What can my mom do?" I inquired.

Avril smiled at me and swung her cinnamon hair back, flipping through a few more pages before finally showing me each image as if she were reading and explaining something to a small child.

"Your mother is the goddess of the harvest. She can manipulate all of nature. Our dad is Zeus. He is the king of the gods and of the heavens and Hertha is his queen. She shares half of his domain and rules half of the skies and half of the earth. Her gifts vary but are often sinister and twisted due to her constant jealousy. Parker is king of the ocean. He has complete power over all the seven seas. He is also partial to causing earthquakes," Avril smirked.

"And what about you? What about Haden?" I prodded, testing his name on my tongue.

An uneasy look swept across Avril's features. She arched her brows and straightened her back before answering.

"Haden is the king of the underworld. He is the overseer of the dead and the god of riches. And as for me…"

She stilled, chewing the inside of her cheek as if she were embarrassed to tell me. I watched her spring up from the bed and drift over toward the bay window. She fiddled with a piece of her cinnamon hair and smiled back at me.

"Isn't it obvious?" Avril asked, her ocean eyes sparkling.

"No," I said, shaking my head.

I got up from the bed and journeyed over beside her.

The setting sun glimmered down on both of our heads, causing the red in our hair to glisten like ribbons of fire in the light.

Avril sighed in deeply and caught my hand in hers, interlacing our fingers before closing her eyes. I watched her curiously and then surprisingly felt my breath hitch in my throat.

As the light from the sun spilled in through the window, Avril's pastel bedroom began to fade, bit by bit. Darkness swirled in from all around us, inundating the space until only Avril and I remained, shining like two polished opals in a massive garden. The same sun was lowering there too, casting hues of orange and pink on all of the different shrubs and trees. Flowers and vines of every sort dangled and sprouted from every surface of the mossy room. Birds chirped off in the distance and the sound of rustling water and the deep croaks of frogs livened the silence.

"Where are we?" I asked, twirling around in alarm only to find that Avril and I were engulfed in a maze of green and glass.

Avril said nothing, nor did she move.

A look of sadness danced across her features as she motioned for me to move forward.

CHAPTER 12

THE GREENHOUSE

I did as she said and hesitantly walked through the garden. A set of low marble steps led the way up to an elegant platform. Rows of junipers lined the stairs, and clusters of purple geraniums dripped from the iron railing. I drug my fingertips along the foliage and ascended the steps in awe. It was completely and utterly breathtaking. Never in my life had I seen so many flowers...*so many different colors.* Whoever owned this sanctuary must have loved it dearly. Each plant glowed with a certain amount of fondness. Oh, how I longed to smell each blossom, to press petals between pages and nurture the vibrant collection of perennials into brilliance. I knew without the slightest hesitation I could easily lose myself in this green and sketch for hours without disruption.

I was seconds away from touching a yellow tea rose when the sudden *SNAP* of a twig broke me from my thoughts.

I twirled around and felt my heart stop all at once.

Standing before me was a startlingly handsome young man. He was tall, with lean muscles and olive skin. He had a dark beard that gave prominence to a chiseled jaw and the most tempestuous gaze I'd ever seen, with eyes the shade of burnt umber. He was dressed in diverging shades of black, every inch of him flawless except for the thick wisps of unconquered chocolate curls atop his head.

Quickly I stammered a mix of apologies. I was an intruder, a *trespasser.* How could I justify being here without sounding insane? Thoughts of enchanted gardens and cruel princes skipped through my mind. Would this stranger be angry? *Would he call the police?* How would the near touching of a rose affect the rest of my future?

Much to my surprise, the man didn't say anything. In fact, he didn't even stir. It was like he couldn't see me, yet I was so close I could bump into him if I moved another step.

I bit my lip and froze, trying my best to hear over the pounding of my own heart.

He seemed to be strolling aimlessly through the garden, his obscure gaze drawn to a red item in his hands, a pomegranate. He shook his unruly hair out of his eyes and continued to walk past me, rolling the fruit somberly over and over in his large hands, his dense gaze momentarily meeting mine and then darting back down to the pomegranate.

The urge to scream, to cry, to faint, to do something was nearly unbearable!

This was him. After all this time, the man from my dreams, the face on nearly every page of my dream journal was merely inches away from me. He was real! *Haden was real.*

I placed both of my hands over my mouth in shock but as soon as my fingers broke away from Avril's the connection was lost. The garden faded and we were standing back in the middle of her room.

Immediately whimpers fled from my lips and warm tears streamed down my cheeks. That hidden feeling, that relentless ache carefully contained within my head, burst free. I was blinded by the surge. I was drowning in it.

I had no clue who he was, whether he was a martyr or knave. I had no inkling where he lived, or where to find him, but I knew one thing for certain.

From the very first dream, he had left a mark on me, an imprint of some sort that made his existence nearly impossible to forget. I loved him as I had never loved another before in my entire life. Something told me I always would, no matter what, even if I didn't know entirely who he was, or how we came to be in this mess.

"Love," I sobbed. "You are the goddess of love.

CHAPTER 13
WIDE AWAKE

Avril nodded at me apologetically, and for a moment, there was silence. I stood before her, crying and shaking until my legs gave out. I slid against her bedroom wall as if I did not have a single bone in my body.

I felt cold and dizzy. Quickly, I pressed a hand against my lips, sick to my stomach.

This was too much, too consuming. I couldn't withstand these unfettered emotions. I couldn't decide whether or not to rejoice in the knowledge or beg for my ignorance back.

Nothing about this was reasonable…but I couldn't doubt it. I couldn't write it off as a lie or run away from it.

I had just seen what Avril could do. I had just seen him. This was the truth. This was real.

Avril's pink lips wilted into an even deeper sulk. She crouched in front of me and brushed my bangs from my eyes, wiping away my tears before pulling me into a hug. I clung to her, sobbing until the gorgeous shoulders of her designer blouse were ruined by my tears. Avril said nothing. She didn't seem to mind. She just clutched me tighter, gently rubbing my back until my breathing returned to a somewhat regular pattern. I peeked up at Avril with stinging red eyes and tried to thank her but only managed to choke on my tears. Every sentence I tried to form clumped up in my throat, strangling me.

To be the goddess of love, she had introduced me to a pain so…excruciating.

I had answers now. I had just a few pieces of the broken picture in my mind, and the shards were slicing me to ribbons.

Avril pulled back from me and wiped at my eyes again.

"I am so sorry, Perrie. I had to show you somehow, though." Her voice was a whisper, nearly to the point of tears herself.

I tried my best to nod, to show her that I understood, but only more tears came. No matter how valiantly I tried to think of something else–anything else, I couldn't shake him from my thoughts. He was etched onto the back of my eyelids, engraved in my memory, haunting me with those deep-brown eyes and that saddened expression. It felt like he was in my very veins, coursing through me.

Mom loved me. I knew this undoubtedly. She had always wanted the very best for me…but why would she lie to me? Why would she disapprove of him, knowing how happy he had made me? What could possibly persuade her to keep me hidden from the immortal world for so long? She would have had to have known it would break my heart, that this pain was unavoidable. She wouldn't put me through that, would she?

"What happened?" I finally muttered, raising up. "Why aren't we together? Why can't I remember anything? Why do each of you have different names?" I grappled, tugging at my hair in frustration.

Avril tossed me a look, signaling that I needed to calm down, and I let out a shaky breath, doing my best to oblige and mask the very evident impatience boiling inside me.

"With each generation, the power lessens. Titans lost the ability to reproduce, so Rhea alone created five lesser beings–gods but not Titans. You, our siblings, and all of their children are known as 'lesser gods'. Olympians still, but nowhere near as powerful as our forefathers."

"I don't understand. Why would that require us to have so many different names?"

"Because," Avril exhaled impatiently, "humans have an afterlife when they die. Gods do not. We fade. We need humanity's praise to keep from vanishing. If you are a lesser god, your chances of fading are higher than that of an older deity. Think of it like this, why would you sacrifice the better half of your cattle to appease two sun gods when you can offer less to one primary god and have food left over to feed yourself and your kin? The price of our immortality is not without cost. We cannot afford to be forgotten."

"That's why you all have different names…so, you won't be forgotten."

Avril shrugged her shoulders and smiled dismissively. "The people of today...they aren't very religious. They think they are too smart for prayer and too clever to believe in divinities. Little do they know, other ways exist to obtain their worship."

I watched my sister spring up and strut over toward her crowded vanity. She plucked three tissues from a box and primped her cinnamon-colored locks twice before twirling back around to face me.

"I've been a model, an actress, an influencer. I can't tell you how many times I posed for Sir Lawrence or wore something ridiculously scandalous for Gianni–fates rest his soul. We've all been the face of something flashy, something famous and new. Mortals live for their idols, especially those that are celebrities."

"That would explain all the wealth and why Dad is–"

"A trillionaire? Absolutely! He's had his hand in everything since the very beginning. Every multi-million-dollar enterprise is run with his stamp of approval. There's been no fear of fading, unless by choice, for decades now. At first, we didn't even think fading was possible until it happened to you," she softly trailed off.

"Me?" I repeated.

Avril bobbed her head and handed me the trio of tissues.

"After you ran away with Haden, Demi went berserk. She refused to let anything on Earth grow. She threatened to starve all of mankind if you were not returned. Like your mother, you are a nature goddess. Your power derives from the earth itself. When she started to kill everything, she only started to poison you. Mortals everywhere were dousing Demeter in praise. In their means to quell her anger, they forgot about you. They forgot about all of the other immortals tied to the land. When you volunteered to leave, it was too late. You were near death. On your way from the Underworld, you fainted. The last thing Haden had mentioned was that you had eaten six seeds of a pomegranate willingly...meaning Demi had to return you. It was the law. You were his wife. However, your marriage was never acknowledged because Hertha refused to bless the nuptials. She said there was no way of proving the arrangement was a mutual intention. You were unconscious when they brought you to Olympus, and you would not rouse."

My heart dropped. One word in particular echoed inside my head for what felt like hours. The sound of it was deafening. *Wife. Wife. Wife. You were his wife.*

I had been married to a god. A king. The king of the dead. I looked up at Avril with what I knew was a startled expression and then began to unconsciously shred the tissue in my hands, overcome with anxiety.

It couldn't be...it just couldn't! All my memories, half of my existence, all had been robbed from me...and my mother was the thief. She, the one who had given birth to me, clothed me, loved me, and sheltered me in my darkest of hours, had shot down my sun for her own benefit.

"You stayed like that, lifeless for months, and then one day, you were gone. Demi had taken you and vanished. No one could find her. She vilified Haden for your condition and blamed Daddy for turning a blind eye," Avril muttered.

"And Haden...is he fading too?" I numbly asked, my mind wandering back to yesterday, to that fleeting moment in the Flower Patch. Avril had mentioned that he wasn't content with not having what was promised to him. Him, being Haden. He was demanding to fade, and our father was not allowing it.

Avril glanced up at me with a look that said everything, that made me feel as if I had been hit in the stomach with a wrecking ball. I squeezed my eyes shut and shook my head, trying to fight back the sudden bouts of pain in my chest and breathe. Breathing, such an easy task, suddenly felt impossible, like moving an anchor at the bottom of the ocean. No matter how hard I tried to get a grip and relax, my spinning mind would remind me of my current predicament, about my deceitful mother and my ancient forbidden romance, and the true immortal nature that I had no idea even dwelled inside me.

"We have been looking for you for a very long time, Perrie. Some—most—haven't seen you since you ran away. They've only heard rumors, little tales that time has twisted and changed. Most think you have faded. Your mother has kept you very well hidden...and Haden, well, he has a flair for the dramatic. He doesn't want to go on without you. It's all quite romantic of him, actually. Kind of like Romeo and Juliet," Avril explained, causing my heart to constrict in panic.

Quite romantic?! Like Romeo and Juliet! Nothing about this was romantic! This was confusing and serious and a matter of life and death. A matter I could no longer sit in the dark and be quiet about. I had to go to him. I had to get this all straightened out. But how? How could I when I didn't even know which direction to step foot in?

"I-I have to go," I unexpectedly blurted, my teary gaze flickering over toward the window and then back up at Avril. "If I'm not home soon, my mom might freeze the earth again," I grumbled, standing up from Avril's bed and waiting for her to stand up with me.

She nodded at me and guided me outside of her room. "You'll come back with me, though, right?" she questioned, her gaze fretful. I bobbed my head and wiped my eyes yet again.

"Yeah, yeah. Of course. I…I need to find him and make things right."

Avril smiled at me and nodded, brushing my hair out of my eyes and hugging me close.

"Trust me, darling, that is in the plan. Haden mustn't fade," she replied.

My heart stopped at the thought, and I shook my head violently. "I will not let that happen," I sternly answered, following Avril downstairs.

The atmosphere of the living room had shifted drastically since my first step inside the house. The air still smelled of lavender, and the temperature was still cool enough to raise goosebumps, but something about the space seemed too tight. Slouching on the sofa in a snug green dress was none other than Hertha. She had her hair pinned up and yet another glass in her hand. Standing in front of her was Cam. They both had the appearance of two people who had been bickering, but as soon as my feet hit the last two steps, Hertha dusted herself off and sat up straight, a smile on her lovely face, the liquid in her glass now a vine green.

"Well, well! Doesn't somebody look quite the more…educated." Hertha grinned.

Avril beamed back at Hertha, and I stood straight, fists clenched. Even though I knew I should've shown some indication of respect toward my aunt, I couldn't manage a snicker in her direction. Queen of the gods or not, it was partially her fault my mother hadn't been forced to return me to Haden. It was just as equally her fault that the thought of fading had even crossed his mind.

"I did try my best," Avril sweetly responded.

Hertha uncrossed her legs and sighed, brushing away a piece of imaginary lint from her dress before pulling out a green iPhone.

"I suppose I should break the news to Zane, shouldn't I? He'll be happy to hear he doesn't have to pair us into these ridiculous search parties anymore." Hertha snickered.

"Yes, I think that would be very helpful," Avril replied. She sashayed toward the monstrous bookshelf, plucked a book from the middle section, and handed it to me with a gentle smile. "To fool Demi," she suggested.

I looked down at the copy of Jane Austen's Persuasion in her hands, a first edition, and pushed the book back into Avril's hands. "Forget fooling her.

I'm going to let her know that I know everything," I said, causing a storm of laughter to flutter out of Hertha.

"My, my. Would you listen to that?" Hertha purred, her icy eyes keenly looking me up and down, an amused smirk tugging at the corners of her lips. "I must admit, I had my doubts that you'd be able to process it all, Persephone, dear. It sounded quite shaky up there, and you did look dreadfully mortal when you first entered the house. Now, look at you, though! Hurt, betrayed, a goddess once more, only this time you've been torn apart and made anew by the very answers you so dreadfully desired. Tell me, sweet, were they worth the misery you've just released upon yourself? Does it feel as attaining as you had hoped to learn your mother has a nasty habit of cheating those she claims to love the most?" Hertha chuckled, her voice ending on a serious note at the end.

Somehow, I managed to throw the queen of the gods a smile. A broken one, but still a smile. She was right. I had wanted this. I had so greatly longed for the truth, not caring what I might find…not expecting to discover anything as upending as this. Now, I had my answers. I had obtained them at the cost of my certainty. Nothing would ever be certain again. My mom was no longer the selfless mother I had thought her to be. Real-life monsters roamed this world, and the life I had recognized as my own had been nothing but a cozy lie.

My chest ached with the realization. I felt hollow. Angry and betrayed, but I would not let myself be maddened by this knowledge. I would not let the overcoming truth shatter me. I was bent on saving Haden, on reclaiming the life that had been kept hidden from me. I wanted Mom to know I was done walking about in a dreamy haze. I wanted her to know I was wide awake, ready.

"Yes, Aunt Hertha, they were," I answered, not lingering to catch my aunt's expression as I walked out the door with Avril trailing behind me.

CHAPTER 14
CONFRONTATION

The drive back to the cottage wasn't quite as rebellious and fun as it had initially been riding to Avril's vacation home. Silence hung in the humid island air like a strangling gag, despite Avril's best attempts at breaking the tension by letting the top of the car down and turning on the radio. She flipped through several stations, complaining and grumbling here and there about how today's music was dreadfully unoriginal, and then finally landed on a station playing Madonna's *Like a Prayer*. A wistful smile skipped across her lips. She tapped her fingers on the steering wheel, singing along with the lyrics rather cheerfully despite my crabby attitude.

"Did I ever tell you I knew Madonna?" Avril asked, raising a diverting eyebrow in my direction.

I shook my head.

"Well," she started dramatically. "She is one of the only mortals I could stand that Holland dated."

"Holland?" I repeated.

"Hermes. God of thievery and direction. The guy who returned you to Olympus after you collapsed. The one and only Olympian your husband despises with a fiery passion," she clarified, steering the Corvette swiftly down my road.

I shivered yet again at the word husband and looked down at my interlaced fingers.

"Why does he hate him?" I wondered out loud.

Avril chuckled and parked the car in front of my driveway. She smiled up at me and shrugged her shoulders. "The strife between Haden and Holland goes way back. To spare you every measly detail, I'll just say they are two *very* different gods. Holland was one of the many Olympians bidding for your hand in marriage. He felt that he was entitled to you, while Haden felt that no one was worthy of you, that you should pick a partner of your own choosing. After that, Holland has had his eye on Haden's throne. Lately, he's the only god who isn't completely against Haden fading."

"What?! Why?!"

"Well, for starters, there's no threat of elimination for the king of the dead. If every human on the face of the earth expired right this second, Haden would still have to care for their souls. While the rest of us would fade off into nothingness, he'd receive praise from his dead subjects. Do you understand? He's the only god with an assured chance of not fading," she explained in a lowered voice. "Holland is no lesser god, but he is also lower down the hierarchy than he'd prefer to be. He has been the messenger of Olympus for centuries and has escorted the souls to Charon, the boatman of the Underworld, for even longer than that. If Haden were to fade–"

"He won't fade," I said in a determined tone.

Avril reached across the center console to give my hand a heartened squeeze.

"*If* Haden were to fade, the job would fall upon Holland. Haden has no children to inherit the crown. The council has not yet recognized your marriage, so you could not claim the throne. Holland, however, has shown keen interest in the Underworld, and no one has risen to oppose him."

"Who would usher the dead through if Holland becomes king?" I asked.

"One of his sons, I suppose. Pan would probably take over his father's position at ushering the dearly departed."

I unbuckled my seat belt and shook my head.

"That won't happen. I'll show Haden that I'm here…and that I'm alive and everything will be alright," I said, fooling myself into thinking that I was only reassuring the goddess next to me and not trying to convince myself. Deep down, I knew the truth. I knew my words held nothing but empty air. I had no earthly idea how any of this would pan out…or if I could even make a difference.

The thought of it not ending well frightened me. It left me with nothing but a sense of raw panic that went all the way through to my bones. I couldn't allow myself to think negatively. It would go well. It had to, for both his and my sake alike.

Avril opened her mouth to speak when the jarring sound of a screen door slamming shut disrupted the silence. I groaned, and we both looked up. Through the windshield, I could see my mother tramping down the front porch steps, angrily marching toward the Corvette. She was dressed now, her strawberry blonde hair messily clipped atop her head. A light dusting of dirt was smudged across her disgruntled face, and I noticed that she was wearing her gardening gloves.

Avril cleared her throat and tossed my mom a homecoming queen wave that Mom instantly shot down with a furious glare.

"Hello, Demi," Avril sweetly chirped.

"Save it, Avril. Perrie, get out of the car, *now*!"

I did exactly as she said, suddenly aching to let loose every hurt and angry emotion that I had kept tightly pent up throughout the years. I balled my shaking hands into tight fists and walked over toward my mom, my entire figure trembling with rage. She looked me over with a fleeting look of relief and then instant shock once she noticed my set jaw.

"What did you do?!" she growled, shoving past me and toward Avril.

"What she asked me to," Avril replied, calmly stepping out of the Corvette.

Mom shook her head and started to laugh, her eyes darkening with detest. "That's impossible. She couldn't possibly ask you anything when she doesn't even know what to ask!" she roared.

I chimed in, "I knew," drawing Mom's attention back to me. "I think I always knew something wasn't right, and now I understand. I know the truth. I know what you are...what *we* are. I know what you've kept from me."

Mom's angry posture collapsed. A battered gasp fluttered out of her mouth as if somebody had stabbed her in the back. She looked up at me with tears pooling in her eyes. The weakened sight of her, of the woman who had raised me and loved me so profoundly, nearly cracked my armor of determination. A part of me wanted to run to her and apologize. It had always gutted me when my mom was upset. Another part of me, an older fraction, chose to shake off any feelings of sympathy toward her and cling to my anger.

She had lied to me. She had selfishly kept me here when she knew of the pact I had made. Worst of all, she had led me to believe that I was some broken, crazy thing, born shattered inside with a void that could never be filled.

"Perrie, sweetie...you don't understand," she whimpered.

"What do I not understand, Mom? That you are a liar? That you always have been? Yeah, I guess I don't understand that!" I barked.

She looked up at me with a startled expression and then burst into tears.

I shook my head, trying my best to keep my composure. Just this once, I didn't want her to see me break down. *Just. This. Once!*

My stubbornness served me no good. I caved in like a house of cards, fresh tears streaming down my cheeks. She motioned to comfort me, but I pushed away from her open arms, distancing myself from her broken form.

"No. You don't lie to the people you love!" I cried out, hearing my own voice crack.

"You do if you think it'll keep them safe!" she shouted back.

I didn't say anything. Mom opened her mouth several times, as if she had a reasonable explanation for her behavior, but never said anything aloud, nor did Avril. The silence and the tension had only grown thicker and worse than before in the car.

A drop of something wet hit my shoulder, followed by another wet drop. I glanced up and took notice of the gray storm clouds rolling above us. Rain started to pour angrily from the sky in sheets, soaking my hair and clothes.

Avril let out a squeak of disapproval and raced up the steps of our porch to take shelter under the awning. Like a pampered cat, she looked rather annoyed, all wet and shivering.

I lifted my face to the rain, allowing the drops of water to race down the surface of my skin, onto my lips. The rain was the final convincing piece of evidence I needed. Instead of feeling icy and tasting like regular water, the raindrops racing across my face were warm and tasted like salt…like sorrow-filled tears.

"What were you protecting me from, Mom? *Grief?* I've felt that," I acknowledged, finally lowering my head, and squinting my eyes to keep the rain out of them.

Mom rubbed at her arms and sighed heavily. The corners of her mouth lifted in a weak smile, and she merely shook her head again, meeting my gaze and then Avril's.

"You wouldn't understand, Perrie. You've never understood. You've always, *always*, ignored what's best for you." Her pink lips wilted into a frown, and she trudged up the steps, distancing herself a few spaces from Avril before leaning back into one of the old creaking rocking chairs. Avril rolled her eyes and continued to wring her cinnamon hair out daintily, pretending to be preoccupied with her now kinky curls.

I scoffed at her comment and then walked up the steps myself. Instead of sitting by either of the goddesses in front of me, I decided to lean against the railing and pick at the green kudzu growing between the lattice.

"What do you mean, Mom?" I asked, this time in a softer tone.

I hated seeing her like this. I hated feeling this way...so torn and emotionally shaken.

Mom drew in a shaky breath, and Avril stood up and stopped playing with her hair. Both exchanged careful glances, and then Mom finally looked up at me.

"When your father decided to rule over mankind, he said we'd be...not like the Titans. He said we'd be pure. For a while, he was true to his word. I believed him. We all did. He married Hertha and spoiled her. They even had five beautiful children together. Things were looking promising, but then one affair led to another. Mortal women started naming Zeus the father of their demigod children. New lesser-gods were also appearing out of thin air," Mom whispered, her navy eyes flickering over toward Avril.

"These affairs drove Hertha crazy. Whatever gift my sister had before...she has no longer. Her jealousy tarnished it, her hatred corroded it...and I... I intensified her thirst for revenge. The very humans we all swore to rule justly she has murdered and cursed and tortured for ages. Not even some lesser-gods have escaped her fury."

"My poor Hephaestus," Avril blurted, her now teary eyes fixed on something off in the distance. I looked up at Avril in confusion and then instantly shut my mouth. *Later*, I chastised myself. Right now, there were more pressing things to know, more secrets to spill.

"That is why when I realized I was pregnant with you, I left. I did not want her anywhere near you. I felt guilty for what I had done, so I exiled myself. I wanted to give the earth...give humanity...a pure nature goddess. The deity I couldn't be," Mom said, smiling up at me lightly. "You just so happened to have abilities similar to mine. You excelled at blossoming flowers and ripening fruit. You were dubbed the goddess of spring."

"She wanted you to be a virgin goddess. She wanted you to be oblivious to love–as if that is possible," Avril mumbled with a snort of disapproval.

"Not oblivious," Mom corrected, her tone clipped. "Just limited. You've caused your fair share of tragedies, Aphrodite. Some beyond even your control. Am I wrong for wanting to spare her? There is only one form of love in this world that isn't toxic, that isn't deceitful. One that can recover even from the deepest of wounds, and that is the love between a mother and her child. Even you should know that."

Shockingly, an expression I was all too familiar with flashed across the goddess of love's beautiful face—a look of pain, of stinging remembrance, of heartache.

It made my heart sink to see such a sudden gaze of despair darken my sister's features for even a second. She bit her lip and froze and then finally looked up at my mom with the first remote look of resentment I had ever seen on her face.

"No. You don't get to mention him. He was different."

"He was your first love. There is no difference," Mom argued.

"Ares was…" Avril started, her voice trembling off into silence.

Mom bobbed her head toward me with a contented grin on her face.

"It would seem Avril has failed to mention all of the possibilities that can occur when you choose to listen to your heart rather than your intuition. She, much like yourself, fell in love with her opposite, the god of war. Their very gifts should've been enough to tell them that it would have never worked, but just like you, Avril would not listen to reason. She ignored all the warning signs. She swore that they shared a love blessed by the Fates, so together she and Ares fled from Olympus to the island of Cypress, where they intended to build their own happily ever after." Mom stood from the rocking chair, a faraway look in her eyes. "Undoubtedly, there was some great and powerful love shared between the two. Never had there been such a passionate coupling, such a driven set of two immortals. Their attachment lasted far longer than any of us had expected it would, but gods do not love as mortals do. A life-long relationship between humans is but a dalliance to the Olympians. It wasn't long before the god of war became restless. He could hear the prayers of bloodshed made in his name from across the sea, from across vast continents. No amount of affection or desire could drown out his hunger for violence. Ares left her, alone and with child, to fight in a war that would last for years. To love a soul different from your own is only to give rise to your own misery. You'll never understand why, no matter how hard you try. You can never be compatible. It'll only be harder once you realize that. Maddening even, like with Hertha and Zane. The more you try to force it, the more pain you'll only bring down upon yourself. Avril knows that. If I had not intervened, you would have shared a similar fate."

Avril shook her head back and forth, her entire posture suddenly stiff with sternness. She, too, jabbed her manicured finger in my direction, making me shrink away in suspicious confusion.

"*They* are different. I've felt it, Demi! They have something Ares and I never did, that Hertha and Zane never possessed. They really are fated, and *they* are not *us*," Avril quickly reasoned.

"And what makes you so sure, Avril? Apart from your son, what good did your love ever do? To this day, you still wear that indefinite scar across that big, beautiful heart of yours. Tell me, will it ever truly fade? Not all the beauty in the world could erase that fear of abandonment he left carved in you. I do not want that for my daughter. Just listen to yourself! Haden is the king of the dead, while Perrie is the goddess of spring—of life itself. I do not wish to see her grieve for centuries!"

"I already have," I spoke up, causing both of the arguing goddesses to stop and stare at me. I dusted off their looks of pity and instead shoved my way between the two of them.

CHAPTER 15
AN AGREEMENT

I twisted the doorknob open and made a beeline to the stairs, taking two at a time before finally entering my tiny bedroom. It took less than a peek to confirm my earlier suspicion. My room was unmistakably the size of Avril's closet. Everything looked just the way I had left it. Messy, yet in an odd way organized, like a wrinkly shirt hanging on a clothes hanger.

I glanced at myself in my standing mirror and cringed inwardly, noticing my soaked clothes and drying red hair. I looked horrible. My freckled face was blotchy. My green eyes were swollen, from all the tears I had shed. I had a gut feeling I would more than likely cry enough to fill an entire Olympic swimming pool before this was all said and done.

I reached underneath my pillow and pulled out my bent-up journal. I gripped the cover in my hands and took a deep breath.

What was the worst that Mom could do, take it? *So what?*

She already knew I knew all her secrets. There was nothing really to fear but her reaction itself, and I had already made her cry. It couldn't get any worse than that. I peered up at my reflection one last time before walking out of my room.

Once downstairs, I was shocked to find Avril and Mom in the kitchen. They seemed surprisingly civil, sitting across from each other at the kitchen table without so much as a threat or nasty glare in the other's direction. Mom merely sat with a cup of steaming tea in her hands, staring off into space with a fretful expression. Avril was focusing on her nails, her tongue hanging out slightly with focus as she magically made each of her French-manicured nails turn a bright crimson. I cleared my throat and both goddesses sat straight forward in their chairs, immediately alert. I walked forward and dropped the journal in front of my mom. She instinctively reached for it and began to flip through the pages. She stopped once she noticed a picture of a hand offering a pomegranate, her face paling. She shook her head at me with a horrified expression, as if she had just discovered the diary of a serial killer.

"What is this, Perrie?" she asked.

I sat down beside her and slid the journal back toward myself. Furiously, I began to flip through the pages. I stopped on a poorly drawn sketch of a dark figure I had done right after waking up from the accident and pointed down at the date written below in ink: *2/03/2015*. I continued the process, turning page after page and noting each date scribbled alongside my signature.

"How long have I been asleep, Mom?"

Avril cut in. "I've always been able to feel Haden's love for you, you know. Yours came in fragments for a long time until recently. That's how I found you."

My heart did a giddy flip at her words. After all this time, she still felt his heart longing for me, even when there was a possibility that I could've faded. Mom gulped and pushed back an escaped tendril of hair before looking at me.

"You've been asleep for a little over two thousand years," she quietly answered.

"Two thousand years?!"

"You woke up sometime in 2015. I told you that you had been abducted as a teenager and had suffered severe head trauma while being held captive."

I crashed back into my chair in absolute shock. I couldn't believe what I was hearing. Mechanically, I flipped through my journal. I eyed each drawing in profound bafflement, drinking in every little detail, all of the random words I had woven into titles for each of my drawings.

The more I peered down at my sketches, the more they seemed to come to life, like a bunch of scrambled recollections from a time long ago, from a time I had lived in. These were not just dreamed-up fantasies; they were memories interlaced with importance. They were moments my mind had held on to…moments my mind refused to let fade no matter my physical condition. They were pieces of me.

Just minutes before, I had stared at my reflection. I was two thousand years old, yet I appeared like any other young woman in her early twenties.

How long had I looked this way? How long had I been twenty-three?

Reluctantly, I tore my gaze from my journal and looked up at them. Mom looked back at me with an anxious expression while Avril grinned cheekily to herself.

"Told you you weren't fourteen," Avril boasted.

Mom snorted and tossed her an indignant glare. She reached across the table and took my hand in hers. Despite Mom always meddling around in the garden, tearing out weeds, and clipping off thorns, she had relatively soft hands, nice and warm and familiar. She lifted my chin and smiled at me tenderly, her blue eyes pools of sincere regret.

"Perrie, what I did, I did not do to hurt you. I didn't think you could miss what you could not remember. Humans live such careless, easy lives. The life you would have had with Haden...as a goddess... It would've done more than take you away from me. You would have been a queen. A rival to Hertha. She already dislikes you; if she were to hate you, I fear I'd have no daughter at all."

"It would be against Hertha's jurisdiction. Besides, Perrie would be queen of the Underworld, not queen of the skies, more or less the gods. The life of a human is no safer, either. You yourself mentioned how she has slaughtered billions of mortals over the eons out of spite," Avril retorted.

"Hertha doesn't care about jurisdiction. If Perrie were to annoy her in anyway... Why am I even explaining this to you? You know our ways! You know how the gods are. For your son to have his bride, you had the poor girl prove her worth by dying for him, for Fate's sake!" Mom snapped.

Avril rolled her eyes and flipped her hair back, looking like a ticked-off mean girl. She smiled at Mom with a look of absolute innocence.

"Alright, Demi, point taken. I had just had my heart shattered, and I did not want the same for my son. We all were a bit...theatrical back then, wouldn't you agree?" she shot back, her lips pursing at the word theatrical as if it had taken her a few moments to select the proper word.

She then laughed musically to herself and waved her hand in the air dismissively as if to fan away Mom's previous comment.

"Besides, was it not *I* who convinced Daddy into turning Prilla into a goddess afterward? With the help of your daughter, of course," Avril noted.

I glanced up at Avril in disbelief. Even though I knew it was true, I couldn't believe I had already met the lovely auburn-haired goddess facing me. Before Mom could fire off another response, I stood up from my seat and cleared my throat.

"It doesn't matter," I said sternly. "I am a goddess. If my place is with Haden, then I will be with Haden. I am not about to sit in that shop and dabble around upstairs on my laptop, pretending to be less than what I am when my husband is considering fading."

Mom bristled and ground her teeth as if it were taking every ounce of her self-control to refrain from retorting at my use of the word *husband*. Avril stood up and clapped her hands, smiling brightly at Mom and me.

"Well, I'm glad we could all reach an agreement! We are expected to arrive at Olympus in two days. Daddy has called for a meeting, and every Olympian is expected to be in attendance, including us–*especially* us–to discuss all of this," Avril smoothly declared, leaving my mouth open and Mom jumping out of her seat.

"He's not even her husband! They weren't properly wed! Hertha never blessed the marriage, and Zane only acknowledged it, therefore–"

"Therefore, Hertha will marry them in front of every god and goddess when the couple is reunited," Avril smirked.

A look of horror swept across my mother's face.

"When did Zane declare this meeting?" she skeptically quizzed, her brows knitting together into that familiar distrustful scowl.

Avril rolled her eyes and reached inside the back of her shorts pocket. She retrieved a neon pink bejeweled smartphone and pointed to the screen covered in different colored text bubbles. Mom's eyes squinted in distaste as she collected the phone indifferently with a sour face.

"Here we are, the most powerful beings in the universe, using human gadgets just as they do," she griped.

"Don't be such a tree-hugger, Demi," Avril said exasperatedly.

Mom snorted and began to read, holding the fragile iPhone as one might begrudgingly handle a bag of manure.

"In two days, the council will gather to discuss Haden's plea to fade. This will be the last meeting before a final decision is made. It is also the last day to prove you have not faded, thus, to change Haden's mind," Avril clarified.

My heart slammed to a jarring halt, only to relaunch at a breakneck pace at Avril's words, my stomach nervously tying itself into nauseating knots. *Two days*. The words siphoned every other noise from the room. In two days, I would meet my father for the first time in years. The god I hadn't seen in so long I embarrassingly couldn't remember the color of his eyes or even the sound of his voice. In two days, I'd be brought before the entire other family. No, not just my family, all of the Olympians. More importantly, I would finally be reunited with Haden—my *husband*.

If I truly agreed to this, I'd no longer be the daughter of a hermit florist.

I would become a queen. Everything I had ever known, everything safe and familiar would be replaced, pushed aside for the life I had left behind. *Could I do that? Could I marry a stranger?*

"*This Wednesday?!*" Mom shrieked. "You want me to march back into Olympus with Perrie in two days?" A look of complete bafflement flushed across her features.

Avril smiled at me with a reassuring sparkle in her ocean-blue eyes and then shrugged her shoulders sassily at Mom.

"You have had her for two thousand and something years…"

"A-and I'm ready to go," I answered with all the audacity I could muster.

My rather bold, perhaps *too* bold, statement drew both goddesses' attention to me, making my face grow warm and the need to fidget and squirm nearly unavoidable.

"No, you aren't," they bluntly said in unison, causing an unexpected gasp to escape all three of our lips.

While Mom and Avril looked at each other in perplexed shock that they had actually agreed upon something, I couldn't help but feel the heat in my face from embarrassment flare back up in spouts of temper.

I was dumbfounded. Of the two, I had at least expected Avril to be in my corner. She, after all, was the one who had introduced me to this new world, to my old life. It was all her fault I didn't believe I was some miserable young shut-in anymore. She was the one who had induced this very conversation we were having now, and *she* wanted to agree with Mom and say that I wasn't ready?

Avril instantly noticed my wounded expression, despite my best attempts at masking it, and shook her head apologetically.

"Perrie, darling, not to side with Demi, but you've just realized you're immortal. You don't remember how to use your powers or even our in-depth family history yet. You smarted off at Hertha today, for Cosmos's sake!"

Mom blanched, her eyes growing large in disbelief.

She looked back at Avril and then up at me and began to nervously pace the kitchen, her fingers raking through her strawberry blonde locks in distress.

"Oh, no. Oh, no, no, no. She mouthed off at Hertha? And here you are telling me she will mind her jurisdiction when my daughter could've started another immortal war under your care!" Mom shouted, whirling around, waving her finger at Avril furiously.

"Demi, honestly. Relax!" Avril grumbled.

"Relax? *Relax*?! Avril, do you realize what you are asking of me?"

She stopped her pacing and nail-biting and slumped against the kitchen sink, making the hanging planter above her head shake. Mom closed her eyes, sucked in a deep breath, and stilled the plant from its rocking motion, then shook her head in an expression of defeat.

"Demi," Avril whispered.

She smiled tenderly at my mother and nodded in understanding, a look of sympathy dancing upon her angelic face.

"I do know what I'm asking of you. I understand what it is to worry and want the best for your child. I felt your heartbreak when you thought you had lost her, and I grieved with you just as the earth did all those years ago. Do not forget that I feel all love, Demeter, just as you feel all life in nature," Avril answered in a delicate voice.

Mom opened her eyes and glanced up at Avril with tears rolling down her cheeks. Once the tears hit the floor, they shockingly turned to ice.

"I feel your daughter's sorrow too, though, Demi. I feel it now, leaching at her inner light. She needs to be with him. I know you only want her to be safe and happy, and I promise you on the River Styx, that is my only intention."

Mom wiped at her eyes with the square of her palms and then looked up at me, her sobs causing nips of sadness to ripple through me.

"That is all that I've ever wanted," Mom replied, looking me over, a fond smile lifting her tear-stained cheeks. "I want you to be happy, Perrie."

I ran into her arms and clutched her close, hiding my face in the crook of her neck. She held on to me just as tightly and ran her fingers lightly through my hair like she had done countless times before.

"She will never be that way if he fades, Demi. The world will no longer be a safe place for even humans if the dead are not escorted properly. Someone else is looking for her, someone with a less-than-adoring purpose. She is being hunted by Harpies," Avril said quietly.

All of the color drained from my mother's face.

"Harpies," Mom repeated. "Who would…"

"I don't know," Avril admitted.

Mom pulled back and frowned lightly to herself, a trouncing look of discernment furrowing her features.

She kissed the top of my head and then nodded at Avril firmly.

"Then it will be done. We'll leave tomorrow," she tonelessly answered, her voice void of any emotion.

Avril smiled lightly and patted Mom's shoulder encouragingly.

"You made the right choice, Demi, I promise."

Mom bobbed her head and then wiped at her eyes one last time before wiggling out of my embrace and rushing upstairs.

Guilt spilled inside me at the sight of my mother's retreating form. A sour taste developed in my mouth, and the bout of queasiness I had felt earlier returned sevenfold.

Briskly, I walked over to the kitchen counter and busied myself with making a cup of peppermint tea. I swiveled on my favorite burner and filled Mom's whistling kettle to the point of brimming over. I pilfered through the cabinets, moving aside jars of ginger root and ground chamomile, searching for the right ingredients to soothe my battered nerves. I tossed in my finds and barely gave the tea time to steep before I downed it, the liquid scorching my throat. I gripped the counter, my gaze fixed on the drain in the kitchen sink.

Throughout the years, I had been my mother's only friend. She had been mine. No one could ever fill my mom's shoes. To me, she was irreplaceable. I loved her indefinitely. I hoped she realized that...I hoped she understood. This wasn't going to be easy for her, for either of us. I was going to hurt her by leaving, but what other choice did I have?

Soft fingers met my own, gently unfurling each of my digits from around my empty mug. Avril took the cup from me and sat it in the sink. I turned to face her, the air in my throat hitching uneasily. I peered up at her, teary-eyed, and she frowned and pulled me into a half hug.

"She'll be okay," Avril mumbled.

I brushed the tears out of my eyes and shook my head, feeling my heart splinter.

"I'm all she has," I whimpered.

A faint smile scampered across Avril's beautiful features.

"Come on."

Avril took my hand and guided me slowly up the stairs and into my small bedroom. I glanced around my room, suddenly feeling faintly self-conscious. I had not been expecting company. I knew it could not hold a candle to her beautifully designed boudoir on its messiest days.

If the lack of luxurious items bothered the goddess of love, she didn't seem to show it. Her expression never changed from that of corroborative and friendly.

"It won't be as scary as you're thinking," Avril said, disrupting the silence. "You'll still be able to see her. You won't be confined to the Underworld. You will be able to come and go as often as you please," Avril spoke, turning her back to me and opening my dresser.

She instantly wrinkled her nose in distaste, pulling out nightshirt after nightshirt, comparing them, then finally standing with her finger on her chin for a few seconds, tapping her foot in frustration.

After what felt like hours of pondering, she let out a defeated huff. She selected an old baggy shirt and a pair of flowery pajama bottoms from the pile of clothes. She handed them to me with a smile, and I couldn't help but grin at her. I knew my conservative selection of modest shirts and loose-fitting joggers must've been driving the colorful fashionista to the edge of sanity.

I took them from her, sniffling, and then glanced down at the stack of pajamas she was now folding back into my drawers.

"Should I be packing?" I quietly asked.

"Oh no!" Avril quickly answered. "You had more clothes than all of the immortal queens combined in the Underworld. They are, of course, a little dated now since you know... I'll take care of that though, darling. Don't you worry." Avril grinned, a gleam of excitement sparkling in her blue eyes.

I nodded and then walked into the half-bathroom. Slowly, I shimmied out of my wet clothes and slipped into the comfy, dry pajamas Avril had picked. They smelt like the cleaning detergent Mom made from a bar of soap and the grater. I smiled lightly and quickly wiped away the tears rushing down my face. Even the small things like our stupid homemade washing detergent made me feel homesick, and I hadn't even left home yet.

Once dressed, I walked out of the bathroom to find Avril sitting on my bed with a smile. She held my brush and motioned for me to come forward. I did as she said, feeling incredibly grateful for her sweet gestures. I needed them terribly tonight. I doubted I'd get any sleep.

I sat on my squeaking mattress, and Avril collected my damp red hair in her hands. She hummed to herself as she crossed and weaved each strand of my hair together.

"I've never seen her so...upset," I finally blurted, feeling the lump in my throat rise.

Avril sighed heavily to herself and finished fishtailing my hair. She twirled around to face me, her face a lovely work of sympathy.

"She's just worried, and rightfully so. The immortal world can be a dangerous place, even for us, but I have faith in you." She squeezed my shoulders encouragingly.

"You do?"

"I do." She beamed. "Hertha is hell to deal with, but we all can be. Even you." Avril giggled.

"*Me*?". The confusion in my voice was evident.

"Yes, even you." Avril smirked. "Being the goddess of spring might sound inconspicuous, but you weren't all sunshine and daisies every day. Sometimes, you could be a real whirlwind."

I grinned back, finding it unbelievable that I had ever held such power.

It seemed against my nature, but then again, I barely even knew my nature. I was a shell of the goddess I used to be. I pulled my knees up to my chest and glanced at the cinnamon-haired goddess before me.

"What was I like?"

A crazy smile flashed across Avril's face, and she covered her mouth to keep from laughing.

"A lot like you are now—bashful, sweet, one of my best friends. I could tell you anything, knowing you'd never think less of me. You were dependable and brave and, best of all, a romantic. I would have never got Adonis back from the Underworld if you hadn't convinced Haden that you could send him back to me as a flower."

"Adonis?" I wondered aloud, resting against my mattress, my head softly colliding with my pillow. A smiling Avril tumbled down beside me, reminding me of that best friend I had always daydreamed about having sleepovers with.

"Oh, yes." Avril blushed. "Adonis. He was one of the most gorgeous men I had ever seen. After Aaron, I... I had a few short-lived trysts with others. Gods mostly, but I wasn't above sharing a bed with a human now and then. Adonis was the ideal distraction. He was young and beautiful and so very impassioned about everything he said and did. I got reckless and did little to hide our entanglement. It enraged Aaron. He wanted me back, but I refused him at every opportunity. I told him I'd rather waste my time with a mortal than with him ever again. In his rage, Aaron transformed into a boar and sought out Adonis. He found him hunting in the woods and impaled him with one of his tusks. By the time I caught wind of what had happened, it was too late to save him. I didn't love Adonis, but I didn't want his death either. I felt responsible for what had been done to him and couldn't live with the guilt, so I did the only thing I could think of: I rushed to the Underworld and begged Haden to release his soul, to give him a second chance at life. He told me it wouldn't be advisable...that returning his shade to the mortal world after such a traumatic death would be more a cruelty than a gift. He informed me that he would never be the man he once was and I should just let him rest. I continued to plead, entirely deaf to reason. I felt so repentant, so ashamed. I needed that feeling gone. Eventually, you took pity on me and figured out a way to appease us both. You drew Adonis's spirit into a seed and told me to plant it somewhere I thought he would be most happy. He would not live again as a man, but he would continue as a flower."

I lay beside her, quiet for a moment before finally asking, "Who is Hephaestus? You mentioned him earlier, out on the porch."

Avril smirked, and the mood around us lightened tremendously.

"Hephaestus is my husband."

"The goddess of love has a husband?" I countered, the corner of my mouth quirking upwards into a stunned grin.

"Yes," Avril gaily answered, resting her head upon her hand. "As a matter of fact, she does. He is the god of blacksmiths and Olympus's master tinker."

I raised a brow in consideration. "Fancy," I quipped, earning a barely-contained laugh from Avril.

"Indeed. As a child, he was cast from Olympus, thrown from a window by Hertha. She saw herself as teaching our father a lesson, but all she really did was mar her own son. Later, as compensation for allowing such suffering to happen, Daddy gifted me to Henry. I was to be his bride, a pretty bauble to ease any strife still felt on Henry's part. As you can imagine, I did not want to marry him. I barely knew him, and I thought myself already in love with his brother. I was a young goddess then, foolish. I hadn't yet realized that each love has its own language. All I ever knew was Aaron…his emotions and desires. Where he was molten and possessive, Henry was patient, steady. His wasn't the sort of love to consume you, but one that nourishes you, that consoles and heals and feels like home. Henry never demanded anything more from our union despite his feelings for me. He left me to reflect, to live and learn on my own until I was ready to accept the sort of love he had to offer. I have since come to regret every moment I spent running from him, from the love we now share. I couldn't have asked for a more perfect immortal to be fated to," Avril admitted, smiling at me softly.

I returned her smile, her story bringing me both a sense of bliss and jealousy. I wondered if I would ever feel that way again, if I would ever be truly happy and utterly in love.

Avril motioned to get up and leave, but I quickly reached out for her, grabbing the back of her top. She turned around and looked back at me with a puzzled expression.

"Sweetie, you're going to need your rest. Tomorrow is a big day."

"Stay," I murmured. "At least until I fall asleep."

Avril's perplexed expression instantly evaporated and transformed into a mask of honored obligation. She patted my pillow twice and then laid down with a smirk.

"Alright. I'll stay. Somebody will need to help you get all dolled up anyway; it might as well be me." Avril boastfully grinned.

I smiled back at her and quickly found myself getting sleepier and sleepier by the minute.

CHAPTER 16
THE END OF AN ERA

SNIP! SNIP! SNIP!

I sprung up in my bed in groggy confusion, looking around for the source of noise that had drawn me from my sleep. A sense of panic wedged its way through my chest. *Where was I?* The room around me was not my own, but grand in size and unimaginably beautiful, like a garden-themed room for a princess. A tiny sliver of light shined through a cracked door with elaborate wooden flowers carved into its ivory frame.

I tossed back my silk sheets and slowly padded toward the door, pushing it aside and wandering out into an enormous foyer. Crystal chandeliers hung from the ceiling like something from a fairy tale, bathing the hallway in a silvery light. The floor, cold against my bare feet, had a soft sheen and looked to be made of pearl glass and marble.

I followed the sound of heavy sobs to a doorway. I paused, worrying my bottom lip in hesitation before entering a large, golden washroom. Steam drifted through the room, along with a thick cloud of sticky humidity. I could hear the splashing of water pouring into a tub, along with the doleful sobs of a woman and the frantic snapping of scissors. Cautiously, I proceeded further into the room when a slender woman dressed in a satin blue nightgown rushed past me, her shoulder bumping mine.

I let out a frightened gasp and immediately released a slew of apologies. I braced myself, waiting for the woman's reaction to my unexplainable intrusion, but she didn't even toss me a second glance.

"Oh no, *Hera*..." the woman uttered in an alarmed voice.

I knew that voice!

I followed the woman into the washroom with frightened determination and then nearly stumbled back in astonishment. There crouched before me was my mother…but not the Mom I knew.

Here, in whatever reality we were in, she was a breathtaking vision in blue. Her skin was still a dewy shade of white, and her eyes were like gentians. However the laugh lines I had always resonated as a part of her were nowhere to be seen. Gone were her hooded lids and the slight crinkles at the corners of her eyes. She appeared to be about my age, her strawberry locks a billowing cascade of red down her back. But she wasn't alone.

I stepped forward and then immediately stepped back when I'd noticed that I had stepped on something soft. A lock of hair…*a lock of frosty blonde hair*. A trail of shorn-off curls led to the massive bathtub, where a younger version of Hertha sat, weeping into her arms. Her long, fair hair was nothing more than a butchered mess of short, uneven layers.

Despite knowing Hertha, despite hearing everything my mother and Avril had said she was capable of, I couldn't help but feel pity for her. This version of Hertha didn't look capable of inflicting pain upon anybody but herself. She wore the expression of a woman who had just had her heart ripped right out of her chest. Her eyes were swollen from ceaseless tears, her entire body trembling from her heavy sobs.

"H-he has another mistress," she, out of nowhere, hiccupped.

The knotted tension in my mom's shoulders lessened as soon as she noticed her sister's grieving blue gaze upon her. A look of sincere concern swept across her features. She brushed her fingers lovingly across Hertha's bare shoulder blades in soothing rotations.

"Come now, Hera. Let's get you out of this water and back to bed. We can talk about this later," she coaxed, her voice motherly and sweet.

Hertha shook her head and started to laugh uncontrollably in-between her sobs, splashing water every which way, like a madwoman. Her beautiful, disheartened expression shifted into a seething look of rage, and she began to pound her fists angrily into the water, causing my mother to leap back in horrified surprise.

"Hera…Hera, stop! You're going to hurt yourself," Mom worried.

Hertha paid her sister no attention. She hammered her fist into the sloshing water, again and again until the tub was near empty and most of the water that had been in the basin spilt out onto the washroom floor.She screamed furiously, and then with one final hit, cracked the tub in two with her knuckles. She crashed back against what remained of the porcelain, sobbing once again and cradling her bleeding fist against her breast.

The golden streaks of blood running down the goddess's arm vanished almost as quickly as they had appeared. Her evidently broken knuckles realigned as well, and she didn't let out even a tiny whimper or grunt of pain. Eventually, she relaxed, her chest rising and falling in weariness.

Once she was calm, Mom sidestepped the pieces of broken porcelain and helped Hertha to her feet, guiding each of her arms into a silk bathrobe and loosely tying the sash around her waist.

Even in her rage, in her madness, Hertha appeared as lovely as ever, yet something about her seemed off. Something had, without a doubt, snapped. You could feel it radiating from her…you could see it like heat rising off pavement. The stunning goddess of marriage had reformed for good this time into something jagged, something bent. Her precious china doll heart had taken its final, fatal crack. Now she was a force to be reckoned with. She was an idol reborn.

"It was a goddess," Hertha replied, her voice venomous.

"A goddess?" Mom deftly repeated, her facial features creasing in fret, her hand anxiously lowering down to her flat stomach and then back down to her side.

"Zeus's new wench," Hertha answered, her lips curling into a wickedly beautiful smile before she marched out of the damaged washroom.

Mom said nothing. She merely followed her sister out of the bathroom, keeping her face blank of expression. Outwardly she seemed collected and calm. Her eyes, though, were navy pools of fear, of apprehension. *She was terrified.*

"No lesser goddess could ever compare to you, sister," Mom offered with a weak smile.

Hertha grinned crazily to herself. She ran her fingers through her choppy blonde hair, causing the longer pieces she had missed to fall off at her feet. She shook her head and shrugged, smiling even wider at her sister. The spiteful, chary, animalistic glint hadn't faded in the slightest from her blue eyes, causing the fear in my mother's eyes to increase.

"Oh, Demeter," Hertha exhaled, "I don't give a damn about Zeus anymore, or any of his insignificant little *pets*. He can have all the mistresses he wants for all I care. My honor as queen, though… *That's* what I care about."

Mom looked Hertha over and nodded in understanding, following her sister down another hallway. Together, they entered a dimly lit room that I soon registered as a nursery.

"That is understandable," Mom agreed, her white fingers lacing together in worry.

Hertha nodded excitedly and strode to a crib where two baby boys lay– one with chocolate curls, asleep with his fist in his mouth, the other lively and brown-headed, awake and playing with his feet. His innocent little face lit up at the sight of his mother, and Hertha smiled down sweetly at her smaller son. She scooped the infant into her arms, bouncing him and singing to him, causing the baby boy to grin from ear to ear.

"He'll never make a fool of me again without I doing the same to him," Hertha affirmed, walking toward a window, and pushing it open with her shoulder.

Mom's eyes followed her from across the room. Anxiously, she bit down on her lip and twisted her blue nightgown in worry.

"D-do you really think it's a good idea to test the king of the gods, Hera?" Mom hesitantly asked.

Hertha twirled around and met my mother's concerned gaze with a vicious look glazed over in her gemstone blue eyes.

"No," she acknowledged. "But it's not a good idea to test the queen of the gods either." Without warning, she turned and dropped the smiling infant out of the window.

"No!" I screamed, bolting upright in my bed, my heart hammering and my eyes darting over every inch of my room in wariness.

I was still in the cottage. It had all been a dream…*a nightmare*. I shook my head and sucked in a shaky breath, trying my best to calm my racing heart. The early rays of sunlight were seeping in through my old white shades, making my hair glisten like embers. The spot beside me was empty, and my sheets were twisted from where I had been kicking and tossing in my sleep.

Memories of Hertha's fox-like grin haunted my thoughts and *my mother…* My head flicked up the second I heard commotion downstairs. Somebody was awake. I breathed in a sigh of relief. Surely some idle chit-chat would keep my thoughts at bay. I motioned to dig under my pillow for my dream journal and then stopped. I didn't have to secretly jot down my dreams anymore. *Right*, I snickered to myself, *that would take some getting used to.* I inhaled deeply and climbed out of bed..

From the top of the stairs I could spot Mom in the kitchen. She was busy at the stove flipping pancakes, her long hair braided to the side and her floral bathrobe baggy on her tiny frame.

She hasn't made pancakes in forever. I watched Mom in silent curiosity as

I padded down the rest of the steps. She was now standing in front of our open refrigerator with a look of fleeting annoyance rolling across her face. She clucked to herself in irritation and snapped her fingers. In an instant, a bowl of diced strawberries appeared in her grasp. She was starting to tip the bowl of berries into the pan when she caught my gaze upon her. She smiled lightly and scraped the fruit into the sizzling batter.

"Good morning, sunshine," she murmured. "Sleep well?"

I shrugged my shoulders, and a slight frown scampered across her face. I pulled a chair out from underneath the table and sat down.

"Have you always made pancakes that way?"

A slight snicker shimmied across my mother's lips as she shrugged and flipped the pancakes in the sizzling pan.

"If you are referring to the strawberries, then the answer is no. I've been living like your average, everyday, single parent for quite some time. No glamours, no powers. Just us, living normally. Now that the cat is out of the bag, though… I figured I might as well brush up on my abilities."

I nodded and looked about the house. *Where had Avril gone?* Mom placed a plate of steaming pancakes in front of me, along with a cup of orange juice and a fork. I looked up at her, perplexed.

What was she doing? She hadn't served me my food and laid out my utensils in ages! Mom caught on to my gaze and quickly averted her stare, turning on her heel and sniffling down at the sink.

"Eat up, Perrie. We'll be leaving soon," she ordered, her voice cracking only slightly.

"Only if you'll sit with me.".

She tossed me a glare and then finally softened and sat down in the chair facing me. Her eyes were red and I knew she had been up all night crying.

She looked tired and even a bit older than when I had seen her last, as if yesterday's ordeal had aged her overnight. She inhaled and snapped her fingers again, and a cup of hot herbal tea appeared in her hands. She cautiously took tiny sips and looked at me expectantly, waiting for me to take a bite.

I blinked back the tears in my eyes and finally stabbed at my plate. I popped the fork into my mouth, savoring the sweet syrupy combination. I shook away the creeping sadness inside me and instead returned to my first curious thought.

"Where's Avril?"

Mom scoffed into her cup and then smiled at me with an amused twinkle in her eyes.

"She went back to their rental to pack and get a stack of your father's money."

"Why money?"

She smirked again and pointed down at my pajamas.

"You cannot wear *that* to meet the council. Once in Olympus, it's tradition to dress with elegance. A queen-to-be does not show up to her coronation looking like some slouchy gardener."

I looked down at my comfy pajamas and then back up at Mom, who was smirking. She herself knew how fondly I favored comfortability over style.

I was no trend-chaser. I knew very little about mortal fashion, even less of proper god attire. I usually found myself dressed in some sort of half-tomboy, half-girlish motley, my closet consisting of a lot of worn denim, conservative cardigans, a handful of thrifted tees, and the occasional slip dress.

The thought of wearing some horribly frilly contraption had me cringing internally. I took in a shaky breath and looked down at my plate. I jabbed at my pancakes again, pushing a hunk of strawberry around with my fork in worried thought.

My coronation? That probably meant I'd be the center of attention even more than I already thought I'd be. I gulped and watched Mom stand up. She walked over to me and took my hands in hers. She beamed down at me lovingly and kissed the top of my head, making the fear inside me evaporate bit by bit, but then it reappeared like an enraged inferno.

"Will Hertha be at the crowning?" I worriedly asked, peering up at my mom in concern, my mind jumping back to my dream...to that vicious animal-like cruelty in the queen of the god's icy eyes.

Mom smiled lightly and nodded, but I could see the real panic coursing beneath her in her every movement.

"Yes, she will. It is your crowning and your wedding, her specialty..." Mom trailed off, wandering back over toward the sink.

"*My wedding*?!" I choked. "I thought this would be–"

The front door swung open and in paraded Avril, an assortment of colorful bags hanging from her dainty arms as if she were a living display rack. She cleared her throat, and the door behind her instantly clicked shut. Gently, she shrugged off each bag and dropped them onto our little green sofa with a proud, energetic smile stretched across her face. She sighed happily to herself, dusted off her hands on her little black dress, and then twirled around to face us, removing her sunglasses, and swooshing her curly auburn bangs out of her eyes.

"You are going to *LOVE* what I got you!" she happily sang, clasping her hands together in excitement.

The more I tried to look enthused, the more I could feel my brows furrowing and my lips drooping into a stern line of confusion. Avril's cheerful mask faded into that of a look of sheer bewilderment, sending Mom into bouts of laughter. She eyed my mother in aggravated misunderstanding and then jabbed her finger in my direction.

"Okay, what have I missed in the past four hours?" she asked, looking at me and then at my mom before propping against the back of the sofa.

"I'm getting married?!" I exclaimed.

"*Officially*," Avril clarified.

"But I thought I was already married."

"Elopement isn't recognized in Olympus. There are certain protocols one must go through first before becoming justly wed. Both I and Hertha must be present at the ceremony for starters, or else the marriage is void."

"I know. I just... I thought there would be more time actually to get to know him first," I confessed.

Avril smiled at me again, this time with empathy, before turning her back to me and walking toward the horde of shopping bags she had left lying haphazardly on the sofa. From the mountain, she selected a striped box the size of a large suitcase.

"I know this is all very sudden. Normally, I would prefer to bring two people together under better circumstances...but in certain instances, Fate intervenes. Fate is never wrong, my dear, and it has always had a very active part in your relationship with Haden. In due time this will all make sense, and it won't seem so...thrown together," Avril said encouragingly.

She handed the box to me. Cautiously, I took it, thinking her words over before looking down at the striped object in my hands. My eyes skimmed across the fancy logo.

Arachne Couture?

I undid the white ribbon on the box and lifted the lid. Inside, past several flimsy sheets of protective paper, was a beautiful blush-colored wedding gown.

I lifted the dress from its box, watching the delicate fabric unwind from its perfectly folded shape. Voluminous layers of blush tulle flowed down to my feet, like a pale pink sunrise. The neckline of the gown was cut into a lovely sweetheart shape, leading down to a snowy-white torso. The upper half of the gown was adorned with beautiful white mesh flowers, trimmed in crystal beading. Just the right amount of flowing white lace embellished the sheer sleeves, like a flowery illusion.

I smiled lightly to myself as I ran a finger down the array of pearls that embroidered the gown's train. *It was gorgeous!* I'd never seen a more perfect dress. It captured the very essence of spring with its perfect blend of pristine colors and its enchanting design.

"Do you like it?" Avril asked, her beautiful smile contagious.

I hugged the silky dress close to my chest and nodded with a genuine smile.

"It's the most beautiful gown I've ever seen."

I twirled around a few times, watching the flowing pink skirts curve along with me, imagining that I was dancing under the Sistine chapel.

Avril nodded her head in agreement, trailing her fingers down the edge of the dress with a fulfilled look about her as she peered up and met my gaze.

"There was a time when you owned finery far more flattering than this. However, after the fall of the Romans, it has taken humankind nearly a millennium to get back in touch with what's glamorous and what's sheerly breathtaking. You wouldn't believe how long it took me to track down an actual decedent of Arachne. Anyhow, I tried my hardest to find a dress that would put my own beauty to shame," Avril jokingly responded, a twinkle in her sea-blue eyes.

Before I could throw back my head and laugh at her remark, Mom walked up and ran her fingers alongside the fabric of the dress as well. She eyed it with a look of distaste.

"It's pink!" Mom grumbled.

Avril smiled to herself, and with a bat of her eyelashes, the dress evaporated from my hands and neatly folded itself back into its box.

"Only the bottom half is pink," she corrected, guiding me by my shoulders toward the bathroom. "And she is technically already a married woman!" Avril shouted from the hallway.

I could have sworn I heard Mom choke on her tea.

Once in the bathroom, Avril marched over to the bathtub. She pushed aside the polka-dotted shower curtain and fiddled with the knob. Pleased with the temperature, she turned her attention back to me.

"I know this is like asking a fish not to swim, but seriously, try not to worry, Perrie. You owe that much to yourself."

"I'll try to keep that in mind," I murmured.

"Good, because from this point onward, there's no going back. We've got a schedule to stick to." She gestured for me to get into the running shower. "Wash off and meet me in your room. We need to be leaving in an hour," she bossily ordered before cracking the door and walking out, leaving me alone in the humid bathroom.

As soon as I knew there was no one lingering about, I slid out of my undergarments and stepped into the shower. I ran my fingers through my wet hair and closed my eyes, trying not to think, but of course that proved to be impossible. I was tense, even under the hot water. I raked my mind desperately for even the dimmest memory of Haden and what he might be like. Who was this god I was marrying? I had married him without hesitation before, but now… *Now* I couldn't wrap my mind around how it could be possible to love someone I didn't even remember entirely. I knew what he looked like. I could tell from both my dreams and the vision Avril had shown me that he was a very handsome, exceptionally handsome god. His physical attributes, however, revealed nothing of what I needed to know about his character. Did he have a bad temper? Was he kind and thoughtful, or cold and dishonest? Did he possess any crucial weaknesses or deadly secrets that I should automatically remember?

I was certain of two things. It seemed likely that my only way of truly knowing Haden was to meet him firsthand, face to face, and that my fear of marrying a stranger paled in comparison to the fear I felt for my mother. I could only imagine what type of horrible grudge Hertha still held against my mother. Even after all this time, how could she not be enraged? It had been her sister. The same goddess whom she had trusted, had also become a turncoat right under her nose. I shivered at the thought and quickly finished showering. Once dried off, I did as Avril had instructed and walked back upstairs with one towel wrapped around my body and another drying out my long mess of ginger hair.

Just as I was reaching out to touch the doorknob, the door opened, and Avril snatched me in. I stumbled to regain my balance, my eyes already searching the room for the outfit I knew she had selected. Much to my surprise, there was no special outfit to be found. Avril looked me over with a look of concentration.

"Hmm," she pondered aloud.

I watched the goddess circle me in deep wonderment. Several rotations later, she finally decided to tap on my shoulder. Seconds later both of my shoulders began to glitter, and a warm, ticklish sensation swept across my skin. I eyed my shoulder in wonder and gasped. From the luminescence came a lacey white bra, materializing underneath my towel and across my chest. She made the same gesture toward my hips and before I could blink, I was in a matching pair of lace-trimmed panties. I looked up at Avril in surprise and smiled widely.

"How did you do that?" I asked, curiosity charging through me.

Avril smiled up at me and twirled me around to where I was facing my bedroom mirror.

"Darling, we are gods. We can do anything. I'd say mainly imagination though," she playfully answered, and then snapped her fingers.

In the blink of an eye, the towel wrapped around my body vanished, waning into a flickering display of tiny iridescent lights. From the colored lights appeared a dainty eyelet dress the color of vanilla that stopped just a few inches shy of my knees. I resisted the urge to fidget as the ticklish lights continued their quest, gliding down my arms, and forming a pale pink sweater with sleeves as light and wispy as wisteria. They took to my hair next, raising each fiery lock above my head. In a swirl of colors, my wet hair dried on its own accord. I watched, completely bewitched as each strand twirled and magically twisted into a braided bun. The lights came to a shimmering stop, taking the final form as a pink ribbon that interlaced itself into my hair.

I eyed my reflection in pure fascination. What would've taken me hours to do normally Avril made happen in a matter of seconds. Even small amounts of makeup had somehow ended up on my face. I looked pretty for once, delicate, and prim and not as shy and unsure as before. I felt like a modern-day Cinderella.

Before I could open my mouth to thank Avril, something bumped into my ankle. I twirled around and noticed two pink flats. I picked them up with a huge grin on my face and slipped them on each foot.

"Avril…" I started when a puff of hairspray shot out at me from one direction and squirts of perfume appeared from another, leaving me in a cosmetic cloud so strong I feared my eyes might water. I coughed and fanned away the scents and found myself being dragged back out the door by Avril.

"You're welcome," she responded with a princess smirk.

We walked down the stairs and through the living room. The house looked as it always did, restful and neat. Mom had put away the remnants of breakfast and shut off all the lights. As we approached the door, I realized this would be the last time I'd ever lay eyes on our little two-person cottage. I blinked back tears and followed Avril out the threshold.

CHAPTER 17
MADAME CECILY'S HOUSE OF CONJURATION

My heart made an instant hurtle into my throat as I caught sight of the commotion outside our house. Idling in our driveway was a sleek black Volvo. A group of men, all of whom were dressed in impressive black suits, were hauling suitcases from the porch to the trunk of the automobile.

Mom abruptly stood up from one of the porch rocking chairs, her arms folded across her chest.

"You look beautiful," she said, notedly taking in my dress and the bit of blush on my cheeks. She toyed with a tendril of my hair, a dim glimmer shining in her eyes, and I offered her a half smile, sensing her disapproval. I knew how she detested makeup.

A thousand words spun inside my head, followed by a thick cloud of mixed emotions, none of which I dared to speak or show upon my face. There were so many things I wanted to say, so many things I *needed* to say. Some part of me was still angry...still hurt by her decision to withhold the truth.

"So do you," I replied instead, looking my mother over from head to toe.

Even she didn't look quite herself, dressed in a dazzling blue tent dress with her strawberry-blonde hair gliding down her shoulders in tight, golden ringlets. It was odd seeing her this time of the day without her gardening gloves on. *Who was I kidding?* All of this was odd. Dreamlike even.

The unexpected sound of a car door snatched me from my thoughts. One of the men had parted from the others and had finally opened a door for us.

"We're all set!" Avril sang, clapping her hands in excitement.

She waltzed to the car, leaving Mom and me behind. We glanced up at each other, both of us looking a little uncertain.

"Come on," Mom finally encouraged, a faint smile tugging at the corners of her lips. "It would be an awful disgrace to keep your father waiting."

Nervously, I nodded my head, and together, the two of us sauntered down the front porch steps.

Avril stepped into the Volvo with ease, looking out at the two of us with exuberant eyes.

Mom slid into the backseat begrudgingly. I lagged behind both of them, doing my best to mentally catalog the front yard and its many wind chimes and flower beds before it was hustled from my memory, replaced with something otherworldly. Nervousness nipped at my fingertips, causing them to tingle and my palms to sweat. I knew my father was the head of an affluent company, but I had never taken him for the type to send out drivers to pick up his ex-mistress and estranged daughter.

I peeked up at the suited man holding open my car door. He looked ordinary, dark-skinned, and stoic. The man bowed his head toward me, and I found myself gasping. Protruding from his thick, curly hair were two horns. He grinned at me, and suddenly I noticed not only did he have the curved horns of a ram, but dark, horizontal pupils. Frightened, I stumbled backward. *What were these things my father had hired?*

Fingers interlaced with mine, tugging me forward.

"Come along, dear," Mom encouraged, helping me into the Volvo before climbing back in herself.

I took a seat beside Avril and watched the creature shut our door. I looked at them both in bewilderment and pointed a finger toward the outside.

"H-he has horns," I stammered.

Mom nodded her head, and Avril waved my statement away with her hand as if the topic was ancient news. Which to them, and everybody else, *I supposed it was*. I was the only goddess who had foolishly mistaken herself as a mortal.

"They are called Satyrs. They also have the bottom half of a goat. You don't want to get involved with them, sweetie," Mom tersely summarized.

"Why not? Why are they here?" I asked, my fingers fumbling around for my seatbelt the instant I felt the car start to jut forward.

Avril crossed her legs and began to brush her shiny red nails on the front of her dress, pulling her hand back to examine them before meeting my gaze and answering.

"They are here to help us along on our journey. Consider them the hired help of the gods."

"Are they dangerous?"

Mom and Avril shared a look before redirecting their attention back to me.

"No more dangerous than man," Avril said decidedly. "Satyrs are well known for being promiscuous drunks. Before the founding of Olympus, the Satyrs were nothing more than a tribe of boorish creatures. They did as they pleased and took whatever they desired. The Satyrs you see today are far less barbaric. They have evolved a great deal from their tribal ancestors. Nonetheless, old habits die hard. There's nothing more fascinating to them than a set of pretty young legs," she truthfully answered, causing Mom to raise her eyebrows in an irritated manner.

Avril only stared back at her with a mischievous tint sparkling in her blue eyes.

"*What?* Honestly, Demi, you can't sugarcoat everything. She needs to know what our world is like. That includes all of it. Even the less than proper beings in it," Avril said sweetly. "Besides, you wouldn't want her to make the mistake of lingering around one for too long, now, would you?"

"No," Mom agreed. "But I would prefer to keep her innocence intact without scaring her senseless."

Whimsical laughter erupted from Avril, and she only shook her head at Mom and tossed her a sensual grin.

"Your daughter is an Olympian. None of us are innocent for long," Avril reasoned, winking at me.

Mom scoffed, pretending she didn't hear Avril's words. She turned her attention toward the moving scenery outside her window.

I sucked in an anxious breath and then glanced over in Avril's flawless direction. Yet again, she looked unruffled.

I huffed in envy. Oh, how awfully I wished to be just as rosy as my sister. My mind was a wasteland of jumbled-up thoughts and volatile fears. Try as I might, I couldn't manage to pull myself free from the brambles of doubt. Not only was I going to meet a god I had once known and loved in one aspect, *but on the flip side, also a god who had known me. What if time had changed me? What if I wasn't all I used to be?* I knew without question I sounded incredibly dense. *Would Olympus see me as a half-wit?*

I reached up for my bangs to nervously twirl and then caught myself scowling once I realized they were braided back.

"Will you calm down? You're going to mess up your hair!" Avril grumbled, her gaze never lifting from her nail file.

Reluctantly, I lowered my hand and set it back in my lap, drumming my fingers on my knee. I peered out the window. We had traveled farther out of town than I had come to notice. The cottage where I had spent what felt like most of my teen years was long gone and far out of sight. In its place was a clearer view of the ocean and East Beach. The neighboring houses only seemed to grow in both size and beauty.

We were close to the gated community where Avril and the others had been staying when I noticed the driver easing the car further down an unknown road.

"Is Olympus close?" I wondered.

"Not exactly," Avril replied. "Olympus doesn't really exist on Earth. It resides somewhere… in between."

"In between?" I repeated, my brows furrowing in confusion.

"Yes. The world you know actually consists of two separate domains. Everything you see around you is the Realm of Man. Beyond this is the Land of Immortals," Avril clarified, the ends of her mouth curling into a dashing smile.

"We can't drive there…can we?" I asked, all the color draining from my face.

"I'm afraid not, love. Don't worry, though. There are several ways to get to Olympus."

"Which *way* are we taking?" Mom asked, her tone mistrustful.

"Well, first, we are going to pay a little visit to Circe."

"Circe!" Mom laughed, "You're joking. No mortal can survive centuries, not even those well refined in the craft."

"Circe is more than just well refined. Her little stunt with the king of Ithaca impressed Hecate immensely. Just as I bestowed the gift of immortality upon Psyche, she turned Circe's thread to gold," Avril stated.

Mom shook her head and crossed her arms in outrage.

"That was foolish on her part. Circe was a guileful mortal. I can only presume time has made her an even more untrustworthy goddess."

Yet again, Avril shrugged her shoulders, her cherry-colored lips curling into an exquisite smile.

"*Neither* of you needs to worry about Circe," Avril reassured.

"Oh, and why not?" Mom asked, her tone uneasy.

A tawny-colored sack appeared in Avril's grasp. She held the purse up, loosening the twine around the pocket to show us a bundle of silver coins.

Mom's eyes widened.

"Where did you get those?" she questioned.

I watched her pluck one of the coins from the bag. She turned it over in between her fingers, scrutinizing the bit of tarnished metal the same way one would an irrecoverable item before dropping it back into the satchel.

I monitored the coin, watching it sink into the pile of discolored hunks of silver. I knew these were no ordinary dimes. The ferocious heads of lions and other strong animals looked far more intimidating than the broody, over-exact faces of former presidents. Several unfamiliar runes also decorated the coins, stating words in some foregone text.

"For a while, Daddy was obsessed with collecting all of the old currencies. He sent countless demigods to their deaths in search of these hideous coins," Avril admitted, her eyes glazing over in distaste. "I couldn't fathom what type of worth just one of these drachmae held, but then I caught word of some of the rituals witches were performing with them. I'm still not quite sure of their value…but on occasions as vital as this, I'm hoping they come in handy,"

"I hope you know what you're doing," Mom grumbled.

A confident look danced across Avril's face. With a flick of her wrist, the purse of drachmae vanished in a swirl of effervescent sparks.

"Always, darling," Avril simpered, looking quite sure of herself. "Always."

***

The Volvo coasted down idle roads and bustling highways for hours, hastening through rural towns and cities, stopping only for gas and requisite breaks. Our destination, it turned out, was none other than the infamous voodoo capital of the South, New Orleans–the perfect home for a two-thousand-year-old enchantress. Infrequently, someone would break the quiet. Usually, Mom or Avril inquired whether or not I wanted a snack or if I needed to stretch my legs. For the most part, I refused, set on making it to New Orleans before nightfall. Realistically, I knew the odds of us arriving there any earlier were unlikely. Like a child, I fought the urge to ask if we were getting any closer. I distracted myself by peering outside my window, watching landscape after landscape fade into one moving image of grass and power lines. We had traveled quite some distance from Saint Simons, not a single shop or house to be seen, just miles and miles of sizzling asphalt. Spanish moss flowed freely from the trees like virescent curtains, taking on a more sinister look as the sky darkened and the sun traded places with the moon. After some time, I opened my lips to speak, a whirlwind of disquiet emotions rising inside me when the

Volvo finally stopped. I scooted closer toward the tinted window, my eyes drinking in the countryside around us.

The land had turned to mossy marshland. I stared out at the gnarled trunks of tupelo and cypress trees, wondering just how far the undergrowth swept out to meet the endless stretch of the salt glades surrounding us.

Ahead of us, hiding in the shadows, stood a massive black gate covered in green ivy. An elaborate C sat between the wrought iron bars, decorating the gate's center like a rusted centerpiece. A being stood before the entrance, safeguarding the property in a white suit.

The figure was gargantuan, with all the hard features of a man and the unnerving height of a mountain. The giant approached the car, stooping down to face the chauffeur's window. The driver rolled down the window, letting in a bustle of stifling bayou air. Curiosity buzzed through my veins, and I couldn't help but lean forward in my seat. I was no better than a marionette, my thirst for knowledge tugging me forward. *Was this figure a man or yet another monster?*

Instantly, I found my breath hitching when a single pink eye centered in the being's forehead fixed on me, glaring. Avril yanked me back before a sound could escape my lips, and Mom shook her head at me.

"And you said you were ready," Mom lowly scolded.

"Ground rule Perrie, no staring! Some find that highly offensive," Avril also chimed in.

"What was that?" I asked, my entire body quivering.

"A Cyclopes," Mom replied.

"A cousin of ours." Avril smiled. "It'd probably be for the best if you didn't look up or speak to anyone just yet, not unless directly spoken to, at least," she suggested, gently squeezing my hand.

"For Fate's sake, you must remember your manners, Perrie! These are ancient beings you are dealing with, sweetie, not civilians. Powerful, easily offended beings. They do not excuse gawky behavior in the same way humans do," Mom construed.

I nodded at both of them in apologetic understanding, doing my best to look attentive. The need to fidget, however, had gotten exorbitantly worse.

The acrimonious Cyclopes stepped away from the car, and the large black gates creaked open. The quiet hum of the driver-side window ascending back into place was near deafening. My heart felt like it was about to burst with every gyration of the vehicle's tires. The Volvo proceeded its journey up the silty path.

Trees veiled in Spanish moss lined each side of the driveway, with wild, unkempt bushes shrouding the estate from afar. Further beyond, you could see the shimmering surface of the salt marsh surrounding an old white plantation house. Not a soul roamed the grounds, leaving an unsettling sensation in the pit of my stomach. I sunk my nails into the sides of my seat, worrying my bottom lip in dismay. I had yet to learn what we were about to come across or even what type of beast Circe might be. Images of the harpy overwrought my mind. I couldn't let myself think of that. I couldn't dwell on the foreboding notion of not making it to Olympus with our lives.

Mom didn't seem to trust this Circe, and even Avril looked a little antsy now that we were beyond the gate. Up close, the manor was far less alluring than it had appeared from a distance. Creepers wrapped around the ivory columns, and dark patches of algae marred the alabaster facade of the once luxurious home. The car veered to a stop, angling us in front of an aged porch. The driver hopped out. I watched as he and another suited Satyr walked around the Volvo to open each of our doors.

I gulped and unbuckled, shrugging off my seat belt. Avril slid out first, graciously stepping out of the back passenger side door closest to the manor. I decided to scramble out the other side, taking a few extra steps to gather myself. Mom was right on my heels, walking behind me watchfully as if she expected us to be ambushed.

We joined Avril by a murky-looking fountain. She smiled at us and gestured toward the weathered entrance.

"Shall we?" she asked, her eyebrows arching optimistically, although I could tell the goddess wasn't exactly thrilled with her environment.

I nodded my head, and together, the three of us ambled up the porch steps. We stopped before a set of old double doors, a dingy sign fixed to the wood that read MADAME CECILY'S HOUSE OF CONJURATION: NOW ACCEPTING DEBIT. Avril sniveled to herself in reluctance before reaching up and tapping on the door with a rusty door knocker. She thumped on the door thrice before quickly snatching her hand back and wiping it in distaste on the side of her dress. Moments later, both doors burst open, flying back to reveal a darkened foyer. No one lingered in the entry. No Cyclopes dressed as a butler or Satyress scullery maid. The only hint of life was the cobwebs hanging in the corners. Avril walked into the house, looking around curiously before waving us forward.

"Does she still live here?" I wondered, observing the old gothic wallpaper and the tattered Persian rug below us.

"I think so," Avril responded from over her shoulder.

"You *think* so?" Mom groused, her eyes narrowing in agitation.

"I know so!" Avril fired back, sassily marching through the foyer.

"Hello?" Avril called out sweetly. "Circe, it's me, Aphrodite. Surely you remember me." She smiled, waiting for a response.

There was nothing. No noise whatsoever. Avril pursed her lips.

"I'm sure she just didn't hear us," she offered.

Mom rolled her eyes and fell into place behind the brassy young goddess, arms crossed regrettably. I smiled to myself and maundered behind both, my attention drifting.

Oddly, the manor was as pretty as it was unsettling. The home was littered with all sorts of eerie antiques and romantic archways. I drifted over toward a fireplace, my gaze fixed on a trio of shattered porcelain dolls sitting lopsidedly on a dusty mantle, when suddenly something slipped from the shadows, something big and burly. I bit down on my lip in apprehension, curling my hands into uneasy fists. *Had I really just seen something, or could it have just been a trick of the light?* I backed away from the hearth, walking a bit more briskly toward Mom and Avril, who were now standing in a large sitting room. I froze the moment I heard hooves scuffing behind me. *I surely hadn't imagined that.* Something wriggled past me, nearly knocking me over. Its coarse fur brushed against my naked legs. I immediately averted my stare. My eyes fixed on the dusty floors below in fear of offending some other great mystical creature with my unintended insolence. I lowered myself, attempting to look as meek and compliant as possible. I did my best to calm my galloping heart and stood perfectly still, even going as far as holding my breath. Nonetheless, a spooked noise flew from my lips, causing both Mom and Avril to cease their bickering and redirect their attention back to me. I waited for the creature to pass before rising back up. In between us stood a dark-haired hog. Mom tossed Avril a zealous look before rushing past the pig and grabbing hold of my wrist. The pig only watched us as Mom hurried across the room. She shouldered me between her and Avril, and I gladly stood between them. Avril merely stared at the animal as if she expected it to give her the directions of Circe's whereabouts.

"Well, well, well," a lovely Cajun voice snickered. "What do we have here? Two pretty little flowers and a troublesome dove."

"*Troublesome*?! Why, that's no way to greet an old friend," Avril exclaimed.

"I suppose not," the voice replied, drawing nearer. "Although to be quite honest, I've never considered you much of a friend."

Suddenly, a bewitching woman dressed in all black entered the room. Another pig trailed behind her, this one much smaller and speckled.

It settled next to the other sow, oinking quietly. The enchantress laughed to herself peculiarly, bending down to pet the hog at her feet before sinking into one of the velvet winged chairs.

"By all means, sit," Circe insisted, her dark eyes lifting to meet mine. "The furniture won't bite."

I looked at both Mom and Avril suspiciously before sitting down on the velour settee. Mom sat beside me while Avril drifted to the seat closest to Circe. The enchantress smiled crookedly as we each took a seat. She turned to the candelabrum beside her and whispered some chant into the air. Violaceous veils of vapor drifted from her hands toward the set of candles. One by one, tiny little flames danced upon each candlestick, brightening the darkened room. She turned her attention back to us, resting a hand in her wild sangria locks.

"What has it been, nine-hundred…seven hundred years since we last saw one another?" Avril asked, her cherry-colored lips twisting into an uncomfortable smile.

Circe sniggered, her dark eyes sparkling with some seething light.

"I swore to turn you into a bird if I ever saw the likes of you again. You must be in quite the predicament to come crawling to my doorstep." The enchantress grinned.

"S-she's not," I answered, the words flying out of my mouth before I could even weigh the cost of my outburst. "I am," I continued, ignoring both my mother's and Avril's frantic stares.

A look of utter interest flickered across Circe's face.

"Oh?" she purred. "And why would the daughter of Demeter require my help? This is not the place for sweet little flowers. Any aid you receive from me will come with a price, and I do not take kindly to those who cannot pay their debts."

Every inch of my being begged me to be careful, to shrink back into passive silence. I had already ignored Mom and Avril's warnings. Any further contempt could have damning consequences.

"Are you familiar with drachma magic?" I asked, struggling to sound valiant.

An amused gander swept across the goddess's face. Circe reclined back in her chair, crossing one leg across the other lazily.

"Do I know drachma magic?" Circe quipped. "Of course I do, girl. I know all magic."

I turned back to Avril and Mom with relieved eyes and then returned my recognition to the enchantress. Before I could even open my lips to carry on, Circe held up a hand, deterring me into silence.

"Don't take this the wrong way." She paused, summoning a cigarette from thin air.

I watched as she brought the black stick to her lips and lit it with a blaze of purple flame. She took a smug drag and blew out a hazy cloud of smoke that smelled oddly enough like plums.

"But, I think my services are a little beyond your budget, *little fleur.*"

"Oh, I wouldn't be so sure of that," Avril sweetly interrupted and then flung the purse of drachmae in Circe's direction.

The pouch of drachmae slid across the coffee table, scattering several tarnished coins in its wake. I watched one of the discolored disks spin before finally landing back on its side with a gentle *clack*. Circe watched it too, the cigarette between her fingers loosely dangling, as if the shock of seeing the tiny bit of metal had caused her to lose her grip on the smoking cylinder in her hand. Her big, brown eyes widened, and her pouty lips transformed into that of a stunning gape. Even the pigs at her feet squealed in upset.

Avril cleared her throat, practically teeming with satisfaction. "Is that acceptable enough payment?"

Circe tore her gaze from the pile of coins and sat up straight in her seat. She began fussing with a pendant around her neck with her free hand, thinking.

"Nearly," she finally answered, taking a final puff of her cigarette before snapping it out of existence.

"*Nearly?*" Avril repeated, a look of aggravation sweeping across her pretty features.

"Drachma magic is costly. One doesn't use it without first giving a sliver of themselves along with it. The spell will require an offering from the recipient," Circe explained, her dark stare landing on me.

A frightened gleam shone in my mother's eyes. She held my gaze pleadingly. I knew what she was thinking. This was too steep of a price, too rickety of a bridge for her to watch me cross. I looked away, turning my attention toward my interlaced hands. *Could I do it? Could I really bring myself to make such a bargain? Was one stranger really worth the indefinite?*

I lifted my head and met Circe's dusky stare. I knew the answer, no matter how much it tugged at me. Whatever the price…I would pay it. For him, I would do anything. There was no cliff too high or river too deep.

"I am willing to do whatever is required."

"It's settled then." Circe smiled, her lips curling into a twisted grin.

She stood up from her seat and smoothed the wrinkles in her web-like dress, looking every bit as shadowy and cultivated as Marie Laveau or perhaps even Salem's Tituba.

"Come," she called, offering me her outstretched hand.

Before I could even come to a complete stand, fingers grabbed for mine, anchoring me in place. I whirled around to find my mother, her face a steely mask of power.

"What *sliver* will you be collecting?" Mom asked, her voice calm and almost *too* collected.

"Oh, just a little trifle. Nothing of major significance. Clients rarely miss whatever the magic claims," Circe assured, her eyes glittering.

"For your sake, I hope so," Mom noted, her fingers unfurling from around my wrist.

I rose from the settee and walked across the room. Circe waited for me by an odd-looking grandfather clock, the pigs at her feet restless.

"Come along, my belle petite fleur," she cooed, draping her arm around my shoulders. "We've got quite a bit of work to do."

CHAPTER 18
THE BARGAIN

I followed Circe further into the house. We passed through several mysterious rooms, each old and trimmed in a faded, damask-style wallpaper that I imagined had been sumptuous once but now appeared more unsettling than anything else.

Strange objects, along with all sorts of peculiar animals, seemed to inhabit most of the manor. Unfamiliar glyphs were written above crumbling archways, drawn up in what appeared to be chalk, and a number of unusual trinkets littered shelves and bureaus. Items like old, knotted fishing lures, hand-fans, and other keepsakes that seemed far too out of place to pass as just eccentric decor. I pretended not to notice a rather scrawny, one-eyed cat lounging about on a trunk and chewing on a marred glass eye.

Circe dropped her arm from around my shoulders and drifted ahead of me, humming to herself as she ascended a set of mahogany stairs. I kept behind her, maintaining a respectful distance between myself and each of the ginormous hogs at her side.

"Don't worry about them, dear," Circe called, as if she could sense my uneasiness without even directly looking at me.

"Aeetes and Pasiphae are extremely well-mannered. They wouldn't dream of harming any of my guests."

"Aeetes and Pasiphae, " I repeated. "What…unique pet names," I uttered, failing miserably at small talk.

Circe chuckled strangely to herself, twirling the pendant around her neck once more.

"Oh, they are not my pets, little fleur." She stopped before a large door made of oak. She curled her fingers around a bedecked doorknob and jerked it open. The beasts scurried ahead of us, rustling the ends of their mistress's gown as they darted into the room. "They are more like…collateral." Her dark eyes teemed with some wicked light.

She pushed the door open even wider, and wafts of cold air glided out into the hallway, along with the overwhelming scent of bayberry. I lingered by the door, fiddling with the ends of my wispy sleeves. *This was it…the final room.*

I hurried across the threshold, driving myself forward before I could think better of it. Circe trailed behind me, clicking the door shut with the mere flick of her wrist. She repeated the same mantra as she had before, brightening the room in a pleasant glow. I glanced around, not quite sure what to expect.

The walls were paneled, painted a dreary shade of maroon. A table sat in the center of the room, made out of what appeared to be a cluster of geode and dark druzy amethyst. Underneath the table lay a colored rug with varying phases of the moon on its celestial surface. Vials of crushed herbs and colorful liquids sat on floating shelves, along with different types of crystals and a chilling assortment of tarot cards. Skulls and jars occupied a bookcase, crammed tight with all sorts of books and stumpy-looking candles. A set of mixing bowls sat neatly next to a collection of pestles on a black countertop, looking like something from a James Whale movie.

I inadvertently backed away, my eyes wandering back to the closed door. *What had I gotten myself into?*

Circe waltzed past me, humming to herself as if she had just stepped into a cozy studio, and not some arcane room used for magic. I watched the enchantress walk around the ebony countertop, digging inside the cabinets until she finally retrieved two cut crystal glasses.

"Do you drink?" Circe asked, selecting a pitcher filled with a swirling, dark liquid.

I shook my head no, causing the unruly-haired goddess to snort into her beverage.

"Pity," she retorted, taking a deep swig. "A little wine is always good for the nerves."

She placed the glass back on the countertop and wandered toward the amethyst table.

"Well, come along then. We need to get started," she said, bobbing her head toward one of the black sweetheart chairs.

I stood still, eyeing the intimidating slab of geode.

"W-what about mom and Avril?" I asked, my voice trembling as I slowly approached the casting table.

Circe stood up from her seat at the head of the table. The corners of her lips lifted into an aggravating smirk. She smiled down at me, her eyes still shimmering with some sort of wicked amusement.

"Aw," the goddess cooed. "You're frightened for them. How selfless you are, little fleur!" She pinched the side of my cheek and chuckled as if I were some ridiculous little pet. "Quite smart too!" she notedly added, giving my cheek a slight shake before retracting her hand to her side. "They will be joining us shortly. You're my honoree client for the day." She looped her arm through mine.

A chair whipped out from underneath the table on a phantom wind and Circe escorted me to it, sitting me down and scooting me closer to the table. The enchantress materialized back into her own chair, the purse of drachma now tight in her grasp. She released her hold on the bag, loosening the strings around the top before turning the sack upside down. Hundreds of tarnished coins fell from the purse, showering down onto the tabletop. A metallic scent lifted into the air as the coins collected into a silvery heap.

"Now," Circe said, her dark eyes growing even blacker, "the real fun begins."

She flashed a smile, and I could have sworn each of her teeth had lengthened into little white spikes. The goddess swayed her arms around the table, combing her tattooed fingers through the coins as she uttered a harsh-sounding chant. She quickened her movements, raising her voice to a vigorous crescendo as if she were calling out to someone. Something unseeable, something ancient. The portraits on the walls began to shake, and the lights started to flicker. Goosebumps pimpled my skin, and I could feel each of the hairs on the back of my neck coming to a stand. I watched in suspense as she continued to recite the words, her soft features changing into something more ghostly. Inky black veins sprung to the surface of her mahogany skin, and her wild sangria locks began to twist and curl as if she had stuck her finger inside an electric socket. She looked terrifying, like an otherworldly beauty.

A sudden gust of heat erupted from the center of the table, and then, without warning, everything in the room went still and the drachmae caught flame.

Circe stopped moving. The white of her eyes returned, and hints of color returned to her cheeks, making her look a little more like herself. She straightened in her seat and smiled at me crookedly, the ends of her hair returning to their rampant state.

"The rest is up to you, little flower," Circe declared, her chest rising and falling from exertion.

"Me?" I blanched. "I don't know any–"

"You don't need to know any magic. What I need from you is far more straightforward."

I eyed the enchantress in confusion. "What do I need to do?"

Circe smiled a knowing smile and then reclined back into her seat. "You and I need to strike up a deal, chérie. You tell me what you want most, and then the magic will choose what it wants from you."

"I–"

"Ah, ah, ah!" Circe clucked, wiggling her finger back and forth. "You must whisper it into the drachma," she instructed, waving forth a single smoldered coin from the flames. I watched the coin skid to a halt, landing on its side right in front of me. A trail of smoke billowed around it as I eyed it hesitantly before picking it up. The rim of the coin had turned a charred black. It felt hot in my hand, almost like a car lighter.

"Try to be very specific. I like you, *sweet*, but I do not give refunds." Circe grinned, resting her chin against her steepled hands.

I nodded nervously and then cupped my hands around the bit of burnt silver. I brought the coin to my lips and closed my eyes.

"I want to be at Olympus," I whispered, thoughts of Haden rushing through my mind.

I'm coming, I promised. *Hold on just a little bit longer!*

I opened my eyes, and the coin was gone. Circe had the bit of metal between her fingers, rotating it with slight interest before tossing it back into the flames.

"Star-crossed lovers really do make the *absolute* best clients!" she purred, her dark eyes brightening greedily. "There isn't much they aren't willing to pay to be with their bien-aimés."

I tried my best to look contained. This had been the moment I had been dreading. I could only imagine what she would ask of me. A portion of my beauty, perhaps. Or maybe even some sort of lease on my soul. *If goddesses even have souls.* I tried to steer clear of thinking. For all I knew, she could be reading my thoughts, waiting for me to conjure up my own personal trial. I wanted nothing to do with the kind of pacts that would leave me with no choice but to choose something gruesome.

Circe stood up from her seat. She glided over toward me, draping her arm around the back of my chair. "Did you know there are fewer goddesses of the craft than there are sons of the wind? Even the Muses outnumber us.". The enchantress straightened and tucked her hands behind her back. "It's quite a shame, really."

"I-is that what you want?" I wondered. "Do you want me to become a goddess of the craft?"

A bray-sounding laugh drifted from the enchantress. She threw her head back and howled in amusement.

"*You*? A goddess of the craft?" Circe snorted, shaking her head in disbelief. "Elysium, no! Don't get me wrong; there is all sorts of untapped darkness in you, but nowhere near enough for the sisterhood. You are far too noble-hearted. Not even a crown of bones can remedy that, I'm afraid. What I want from you is a goddess already accustomed to the arts."

"Any goddess?" I asked, my thoughts gravitating toward Avril.

I didn't like the thought of enlisting another person into a strange cult of enchantment and witchcraft, but I didn't have much of a choice. The debt had to be paid, and Avril may know someone…maybe even somebody willing to dabble in magic. Circe shook her head, dissatisfied with my suggestion.

"No! No!" she dismissed. "Someone of noble blood. Someone…" The enchantress trailed off, a dirty look dancing across her face. "A daughter," she decided, an awful smile tugging at her lips.

"A daughter?!" I exclaimed, "What if I have no children?" I asked, my stomach suddenly twisting with fear.

Circe shrugged. "Then, there will be no debt for you to pay."

"And if I do…" I pressed.

"If you do, then your daughter will be born a pretty little nightshade and not a blushing little begonia. It would be best if you considered yourself reasonably lucky. Most of my clients are faced with much nastier bargains to pay than yours," Circe disclosed.

I stared at the goddess with what I knew was a tortured look of affliction. I couldn't agree to a bargain like this, *could I*? It felt wrong, almost like overstepping some primeval boundary. This was not my future to tamper with, and yet, in a muddled way, it was. I couldn't risk Haden. Time was running short. Every second I spent here, mulling over some uncertain future was time wasted. I had to get to Olympus. I had to convince him not to fade.

"Okay, " I said at last. "We have a deal."

Circe grinned cheekily to herself. "I knew you'd come around." She smiled, summoning a long pair of shiny scissors. She twirled her finger around an escaped tendril of my hair, watching it bounce back into place before cutting the fiery strand off. With curious eyes I watched as she tossed my severed hair into the flames. It melted into the coins, adding a heavy burning scent to the air.

"It's done," Circe announced.

The enchantress glided over to the table and held out her hand. She made a fist with one swift motion, and the flames dispersed. She picked three warped coins up from the ash and dropped them in my hand.

"These will take you straight to Olympus," Circe murmured. "There is only enough magic for one trip, so don't expect them to work after this initial journey. To activate the magic, visualize your destination. Try to stay focused. Any stray thought can catapult you lightyears away from where you want to be. To arrive as a group, you must toss each of your coins at the same time. Comprendre?"

I nodded my head and followed her toward the threshold. The enchantress opened the door, letting both Aeetes and Pasiphae trample ahead of us before turning out into the hall. To both our surprise, Mom and Avril were outside waiting.

"Perrie!" Avril cried, her pretty features tousled with a sudden look of worry. "Something has happened. I can barely feel him anymore. It's like his heart has gone still. He doesn't believe you're coming."

CHAPTER 19

OLYMPUS

"W-what?" I stammered, unable to think straight, to give credence to Avril's words.

She had to be mistaken. I couldn't be too late. *I couldn't be.*

Mom took a few wary steps forward. She held her arms out to me with a rueful expression upon her face as if she couldn't quite decide how best to comfort me.

"Perrie," she called, but I found myself taking an unbelieving step back. *No. No, no, no.*

I turned my attention to my sister who stood quietly behind her, a sense of shattered loss welling within her ocean eyes that had my chest aching. I shook my head despairingly and backed away from the two of them, panic seizing my lungs. *This couldn't be happening. I had just made a deal. A magical pact. I was on my way!* I gripped the drachma in my hand, squeezing the bit of scorched metal until sparks of pain began to bite at my palm. With the pain came a sense of clarity, and like lightning, it struck me. *They may have lost hope…but I hadn't. I refused to.*

Hastily I tossed Mom and Avril their coins. They both lunged forward, nearly missing the enchanted bits of tarnished silver. I sucked in a shaky breath and then without a moment's hesitation threw my drachma onto the ground. It landed on the floor with a subtle *CLINK*, and then everyone else in the hallway vanished.

An eerie mist surrounded me, darkening my view of everything. The walls shrank into the shadows, and the floor turned into a murky pool of black.

Somewhere far off, I could hear my mother's screams, an awry echo-like sound against the quiet nothing. A sudden *POP* resounded within my ears as if I were underwater. The ground drastically shifted, slipping out from beneath my feet like sand. I was falling, spiraling down into a dark abyss. I could not scream or writhe away. I was paralyzed, left to the will of this invisible force. Gusts of cold air wrapped around me, whipping through my hair and my clothes as I fell.

I had determined this was my end, my miserable undoing, just as a streak of light tore through the darkness. In a matter of seconds, the wind around me lessened, transforming into a gentle breeze. The mist softened, ebbing away to reveal a beautiful indigo sky. Thousands of silvery stars illuminated the night, shining their soft light onto a stretch of land. I found myself standing in the middle of a magnificent bridge. The ground below me was solid, made of cobblestone. Vines of pink clematis hung from the ivory beams, and the quiet babble of a stream rippled below.

I was alive. The spell...*it had worked*! Circe had upheld her end of the bargain. I ventured forward in disbelief, my arms and legs unsteady. I was charged with adrenaline, trembling, and restless as if I had just finished a marathon. I gripped the intricate railing until I was ankle-deep in the grass. For a moment, I was certain I had condemned myself to an eternity of darkness. I had thought I would never see another sunrise or ever feel the dampened earth between my toes again. Yet, here I was, breathing in the scent of gardenias and staring out into a beautiful courtyard. I was no longer wavering between realms or lingering about in Circe's gloomy manor. No, I was somewhere else entirely, somewhere far more divine.

Here, the world was as bright as technicolor. The air seemed smoother, the grass softer. Statues made entirely of marble stood in oversized flowerbeds, and orbs of golden light twinkled from the treetops, lighting a grassy trail made of stone. I eyed the path thoughtfully. Could this be the road to Olympus? I started to move forward but then found myself lost in contemplation. A smarter goddess would have waited for Mom and Avril before leaping into a hazy vortex. So far, I had proven to be quite the opposite of smart, more like reckless. I was out of my element here, an outsider in a foreign new land. This wasn't Saint Simons. Without them, I couldn't possibly dream of navigating through the woodsy garden, let alone find my way to Mount Olympus.

I debated waiting for them and then convinced myself that it didn't really matter whether or not I knew the land. I had dawdled enough. The only thing that mattered now was finding Haden. I stared at the path ahead one last time before sprinting forward onto the trail. Lofty cedar trees lined each side of the road, casting shadows onto the cobblestone below.

Strangely enough, I wasn't afraid. A sort of peace blanketed the courtyard. It was quiet here. No blaring car horns or chatty tourists to take away from the tranquility. The fear of larger, more vicious predators lurking in the brambles was all but imaginary. Only the occasional flicker of fireflies and the quiet chirp of crickets livened the night.

After several moments of brisk walking, I stumbled upon a marble colonnade. Columns of ivory stood on each side of the covered walkway, winding out into the darkness for what seemed like an eternity. I journeyed up the steps, rubbing my arms. It was cooler underneath the pillars, lit only with moonlight. I proceeded further down the breezeway, stealing quick glances of the rolling hills and grassy valleys through the columns. Beyond, I noticed an ocean glittered as inky blue as the starry sky.

My breath hitched inside my throat the moment I caught sight of something glowing. Looming ahead sat an enchanting palace. It was magnificent, with grand ivory towers and cathedral-like walls carved straight from the side of a mighty mountain. Several windows illuminated the structure, coloring the exterior like reflective jewels. Scaling up the side of the palace were multiple flowery balconies, like something from a fairytale, and near the grand gates were two waterfalls that poured down into a misty haven. This was nothing like the Olympus I had envisioned from the books. It was a home truly fit for the gods, exceedingly so.

I urged myself onward, hurrying through the colonnade until I was once more fleeting through ticklish grass. The walkway spanned into a great backyard, so close to the palace I could make out the pale balustrades' raveled designs. I ducked under olive trees and sprinted through leafy mazes until I ran headfirst into something hard. I glanced up and noticed a group of bearded Satyrs and one rubbing his head, with several bags of vegetables spilled out onto the lawn. They waved their fists angrily at me, spitting foul-sounding words in a tongue I was unfamiliar with. I didn't bother with an apology. I had no time. I sprung up and willed my legs to go faster, running and running until I approached an open door. I darted into the large Olympian home.

"Haden!" I screamed, my voice bouncing off the walls. No answer."Haden!"

I spun around, my green eyes curiously observing every inch of the sumptuous room. It appeared I was standing in the midst of the servants' quarters; wooden barrels, and tables utilized the space. I shot through an open archway and out into an enormous foyer with rows of stained-glass windows positioned alongside the walls. The hallway was empty, save for a handful of lavish flower vases and the occasional entryway table. I walked further into the palace, intent on finding a set of stairs or any possible corridors that could lead me to Haden. My ears strained to hear other voices. There were none. Only the lulling sound of Beethoven flooded in from somewhere as if hidden nearby; an invisible orchestra was playing passionately. Gilded canvases hung from the walls, depicting beautiful men and women of every era watching me with oil-painted eyes.

The portrait of a bearded man snatching a flaying young girl by her thighs seemed to stand out the most. The man looked so cruel, so ruthless, and the girl seemed so sorrowful and terrified, her arms clawing up at the surface for dear life. Something about the picture did not seem right. It was like trying to decipher the meaning of a book while several of the pages prior had been ripped out. I couldn't put my finger on it, but something was missing. I tore my eyes from the painting and paced onwards, hoping to find an entrance I had perhaps missed. My heart leapt at the sight of a door, only to plummet at the discovery that it was just a broom closet.

Fear began to pulse through me, causing that awful familiar lump to form in my throat. I blinked back tears and carried on with my search, my shoes clacking noisily against the checkered tile with every hurried step I took. I veered to the right and found myself letting out a loosened breath. Ahead of me, a brass-colored elevator, scissor gated to look like golden vines, came into view, the doors creaking open. I slammed to an abrupt stop, crashing into somebody, someone warm that smells woodsy…like apples and cardamom.

I peered up and found myself staring into the eyes of a lanky stranger. The god had dark blonde hair and golden skin. He was well dressed, with slicked-back hair and a clean shaven face. He wore an expression of surprise as he steadied me. A handsome grin flickered across his lips, catching me off guard. I didn't like the looks of it.

"Persephone," he gasped, a tremor of shock present in his voice.

"Per–" I tried to correct when I found myself momentarily being lifted off the ground and twirled about.

"I can't believe it!" the god exclaimed, sitting me down. "There had been rumors, but…"

A Satyr appeared behind the young god and waved an angry finger in my direction, barking out displeasing-sounding words, cutting the god short. I paid neither of them a lick of attention. My gaze was locked on the elevator.

I had to get into it. I had to find Haden. *Perhaps I should've waited for Mom and Avril after all.*

"Alright, alright, enough of your griping. I'll see to it Zeus is aware. Go and assist the others and collect any belongings the goddesses might have brought with them," the god instructed, sending the grumpy Satyr back out into the night.

I resurfaced from my revere of escape when I felt the god's hazel eyes boring into me. He watched me, mystified, as if my standing here was something to behold.

"Where's Haden?" I quickly questioned, my heart constricting with fear. *What if he had already left? What if I were too late?*

He chuckled loudly and shook his head at me as if I had said something amusing. "Well then, after all this time, you are still not one for small talk, huh?" The god grinned.

I only stared at him, trying my hardest not to show any signs of growing agitation and instead to school myself into having tolerance. Here stood yet another god with memories of me from another life, remembrances we no longer shared. He did not know that, though, and short words would get me nowhere.

"I suppose not. I apologize," I said guiltily. "I'm lost and in a bit of a hurry. Could you please escort me to my husband, sir?" I softly implored, remembering to mind my tongue and be polite.

A mischievous glimmer irradiated in the god's eyes, causing me to tense.

"Sir," the god repeated, a pert smile toying at his lips. "Whatever has the world done to you, Seph?" He chuckled at me once more and then lifted my hand to his face, lightly brushing his lips across my knuckles.

"Have I ever been able to deny you anything?"

Before I could part my lips to respond, he bobbed his head agreeably and walked over to the elevator. "But of course, right this way! It would be my pleasure."

Hesitantly, I followed behind him, watching as he unlocked the doors with a golden key. The rattling doors instantly opened, and the god offered me his hand. I took it respectfully and boarded the elevator, standing as far in the corner as I possibly could. The doors clicked shut, and up we went.

"Forgive me if I am assuming incorrectly, but you don't seem all that well acquainted with Olympus," the god said, a hint of a simper to his words.

I shook my head and forced a smile. "I'm not," I admitted, color rushing to my cheeks.

"So, it's safe to surmise that you don't remember me then?"

I looked at the golden-haired god and nodded, a new sense of panic beginning to gnaw at my nerves. I picked at my cuticles and watched his posture, searching for any indication that he might throw me out. A look of disappointment nipped at his face but was quickly replaced with a cheeky smile.

"Well then," the god remarked, "allow me to reintroduce myself. The mortals call me Holland Ermis, but you may remember me as Hermes, the god of direction and thievery." He gave a bow. "We were something like friends."

Holland. Friends.

A strong sense of disbelief washed through me, hard enough it seemed it could topple me over. I struggled to imagine how I could ever befriend anyone willing to watch another Olympian fade. I tried my best to appear unchanged, although I couldn't help but feel each of my thoughts directed towards him changing into something bitter with every passing second spent in the elevator.

"Thank you, Holland. Oh, and please call me Perrie," I replied.

"Perrie?" Holland repeated, his lips curling into a grin. "Is there a reason you shrink away from Persephone?"

I smiled at him weakly, wishing he'd shut up, and shrugged my shoulders awkwardly, looking more like a young girl than an ancient goddess.

"I've never gone by it. For as long as I can remember, I've always been just Perrie."

The elevator stopped, and the god of thievery chuckled as he reached for the key to unlock the doors. I anxiously watched his hands, waiting for the moment the doors would slide open and I could dart out.

"Names are quite important, you know," Holland added, opening the doors and gesturing for me to move forward. "To give something a name is to allow it to have power. For entities such as ourselves, power is everything. You are so much more than *just* Perrie. Right now," he muttered, shoving the keys back in his pocket, "you are a goddess worth more than a king's immortality."

I looked Holland over and gulped, suddenly remembering why I was even there to begin with: Haden was willing to trade his very life and kingdom for me. The thought made me shiver.

Never in my wildest dreams would I have ever thought there could be someone out there who cared that deeply about me. Slowly, I moved forward, listening to Holland's footsteps behind me, and then stopped once I found myself standing unexpectedly in the same enormous marble hall as the one in my dream.

Facing me towered a set of Levantine doors inlaid with gold and mother of pearl. Behind them, I could hear what sounded like all hell breaking loose. Claps of thunder shook the portraits on the walls, and sparks of fire flew out from underneath the door. I looked back at Holland, and he only smirked at me crookedly.

"Your husband awaits."

CHAPTER 20

HADEN

My heartbeat pulsed heavily within my ears, growing louder and louder with every nearing step. I took a breath and reached for the handle, my skin prickling. *One,* I counted in my head. *Two.* I squeezed my eyes shut. *Three.* I yanked open the doors with shaking hands and forced myself through the entrance.

A furor of voices filled the space, each clambering over the other in a blustery dispute. I opened my eyes only to discover that I was standing in an enormous throne room. White columns lined each side of the gilded chamber, stretching up to a vaulted glass ceiling. Several golden gasoliers hung suspended from the rafters, twinkling brightly in the dark. Below, spiring wrought iron windows bordered the cerulean walls, allowing in glints of silver moonlight and an expansive view of the palace grounds. Throughout the chamber, several gods and goddesses sat scattered in an impressive gallery, their ornate chairs encircling both sides of the great room, like a gilded senate. They did not notice as I crept further into the room.

"Don't be daft!" an Olympian with olive skin and aqua eyes cried out.

"An original cannot fade," another god protested, this one with hair the color of honey.

"It has never been done *purposely,*" a goddess muttered, her ebony braids swaying with every emphatic gesture.

"Nor shall it!" a voice like thunder bellowed. My gaze landed on the last speaker. An intimidating god with wavy blonde hair and sharp angular features sat on an enormous dais. He was impeccable, with a kept beard and stormy, cyan-colored eyes. His throne was positioned higher than all of the others, a sheer crest to his power. Beside him, sitting primly on a slightly smaller throne, I recognized Hertha. She was dressed in a gown of pearls, white peacock feathers pinned in her hair. A gripping sense of realization battered through me. This god…he was Zeus. *My father.*

Everyone quieted as Zane rose from his throne and proceeded down a set of steps.

"Your position on this council is of too great importance to be dispensed upon some lesser god," Zane affirmed, his gaze settling on a figure shrouded in the shadows.

My heart stopped as I followed his stare, something within me waiting…*hoping.*

From the darkness, a man arose, disheveled and dressed in all black. Hues of umber showed in his tangled curls as he crossed the room, his face rugged and unshaven. Grief clouded his features, underlining his eyes with dark, tired, circles…circles much like my own.

"You've never seen me of value before, I don't see why my presence is of such grave consequence now, *brother*," the god bit back.

I froze, recognizing the sound. Even in such a harsh tone, his voice was euphonious. I realized I'd know it anywhere…it was impossible not to. I had been enraptured by it. A fluttering sensation bloomed inside my chest, sweeping throughout my body and pulling at my core. Like a moth to a flame, I found myself voyaging ahead, needing to be closer. *It was him!* Haden. I hadn't been too late.

"Once your acceptance was all I sought after. I would have reveled at this opportunity, at the sight of all your groveling and decadent overtures. Once, but no longer," Haden acknowledged, a ghost of a smile tugging at the corners of his lips.

"Hades…"

Haden shook his head, refusing to be quieted. "Life has become so trivial…so meaningless. Nothing holds enough significance to make me rethink this choice. Without her light, I am not the sovereign I should be. I do not want a seat on this council. Nor do I care about being looked upon as your equal. Every second I exist is torture. Do not condemn me to another forsaken millennium. Please," Haden begged, his voice raw with affliction. "Let me seek her out."

A vehement look of regret settled in the King of the Gods' jaw. "Reconsider," he demanded, his voice stern.

"No."

"Last chance, Hades. Reconsider."

"No."

"Granted," Zane thundered, wounded malice lucent in his eyes.

"I have offered you all I can think of, power, women, equality. So be your decision." He turned his back to Haden.

The brief sense of relief I had begun to feel rusted in my veins. I faltered, the finality in my father's words knifing me through.

I watched in horror as he summoned three wraithlike women from the shadows. They glided across the room like vultures, thin strands of silver hair peeking out from underneath their tattered cloaks. One by one each of the stooped sisters bent in front of my father, dipping their heads amiably. Together, they pulled back their hoods in eerie unison, revealing the translucent skin and gnarled hands of storybook witches. It was *they*, I realized, who had enchanted Shakespeare's Macbeth, who inspired The Brothers Grimm, and every other ominous legend. The same three old women who had reared my father in a hidden cavern.

A startled gasp flew from my lips as I studied each of their weathered faces. Thick twines of greasy black thread jutted through their wrinkled lids, weaving them completely shut, like the sewn eyes of a corpse. The tallest of the sisters wore what appeared to be a ratty cord around her neck. A single cloudy eye dangled from its end, swaying like an accursed jewel.

As she faced Haden, a blackened smile chased across the old woman's lips. She splayed stained fingers across his forearm, soft at first…then searching. She stopped at his wrist, gripping until a notable blue vein leaped to the surface. Behind her, the other two moirai waited impatiently.

The eldest Fate drew back, only to plunge her fingers deep into his flesh, *digging* as if she had just dipped her hand within a jar and not a turnpike of capillaries and muscles. Gleaming rays of golden light burst from the tear. I stopped breathing, petrified by the sight. To my astonishment, Haden remained perfectly still, his face a guise of solemn indifference.

From his wrist, she plucked a long scarlet thread, tugging and wresting until it spiraled down to his elbow, shining like a stolen star. His complexion paled significantly once the thread was free. Swiftly, I noticed his dark hair was waning, turning an ashy gray. His fiery-brown eyes lost their luster, dimming into dull orbs, but still something within them blazed, revealing some great and horrible emotion that clawed at my insides, urging my feet to move. *Pain*. He was feeling pain.

The next beldam hurried forward, gathering the glowing thread in her hands, holding it carefully still while the last, the shortest of the crones, motioned to cut it with a long pair of rusty scissors.

Haden's head lolled the instant the sharpened blade grazed the thread, his knees buckling.

"Stop!" I cried, my voice a gut-wrenching scream that echoed off the marble walls and tore through the gallery.

I raced across the massive throne room, shoving past two of the Fates, not caring that I suddenly had every Olympian in the room's attention.

"Please," I pleaded, my eyes landing on the tallest of the Moirai. "Stop!"

The Fate holding the golden thread instantly lost her grip, causing Haden's swaying body to still and the slash in his wrist to knit itself back together, taking with it the golden thread.

Gasps echoed all around the room as color bled back into Haden.

"Persephone!" my father exclaimed, surprise flooding through his words.

A surge of baffled voices filled the gallery, loud musings, all demanding an explanation. I, however, could barely hear them. All I could discern was Haden. Here he stood a mere foot from me, breathing, solid, *alive*. I inhaled a jagged breath of panic, something in my chest aching. Tears pricked at the corners of my eyes as my mind began to race. What if I had waited too long to make my presence known... What if some sort of irrevocable damage had been done... *What if...*

I opened my mouth to speak and then briskly decided to shut it. There was no point wrestling for the right words. I was past the point of speaking.

Haden was across the room in two strides, shortening the space between us. A whisper of cedar and smoke lingered in the air around him, along with a sense of flaring heat. His russet eyes bore into mine, locking me in place. Restlessly, my pulse quickened as I watched him observe me, unearthing me to what felt like my very last atom. With a stare that intense, *that lionizing*, surely, he must've been able to see the very colors of my soul.

My breath hitched the moment I felt his skin on mine. Gently, he traced the lines of my face, his long fingers sweeping down my cheeks and then wandering up through my hair as if he couldn't quite fathom how I could be real. Slowly, he tilted my chin upwards, and then his lips were pressed against mine, drawing me away into some secret world, someplace devastating and alight. Kissing him felt both soft and stirring, infinite and true. It was everything and nothing like my visions. He held me with a certain recognition that spoke of great dolor and deliverance, and I allowed myself to be swept away in him, in his embrace and in his smell, as I was never allowed to be in my dreams.

The spell between us was not easily lifted. Haden did not break our kiss, not until the sound of someone sassily clearing their throat filled the air. We both peered up only to find Avril and my mother standing in the doorway. At once, I could feel my cheeks flushing a disagreeable shade of pink. Avril, for all intents and purposes, was glowing. A rather radiant smile showed upon her rosy lips, and her eyes glistened with pride. Mom stood rigidly beside her, a look of horror splashed across her face.

"Well," a voice echoed, queenly and disrupting.

All eyes swept toward the queen of the gods as Hertha gracefully rose from her throne, her lovely features cast into an uninterested evince of boredom.

"It would seem I was right. There will be no further need to discuss this dreary topic any longer. Send the Fates away, dear; your pretty little bastard is here to grace us with her presence."

Zane stiffened, lightning storms raging in his eyes as he forced a smile in his wife's direction. "It would appear so. Forgive me, my darling; I was wrong to dismiss you."

Hertha snorted in contempt, turning her attention toward Avril as Zane sunk into a playful bow.

"And forgive me, Avril, my dear. It looks as though you have done what none of my other kin could. You have recovered our most precious lost flower." Zane grinned, the corners of his eyes crinkling in satisfaction.

"All in a day's work," Avril spoke, turning to cast a playful wink in my direction.

Haden's grip tightened around me and then loosened as he ventured closer toward the center of the room, a horrid chill already kissing up my skin without his touch.

"With your approval, brother, I would like to acquire the support of both Hera and Aphrodite," Haden suddenly spoke out, causing my heart to gallop.

He, like my father, had a demanding voice, sharp and exquisite, like any king would, I imagined. "I believe it is time I took a bride."

"Nothing would please me more," Zane affirmed, his voice growing ever silverer and adorning as he turned to address the host of immortals around us.

"This is a day to be remembered! Persephone, our goddess of spring, has returned to us. After centuries of displacement, she has arisen from a sleep-like death, only to defy the Fates and to refuse the celestial arms of Khaos. She has returned to us not only as a survivor but as an idol reborn, a true daughter of Zeus. She has spared the life of an Original, saving my beloved brother, and for that, they shall be wed by Eos's first light." His cyan eyes landed on me and then flickered toward Hertha and Avril. "Have the Queen of the Underworld ready and dressed for her ceremony."

Hertha acknowledged him with a look of heedlessness, and Avril skipped over to us with a smile as bright as the sun.

"Come, daughter," Zane said, signaling me out. "There is much for us to discuss."

CHAPTER 21
A MEANS OF WORSHIP

My father was gone in an instant, disappearing through a curtained entryway, leaving behind both I and his garrulous court. Gods poured from the gallery, each wearing garments colored to match the sky as they noisily abandoned their decadent chairs. Discursive whispers and catty titters soon surrounded me, twining around the room like a heavy mist. I could feel their stares, their disconcerted smiles as they passed me by. I remained still, my body a listless vessel, too shaken to move. So much had happened within the last forty-eight hours. *So much*, and yet...

My heart began to hammer as a hand drifted down my spine, stopping respectfully at the junction of my shoulder blades. A hint of cedar scented the air, along with a wreathing smell of earthy smoke. *Haden*, my blood seemed to sing.

Quietly, he guided us in the opposite direction, away from the other Olympians, and I felt the tension in my shoulders begin to wane. Somehow, I managed to walk alongside him without stumbling. I suppressed the desire to stare at him ceaselessly. He was beautiful. Arcane and deft on his feet...like a breathing shadow. We stopped near an empty alcove, and I veered around to face him, determined to say something, anything to atone for our first encounter.

"There is much I must attend to," he spoke, his voice low, gravelly. "I have to leave. I'll be back before you wake."

"B-but..." I stammered, something within me feeling steeply jilted.

Haden shifted closer to me, lifting my chin once more with his fingers. His umber eyes swept over me, lingering on my face. Resultantly, my breath hitched, and a searing blush crept across my cheeks. Would he kiss me again? *Did I want him to?* Ebbs of embarrassment sprung to the surface as I recalled our kiss. *Oh, that kiss.* I could still feel how it had left my lips swollen, how his bristly stubble had caused my mouth to tingle. It had roused some carnal sensation within me, turning the butterflies in my stomach into fiery red admirals. I urged myself to reel in my emotions, picturing just how wanton I must have appeared in front of the council. I don't know what had come over me. Being near him was like being entranced and I couldn't help myself. I wanted to be closer to him.

A slight smirk tugged at the corner of his lips as if he knew what I was thinking and was entirely remorseless of our nature. He then pressed a gentle kiss against my brow and stepped away.

"I promise, Persephone.".

"Perrie," I corrected, my voice a timorous assertion. "I go by Perrie now."

He lifted a brow and smiled again—a slow puckish grin that sent shivers down my spine.

"Perrie," he repeated.

I smiled at him and nodded, watching our hands drift apart and him stride away, his lean shape a stark wraith amongst all the gilt and cerulean until he was no longer visible.

"I haven't seen you this antsy since, well, the first time you saw him," Avril suddenly announced, her sing-song voice rattling me from my thoughts.

I jumped, my cheeks once again reddening. Avril gleamed at me and then let out an excited squeal. She snatched me in her arms, pulling me into a joyous hug.

"You did it!" she exclaimed, bouncing us around in gleeful circles.

"I did, didn't I?" I mused, her delightful smile contagious.

"I wouldn't be celebrating just yet," a voice cautioned.

A brusque youth stepped from around a pillar. He was handsome in a macabre sense, with closely cropped nut-brown hair and a herculean stature. His eyes were a cruel amber that seemed to glow saffron in the light as he observed us fiercely. Avril stiffened beside me, her smile waning into a reserved grimace as the male drew closer. Finally, she gripped my arm and held her head up high, slipping into an alluring bravado.

"Hello, Aaron," Avril greeted, lowering her lashes in a movement that was so beguiling it was no wonder Botticelli had chosen to paint her rising from the ocean foam into the arms of her countless admirers.

The god smiled, a vicious flash of teeth, and nodded his greetings.

"Hello, Avril," he returned, shifting his keen interest towards me.

He conceded into a low bow, rising to glance at me with an overlying sign of disfavor in his features.

"Word has it that you have no recollection of your sanctity," Aaron put forward.

I studied the god facing me, noting the pretentious way he chose his words as if he were whetting daggers to cut me down with. I gave him a sweetened grin before nodding my head in admittance.

"You've heard correctly," I confirmed.

He snickered and straightened his back.

"Well, for what it's worth, I owe you an apology. I'm afraid I presumed you faded a millennia ago," the god said tersely.

My smile remained, a good-natured show of understanding, while Avril all but seethed next to me.

"I am Aaron Bennett," he carried on. "You may remember me as Mars, or Ares, god of–"

"War," I finished for him, my stare wandering back to the goddess next to me, toward Avril and her cautious appearance.

Aaron followed my gaze, and a hint of something like pining rose and fell in his eyes.

"You've heard of me then," Aaron noted, his face hardening back into that brow-beaten scowl.

"Yes," I said quickly, my thoughts straying back to Mom and what she had admitted earlier at the cottage.

To love a soul different from your own is only to give rise to your own misery.

"Then you know that as the deity of war and as commander of Olympus, I felt compelled to vote for the greater good of our ménage. There was no malice behind my decision, only commiseration. Your betrothed has been living a life of self-sabotage for centuries now, abandoning his dealings in the mortal land, and barely attempting to evolve with the times. It was all we could do to convince him to change his name. He was still living by many of the old laws, and by doing so, has lost great arrears of worship. I did not want you to assume me to be a careless elector."

I inclined my head, squeezing Avril's arm in what I hoped was a subtle, reassuring gesture.

"I appreciate your honesty. I'll do my best to do right by our family," I admitted, trying to sound stouthearted and not at all as touch and go as each fiber within me seemed to bustle.

Before another word could be said, Mom made her presence known. She looked every bit a distinguished goddess, equable and prepossessing, as she smiled a genteel hello towards Aaron and then turned her navy focus upon me.

"Come along, Perrie. It is ill-mannered to keep your father waiting," Mom beckoned.

Knowingly, I bobbed my head, and together Avril and I wended our way over to Mom. She steered us toward the curtained entryway, away from the tinseled blue walls and the bearish god of war.

"Good luck," Aaron called out, his voice echoing across the throne room. "You are most certainly going to need it, sister."

Avril quickened her steps, her cinnamon hair swaying as she drew me closer, refusing to give Aaron another glance. From over my shoulder, I could just make out his pointed smile and then the shift of his body as he strode in the opposite direction.

"Hey," I said, jostling to keep in pace with my fast-moving sister. "Are you alright?"

Avril paused for a moment, stopping at the threshold to hold back the taffeta curtains. Then, she offered me a comely smile that took a second to reach her eyes.

"I will be," she resounded. "It's always a bit jarring to see him again. Even though Aaron and I long ago made our peace, he still reminds me of another time, of the goddess I used to be. I'm not proud of who I was then. Remembering that version of myself and all the hurt we caused each other, it makes me feel a little...out of sorts. It's nothing my Henry won't be able to fix, though, darling. Oh, I can't wait for you to meet him!" Avril beamed.

I smiled at her and drifted past the palls of silk and out into an open antechamber littered with dozens of lofty wrought iron windows. We found Mom waiting for us in the hallway, her spine straight as she gazed up at a set of towering oak doors.

I sucked in an anxious breath, my pulse racing as I beheld the entrance. The same swirling iron that trimmed the windows entwined the polished wood. I knew what awaited us beyond those doors. It was time to meet my father, to claim my future as a goddess.

An animated grin dusted across Avril's rosy lips as she sashayed forward, fearlessly shoving open the doors and losing out a gust of heat.

The space we entered next was not at all as I had expected. The room was large and ivory, bedizened with several tawny-colored columns. Below, the floor was marbled, and an impressive map of each of the four kingdoms was raveled against the stone. A far-stretching table occupied most of the chamber, drawing out to meet a broad fireplace. Two sallow-colored eagles sat astride the mantle, their carved wings outstretched as if they might take flight one day. Books of all shapes and sizes bordered the walls, living upon alpine shelves, infusing the air with the comforting smell of old paper and leather.

I walked further into the room, counting twelve high-backed chairs that sat around the magnificent table. Each of the chairs was occupied, seating nine divine Olympians. All but three were empty, and I quickly gathered whose they must belong to. Mom moved ahead of me, her fingertips lightly grazing mine as she strode toward one of the chairs. Avril pursued her, mouthing the words, "You've got this," and then prettily situating herself next to a god with a gruesome scar.

I felt their absence like a bite. Suddenly I was exposed, like some poor insect wriggling underneath a magnifying glass. Panic flowered inside me, twining around my lungs. I fought the urge to nervously muss my hair, choosing instead to clutch and release the gossamer sleeves of my sweater. I realized this would be my last trial–the final test before infinity. I refused to be seen as anything other than determined. *I could do this. I was a goddess.*

"Persephone," a voice rumbled, turning my attention toward the tallest of the chairs. Rested at the end of the table, my father reclined, his body facing away from the daunting fireplace.

"Come here, girl. I want to take a look at you," Zane ordered, his tone jovial and pleasant.

I did as he instructed, walking toward the end of the great table and then stopping once I was in his line of sight.

As a girl, I used to fantasize about meeting my father. I had wondered what his life was like, picturing him in giant skyscrapers, promenading about the busy city streets of New York or Chicago. I often thought about his world while I was tied up in my own, snapping green beans or shooing pesky grubs from the vegetable garden. Mom had called him a mogul once, a tycoon of business, and I reckon the Gatsby-like image I conjured of him stuck. It wasn't until I was a few yards from him that I realized how wrong my imaginings had been. Like my mother, Zane appeared middle-aged. He was handsome as only a god could be, exuding a sense of witty charm and excellence. His suit was perfectly tailored, and his sandy hair and beard were thoroughly kept, shaped into a modern cut. His cyan eyes were flecked with the same greenish celadon as my own, and I found that I had his exact snub nose and dimpled chin.

A hearty chuckle escaped his lips as he stood and offered me his chair.

"Why, what a radiant beauty you have become, Persephone. You are a near miniature of your mother, save for those eyes and that chin! Those are quite mine, wouldn't you agree?" Zane doted, peering about the room with an exultant look about him.

An assenting murmur of voices fluttered about the chamber as he again offered me his place at the head of the table. Sheepishly, I took it, lodging myself on the edge of the cushioned seat. I pretended not to notice the blackened glower Hertha threw my way as I scooted closer to the tabletop.

"Now," Zane began, leisurely strolling about the room, "we must discuss several things. You, daughter, must understand the delicate structure of our being. Without a firm discernment, I'm afraid you may have yet another run-in with Khaos."

He paused, carefully considering his next words, and then stated in a very astute voice, "Humans eat food, breathe air."

He made a show of inhaling, breathing in deeply through his nose and then out through his mouth as he walked over toward a large glass window. I watched as he peered outside the window, crossing his arms behind his back.

"They survive, and then they are turned to dust, but that is not the end of their journey. No, nowhere near it. They are given an afterlife. We are dissimilar. Gods know no end. We know only forever. Or so we thought. We immortals can live for eons, impervious to age or human disease, but we are not lost to time. It would seem without the worship of mortals our eternal threads begin to wear thin. We become frail and sickly, our bodies deteriorating until we are barely more than wisps in the wind. When your name is forgotten and your wells of prayer run dry, that is when you cease to exist. That is when you fade, and there is no great beyond for us." Zane grimaced, his demeanor suddenly stripped of its breezy cheerfulness.

Goosebumps rose on my flesh, and a rivulet of hazy memories began to stir within my mind, each reminding me of a ruinous cold…one so penetrating, so frost-bound that my bones began to ache.

"The world is not as you left it, Perrie. Humans no longer worship and idolize deities; they adore those who wear flawless acquainted faces. Young girls don't want Apollo. They want Harry Styles. They don't want to be as bewitching as a goddess. They want to look like a Kardashian. To survive, we had to adapt. We had to become reputable. Before you are some of the world's most thriving business heads." Zane waved his arm out to present each of the nine Olympians present.

He abandoned his window and sauntered to Avril, placing his hands on her slender shoulders.

"My beautiful Aphrodite, once worshiped by all of Greece and Rome, is now Avril Jones. She is a world-renowned supermodel, fairer than any other in the industry, featured on Sports Illustrated, Playboy, Vogue."

He moved across the room over to a chair holding Aaron. Roughly, he clasped him on his shoulder in that proud fatherly manner I had often seen dads do to their favorite athletic sons when conversing at the grocery store or at a concession truck.

"My eldest son Ares, the god most praised during times of violence and hardship, is now the United States five-star general, Aaron Bennett. He trains half of America's armed forces."

Zane made a confident circle, trekking back around to softly tousle the hair of the scarred god sitting next to Avril, a fleeting look of pity in his eyes before he spoke.

"Henry, the god who once constructed all of my lightning bolts, is now the world's greatest inventor, working alongside and guiding some of the brightest minds in history. You may have heard of some of his pupils…Archimedes, perhaps? Or De Vinci? Tesla? Who do you think it was who *actually* invented the atomic bomb?"

He continued his saunter over to the male I had seen earlier in the throne room, the god with bright aqua eyes and golden-brown skin. A wide smile spread across his face as the two roughly shook hands.

"The mighty Poseidon, king of the seas, is now the head CEO at N.O.A.A. Without Parker Scott, there would have been no hope of cleaning up that dreadful oil spill in 2009."

Zane bobbed his head toward several of the others, and Holland winked at me from across the table.

"Hermes, or Holland, has been in the music industry for years. He also is your man if you want anything illegal smuggled to the public. He was over the delivery of moonshine during prohibition, and now Sony hacks and the leaking of celebrity nudes seem to be his hobby."

Zane's cyan gaze shifted onto the devilish figure of a handsome god, sitting with his feet propped against the tabletop, a vibrant violet boa scarf slung around his neck, and a collection of piercings glittering in his ears. "Beside him is Daniel Ricci. Daniel, once a god known for ritual madness, is now a grand event organizer. He owns numerous vineyards throughout the globe and throws untamed parties for the rich and famous."

I watched as Zane presumed his traipse, calling out name after name, pointing in the direction of a great many alluring faces. The goddess Artemis, now known as Aryanna Bishop, a popular track star. Her golden-haired twin brother, Arthur, once an authoritative sun god, now an esteemed surgeon. Athena, the goddess I had seen with the flowing ebony braids and prominent gray eyes, presently a notable architect, working under the licensed name of Alivia Laskaris. Finally, his gaze settled upon two goddesses, both blue-eyed and fair skinned, one with hair the color of spun gold, the other with wavy strawberry locks.

"Hera, my beloved queen, is an esteemed wedding planner. It was Hertha Windsor who managed everything from the flowers to the five-foot-tall fruitcake Lady D and the prince of Wales had on their wedding day." He spoke softly, the liking in his voice causing Hertha's posture to stiffen, and her features to frost over.

After a moment, he tore his stare from his incurious wife and offered a faint smirk in my mother's direction.

"Your mother, Demeter, has proven to be quite the changeling, living countless different lives throughout the years, going about as a spinster in the seventeenth century, running several secret apothecaries, faking her own deaths on multiplel occasions. Isn't that right, Demi? Or should I say Giulia Tofana? She has since opened several flower shops and dispensaries, relocating when the mortals become suspicious, or when our search parties happened to get too close for comfort. Somehow, she has managed to gather just enough admiration from the humans to sustain both you and she alike without being too conspicuous," Zane revealed, causing my eyes to widen in shock.

I looked over at mom who was quietly sitting with her hands folded in her lap. She didn't bother denying it. Waves of contrasting emotion seemed to be warring within her mind, telling on themselves through the disquieted purse of her lips, and the shameful lowering of her lashes. I couldn't believe it. My mom, a brilliant murderess…an ageless mistress of disguise.

Zane let out a troubled sigh, shaking me from my shock. He raked his fingers through his sandy hair and leveled a condoling glance at my mother.

"A god cannot undo the workings of another god. You've caused quite the ruckus, Demeter, and broken one of our most sacred laws. By not honoring the pact made between Hades and our daughter, the world has fallen into disorder. Parker tells me that the ocean surface has been plagued with red tide. The snow nymphs are worried that they may not see the next millennia, and famine has run rampant in certain parts of the globe. You've been neglecting your duties for some time now, and there are many here within the realms who wish to see you punished for your crimes. I, however, will not make a villain out of you for acting as a mother should when she believes her child to be abducted. I am partly to blame, and will take accountability for my actions. I should not have allowed Haden to steal away with our daughter. She is the child of two originals, and it is a dishonor to us both for her to marry in such secrecy. However, she must return to him, Demi. They must be rightfully wed," Zane noted, earning a slight nod of understanding from Mom.

"I know," she answered. "You have my word. As long as our daughter remains safe and happy, I will not interfere in their lives."

Zane nodded his head, giving his beard an accepting stroke.

"Fair enough. Consider yourself pardoned and forewarned. Should you go back on your promise a second time you will not be so easily forgiven," Zane professed, his serious stare meeting Mom's.

Again, she inclined her head. "Thank you, brother."

Seemingly pleased with her response Zane then returned his attention back to me, clearing his throat.

"The days of old are gone. We cannot have temples built in your honor, and have offerings sent to you in the libations of grain, or the burning of oxen. After tonight, Perrie, you and Haden will have shared sums of praise, if he so permits it. Your mother has also agreed to continue and portion some of her tributes with you, as well. However, as a precaution, I advise you to seek your own way of obtaining worship through whatever means you see fit. Understood?"

"Yes," I answered, my throat suddenly feeling dry from the immense weight of my acknowledgment. "I understand."

"Good," Zane exclaimed. "Good!" A delighted smile stretched across his face from ear to ear. "Then everything is resolved!"

"Not quite," Avril suddenly spoke up, drawing everyone's attention upon her. "The day before we arrived at Circe's, Perrie was marked by a flock of harpies. It would seem whoever sent them is not very accepting of this union and went to great lengths to prevent it."

Zane's smile vanished and something like shock darkened his eyes.

"Well," Zane muttered, once more stroking his beard. "That is a fair cause for concern, isn't it? Not to worry, though. I'll schedule an audience with Chiron. He'll know if any of the Creatures have been acting out of sorts, and we'll find these harpies."

Everyone watched as the king of the gods strode across the room and stopped at the large oak doors of his study.

"Oh, I almost forgot. There are two tasks I require of you, Perrie. The first will be to get examined by Mnemosyne. Only she is truly capable of aiding you in the restoration of your memories. The second is to be tutored by Alivia. As an Olympian and an immortal queen, it is important for you to understand our history, and it is of great consequence that you learn to control your powers. You will be allowed four weeks to enjoy your time as a newlywed before being called upon to complete these charges." He gestured toward the outside and yawned, a drowsy look underlining his features as he looked down to read the time on a golden pocket watch. "It has been a boisterous few days, and I would very much like to retire for the evening. I suspect the lot of you would as well. I shall see you all bright and early in the morning." He turned to leave.

Gods stirred around me, each rising to leave the enormous room, and once more I remained motionless, my mind still whirling with the frenzied words of my father's consultation.

Powers. Training. *Ha! I* knew if I hadn't been so wracked with fatigue, I would have surely found the terms laughable, visualizing myself decked in some ridiculous latex suit, dodging laser beams, and shying away from shards of kryptonite, as if I were some silly comic book character. Instead, I found myself sinking further into my father's chair, my eyes burning for sleep.

Just before my head began to dip, I was on my feet, with an arm snaked around my waist. The smell of honeysuckle stirred the air, and the warm ticklish sensation of hair sweeping across my cheek pulled me into awareness. I was leaning against Mom, my feet padding down a moonlit hallway. Avril was a capering sum of cinnamon curls and flashy red stilettos as she guided us up an ornate staircase to Mom's old chambers.

CHAPTER 22
BRIDE TO BE

The next morning, I awoke to the twittering sound of voices outside my bedroom door. A congenial knock ensued, followed by a mishmash of girlish laughter. Groggily, I sighed into my pillow, and tugged the covers over my head, and then immediately bolted upright, a frantic realization jolting me awake. I wasn't in my bed. *No*, I was at Olympus. It was daylight! Hastily, I scrambled out from underneath the sheets, blindly pushing aside the silken tassels of a canopy, and then tottered to a stand. My breath hitched the moment I was coherent enough to truly observe my surroundings.

All around me, the walls were a gleaming shade of ivory paneled in shimmering gold. Beneath me, the floor was a dusty marble, attired by a viridescent rug that seemed to frame the bed in a furl of floral-patterned carpet. The bed was a massive four-poster, positioned atop a small platform and teeming with lots of satiny pillows. The coverlet was a brilliant reseda green, ruffled, and downy, like a mullein plant. Curtains of the same earthy shade decorated the room, wreathing gilded windows and even a set of shining gold-plated balcony doors. Below, the room appeared to go on forever, coming across more like a grand suite than a bedchamber.

Curious, I wandered toward my bedroom door, interested to see just who expected me in the hallway. I jumped the second I heard the familiar creak of another set of doors whirling open behind me. Minutes later, Mom appeared through a hidden doorway, the entrance disguised as a lovely woodland mural of two magnolia trees, one a blossomy pink, the other a pearly white, their branches intertwined. Behind her, I noticed the botanical design of a brass footboard and the rumpled layers of an unmade bed.

A subtle ache settled in my chest as a swell of recognition shot through my mind. Mom and I... *we* had adjoining bedrooms. Once, this had been my sleeping quarters—a place made explicitly for us. Someone had taken the time to fit my room with furniture and other sorts of glittering baubles and flowery bric-a-brac. None of it suited me. As resplendent as it all was, it was a bit too gaudy, too luxuriant, and yet it was this thought that unsettled me: in another life, I had been meant to grow up in this room, live in this palace. As if I were a princess... as if I were a daughter of Zeus. Avril's words at the Flower Patch suddenly fluttered through my mind. *He loves us all in his own way.*

Mom's yawning uprooted me from my thoughts, drawing my attention back to the here and now.

"If that is Avril, she better have brought something heavily caffeinated with her," Mom grumbled, padding toward the door with a disagreeable look of sleepiness about her that she didn't normally sport.

Out of the two of us, she had always been the early riser, relishing in the wee hours before the rest of the world arose. I credited her crotchety attitude to a lack of sleep. We had all stayed up well past midnight, and she had more reasons than most not to feel comfortable here.

Mom groaned, drawing both sides of a loose gray cardigan around herself before opening the door. A swarm of giggling girls entered my room, each adorned in delicate light dresses and matching armlets. Some, I noticed, had long pointed ears that peeked through rivulets of curls. Others had unusual eyes, dazzling and sharp, like the eyes of a feline. They all seemed to have the same extraordinary hair, each possessing a head full of vibrant locks more colorful than the last, as if they had all dipped their heads in a radiant pool of rainbow. Once inside, all the girls dropped into spirited curtsies.

"My goddess," they greeted, their voices sweet and sprightly, like the lilting sound of wind chimes or the tuneful rattling of reeds.

I stared at them, transfixed. Never had I seen hair so bright or complexions so shimmering and unearthly. Who were these girls? Why were they here? The painter in me yearned for my sketchbook, for my watercolors, and shading pencils. The well-mannered part of me worried for their ankles that remained crossed and their hems that still kissed the ground.

Why did they suddenly appear so meek, so quiet when I had just heard them laughing moments before? I glanced over at Mom. My lips parted in question when a show of cinnamon hair filled my peripheral, and the hickory smell of bacon and raspberry muffins infused the air. Avril cheerily sauntered inside, an exciting ambiance about her as she came to a stop beside me, bringing with her a steaming tray of breakfast.

"Good morning!" Avril cheerfully sang, venturing across the room to set the tray down on a small, round tea table.

I watched as she dusted her hands on her hips, twirling about to face us.

"And how are my two favorite nature goddesses? Did you sleep well? Are you excited? Never mind that last question. Of course, you are!" She shone, popping a piece of bacon in her mouth.

She turned her back to us once more, busying herself with filling two porcelain cups with what smelled like dark roasted coffee. She twiddled with the sugar, dropping in at least three of the gritty cubes before pouring in the creamer. Contented with her ratios, I watched Avril skip over toward us, offering Mom and me a scalding teacup.

Mom grabbed her cup, sipping the liquid, and then crinkled her nose, evidently appalled by the concoction.

"I slept fine," I responded, carefully gathering the teacup in both hands. "Who are your friends?" I questioned, bobbing my head in the direction of the colorful-haired girls.

Avril stopped her chattering, her flamboyant movements stilling.

"My friends?" she muttered, her lovely features scrunching in confusion. "Oh!" Avril giggled, tossing her hair back dismissively. "Darling, those are your flower nymphs. They're here to serve as your handmaids." She walked toward the alignment of young women. I watched as she stopped in front of them, her dainty hands laced behind her back as she softly cleared her throat.

"Euphemia, if you and Calandra could please go and prepare Perrie's bath, that would be splendid. Oh, and Hyacinth, I would greatly appreciate it if you and Nara could freshen up the room and perhaps open some windows. The bride-to-be must have a heartening environment before her big ceremony."

At once, each of the girls broke free from their curtsies and began to scatter about the room. Two attended to the bed, stripping back the blankets and replacing them with crisp new sheets. Another set about fluffing each of the pillows, neatly situating them back in place. I noticed a nymph with lavender skin disappear through an open archway. She was followed by another nymph carrying an arm full of towels.

"Handmaids," I repeated, the word an anomaly on my tongue.

"Yes, yes," Avril said. "Every respectable goddess has at least four. They are here to help you get ready, which–" She took the untouched teacup from my hands, sitting it back down on the table with a gentle *clack*. Then, she selected a rather plump muffin, slathered it in butter, and handed it over to me. "We must begin if we are to arrive on time."

I had hardly managed to take a single bite of the muffin before we were moving, gliding through an open archway into a space bordered by the same ivory walls as the ones in the bedroom. A rosewood vanity awaited us, decked with dozens of prismatic bottles and pretty brushes. A flowery dressing screen stood to its right, as picturesque and delicate as a fairytale.

In the corner, beneath a window, a glimmer of something white caught my eye. I turned, my breath catching as I beheld my gown. It was displayed on the body of a mannequin; its blushing pink skirts scattered about the floor like the unfurling petals of a rose. It was even more gorgeous than I remembered, with all its white upper lace and intricate beadwork.

Two shoes I hadn't noticed before sat inches away on a cushioned bench. They, too, were remarkable, with a low inkblot heel and a flowery covering of white satin.

"Gorgeous, aren't they?" Avril sighed, stopping to admire the pair of delicate shoes.

"They're lovely," I responded, my attention drawn to the top line where an array of small, embroidered butterflies sat, stitched out of what appeared to be dozens of sparkling gemstones.

"Holland brought them in sometime last night. He said they are a gift from your groom," Avril stated.

She gave an expressive wink that instantly had my heart leaping in my throat. I tried to summon forth a small smile, to upturn my lips into a modest show of excitement, but instead found myself too nervous to even blink.

My groom. The words felt surreal. Dizzying even, the longer I thought them over. Once more, my eyes settled on my dress, its tufts of pink tulle and its elegant white lace. Behind it, shimmering in the windowpane, I noticed my reflection. I could spot the tautness in my shoulders, the spark of apprehension rising in my eyes. I realized what little reign I held over my anxiety was beginning to wear thin.

Never had I imagined myself as a bride. I was too used to the deception...to the timid girl who accepted dandelions as bookmarks and found companionship amongst the words of Oscar Wilde and Charlotte Bronte.

I had no clue how to be a wife, let alone an immortal queen.

The immediate sound of footsteps stymied the silence, wresting my mother and Avril's attention from the gown. I loosed an anxious breath, glad for a momentary diversion, and turned to see no other than Prilla zipping through the entryway.

She was dressed in a yellow poet dress, her nut-brown hair swept into a loose twist at the nape of her neck.

Her cheeks were flushed as she came to stand beside me, her breaths quick, an indication that she had more than likely raced down numerous flights of stairs to be here.

Still, the goddess of soul managed a friendly smile in my direction before turning her focus upon her cinnamon-haired mother-in-law.

"Sorry I'm late," Prilla gasped, "I lost track of time and—"

Avril harrumphed, taking my hand once more in hers.

"Did you at least remember to bring what I asked you to?" Avril asked, a hint of irritation lacing each of her words as she waltzed us toward yet another set of gilded doors.

"Of course!" Prilla replied, summoning a bejeweled box from thin air.

Avril let out a little sigh of relief.

"Good!" She beamed. "I couldn't imagine the ceremony without it." She nudged open one of the ornate doors.

Thick whirls of humidity met us at the threshold. Through the haze, I could make out the design of an exquisite washroom. Like in the other two apartments, the washroom was ornamented in shades of flora green. Moisture fogged the delicate glass of several gold-leaf mirrors, and the soft glow of dawn brightened the space, making the veins of gold in both the marble flooring and the ivory basin glisten.

A sunken tub, more reminiscent of an extravagant pond than a bath, sat in the very center of the room. Three arched windows stood before it, overlooking the grassy plains and snow-capped peaks of Olympus.

Water poured into the bathtub, falling from a decorative faucet. Slices of grapefruit and the colorful petals of freesia floated atop a sea of bubbles, imbuing the air with the beckoning smell of spring.

"This really is a bathroom worthy of a goddess," I muttered, finding myself taken aback by my surroundings.

Avril laughed beside me and gently dropped my hand. "Good thing you are one, then, huh," she teased, a radiant smile seizing her lips.

Before I could summon a response, I noticed the fabric of my vanilla dress and the wispy sleeves of my sweater vanishing, disappearing in a show of effervescent sparks. A velvety white robe appeared in its place, covering most of my bare skin. The pink ribbon that had been meticulously woven into my hair just yesterday was the last to go, mindfully unraveling itself before vanishing. I let out a little sigh of relief as my hair tumbled free from its updo, falling down my back in a mess of gingery waves.

The nymph I had seen earlier, the one with lavender skin, reappeared. She smiled at me timidly and dipped into another brief curtsy.

"Is the room to your liking, my goddess?" the nymph asked.

"Oh, um…yes. Thank you!" I answered, hating the unmistakable awkwardness that tainted each of my words.

"Excellent. Shall I help her majesty into her bath, then?" She gestured toward the steaming tub.

Promptly, I shook my head no and fumbled back a few steps.

"No, thanks. I think I can manage," I assured, my fingers instinctively reaching for the neckline of my robe.

I knew if I could have, I would have certainly tugged the velvety material up to my nose. Behind me, I could hear a blend of laughter. I turned to find my bridal party giggling. Even Mom, who had managed to keep her facial features indifferent for most of our visit, cracked a half-smile.

"Give us a few moments, Euphemia. We'll call for you when she's ready," Mom spoke up, dismissing the girl.

The nymph nodded pleasantly and drifted out of the washroom. I waited until I knew for certain she was gone before approaching the lip of the tub.

"You better get used to answering questions like those," Mom stated, tossing me a knowing look. "You are the Queen of Hades, after all. Once this marriage is legitimate, you won't be able to so much as sneeze without there being an entire mob of servants there to offer you their handkerchiefs."

"Will I really need assistance bathing, though?" I asked under my breath, careful not to speak too loudly.

Mom smiled at me grimly and futilely attempted to sweep my wayward fringe behind my ear.

"You are a goddess. Your feet aren't required to touch the floor unless you wish otherwise. Forget what you think you know, what I've told you, and listen to your instincts. They haven't led you astray thus far," Mom said softly, a navy glimmer of guilt showing in her eyes.

She gave my arm a loving squeeze and then calmly stepped out of the way, leaving me to stare at the set of closed doors where I knew a team of nymphs waited on the other side.

"You'll get used to it," Prilla reassured, her dimpled smile sweet and uplifting as she trailed behind Mom toward the exit.

Avril was the last to drift toward the doors, a mischievous smirk fixed upon her cherry-colored lips as she turned to face me.

"Do try to enjoy yourself. And don't put up too much of a fight. We'll be back soon. Elysium knows I can't have those two dressing themselves," Avril teased.

I laughed at her words, imagining just how difficult it would be to coax my mom into wearing something snazzy, and nodded my head in a show of readiness.

"Okay," I conceded.

"Okay," Avril beamed agreeably.

She let out a little sigh as if she were readying herself to outfit a bear and then strode away, closing the doors behind her.

CHAPTER 23
FIT FOR A QUEEN

For a few guarded seconds, I continued to stand by the tub, watching a pink petal float atop the sudsy surface before finally deciding to throw off my robe and descend into the bath.

The water felt divine, warm and relaxing as it splashed against my skin. Dozens of ticklish jets shot out from different angles, kneading away the tension in my shoulders as I waded further into the bubbles. I was surprised to find just how deep the tub was, noticing that from my spot, only my collarbone was visible. Pleased with this, I judged it safe to unwind and dipped beneath the foam to wet my hair. When I emerged, Euphemia and another nymph with curls the color of larkspurs waited by the edge of the door. In her arms, I spotted a basket filled with all sorts of crystal bottles and vibrant jars. She smiled at me and then nodded toward the bath.

"Is her Highness ready for assistance?" Euphemia inquired.

I ignored the flaring urge to tell her no and instead bobbed my head.

"Yes," I answered, willing myself into accordance.

Once again, Euphemia offered me a pleasing smile as she situated herself upon the marble steps. I watched as she emptied one of the containers into the center of her hand and then knelt forward to gently massage the liquid into my scalp. I leaned my head back and closed my eyes, appreciating the citrusy smell of lemon verbena and pomegranate as she worked the rest of the lather into my hair. When she was done, and my hair was thoroughly free of soap, the other nymph gestured toward my hands.

"May I?" she asked, lifting an emery board.

I nodded, and the nymph made quick work of my hands and feet, brushing and buffing until my nails shined and all the calluses I had grown used to feeling on my skin were gone. Both nymphs mercifully rose and left to prepare something in the other room when it came time for me to bathe my body, leaving me with a single round sponge to rinse with. Wary of the hour, I hastily turned myself over to habit, scrubbing until I felt decidedly clean and then rising to grab one of the fluffy towels. I still had one foot in the bath when Euphemia reappeared. She helped me out of the sunken tub and down the slippery steps, steering me out of the washroom and back into the open space where my wedding gown waited. We were greeted by another handmaid, this one with the honeycombed eyes of a butterfly. She bent into a brief curtsy, then inclined her head toward the dressing screen.

"This way, my goddess," she directed, waltzing us toward the flowery divider.

Upon their instruction, I slipped behind the panel and noticed the dazzling box Prilla had summoned from earlier. It was no bigger than a hatbox, bedecked in sparkling jewels and lacquered pearls. A small, folded piece of paper was pinned to its cover. Curious, I unfolded the paper and found Avril's unmistakable scrawl written across the page. The words *Open me* were penned in large cursive letters. I smirked at the note, silently bracing myself for whatever item resided within the box, and then threw back the lid.

Inside, beneath a scattering of dried rose petals, a white corset lay. The corset was unimaginably racy, trimmed in a pale pink lace. I gaped at the bit of lingerie, holding it up in the light, and then found my jaw dropping at the sight of the matching pair of panties beneath. Another note sat on top of them, this one written in the same cursive letters.

"To my darling sister," I lowly read. "I had this made for you eons ago. I had hoped to give it to you on your wedding day *if* you chose to marry, and now I am finally able to do so. It is a near replica of my own infamous girdle. Fear not, I had the girls at Arachne Couture give it a few contemporary touches. Wear it well and wear it often. Love, Avril."

A befuddled titter fled my lips. She had to be joking. *I couldn't wear this.* Undergarments like these were meant for prettier females, goddesses like Avril, who were unabashedly beautiful. I was, well…different. I did not possess the same stunning height or sinewy muscles as the goddesses in the throne room. Nor was I as pleasing and shapely as some of the other Olympians that sat on my father's council. I had a soft stomach and narrow hips with a face far too round for my own liking.

"Does her goddess require help with the fastenings?" a voice called, wrenching me from my turns of self-disgust.

I stirred, wriggling into what I could of the lace underwear before stepping back around the divider.

"Yes, please."

Euphemia waved her hand, calling out to the girls in a smooth, whimsical language. Two handmaids instantly appeared, one scurrying behind me, another stopping to straighten the front of my corset. A sudden powerful jerk had my breath catching. I winced as the handmaid behind me tightly crisscrossed each of the ribbons along my spine, silently tugging and towing for several minutes before stepping away to admire her handiwork.

"Perfect!" the nymph declared.

I smiled at her stiffly, hesitant at first to move or even breathe. I wasn't entirely certain I could. The sudden whisper of fabric rustling and the nimble patter of footsteps deterred me from trying. There, in the arms of a single yellow-haired nymph, was my gown.

"If her goddess would care to step forward," Euphemia encouraged, waving me ahead.

Obediently, I ambled toward the center of the room, my heart a frenzied pulsar within my chest. *This was all beginning to feel real. I was actually going to do this.* I sucked in an anxious breath and stepped into the open gown. Euphemia held me steady as the others guided me through the tiers. It was made of three layers, shrouding my legs in a crest of garden pink.

The upper part of the gown brushed across my skin like silk, garnishing my torso in a shower of beadwork and fluorescent lace. The sleeves were as delicate and soft as I had imagined, racing up my arms in an illusion of ivory blossoms, stopping just at my shoulders, and dipping to meet the pale blooms that made up the plunging neckline.

I stood perfectly still as one of the nymphs did up each of the buttons at my back, securing me into the dress, while another fluffed out the train.

"Oh my!" a passing nymph exclaimed, stopping to bring Euphemia my shoes. "You look stunning." A mossy smile spread across her bark-like face.

"Come see, come see!" the girl behind me said excitedly, skipping toward the vanity.

Slowly, I stepped into the shoes, surprised to find just how perfectly the heels fit. I allowed myself a few necessary moments to find my balance before daring another step. The last thing I wanted to do was trip or tear a snag in my gown. Avril would undoubtedly have my head if I did, and I couldn't bear the thought of scuffing the heels Haden had gifted me. Once adjusted to my new height, I carefully lifted my hem off the ground and made my way across the room. Walking in my bridal wear was not nearly as challenging as I had dreaded, and I found myself standing before the vanity in no time.

I purposefully avoided my reflection, identifying all the items atop the dressing table before lifting my gaze to stare into the mirror. I wasn't ready to see how ridiculous I looked…how horribly I spoiled such a lovely dress. The moment my eyes fixed on my reflection, I immediately clasped a hand over my mouth. Gone was the frumpy shopkeeper. In her place stood a goddess, regal and radiant with skin like porcelain. Specks of glitter shimmered across my collarbone, dipping down to elegantly dust the tops of my breasts. The plunging neckline that I had been most concerned about showing too much modestly complimented my figure, reminding me that while I may not have been as tall or voluptuous as the others, I possessed divine curves of my own.

"Stunning, indeed," Euphemia agreed. "All that's left to do is your hair. How would you like it styled, your grace?"

I sat down on the cushioned chair and peered up at my mess of tangled curls, eyeing my drying fringe and loose waves in puzzlement. Most days, I barely did anything with my hair, either weaving it into a loose braid or tying it back. I didn't bother with elaborate twists or fancy knots. It wasn't as if the plants cared how I looked.

"Up, perhaps?" one of the nymphs suggested, raising a glowing finger and spinning my hair about.

Magically, my kinks lifted into the air, each of the fiery strands drying as they bowed and twisted into an exquisite French bun, wisps of loose curls spiraling down to frame my face.

"Or down," another chirped in, snapping her fingers.

Instantly, my hair tumbled free from its updo, each of the upper braids slowly untwirling and falling down my back in smooth, sleek tresses.

"Why not both?" a voice called from the doorway. The familiar clack of heels against marble filled the space, and everyone fell silent as the queen of the gods entered my dressing room.

Naturally, Hertha was gorgeous, dressed in an indigo ball gown fit for a queen. Her golden hair was curled, pinned to the side with two dazzling combs that were crafted to look like peacocks.

She halted behind my chair, shooing Euphemia and the other handmaids away with a glare that could sear flesh. They wasted no time in leaving. A few even tripped in their haste to flee the room. Hertha grinned, a wicked gleam sparking in her glacial eyes.

"Nymphs," she exhaled. "Terrible company to keep. Worse to have as maids, what with all their senseless giggling and idle chatter."

"I thought they seemed nice," I managed, doing my best to sound calm and unshaken.

Hertha made a derisive sound. She toyed with a few of the items on the vanity before picking up a heavy silver brush. Lazily, she examined it, pretending to be intrigued by the motifs on the back. However, I knew her real interest lay beyond the gilded toiletries. She was looking for something else–a jolt of fear, perhaps. Or maybe a shudder of panic. Any sliver of weakness that she could hold over me to make me feel inferior. I would not give her the satisfaction of being outwardly startled. She and I were soon to be equals, two immortal queens. I would not be cowed by her again.

"Yes, they always do..." Hertha agreed. "Don't let their charm fool you, though. They're more conniving than they look."

Tenderly she began to run the brush through my hair, rearranging a few loose waves here and there before conjuring a box of gilded barrettes. I watched as she pinned the golden blooms into my hair, leaving most of my curls down to spiral past my waist in soft, romantic ringlets.

A sense of disquiet hung between us, wordless and smothering as she worked. I sat still, trying to decipher why my aunt would find it necessary to come to visit me. She seemed to be considering the same. Hertha sighed once more, setting the box of floral barrettes down in a show of exasperation.

"Look," she said, abandoning all pretenses of kindliness. "I do not like you. The very sight of you sitting here, under my roof, vexes me. You are as burdensome and infuriating as a pebble in a shoe. However, I am not your enemy."

I held her gaze in the mirror and repressed the urge to shiver. Staring into her eyes was like peering into the heart of a tempest. She was rage and steel, splendor and poison. I was reminded of my dream, of the broken goddess who gave herself over to vengeance. She could slaughter me just as easily as she had summoned those blossoms.

I considered my next words cautiously, weighing their effect before asking, "What are you then?"

A corner of Hertha's lips twitched, lifting into a bitter smile.

"Someone who knows the consequences of the vows you are about to make. Once spoken, they cannot be undone. You will be bound to Hades.

Forever. And he to you. The gods are not like those silly, little mayflies you've lived amongst in the mortal lands. Forever actually holds merit for us."

"I-I know," I acknowledged, cursing the sudden break in my voice.

"Do you?" Hertha instigated. "You may think yourself in love, but you are still quite young. You have hardly lived beyond your mother's shadow. It is easy to make deals when you feel smothered, harder to bear them once clarity sets in and you can breathe."

"I did not make this choice because of my mother," I fired back, a touch of anger now singeing my words.

Did she really find me that pitiful, that reckless to presume that I would barter myself into a loveless marriage just to be rid of my ordinary life, to escape Mom?

"Is that why you did not acknowledge our marriage before, because you thought I was trying to run away?" I asked, the question flying past my lips faster than I could think better of raising it.

Hertha shrugged, a hint of vicious amusement heightening her harsh beauty.

"You were unconscious, unable to speak for yourself. What kind of queen would I be if I condemned a fellow goddess to an unsought union? Binding yourself to an Original is a misstep you will take on your own, lucidly. I washed my hands of forced marriages long ago."

I opened my mouth to ask another question, the words at the tip of my tongue ready to spring free, when the unexpected sound of commotion outside the dressing room invaded our conversation.

Through the walls, I could make out the panicked cries of the nymphs, followed by the quick rap of shoes against marble as my bedroom door creaked open. Mom's distinct voice rose above the chaos, and I knew it would only be a matter of time before both she and Avril were back by my side, ready to gauge me for injuries and shelter me from the queen of the gods.

Hertha hardly seemed to notice the clamor outside. Haughtily, she lifted her chin as if to silently say she had said all she cared to and was now ready for me to be out of her line of sight. In a swoosh of gold and indigo, the queen of the gods spun on her heel to leave. She stopped to linger in the doorway for a minute longer, turning her head to face me.

"Regardless of your sentiments toward me, contemplate our little chat. It has been centuries since you ate that pomegranate. Time changes even an immortal's heart, and it would be foolish to believe that your romance is as you left it. Make sure the choice you decide upon is one you can live with forever." Then she was gone, disappearing to whatever far corner she had come from.

CHAPTER 24
COLD FEET

I had no time to contemplate my aunt's words, to smooth my furrowed brow or organize my scrambled thoughts before Mom and Avril came barreling into the compartment, voices raised and emotions flaring.

Wearily, I sat back in my chair, allowing myself to be swarmed.

"Are you all right?" Avril questioned.

"Did she hurt you?" Mom demanded, an edge to her voice.

"What did she want?" Prilla inquired, her tone the softest of the three.

I opened my lips to speak and then paused, uncertain of what to say. What *had* she wanted? Had her pretense of a warning been genuine, or did she have other motives, greater justifications for wanting me to reconsider my decision?

"I don't know," I muttered, glancing down at the vanity, at the heavy silver brush Hertha had toyed with. "I think she saw herself as giving me marital advice."

"Marital advice?" Mom repeated, an amused bite to her words. "Ha, that's rich coming from her. I knew we should have never left you alone! I knew it!" She shot Avril an accusatory look.

Sensing Mom's building change in mood, I quickly began to shake my head, twisting in my chair to better face my bridal party so they could see I was fine and no damage had been done.

"It's okay," I said. "I'm…"

All thoughts of words, of speaking and forming sentences slipped my mind. Instead, my attention was fixed on Mom, to the hint of gold dusting her lids and the adorning flash of diamonds and pearls that embellished my sister and Prilla's attire.

"...fine," I finally resolved, awestruck. It was hard to declare precisely which of the three goddesses was the most beautiful. Alone, each was radiant enough to steal the air from a room.

Avril, wreathed in a sheer blue gown, looked every bit like a daughter of the sea. Hundreds of tiny pearls were sewn into the marquisette fabric of her dress. She wore no jewelry save for a pair of white drop earrings and a sparkling headpiece. Her long cinnamon hair was swept to the side, braided back in a loose plait.

Next to her, Prilla was a sight to behold, swathed in a long satin gown with a choker of yellow diamonds sparkling around her neck. Her thick, carmel-brown hair was left to cascade down her back in a show of tight, glossy, curls, and her downturned lids were done in brilliant shades of purple and gold, putting me in the mind of a resplendent sunset.

But it was Mom who left me speechless, who appeared so otherworldly and unlike herself, dressed in a backless gown the color of carmine. Stalks of glittering gold wheat decorated the bottom of the gown, and her lips were painted a vivid crimson. She wore a simple, golden circlet atop her head, with her strawberry blonde locks whisked into an elegant, wispy, chignon-style bun.

As if suddenly recognizing my wear, too, Avril let out a little gasp. "Oh, Perrie!" she exclaimed, a jubilant smile upturning her cherry-colored lips. "You look even more lovely than I had imagined."

Mom stopped her pacing, her worried gaze lifting to look at me, to truly look at me for the first time. I watched as her breath caught, as tears pooled in the corners of her eyes and her bottom lip began to quiver. Quickly, she clamped a hand over her mouth and shook her head.

"Perrie, you're... you're..."

"Ah, ah, ah!" Avril suddenly scolded, shoving her way in between us. "No crying! You'll ruin my masterpiece."

Mom tossed her an aggravated look, snorting to herself as if she couldn't wait to scrub all the carefully placed glitter and rouge from her face. Avril snickered back, unabashedly proud of her handiwork.

"Beautiful," Mom admitted. "You look beautiful."

Prilla bobbed her head in agreement, her rosy lips curling into a contagious smile as she settled on the armrest of my chair. "I've never seen a more gorgeous immortal queen," she proclaimed, leaning in to give me a brief hug.

"Thanks," I replied, awkwardly patting her on the back. "I guess I clean up well. All of you look very nice, too," I added, feeling a wave of heat creep across my cheeks.

I wasn't used to receiving such high compliments. Or giving them, for that matter. Prilla only giggled and rose to stand near a potted aglaonema. Mom, however, was right on her heels.

"You shouldn't have said that so loudly!" Mom scolded, her momentary lapse of motherly awe eclipsed by her sudden worry. "Someone could have overheard you and–"

"And what?" Avril interrupted, a defensive twinkle shining in her ocean eyes. "Give Erika the idea to craft a golden apricot this time rather than an apple. Unlike Thetis, I was wise enough to send her an invite. You don't have to fear bewitched fruit or any enchantments brought on by jealousy. Besides, Daddy had Hecate bound the palace for the occasion. Perrie will have a fabulous ceremony, followed by a splendid reception. You have nothing to worry about."

Mom scoffed and crossed her arms, her brows knitting together in mistrust as she settled herself on a tufted bench.

"And this binding spell, I'm presuming it will last for what? A day? A few hours? It takes less than a second for a spy to report back to Hertha or Amara, but never mind that, what marvelous news that you remembered to invite Eris," Mom sarcastically groused. "Have you forgotten how patient Hertha is? Or Amphitrite? If they truly found themselves affronted, they would have no difficulties with waiting to enact their revenge. And let it be known, I'm not too sold on Heather's work. It would seem Hertha still found a way into Perrie's dressing room."

Avril rolled her eyes and stepped away from her place by the wall. Sassily, she walked over to me and gently began rearranging a few of the clips in my hair.

"This is her realm, Demi. I can't have her barred from rooms in her own home. Technically, we are all here as guests. As far as I can tell, Perrie seems fine. No scratches or bite marks. There isn't a single unsightly boil or cloven hoof on her. You know it's supposed to be the bride with the potentially cold feet, right? Not the mother of the bride."

"I don't have cold feet!" Mom insisted, her nervous fingers curling into willful fists. "I swore an oath before the council last night. I do not intend to break my word. It's just... Well, so many things could go wrong. Zane has yet to inform us about those harpies. We do not know their whereabouts or what they're plotting. Their master still remains nameless and could be an

Olympian for all we know, waiting out in the audience. As long as those beasts remain free, she is in danger, and yet somehow, you are as carefree and pleased with yourself as ever!"

"At present, Perrie is the safest she's ever been. Any assailant dumb enough to test their luck against a court full of Originals is asking to meet Thanatos," Avril countered, glancing down at her nails and then up at Mom matter-of-factly.

"And when she's gone? Once she is off Olympian soil, what then?" Mom disputed, throwing her arms in the air.

Curiously, I looked between the feuding goddesses, waiting for an answer. *What would happen to me after the ceremony?* Would I immediately be whisked away to the Underworld, or would my new husband grant me one last day of open air and sunshine?

Avril opened her mouth, a saucy quip forming at the tip of her tongue when Prilla's thoughtful voice interjected, "She'll be with Haden then. He would never let anything bad happen to her."

Once more, Mom's doubtful contemplation landed on the goddess of soul.

"He's a king, Prilla. I'm sure he has his own contestants to deal with. Not to mention there will be days when he must leave her alone for hours and…"

"She will have sentries and Cerberus and–knowing Haden–a blade sharp enough to slay a Kraken!" Avril ascertained. "She'll be fine."

Mom didn't look the least bit convinced. Instead, she seemed inclined to make another comment when the rhythmic sound of someone knocking on my bedroom door stopped everyone short. A wary passing of silence filled the room, and then Mom and Avril were on their feet, marching across the threshold to meet whoever waited for us in the sitting room. Curiously, Prilla and I hustled after them, the hushed rustling of our hems and the clicking of our shoes livening the sudden quiet.

***

Upon entering the sitting room, I was surprised to find an elvish-looking youth lingering near the door frame. The boy was dressed in a simple uniform, his childlike features not so unlike that of the nymphs, save for his pale hair and bright eyes. He bore a nervous expression as he chivalrously bowed at the four of us and then cleared his throat.

"Pardon the intrusion, my goddesses, but it is time. His majesty has sent an escort for the Lady of Spring and her matrons of honor."

"An escort?" I repeated, just as the shape of a well-dressed figure appeared from behind the young courier. It took my mind only a minute to recognize the scent of apples, to recall a pair of steadying hands and a voice that made something like ire and sorrow flutter within my veins.

"My goddesses," Holland formally greeted, stepping through the entryway.

I watched as he took in the room, his gaze sweeping across the furniture, flickering from goddess to goddess before settling on me. For a moment, the god of thievery seemed rendered silent. The lopsided grin he had been brandishing fell, and the playful light in his eyes dimmed, making an uneasy feeling sprout within my stomach. *Why was he staring at me like that?*

Seeming to notice my uneasiness, Mom was quick to step in front of me, muddling Holland's view. Just as fast, the god averted his stare, shifting his attention to the small courier. Lowly, he muttered something to the boy, who nodded in return and vanished in a gust of summer air.

"I have told young Zephyrus to let Zane know we are on our way," Holland said, again smirking. "That is unless the lot of you are plotting a get-away, in which case..." Holland winked but was soon cut short by a miffed Avril.

"Not in your wildest dreams, fly-boy," She responded, arrantly placing both hands on her hips. "We couldn't be more ready. Isn't that right, girls?"

"Right!" Prilla hurriedly blurted, looking back at Mom and me with expectant eyes.

"Of course," I answered, although I could feel all the hidden worry, the infuriating what ifs and daunting unknowns I had strove to bury from earlier humming beneath the surface.

I was a mess of emotions. The thought of leaving this apartment, of being meticulously watched by a chamber full of flawless immortals, was enough to tie my stomach into knots. Nonetheless, I was certain of my decision. No matter how unconventional, I wanted to marry Haden. This was my destiny, my true purpose, but the idea of turning my back on all that once was–The Flower Patch, memories of canning peaches with Mom and spending nights out on the porch watching fireflies–in exchange for something different. An unknown future of riches with a mesmerizing stranger surprisingly wasn't an easy choice to make.

I felt ambivalent. This would be world-changing. I would miss so much. Hertha's deterring words didn't improve matters, either.

Determined not to lose my nerve, I switched my focus to Mom, waiting to hear her final words on the matter. Surprisingly, she said nothing. She merely stood in place beside me, a disagreeing look of compliance written across her face that seemed to assure she'd follow through with her promise to the council, to me, but begrudgingly so. There would be no congratulatory words falling from her lips, no heartfelt smiles of happiness or tears of joy. Today was a day of mourning for her, an admission of surrender, and that was all she was willing to offer. *No more. No less.*

I had expected as much, but it didn't make the knowledge of it sting any less. For now, I knew I would have to acknowledge her approval in whatever shape I could get it, whether it be an imposed white flag or one made of her own love and words. Until then, I knew we would both do what was expected of us. *Together.*

Skeptically, Holland raised a brow, taking in all our expressions before finally letting out a dramatic sigh."Very well then," the god announced, brushing a speck of invisible lint from his jacket. "Since you all seem so insistent, no elaborate escapes. If you would all kindly follow me. We must hurry if we want to catch up with the others."

CHAPTER 25
THE HALL OF PORTRAITS

O*thers,* I thought, wordlessly falling into step behind Mom. *What others?* I pondered, moving across the threshold and out into an open corridor. Bright beams of sunlight shone through the windows, warming my skin as I passed beneath their panes. I contemplated asking Avril about these additional members of our party but instead quickly found myself too stunned to speak as I noticed the door to the guest room magically swinging itself closed behind us, as if some invisible hand had nudged it.

Amazed by the workings of the palace, I couldn't help but to stop and linger in place for a moment, my imagination running wild with the notion of phantom servants and gusts of sentient wind…things I would have once easily dismissed as imaginary. Now I could only stand and second guess. Everything about this world was so different, so alive and whirring with hints of hidden glamor that it was hard not to be dumbstruck.

Time was the only thing deterring me from staying put a moment longer, from finding myself lost in wide-eyed wonderment as I strolled past floating decanters of water drizzling down onto flower arrangements and hovering feather dusters brushing across stern-looking statues. Time and, well, our escort; evidently, Holland hadn't been joking around when he said we would be moving fast. He walked with such urgency that I had no choice but to keep my viewings short or risk falling behind.

Quiet as church mice, we followed the god past various remarkable tapestries. We walked by dangling relics and other gleaming items I hadn't noticed during my previous heavy-eyed walk through the dark. I could hear the distant commotion of attendants going about their day-to-day tasks. Somewhere, there was a scuffling of shoes against marble. Faraway, I could overhear a bleating cough, followed by the tuneful singing of a nymph, trilling in that budded, whimsical language only they seemed to understand. The further we traveled throughout the palace, the more I noticed Olympus was teeming with not only enchantment but life. Through the windows, I could see eye-catching clusters of blue veronicas planted alongside shoots of delphinium in striking flowerbeds. Musters of peacocks strutted about the gardens, and other Creatures resembling gnomes worked alongside sprite-like beings, plucking weeds from the soil and carrying in large batches of greenery. Inside, several smells imbued the air, blowing in from different directions. A sweet, glazed scent from my left; a beefy-caramelized aroma from the right; the unmistakable hint of potpourri from underneath a cracked door.

I wondered whether this bustle of activity was usual for Olympus or if my sudden presence had upturned the palace, doubling the workload of those who served my father. I frowned at the thought, unhappy with the notion. *Did the Underworld employ as many housemen as Olympus? Were all these Creatures happy to have jobs in the palace, or were their labors enforced?*

Fortunately, I was snatched from my thoughts the moment I sensed everyone coming to a gradual halt. We had stopped in front of a massive, curved staircase. Two gold eagles were fashioned atop its caps, and a far-stretching cerulean runner embellished its steps. I watched as Holland approached the stairs. He paused on the first step, pushing back his jacket sleeve to peer down at a silver smartwatch. Swiftly, he swiped his finger across the screen, then refocused on us.

"Nice work, ladies!" Holland remarked, readjusting his sleeve. "Not a minute over schedule. The others are waiting for us upstairs." He donned what seemed to be a pleased smile and then jogged up the rest of the steps.

Avril and I shared a glance before beginning our own ascent. As I climbed each step, I paid close attention to my feet, sending a silent prayer out to the universe that I wouldn't trip and topple backward. What a comical tragedy it would be to make it this far only to meet my doom on a flight of stairs.

After several more breadths of hushed walking, I decided now seemed as good a time as any to ask my earlier question.

"Who are the others?" I whispered, carefully stepping beside Avril, who was deftly holding her own hem off the ground, her ocean-eyes trained straight ahead like a well-disciplined duchess used to climbing such elaborate staircases in all sorts of flowing finery.

"You'll see," she whispered back, an excited smile tugging at her cherry-colored lips.

I looked over my shoulder at Mom, who didn't seem nearly as thrilled as my sister to be visiting the halls of her old home. Her fingers were laced tightly around the winding banister while her other hand was busy wrangling the crimson tufts of her dress out of the way of her feet. At least she also seemed to be having a difficult time maneuvering the stairs in her gown.

***

Once upstairs, I was surprised to find a sizable billiard chamber, this one aligned with numerous towering marble columns and a handful of powder-blue baroque sofas. Matching lamps and other gilded commodities occupied the room, including two ancient suits of shining armor equipped with plumed helmets and glinting swords. A dartboard stuck through with stubs hung on one of the walls, and to its left, an antique snooker table rested in the middle of the room. The noisy clacking of a ball being pocketed filled the air, followed by the rowdy whooping of cheers.

I traced the sound back to a trio of gods, two of whom were crowding the snooker table and another who was observing the game from an armchair.

"Nice one, Casanova," Holland called out, drawing the attention of the first god toward us.

Unexpectedly, it was Cam who whirled around, his flaxen curls a mess, and his face flushed. Promptly he lowered his cue stick back onto the snooker table and scrambled to fix his loosened tie. But it was too late. Avril was already upon him, marching across the room, her slingback heels heatedly clacking as she tramped toward her son.

"Eros!" she scolded, smacking the young god's hands away from his undone tie. "Do you have any idea how much effort your poor footmen went through to get you ready, only for you to go get yourself all sweaty and wrinkled!" She bristled, fixing his mussed hair and rumpled suit in a snap of vibrant sparks.

"I…" Cam stuttered, looking back helplessly at the other two Olympians and then toward his wife, who was disapprovingly shaking her head at him.

"It's my fault, love," an unfamiliar voice answered.

There was a pause as the male sitting in the armchair rose from his seat, followed by several low grunts and a repetitive *TAP, TAP, TAP,* as something wooden struck against the marble floor.

"It was I who suggested we play a few snooker matches while we waited for you lovely ladies to arrive. Don't flay the poor boy," the god continued, stepping into the light.

The first thing to catch my eye was the stranger's height. He was tall, nearly as towering as the Cyclops had been, with an attractive, young face and a kind smile. He had ashy-brown hair that was streaked through with strands of silver, and in his hand, he gripped a cane. The second most prominent thing to draw my attention to the god was the intimidating patchwork of scars that seemed to mottle the entire left side of his face, tapering down his neck and reappearing across his knuckles.

Upon closer examination, I realized I recognized him. *He was Henry!* Avril's husband. The very same scarred Olympian she had seated herself next to in the counsel room and the inventive genius my father had so proudly commended but could not bear to look directly in the face. Any further assessments I might have made of the god's character were promptly cut short, thwarted by Avril's curved frame as she came to stand before her spouse.

"And why in Gaea's name would you suggest such shenanigans? Especially today of all days!" Avril groused, looking very reminiscent of an irritated pixie when standing next to her giant of a husband.

Henry opened his mouth to speak as if he had a reasonable defense for allowing such antics to occur. Then, with a knowing look, he shut it as if he could already predict his wife's unyielding reaction to his response.

"Oh, alright, fine! I'll say it if nobody else will," another voice exclaimed from the very center of the room, capturing everyone's attention. "Bombshell beauty, you might be, but you aren't exactly known for your great and glorious skills in timekeeping, now are you, Aphrodite?"

Still propped against the snooker table, the third Olympian made himself known. He was modelesque, with long limbs and smooth nut-brown skin. I identified him immediately as the flamboyant god my father had introduced as Daniel Ricci. Like last night, the god of wine was clothed rather eccentrically, wearing a patterned suit and a pair of spiked boots. His shoulder-length black hair was crimped, twisted in some half-up fashion, and his tapered eyes were winged in sequins, making him look like a modern-day Cabanel painting come to life. He bore a haughty expression as he continued to chalk the end of his cue stick, pretending to be entirely unaware of the outraged expression that had taken residence across Avril's face.

"How were we to guess you'd actually show up to an event early," he resumed, gently sitting aside his stick with a deviant smirk on his face.

"Early?!" Avril exclaimed, tossing Daniel an indignant look. "I have arrived just when Daddy instructed."

"Precisely my point. You showing up anywhere near curfew should be considered early. Not that I hold your reliable tardiness against you. Fabulousness such as ours should never be rushed."

A muffled laugh escaped Cam's lips, causing Avril to whirl around and pin both her son and husband with an accusing scowl.

"And what about you two? Do you agree with this nonsense?" Avril asked, waving her hand dismissively in Daniel's direction.

Daniel rolled his eyes at Avril, and Henry chuckled, an amused look overtaking his face as he reached out and gathered his seething wife in his arms.

"He might have a slight point," he admitted, brushing a soft kiss between his wife's scrunched brows. "It is only a little out of character."

Avril feigned insult, half-heartedly shoving the god away.

"Quisling." She grinned, a flirtatious glow brightening her pretty features as she spun around to face me.

"Perrie, darling, come here. I want to introduce you to my husband. This is the master tinker himself." Avril excitedly winked.

Bashfully, I did as she asked and crossed the room, offering the god of blacksmiths my hand.

"Hello," I said. "It's so nice to meet you finally."

I watched as the artisan studied me, a joyous smile brightening his features as he took my extended hand in his. Despite his hulking stature and daunting appearance, he had a soft grip, one far gentler than I had anticipated, with a demeanor that seemed to match.

"How wonderful it is to see you again, Persephone," Henry met, giving my hand a light peck before releasing me. "And you as well, Demeter," he included.

Mom managed a faint smile in his direction, her lips parting in response when the sudden, loud tolling of a bell shook the room. Holland, who had been playfully poking fun at Daniel, promptly stood up straight, his eyes flying toward a window where an enchanting-looking clock tower could be seen dinging outside, its gilded arms resting on the numeral seven.

"That would be our cue," he stated. "Shall we, everyone?"

Like before, we all formed a line, each of us now gravitating toward a chosen companion as we motioned to leave the billiard room. Cam had, of course, gathered Prilla's gloved hand in his, causing a radiant blush to spill across her round cheeks. Likewise, Henry had offered his arm to Avril, who gracefully accepted his advance, nestling herself closer to her husband as they wandered toward the door. Holland had, as expected, taken his place at the head of the line, his gaze occasionally flickering back in my direction and then somewhere else as if he wished to ask me something but couldn't quite decide whether he should.

I pretended not to notice, choosing instead to muse over my knowledge of weddings and how they might correlate with my current predicament. I knew most brides opted to wear white, and generally, there was always some kind of bridal march and an exchange of rings. I had never actually attended a service, though. Most of my understanding of weddings came from books or from the frequent orders customers placed for their special days at the Flower Patch, demanding floral centerpieces and bouquets. Realistically, I hadn't the slightest clue what to expect. There had been no sort of rehearsal, no mention of who would be walking me down the aisle or if this ceremony would be anything like an ordinary human wedding. Neither Mom nor Avril had clearly mentioned what the ceremony even entailed, only that it was crucial for both the goddess of love and the goddess of marriage to be in attendance.

A climbing sense of panic flared within my mind the longer I dwelled on my unknowingness. I didn't like being unprepared. Immediately, I did my best to drive the fear back and instead drifted toward the middle of the line, settling myself behind everyone else. Mom naturally gravitated beside me, and Daniel was the last to sort himself in place, stepping behind us.

Taking note that we were all ready to leave, Holland spun around and steered us through yet another open archway. We had scarcely begun to move when I felt one of Daniel's long arms wrap around my shoulders. Awkwardly he shoved his way in between Mom and me, tugging us both close to his sides.

"It would seem Zeus miscalculated just how many escorts we would need for the wedding," he smirked.

"Yes," Mom agreed, an evident tone of annoyance present in her voice as she pushed his arm off. "It would seem so."

"It was heavily implied that *I* was to escort *you* to the ceremony, but seeing as our tour guide has a bit of an unrequited infatuation with the wife-to-be, and I'm still a little sore with you for nearly freezing all of us lesser nature deities off the face of the earth, I think it would be a little bit inappropriate, wouldn't you agree? Maybe you could walk with the Flash, and I'll escort Perrie to her oh-so-handsome bridegroom instead," Daniel proposed, tossing a wink in my direction.

At the mention of Haden, I found my cheeks heating. Mom snorted and chose to loop her arm through mine, jerking me away from the god of ecstasy.

"I think we can manage on our own just fine, thanks," she snapped, tugging me closer.

This spurred a laugh from the god of wine, who decidedly shrugged his shoulders and said, "Suit yourselves."

***

The hallway Holland led us down next was nothing like any of the others we had passed through before. Used to the cloudy blue tones and regency-like furnishings of the palace, I was shocked to find this passage to be rather different, with its dark, velvety red wallpaper and gold leaf sconces. Portraits of all sorts adorned the walls. Some were small in stature and crudely drawn. Others were painstakingly beautiful, with canvases big enough to crush a human beneath their heavy frames.

I paused in front of one such painting, my eyes drawn to the gory image of what might've once been a beautiful man bound to a cliff. Every inch of his skin was tinted crimson, and his mouth was frozen in an eternal scream of agony. Soaring above the man flew an eagle, a bloody liver dripping in its talons.

"Ah, you've found The Painting of Prometheus," Daniel spoke up, causing me to jump in surprise.

I hadn't heard him stop beside me. I had presumed he had journeyed ahead with everyone else.

"He was real, you know. Still is. Poor bastard," he resumed, his voice taking on the hushed tone of a camp leader in charge of telling a ghost story.

"Who was he?" I asked, unable to look away from the awful work.

"A Titan heretic," Holland unexpectedly answered in Daniel's stead.

I lifted my gaze from the hellish artwork to find that everyone had stopped moving. Like me, Holland was now staring up at the portrait, a disturbed look overtaking his charming features as he viewed the piece.

"Once, he was one of Zane's closest confidants. Together, the two created the first race of men. Zane fancied the mortals but not nearly as much as Prometheus, who desired to see them made into monarchs and poets of the land rather than just the simple hunters and gatherers they had been for ages. Our father believed them to be too animalistic to wield the knowledge of the gods. He forbade anyone in the three realms to provide them with any immortal assistance, fearing that they would one day view themselves as our equals if they were to stumble upon our knowledge. Believing Zane's command to be too strict, Prometheus disobeyed our king's orders, stole fire from the heavens, and gifted it to man. He was, of course, caught, and his rebelliousness won him an eternity of torment. He lives to this day chained to that rock, a breathing example to the rest of us not to defy or take the benevolence of our All-Father for granted. This painting depicts his punishment." Holland turned his back to the image and walked further down the hall.

Mom, who had strolled a few paces in front of me, returned to my side, gathering my hand in hers before quickly glancing over the work. She shook her head, disgusted.

She scoffed. "What fools we were to think we could rule this domain any better than the titans."

Together the two of us turned away from the painting and resumed our walk onward, going left when the hallway split into two different directions and then up a set of twisting stairs. As we went, we passed by even odder paintings. Some were of mythical animals, like the cryptic Sphinx and the fearsome hydra, but most depicted small, winged puttos, and other baroque-style children. The image of a curly-haired infant clutching two large snakes in his tiny, baby fists seemed to stand out the most, as well as the picture of a she-wolf nursing twin boys.

Abruptly, Mom stopped to stare at a painting of an exotic woman, her jaw clenched in outrage as she took in the woman's lush frame and the magnificent white swan that wove around her body, its ivory feathers splayed to cover the woman's nakedness. Surprisingly, a troubled laugh fluttered past her lips, causing everyone to stop once again and peer back at us.

With some work, Mom composed herself, fixing her posture before finally explaining the cause of her furious laughter.

"What a doting husband Zane has become, showing off his infidelity and his wife's handiwork with such disregard. I'm surprised Hertha allows for these to be hung up where all of Olympus can see. They're appalling."

Holland shrugged his shoulders and motioned for us to move along.

"These portraits are our history. Some of the works kept here are monumental to our lineage. Others, he finds humorous. To him, they are like caricatures. Very little of the truth is present. Take this one, for example." Holland answered, nodding his head toward a picture of a long-haired youth wearing a pair of winged sandals. Clinging joyfully to his neck, I was surprised to see a young maiden who disturbingly resembled me, with her coppery red hair and vivid green eyes. "I wasn't wearing my sandals that night, and your daughter certainly didn't willingly jump into my arms."

"No," Mom agreed, a deep tone of sadness altering her voice as she approached the painting. "You found her buried beneath the snow that day, near lifeless, nothing like she is here. There was no pink in her cheeks, no smile on her face. Her hair was nearly as white as the ice dusting her skin."

Chilled by her words, I watched as my mother seemed to relive that day. With quivering fingers, she reached out and touched the painted maiden, and I felt my heart break for her, for both of us, as I let her remembrance of that night seep in. Desperately, I struggled to make sense of her memories, to force the pieces of the puzzle to come together. I tried to conjure my own recollections, begging any sliver to reappear. *Good. Horrid.* It didn't matter to me. I just needed something, anything to resurface. And then, all at once…it struck me.

CHAPTER 26
A MEMORY OF ICE

Memories of the night I had been found surged into my mind like ice water, jolting me with a coldness so utterly freezing I could not stop my teeth from chattering. I felt myself staggering, fumbling for something to grab as my vision began to tunnel and I was swept away.

Snowflakes danced in a sharp, wintry wind. I could feel their frosty wetness whipping through my hair, flying beneath my sodden clothes as I fought to stay awake. Far off, I could hear several hurried footsteps crunching through the snow behind me. Somewhere, Mom was shouting—accusing Zane of murdering her only child. He matched her tone, demanding she mind her tongue in a voice cross enough to summon lightning strokes. I paid them little attention. I was too tired, too devastated to catch more than a few sentences. The world around me was white, opaque and overcast. All the trees looked sickly thin. Not a single leaf adorned their poor, stooped branches. The familiar sounds of the forest had gone quiet, as if all the beasts of the wood had vanished. There were no beams of sunlight or hints of flora to be found. A distracting sense of warmth enveloped me, pulling me away from their bickering, from the sudden ache in my chest at seeing such barrenness. I did my best to curl up closer to that warmth. Someone was carrying me—someone who smelled like smoke and cedar. Someone I knew. Haden.

"Perrie?" a voice called, snatching me from my vision and back to the present.

I blinked and found Prilla standing before me, a look of worry racing across her pretty features as she softly shook my arm.

"Are you alright?"

"You look very pale," Cam added, peeking at me from over his wife's shoulder.

I nodded, trying to quell the unexplainable shivers wracking my body. A sharp throbbing accompanied the trembling. It pounded behind my forehead like a bad case of brain freeze. Mercifully the pain subsided after a few deep breaths, and I was able to make out my surroundings again. Somehow, I had ended up across the hall. I was no longer standing up straight and observing the painting but slumped against a wall. Mom had one arm snaked securely around my waist while her other hand was pressed against my brow as if she was inspecting me for a fever. We were sitting on a cushioned bench, and everyone was staring at me with bewildered expressions.

I shied away from their stares, my ears immediately warming in a flare of embarrassment. Never before had I had a memory resurface while I was still awake. *I must have looked so crazy, so out of it.* I pretended not to be bothered, awkwardly rubbing at my arms in an attempt to banish the goosebumps pimpling my skin.

Spotting my embarrassment before anyone else, Daniel whirled around, waving his hands in a dramatic shooing gesture.

"Would you all stop gawking at her? She is fine. The poor thing has just had a bad case of wedding jitters. Nothing to fret over. I have seen this plenty of times. Lots of brides get a little woozy before publicly sealing their fate to another."

"It's not wedding jitters," Avril dismissed, shooting Daniel an exasperated look. "She's remembering. Something in the hall must have triggered a memory."

Mom went very still beside me, her expression growing ever more rueful and apologetic as she turned to face me.

"What did you see?"

"S-snow," I stuttered. "All I could see was snow. I heard your voice and Dad's. The two of you were fighting, and Haden…he was there. He was holding me."

Holland gave an affirmative nod, his gaze turning back toward the painting.

"When I found you, you were at Khao's door. Not in a thousand lifetimes had any of us ever seen anything quite like your condition. It was very disconcerting, to say the least. None of us knew what to do or how to react. We all agreed that you needed to be taken to Olympus, to Apollo or Asclepius, someone with the gift of healing. I focused all my energy on finding the fastest route to get us home. We ended up having to travel through the mortal lands, and Haden carried you every step of the way. When we finally made it home, you were seen by countless gods and goddesses, all of whom tried to revive you and could not. When it was evident no one in Olympus could heal you, I was sent to scour the world for others. I came back with lesser gods, with Creatures and Titans. He was there every time, without fail, guarding your room like some lovesick wraith. The day you disappeared, I arrived with Iaso. It was she who found your bed empty. Haden had been forced to leave his post to attend a council meeting. The legitimacy of your elopement was disputed by many, so numerous meetings were held to determine what should be done if you were ever to wake. When he caught word of your vanishing, his reaction was…"

"Horrible," Avril finished for him, her usually light-hearted temperament darkening slightly at the recollection. "Haden's heartache was a horrible thing to feel. It was as if someone had stolen all the fire from the stars. He felt so lost, so frightened, and overcome with anger. He blamed himself for what happened to you and mourned you with an intensity that could ravage the heavens."

A pang of guilt shot through me, followed by a recognizable throw of sadness. I knew that gnawing ache, that all-consuming sense of being adrift. It felt like being kicked in the chest, like being tossed in some tiny craft, doomed to float in a restless sea. Until our kiss, I, too, shared with him a starless sky. I needed him to know if I had been given any other choice, any other option, I would have taken it. I would have done anything to spare him from that aloneness.

Avril perked up, wrenching me from my thoughts. "That is all in the past, though, darling."

I watched as she waltzed across the hallway, stooping down to squeeze my hands in hers.

"You are here now. In spite of it all, you are here. Everything that has happened to you, to Haden, it was intended by the Fates. Don't dwell on things you cannot change. Today is a day of celebration, of love! You have the rest of eternity to sort out everything else."

She offered me an encouraging smirk, and I couldn't help but to mirror her smile as I stood up alongside her. She was right. I knew she was. This was where I belonged. Faulty memory or not, this was still my fate. I was still the goddess of spring. All I had to do now was finish what I had begun lifetimes ago and marry the King of the Dead.

Raising my head up high, I turned to face Holland, a renewed sense of purpose humming within my veins as I reached out and tapped him on the shoulder. The god shifted, dropping his gaze from the portrait to study me.

"Thank you," I said, smiling, "for allowing us a moment to stop during my—" I paused, searching for the right word to describe my vision. "—episode. I am feeling much better now and would like to proceed to the ceremony if that's alright with you."

A look of amusement played across the god of directions features as he listened to me speak.

"If that's alright with me?" Holland chuckled. "Perrie, you're an immortal queen," he playfully reminded. "Your wish is my command."

He offered me his hand, and after a moment's hesitation, I took it. I was too eager to be reunited with Haden to let something as small as being escorted on the arm of an old acquaintance slow me down. Together, we led the others onwards, walking on and on until finally, we stumbled upon a dead end. Puzzled, I peered around to see if I was missing something and found nothing.

There was no other passageway for us to take, no additional staircase or bronze elevator to lead us in a different direction. Only one giant painting remained, suspended in a gilded frame. Lovely swirls of different colored clouds covered the canvas, captured in a blend of soft hues. Resting atop the clouds were dozens of idols dressed in sheer fabrics and wearing radiant laurel crowns atop their heads. Confidently, Holland approached the portrait and said in a firm voice, "*Aperta ianua.*"

What happened next caused my jaw to drop. Bright rifts of light lit up the canvas, illuminating the clouds and all the tinted idols in a divine glow. Two gold-plated door knobs materialized, and finally, the resplendent outline of two gilt doors.

Holland pushed one of the doors open, and a pure breeze of mountain air fluttered in, perfuming the hall with the crisp scent of conifers and snowdrops. The resonant notes of a harp played across the threshold, as well the airy uplift of a flute. Mingling with the music, I could hear the familiar twittering of songbirds and the distinct sound of laughter and conversation.

Curious, I found myself inching closer, unable to resist the urge to see what lay beyond the secreted door. From my spot, I could just make out the grand design of a gorgeous loggia. Rows of ivory columns bordered the space, allowing in just the right amount of wind and sunlight through a gathering of large, curved arches. Above I noticed a high, vaulted soffit with whorls of pink wisteria dripping from its rafters. Lining both sides of the veranda were stone benches, where scores of gods and goddesses sat, dressed in all sorts of ornate garments and shining jewels. Below, the ground was made of cobblestone, and petals of all shades littered the walkway, leading toward a small platform. Sitting atop the platform was a magnificent stone altar. Garlands of roses and dahlias adorned its surface, encircling what appeared to be two jeweled chalices and something shiny and silver. I blanched, realizing it was not just a glittery bauble but something sharp—a wickedly sharp bejeweled dagger.

A surge of panic bounded within me at the sight of the blade. *What was its purpose? Why was it there? What was I supposed to do with it?* Just as fast as the panic arose, it vanished the second my gaze landed on him.

Standing next to my father was Haden. He was dressed in a regal suit of black. Whirls of gold embellished the cuffs of his sleeves, and a cape as dark as pitch was slung over his shoulder. He was even more beautiful than he had appeared last night. Gone was the anguished look in his eyes, the sad sense of dispiritedness that seemed to haunt his every step. In its stead was a spark of hope, a look of purpose that seemed to cause the heaviness within my own chest to lessen, to fill with promise. He had cut his blackish curls and trimmed his ragged beard, appearing more like the well-acquainted, dark god of my dreams.

All I could feel was that tug. That deep, resounding flutter that announced his presence long before my eyes could place him. My breath caught the moment his stare met mine. I watched as his lips parted, as he, too, seemed to sense whatever pull beckoned us to one another, and for a moment, I forgot myself. I forgot the others. I barely noticed the crowd now turning in their seats to curiously peer back at whatever had caught the king of the dead's eye. For a moment, it was just him and me. I did not fear the foreignness of the ceremony. Nor did I care how I might appear before all of Olympus. I just wanted to be near him. Close enough to count his breaths, to feel his warmth.

I was sick of there always being some barrier, some stretch of space blocking us from one another, whether that be oceans of time or measurements of distance. That ancient, persevering part of me was restive. It begged me to move. To run. To leap. To do anything to end that separation. I was more than willing to give in, to bolt across the aisle. The bond made it hard to stand still.

"Are you ready?" a voice whispered, drawing my attention away from Haden.

I turned and found Avril. As always, the goddess of love was smiling. She bore a knowing expression, as if she, too, noticed the lively force tying Haden and I together and was overjoyed to feel its presence.

Beside her, Mom quietly stood, a similar observation now sparking in her eyes, lighting her features in a way that told me she now finally understood why we were here and why I could never fully forget. Why, no matter the misfortunes, I would never be able to stay away. It was inevitable. He was as essential to my life as oxygen.

Sympathetically, I reached out and took her hand in mine. She laced our fingers together and lifted our joined hands to her lips, offering me a teary-eyed look of encouragement that filled me with an indescribable amount of happiness and relief. Oh, how I had wanted her acceptance. The thought of leaving her unhappy and aggrieved at me had plagued me for days. At last, I could breathe. I could marry without guilt. I smiled at her, blinking back my tears before shifting my gaze to Avril and nodding.

"Yes," I exhaled. "I'm ready."

"Good!" Avril beamed, giving my free arm a cheerful squeeze. "Then there is only one thing left for us to do."

Quizzically, I raised my brow. "And what might that be?"

"Listen for your name." Holland winked, and then he was off, sauntering through the doorway.

CHAPTER 27
THE CEREMONY

A resounding silence swept throughout the gathering, stilling the fingers of the musicians and quieting all the buoyant chatter of the gods as Holland set foot outside the palace. Rakishly, he grinned at each of the guests as he passed them by, proceeding down the aisle with all the forwardness and gall of a performer born for the stage. He stopped in the middle of the loggia and gave a low bow, nodding his head at my father and then at Haden before coming to a full stand.

"Your Highnesses. Sisters." His hazel eyes flitted in the direction of a huddled trio of hunched, veiled figures that I knew to be the Fates. "As requested, I present to you the divine Lady of Spring, Persephone."

With bated breath, I watched as Holland gestured toward the twin gilt doors. As if by command, both blew open, rustling my hair with a gust of mountain breeze. Similarly, beams of golden sunlight poured into the hallway, illuminating the glitter on my porcelain skin and setting my crimson curls ablaze. There was a collective intake of breaths, of soft muttering, and low observations as Mom and I stepped forward and out onto the loggia. *Here we go,* I thought, carefully placing one foot in front of the other. *Time to re-wed my husband.* Together the two of us began our journey down the flowery pathway.

Nervously, I grasped her hand in mine, reminding myself to breathe as we walked further and further away from the Hall of Portraits and closer to that mysterious stone altar. Behind us, I could hear the delicate footfalls of Avril and Prilla. I imagined to the crowd they must have looked like a striking set of shadows, following us with unquestionable poise and beauty. From the corner of my eye, I noticed Cam and the others sneaking away to find seats in the audience. It seemed like more than a hundred gods were in attendance, each one observing me with curious eyes. I spotted several familiar faces in the mass.

The goddess Zane had introduced as Aryanna sat at the far end of a bench, her stunning white hair coiled atop her head in a cluster of intricate braids. Beside her sat her twin brother, Arthur, reclining in his chair and looking positively bored to tears. Parker, the god my father seemed to favor greatly, was seated in a row nearest to the altar, and a stunning goddess with hair as blue as arctic waves and features just as glacial sat at his side, both wearing impressive coral crowns atop their heads with a small legion of other nautical-dressed deities flanking their bench.

Ahead of us, I noticed a flash of indigo and gold as Hertha brushed her way past my father. Gracefully, she stepped down from the platform, her fierce blue eyes staring pointedly at me as she waited for us to approach the dais. Once there, Mom dropped into an immediate curtsy. I did my best to mimic her movements, lowering my eyes and bowing my head as I bent at the knees. After several quiet seconds of staring at the ground, Hertha finally commanded, "Rise," her imperial voice loud enough for all to hear.

Avril flounced past us, her blue skirts shimmering as she came to a stop beside the altar.

"Persephone," Hertha called out. "Goddess of Spring and Maiden of Nature, why do you evoke an audience with your King and Queen?"

The sound of my old name posed in such a sacramental tone threw me off my guard. It was jarring to hear, still so unfamiliar and separate from the name I had known as my own. Eager to rid my face of any expression akin to shock, I fumbled to find my voice, to stitch together a dignified response.

"I-I have come to accept Haden—the God of the Dead's proposal of marriage. I wish to acquire your blessing so that we might be rightfully wed."

"Is that so?" Hertha purred, a peculiar glint shining in her eyes. "And what say you, *sister*? Do you, Demeter, Goddess of the Harvest, approve of this union? Are you here to offer your daughter's hand to the King of the Underworld?"

Next to me, Mom seemed to twinge at the use of the word *sister*, as if the phrase was barbed, and she could not bear to hear it spoken aloud. Heart in my throat, I watched as she peered up at the Queen of the Gods, nervous thoughts beginning to billow in my mind the longer they held one another's stare. *Would now be the time? Would Hertha punish my mother for her betrayal by once more denying me her blessing in front of all of Olympus?*

Regret haunted my mother's every movement as she slowly nodded her head.

"Yes," Mom answered, a light smile lifting the corners of her lips as she turned her gaze back to me. "I do."

Relief flooded my veins the moment the Queen of the Gods' steely gaze shifted from Mom to me.

"Very well," she responded. "Persephone, step forward. The rest of you, be seated!"

Obediently, Prilla gave another brief curtsy and then sought my mother's arm. She motioned for her to follow her out into the audience, but Mom remained rooted in place, her fingers still interlaced with mine. Lovingly, she gave my hand one last squeeze before allowing herself to be tugged away. I watched as the two disappeared into the mass, a small sprout of fright filling the place where Mom's encouragement had been. I chose to ignore it, determined to quash my mousiness. *I was a goddess—a daughter of two Originals. I would not be afraid.*

Alone and with the eyes of hundreds at my back, I decided to hold my head up high and proceed up the rest of the steps to the platform. Once at the top, I found myself nearly scrupling backward. An odd sense of energy, similar to the gentle surge of power Avril had leveled at the harpies, seemed to emit from the altar, coming from each of the items sitting atop its surface. This force, however, I could tell was much older and far more unalterable. The dagger I had spotted from afar was unquestionably bigger up close, its decorative hilt sparkling with dozens of blue sapphires and dazzling green emeralds. Similar jewels bedecked the twin goblets, their gems catching in the light, displaying colorful little diffracted patterns onto the stone slab as they laid in wait to be used.

"Lord Hades," Hertha beckoned, tearing my awareness away from the top of the altar. "Come and face your bride."

With an arresting sense of grace, Haden abandoned his place beside my father. He stood before me in less than two strides, his countenance still alight with that intense look of wonder as he observed me. It was all I could do not to faint beneath that gaze. Being this close to him was like being bewitched. Every part of me burned for him. My body craved to lean in closer, to lose myself in his arms again. Simultaneously my mind yearned for the opportunity to ask him questions, to behold his thoughts, and rediscover the past we shared together. I ached to tell him everything. To show him every haunted sketch, every maddened scribble and oddball word I had done in my dream journal since our time apart.

"Now, join hands," Hertha continued.

At this, Haden seemed to wake from his quiet reverence. His russet gaze dropped from my face to study my hands. He peered back up at me, one heedful brow raised in question as if to silently ask my permission before reaching out to touch me. I gave him a bashful nod, and he gently took my hands in his. As he did so, I couldn't help but look them over. His hands were different from my own, large in size and aristocratic by nature. In contrast to his olive skin, my already fair complexion seemed snow-white. Calluses roughened his fingertips and bits of his upper palms, giving them a ruggedness I found comforting. *He was not an idle ruler then. Nor exceedingly vain.* Perhaps with him, I would not always have to be so smooth, so well-kept and corseted as I have been made to look now.

Against my flesh, he also seemed warmer, his touch both familiar and appealingly unknown. I dared a deeper look into his eyes, feeling the bond between us catch flame. *How? How could something as innocent as holding hands feel just as intimate as a kiss?*

"Turn out your left hand, palms facing up," Hertha instructed.

Compliantly, Haden and I did as the goddess demanded, releasing our intertwined hands and presenting them before the crowd. Curiously, I watched as Hertha turned away from us and approached the altar. Shiftlessly, she picked up the dagger, an odd little smirk toying at the corners of her crimson lips as she admired herself in the blade.

"Do you, Hades, Lord of the Dead, take Persephone to be your Dread Queen?" she mused, turning the dagger from side to side.

"I do," Haden answered, his gaze never drifting from mine.

"Do you consent to share half of your praise with her, as well as all of your riches and the entireness of your Kingdom, so long as you both shall live?"

"I do." He slightly tightened his grip on my right hand.

Another peculiar smile lit up the Queen of the Skies' face as she gracefully swept over toward Haden. A nymph materialized beside her from thin air, one of the jeweled chalices shaking in the girl's grasp. Honey-colored liquid sloshed inside the chalice as the nymph sunk to her knees, offering the cup above her head to Haden.

"Drink," Hertha said, bobbing her head toward the goblet.

Haden took the chalice and drained it completely. A faint glow began to shimmer around him in a matter of seconds, brightening his skin. I glanced down at the empty cup wide-eyed, observing the residual shine that coated the inside of the goblet. I longed to ask what the drink was but remained silent, choosing instead to watch as the same nymph scurried forward to reclaim the chalice and then spirit it away.

Once the maid was out of sight, Hertha drew a step closer to Haden. With little gentleness, she took hold of his free hand and then lifted the dagger. Before I could so much as draw in a horrified gasp, she had the blade pressed against his skin, dragging the serrated metal across his palm. All I could do was stand still and watch, unsure of what to do or how to react as blood began to trickle down his arm, ruining the fabric of his dark suit. The cut was deep. Deep enough that if he were human, it would undoubtedly warrant stitches. He made no show of pain or outrage, though, as Hertha stepped aside to wipe the dagger clean. *Surely, he wouldn't just stand there if this were not some part of the ceremony*, I reasoned, my mind grappling to figure out the rules, to make sense of what I was seeing.

My disbelief was quickly upended, replaced by an even greater shock the moment I noticed the red rivulets of blood rolling down Haden's arm begin to glow a blazing scarlet. *His blood...it was shining like whatever liquid was inside the goblet.*

Like an amused magician staring into the startled eyes of a child unable to wrap their head around a magic trick, Hertha gave me a pithy glance over as she came to a stand beside me, the dagger still firm in her grasp.

"Do you, Persephone, Lady of the Flowers, take Hades as your husband? Do you, as his faithful Queen consort, agree to share with him and only him half of your praise and all your riches for the rest of eternity?" Hertha asked, her blue eyes once again searing into mine, a warning in their depths, reminding me of our recent conversation.

It would be foolish to believe that your romance is as you left it. Make sure the choice you decide upon is one you can live with forever.

"I do," I conceded, not a trace of hesitancy to my words as I said my decision aloud.

At my response, a condescending look flashed across the Queen of the Gods' face. I could tell she thought I was making a foolish mistake. I did not care. *Let her think of me however she sees fit.*

In the depths of my being, I knew my heart had already made its decision. It had chosen Haden eons ago. Even now, after all this time, it still belonged to him. For me, there would be no one else. I would always choose him. Time and time again, no matter the consequences. I would not let my and Hertha's likenesses as consorts to powerful, immortal Kings dissuade me from following my heart.

A light stirring of wind appeared between us, and another nymph appeared in a snap. She hurried beside Hertha, the second chalice shining in her pink hands as she dropped to her knees and presented me with the goblet.

"This," Hertha began, gesturing toward the full cup, "is ambrosia. Only those with divinity in their veins may drink this holy draught and not perish. As is tradition, you must drink this entire goblet to prove you are indeed immortal and worthy of marrying an Olympian."

Nervously, I took the gemmed chalice from the bright-haired nymph, nodding my thanks to her as she stepped away. The cup was heavier than I expected, brimming with an amber-colored liquid that felt hot in my hands, like a giant, steaming cup of cider. Peering into the chalice was like staring into a cup of sunlight. It smelt sweet, like cinnamon and cardamom. *One*, I counted in my head, closing my eyes tightly as I tilted the cup back. *Two*. I brought the rim of the chalice to my lips. *Three*. I opened my mouth and swallowed.

Flavor overtook my mouth. The ambrosia tasted charming, like nothing I had ever tasted before, with citrine bursts and sugary spikes of warm honey. It burnt only slightly as it glided down my throat, warming my insides in a delicious heat. Within a matter of seconds, I could feel my skin heating, the warm sensation spreading throughout my entire body as I emptied the goblet. I almost didn't want to part with the chalice as the nymph hurried back to collect it from me. With unexpected reluctance, I passed it to her and then felt my eyes widen in astonishment.

Strange, new colors of the spectrum swirled around my vision, lighting up everything from the nymph's colorful hair to the air particles around me. It was like taking off a pair of dark-tinted sunglasses. The world around me was so much brighter now. More vibrant and spectacular. Everything seemed heightened. Never had I smelt sweeter smelling roses than the ones atop the altar. Even the wind seemed to sing as an unfamiliar energy rippled throughout my bones.

So, this is what it is to have my true-self set free, I thought, smiling foolishly to myself as I recognized my own immortality for the first time. Once again, Hertha leveled a disbelieving look in my direction as if she couldn't quite decide whether she should snigger or scowl at my naiveté as she inched a step closer. I jumped the second I felt her cold fingers curl around my open hand.

"I must warn you," she whispered, raising the silver dagger and pressing it against my skin. "This is the least excruciating part."

I bit back a cry as she sliced the jagged blade across the center of my palm. Bright streaks of blood, the color of shining rose gold, spilled from the cut. It was over quickly enough, but an unpleasant stinging lingered as she summoned a cloth and began to wipe at the dagger.

"Sisters," Hertha called, stepping away from us. "If you would kindly step forth."

Just as harrowing as the first time I saw them with their tattered black cloaks and horribly sewn-shut eyes, all three of the Fates glided toward us. They grinned unsettlingly, crooning something to one another in a language that sounded as hard and sharp as stalactites. One of the crones laughed in response as if they could smell my aversion to their being there and found the allusion delectable.

"Thread made of shadow…" the spindliest of the Moirai rasped.

"Of fire," another added, an awful, rotted smile visible underneath the sheer fabric of her black veil.

"Of night," the last sister recited, the milky eye around her neck swaying as she reached out to clasp Haden's bleeding hand in her own knotted fingers.

"Remember thy maker, thy sorter, thy cutter," they chanted in unison. "Reveal thyself onto us and meet your destined match!"

They continued to chant, their harsh voices a low drone against the quiet echoes of nature, until suddenly, the steady flow of glowing blood dripping from Haden's hand became blinding. From the light emerged the same scarlet thread as the one I had seen in the throne room. To my relief, Haden did not seem nearly as pained as before as the Fates magically drew the thread into view and left it inertly levitating in the air.

Satisfied with their work, all three of the Moirai turned their keen interest to me. They gathered around me like a triad of hunched condors, each stinking of something like Valerian and mud. I battled every instinct screaming inside me, imploring me to fight, to move away as the one with the eye necklace collected my bleeding hand in hers.

"Thread made of twilight…" she croaked.

"Of blossoms," the second sister resumed.

"Of life," the last intoned.

"Remember thy maker, thy sorter, thy cutter," they again incanted, repeating the last three verses of the incantation. "Reveal thyself onto us and meet your destined match!".

An odd, prickling sensation began to spread across my palm, sweeping past my nerves with every unabating word. It felt as if fire ants had crept into my wound, as if all the circulation from my hand had been suddenly staunched, and all that was left was that uncomfortable stabbing, that building pressure of not enough blood flowing to my fingers. I couldn't hide my wince as the feeling continued to grow tighter. At long last, a flowing effervescent thread burst from my palm, gleaming like a rosy comet. A wide, blackened grin chased across the face of the Fate holding my hand.

"I remember you," she whispered, carefully gathering my floating thread in her hands. "What wonders you are about to set in motion." She muttered to herself, blindly reaching up and plucking Haden's scarlet thread from the air.

"Yes, yes, what wonders," her sisters agreed.

With fascination, I watched as the Fate holding our threads began to wrap our injured hands, crossing my thread around Haden's palm and his around mine until the gashes in our hands were no longer visible and our long glistening threads were overlapping, laced together like a set of glowing, intertwined ribbons. Pleased with her work, the Moirai gave one last smirk in the direction of our tied-together hands and then made her way back over to her sisters as both Hertha and Avril proceeded toward us.

"From this day forth, the God of the Dead and the Goddess of Spring are joined in marriage! I, Aphrodite, hereby bless this love. May all of your years together be filled with nothing but happiness, devotion, and an abundance of passion," Avril heralded, smiling at us both, causing the gods and goddesses in the crowd to clap and shout in hurrahed approval.

The audience's applause died down once Hertha cleared her throat.

"And I, Hera, bless this marriage. May the centuries you spend together be filled with nothing but honesty, adherence, and companionship. Long hail Persephone and Hades," Hertha blazoned.

The kindness in my aunt's blessing took me by surprise. I hadn't expected such well-wishes from her. After all, I was a bastard—a walking-talking reminder of my father's unfaithfulness and my mother's treachery. *Why did she seem so genuine in her respects?* Perhaps there had been no underlying meaning behind her warning after all. Maybe she really did only want to spare me from a similar fate as hers, and my mother simply worried too much.

The crowd, yet again, began to cheer and clap loudly, snatching me from my thoughts. I looked up to find that the mass of delighted gods had risen from their seats. Many had begun to throw flowers at us and chant out our names. A chorus of *Hades and Persephone* and even a few shouts of *Proserpine and Pluto* filled the loggia, the sound of their cheering nearly deafening as the musicians began to play a celebratory piece.

I turned away from the guests, my gaze drifting back to Haden's hand in mine. The glowing threads tying us together were beginning to fade, seeping into our skin like water being absorbed in soil. I marveled at their disappearance, musing over the significance of what we had just done and how our entwined threads signified us as husband and wife.

Did a part of me now exist within Haden? Would it always? I concentrated on that tug between us only to find that the bond seemed stronger than ever, like every beat of our hearts was somehow in sync.

"You look as if you have a million questions," Haden noted, a crooked smirk chasing across his lips.

A searing blush pinkened my cheeks as I met his attentive stare.

"Millions?" I repeated, a shy smile of my own upturning my lips. "Oh no, I have far more than that."

Haden chuckled, and something in his expression softened. "I would imagine you do. Unfortunately, it might be quite some time before I can adequately respond to all those questions."

"Oh," I noted. "And why is that?"

The King of the Underworld grimaced and nodded his head in the direction of my father, who was brusquely descending the dais steps in all his heavenly blue regalia. Beside him, Hertha followed, her arm stiffly hooked through his as they approached Parker and his kindred of seafaring immortals. Soon, the two kings were laughing, and it wasn't long before both Zane and Parker were wandering away from their respective wives and down a set of winding stairs. Noticing their departure, various other gods and goddesses were quick to follow in their steps, excitedly grabbing hold of one another and bustling for the stairs.

"With all the legalities out the way, my brothers can, at long last, have their fun. It has been several eons since Olympus has held a royal wedding. The courtiers are desirous of celebrating, and it is customary for our host to conclude our ceremony with an honorary ball. We shall be made to dance and revel late into the night, or at least until Zeus has had his fill of wooing serving girls and lesser gods."

"A ball?" I blanched, the compelling desire to suddenly slink into the shadows and perhaps find a nice balcony to scramble down becoming all the more appealing the longer I faced the scattered audience. I had zero experience in ballroom etiquette and wasn't too optimistic about my capabilities of keeping up a nightlong poker face. Haden gave me another amused look and then unexpectedly snaked his arm around my waist, causing my pulse to hasten as he pulled me against his side.

"Fear not," he spoke, his lips dangerously close to the shell of my ear as he guided us down the platform stairs and through the throng of cheering gods. "When together, Zeus and Poseidon have a steadfast tradition of drinking themselves into grating stupors. I'd wager good money that by dinner time, they'll be so deep into their cups that they won't even notice if we're in the room or not."

I smiled at him, an entire kaleidoscope of butterflies fluttering in my stomach as I riskily said, "Okay, I'll take your bet, but I have no interest in your money."

Haden slowed, his russet eyes alight with some sort of spirited curiosity as he shifted his head to study me.

"What would you have me wager instead?"

I bit my bottom lip, my cheeks once more flaring with heat as I tried to find the courage to voice my forward, perhaps *too forward*, thoughts.

"Answers," I decided. "If we are able to slip away before midnight without anyone noticing we've gone, you have to answer at least one big question of mine."

Haden grinned. A slow, devilish grin that had my head swimming and something in my lower abdomen tightening.

"Deal," he conceded.

And then we were off, gliding toward the celebration.

CHAPTER 28
FIRST DANCE

Visions of ballrooms, of regency-like banquet chambers and palace concert halls filled my mind as I tried to guess where our reception would be held. I had a suspicion it would be beyond belief, certainly not someplace simple. No, that would be too usual, too akin to that of a mortal venue. Nothing of that world dwelled here, in my father's shining kingdom of wind and snowy mountain tops. Not a single trace, or the faintest semblance to remind me of the world I'd thought I'd known, the world I had decidedly left behind.

As we walked, I stayed close to Haden, following him down stone steps and past flowery alcoves, our fingers still interlaced. Eventually, we encountered a tawny-colored archway that was overcome with ivy. Haden parted the greenery with one hand and motioned for me to walk ahead of him. Compliantly, I ducked beneath his outstretched arm.

To my surprise, a grand pleasure garden lay beyond the leafy archway. Bursts of colorful flowers sprouted from raised flowerbeds, and well-kept hedgerows bordered the space, encircling botanical sculptures made entirely of limestone. Several far-stretching banquet tables sat scattered throughout the courtyard, their elegant tops teeming with all sorts of elaborate trays, filigree plates, and other florid dishes. To the right, a space for dancing had been made beneath the trees and settled nearby, a band of whimsical musicians sat armed with their instruments. They performed vehemently, filling the secret courtyard with jovial notes of music and song. Gods and goddesses were everywhere, spread as far as the eye could see. Some were spinning about to the music, their lavish gowns and fanciful suits a vivid swirl of color amid the lush foliage. Others were loitering about, talking among themselves and enjoying the refreshments. At our arrival, silence fell upon the scene. Zane quickly sprung from one of the banquet chairs, pushing aside a young, antlered dryad who had been sprawled across his lap moments before.

"Gods," he called out, a jaunty smile on his face, "goddesses, make way for our brother and his beautiful new queen. I believe they are owed the first dance."

In an instant, the swaying Olympians hastened to get out of our way, and I fought the urge to dig my heels into the ground. *I couldn't dance in front of a crowd this large. I had no clue how to dance!* I seriously doubted whatever experience I had twirling about to Florence and the Machine while pinning clothes to the clothesline would aid my ability to formally pirouette or break into a ballroom tango. The feel of Haden's hand brushing across my arm had me jolting from my panicky thoughts. I peered up to find him smiling at me.

"Don't tell me you have forgotten how to dance," he playfully whispered.

I shot him a discomfited look and followed him across the grassy pathway. I noticed the dance floor itself was rather pretty, variegated and mosaic-patterned beneath our shoes.

"I'm afraid so," I lowly confessed, a nervous titter flying past my lips as I shifted to face him. Behind us, I could hear the quiet shuffling of the musicians sorting through their sheet music and the controlled musings of the crowd as they gathered around to watch us from afar.

"I suppose I should add dancing to the ever-growing list of talents that have sadly fallen through the cracks since the..."

I trailed off, catching the brief flash of something like disappointment sparking in Haden's eyes. He was fast to hide it, though, choosing instead to lean in closer to me, his body so close I could smell his rich cedar scent.

"I'm sorry!" I blurted. "I didn't mean to— What I meant to say was—"

"No need for apologies," Haden responded, his voice still warm, amicable. "I taught you once before. I have no qualms about teaching you a second time."

I opened my mouth to protest when Haden cut me off.

"First, you place your hand here."

He redirected my hand to the crook of his neck, and for a moment, it felt as if I had been struck with an immense wave of déjà vu.

"W-what next?" I stammered, my fingers brushing against the dark curls at the nape of his collar.

Slowly, Haden trailed his fingers down the curve of my spine. He stopped at the small of my back, and my breath hitched.

"I support you here," he answered, his lips suddenly inches from mine, his russet gaze locked onto my mouth.

"And after that?"

I couldn't take my eyes off him, even as a revitalizing melody began to play, and I felt myself being led into a breezy waltz.

"We dance."

Despite my limited knowledge of choreography, I could tell Haden was a skillful dancer. All of his movements were precise, fluid, and limber as he kept us whirling in time with the tempo. Soon I forgot all about my fears of dancing and found myself yielding to the ambiance of the afternoon. Dancing here in this garden, surrounded by vibrant flowers and in Haden's arms... It was like living in a dream, like finding myself lost in Shakespeare's Faerie.

We glided from hedge to hedge, the ends of my blush gown billowing around us as I mimicked his steps. Only when the song ended did we stop at a table with a tiered crystal fountain in its center, spurts of something like purple punch tinkling into the little glass flutes surrounding it. Haden handed me one, and I graciously took it, urging myself not to gulp it all at once, fearful that it might be spiked.

"Are you still debating ways to escape all of the merry-making?" he questioned, a simper to his words.

I smiled into my drink and shook my head, my chest rising and falling slightly from exertion.

"No. Well, not nearly as much as before. I think I might actually like dancing."

"Is that so?" Haden grinned. "What a shame. I was so looking forward to hearing some of your tactics."

I took another sip of my beverage. It was surprisingly good. Not as flavorsome as the ambrosia, but fruity nonetheless, like huckleberries and grape.

"Did we dance a lot, before...?"

Haden was quiet for a long while. Long enough that I began to wish I could take the words back. Had I already taxed his patience with my questions? Was he like Mom, unwilling to share more than he felt like giving? His memories of us were not like mine. There was no daunting wall of ice to block him from reminiscing about our past, no shadows to hinder him from recalling all of the small, wistful details of our beginning. How agonizing it must be for him to finally find me only to discover I remembered nearly nothing of the life we shared before.

"Yes," Haden finally replied, waiting for me to finish my glass before offering me his arm.

Carefully, I sat the flute on the table and looped my arm through his. He steered us back onto the dance floor, and I let out a tiny surprised gasp as he took my waist in both of his hands.

"There used to be an old law," he continued, gently lifting me up and spinning me about before placing me back on the ground. "For six months, Olympus received all of the eternal-blooded offspring of the gods as guests."

Together the two of us began to circle one another, Haden's hand in mine as he walked me through a slow minuet.

"These young heirs and heiresses would attend debut balls, where many would find themselves either legitimized or betrothed to others living in different realms. In either case, they would receive an eminent title, and shaky alliances between the kingdoms would again be secured, providing peace to all throughout the lands. You were no different. Your mother's protests to keep you in the mortal lands fell on deaf ears, and as a daughter of Zeus, you were expected to spend six months in Olympus after your claiming day. During this time, I, like any unwed immortal, would occasionally visit my brother's kingdom, and we would dance. Like we are now."

He stepped away from me, and I mirrored his movements, coming back to him only to curl my fingers between his and turn round and round with the music, my mind teeming with even more questions than before. *My claiming day? Had that been what Avril meant when she said Zane had thrown me an extravagant birthday party?* Curiosity flowered inside me, but I wrangled it back, choosing instead to rest each of my hands atop his broad shoulders and to simply glide with the music. Now was not the time or the place to pepper him with questions. I would have the rest of eternity to pick his mind. I could endure keeping my mouth shut for a little while longer.

Others soon joined us on the dance floor, and a new, livelier tune filled the space. We danced for hours until the bright blue horizon gave way to an orange and lilac sky. Magic flickers of flame appeared throughout the garden, igniting dozens of gilded candles and outdoor candelabras as the sun descended behind the snow-capped mountains. It wasn't until a sharp, clear *tingtingting* broke through the music that everyone came to a gradual stop. Zane again rose from his seat, a glass in his hand as he cleared his throat.

"It is time to honor our Lord and Lady of the Dead with a feast! Come, be seated. Eat!"

We made our way to the banquet tables. A familiar blaze of cinnamon hair caught in my peripheral, and I was relieved to find both Avril and Mom sitting a few chairs away from my father. The second my sister's ocean eyes found mine, a radiant smile lit up her beautiful face, and she enthusiastically waved us over. Noticing where my attention had drifted, Haden guided us toward the bubbly goddess of love.

CHAPTER 29
THE BANQUET

We chose seats in the center of the table, Haden sitting adjacent to Parker while I sat across from my mother. It didn't take very long for us to find ourselves surrounded. More than a few Olympians were eager to dine at our side, choosing chairs nearby. Once everyone was seated, a line of servers appeared, bringing with them an infinite number of steaming platters on golden trays, all smelling exceptionally mouthwatering. As each server passed us, our plates were promptly heaped high with gracious amounts of glazed meats, roasted vegetables, and rolls swimming in delicious amounts of honey butter. Following them, a team of nymphs carrying pitchers raced from table to table, refilling cups when summoned.

Like any dinner, conversations carried on throughout the meal. My father's deep-bellied laugh could be heard from far and wide as he told boastful tales to all who would listen. He talked about old battles in between bites of skewered zucchini and smoked duck, about his favorite demi-god children, and which of his old paramours he had favored the most. Eventually, Haden and I became the topic of his ramblings. He congratulated himself for wooing Mom with his charm and fathering me.

"Who else could have sired a daughter so fair that even the high-and-mighty King of the Dead would find himself head over heels in love? Certainly not any of you lot," Zane gloated, elbowing Parker and laughing with a trio of older-looking deities that Avril quietly informed me were pardoned, highborn titans.

He also christened himself as a god of incredible genius. After all, it was he who implemented the debut balls. How would we have met if he had not so generously opened his doors and made it law for all of his and the other Olympian's lesser children to come and socialize?

Mom unobtrusively listened with her hands folded in her lap. She'd occasionally respond to others' conversations and roll her eyes discreetly when Zane would get carried away with his retellings. She didn't think I noticed when she'd periodically look up from her bowl of untouched onion soup and eye me with a fretful expression, but I did. I noticed every little stirring made by each of the nearby gods.

Haden, who had been relatively talkative during our time alone, had become increasingly tight-lipped. He wore a stoic guise of disinterest that only a few Olympians were brazen enough to disrupt as the meal went on and our dinner platters were replaced with other exotic-looking dishes. I ached to ask him what the matter was. I wanted to know what had caused this sudden shift of his mood, but I knew better than to raise such questions here and tried to content myself with quietly holding his hand underneath the table.

Sitting farther down from us, Cam and Prilla conversed with a goddess named Isabella. She was pretty in an elfish sense, with vibrant prismatic hair and bi-colored eyes. She had been one of the first goddesses to congratulate us at the table and had cheerfully introduced herself as the patron of the rainbow.

Avril, who was sitting next to me, proved to be quite the socialite. She talked to all the gods around us, stirring up conversations and making jokes while sipping a glass of Rosé. She'd occasionally turn from her conversations to whisper something in Henry's ear. She would then bat her long lashes at him, flirtatiously smile like she knew some alluring secret, and carry on with whatever conversation she had been in the midst of before, leaving her husband red in the face.

Hertha sat at the far end of the table, putting as much distance as she could manage between herself and my father. She played her role as Queen of the Skies as one might expect, with great poise and grace, entertaining all the guests nearest her with a lovely smile. She spoke to my father only when necessary and spent most of her time avoiding his intent gaze with a haughty determination that I felt certain could force the sun to rise in the West. It also seemed, for all her show of disregarding Zane, she had an acute sense of which of the serving girls he seemed to fancy the most. With every nymph that came to my father's beck and call, Hertha would soon summon them over to her side of the table, only to make them burst into hysterical tears without even saying a word. She and the Queen of the Seas made no attempts to hide their staring at me, either. Occasionally, one would whisper to the other and snicker, and I would quickly avert my attention elsewhere.

I had little time to imagine what they might be saying, though, as I was drawn into conversation after conversation. Everyone in Olympus seemed to have some kind question to ask or fond memory of either Haden or me that they wanted to share with us. I would smile encouragingly at whoever was speaking and listen to them go on, both intrigued and saddened to hear their tales. I wondered what the evening would be like if I could remember any of their original names, if I could recall that very first ball where I had met Haden so many lifetimes ago.

I took a brisk gulp of my sparkling water, determined not to fret over what I could not remember. *It would come back to me. In due time, it would all come back. I just had to be patient and meet with this Mnemosyne.* I motioned to place my drink back down and then caught notice of a flicker of something green through my glass. A nymph with the narrow wings of a dragonfly darted in between the tables. I watched as she stopped before Holland's chair and leaned in to whisper something in the god's ear. He nodded in understanding, setting his silverware to the side before coming to a stand. Patiently, he waited for all of the dining gods to go quiet before speaking.

"I hate to disrupt such a magnificent meal, but I have just received some news from the palace maids."

Zane quirked a curious brow in Holland's direction, his lips curling into an inebriated smile.

"Well, go on then, my boy. What do these maids have to say?"

Holland's gaze lingered in my direction, and I resisted the urge to fidget uncomfortably in my seat. Whatever news he had to share, I did not like how it made his eyes darken with what seemed like discontent. Beside me, I could feel Haden's body going tense. Heat radiated from his body in waves, and his hold on my hand tightened as he glowered at the messenger god.

"The bridal chamber is duly prepared for whenever the King and Queen of the Dead wish to retire for the night."

A fiery blush bloomed across my cheeks, scorching me from my ears to my toes as I recognized the meaning behind Holland's message. *Tonight was our wedding night. The night upon which most blushing brides...* I couldn't finish the thought. My heart was beating way too fast. I hadn't planned this far ahead. I had been so focused on making it to Olympus in time, on stopping Haden from doing something unthinkable, I hadn't contemplated much about what would concur after we said our vows.

"Ah, yes! Splendid," Zane responded, sawing into a piece of steak. "I think you'll find the quarters well to your liking, brother. I had the Erotes oversee all of the arrangements." He popped the mignon into his mouth and gave my husband a suggestive wink. In response, Haden threw the King of the Gods an evasive smile.

"I'm sure I would, adelphós. However, you shouldn't have troubled yourself. I made preparations of my own for tonight. I had intended for us to leave as soon as my bride finished her meal."

"Leave?" Zane echoed.

"So soon?" Parker joined in.

A hint of annoyance flitted across Haden's face as he reclined back into his chair.

"Yes. I figured if we departed within the next hour or so, we should still be able to make it to Rome in time to see the sunrise."

Parker looked between Haden and me with a look of utter bafflement written across his features.

"You're telling me you intend on sifting to the mortal realm in the dead of night?"

"No, I had the intention of using a portal," Haden countered.

The sound of someone loftily harrumphing had everyone turning in their seats to find Hertha feigning a look of abashed upset.

"Don't be ridiculous, Haden. I'm sure your pretty new wife is too tired to go gallivanting through portals. After all, she's had an eventful day, and it has only been a week since Avril found her selling flowers in that muggy little excuse for a town. Perhaps you should contemplate a less jarring method of travel if you simply must leave tonight. Maybe one more human in nature? You wouldn't want to frazzle the poor dear's mind any more than it already has been, now, would you?" Hertha sweetly continued. "Oh, I know! The two of you could take a Pegasus-drawn carriage. Wouldn't that be romantic? It would, of course, take quite some time for you to reach the boundary line if you were to travel through the forests, and the centaurs are unfortunately in rut this time of the year, so that might hinder you from taking some of the more scenic roads, but it should get you to the Mortal Lands all the same."

Around her, all of the lovely goddesses sitting at her side began to giggle.

"I don't know," Amara hummed in response.

Absent-mindedly the goddess twirled a strand of blue hair around her finger before turning her crocodile-like eyes toward me. "A Pegasus-drawn carriage sounds far too cramped, and she is unfamiliar with all of the Creatures and beasts that roam this land. Some are quite terrifying, if I might say so myself—especially those that come out at night. Maybe you could ask one of the Anemoi to fly you into the Realm of Man. Or one of our Tritones could guide you on a ship across the border. Most surface dwellers travel in those flimsy airplanes, do they not? And they sail in those dreadful boats. I expect it would suit her nerves better, no? Especially since she was fooled into believing herself mortal."

Shame ravaged my spirit. It colored my cheeks and robbed me of my ability to speak as I was forced to sit and listen to them make light of my broken memory. *What could I say? How could I respond to such allegations?* I ached to disappear…to turn invisible and run as fast as my legs could carry me. I wanted to spring up from my place at the table and go as far from this garden and its many twinkling candles and vibrant blossoms as possible. A formidable urge to cry, to burst into a fit of tears, burned my eyes, but I refused to weep. I would not shed a single tear in their presence. That would only satisfy their desire to see me, my mother, and Haden humiliated, and I would not leave them to fend for themselves.

Across from me, Mom was clenching her spoon so tightly her knuckles were a blazing white. A slight wind had begun to pick up around her, and I quietly placed my hand atop hers, seeking to abate her anger. The gust around her lessened, but she still stared icily at the collection of derisive goddesses.

"Nonsense!" Avril warmly dismissed, helping herself to a generous slice of strawberry cake. She made an appreciative noise as she bit into the desert, licking away a bit of pink frosting from her thumb before returning her attention to Hertha and Amara. "How is it you think we got here? We certainly did not walk. Perrie might still be struggling with a few lingering aftereffects from surviving such a traumatic event, but she lacks no amount of courage. I can assure you of that. She could easily manage to step through a portal as she is now and walk out just as ravishing on the other side."

"Of course, she could," another younger goddess, dressed in a radiant dress of gold, sneered, her tone disbelieving, as she threw a repulsed look my way.

If it were not for her eyes, those very cyan-blue eyes, flecked with the same celadon as my own, I would have thought her Hertha's twin. She was beautiful, with long, fair hair and porcelain skin. Shock barreled through me at the realization that this goddess, who was peering at me with such repulsion in her features, was unquestionably a daughter of Zane's.

"Be that as it may," another goddess continued, her visage nearly identical to that of the goddess in gold, save for her rounder physique and kinder semblance. "I think it would be rather chivalrous of Haden to consider gifting our sister one last evening under the same roof as her mother. Let Demi explain to her what is to be expected of her on this very special night now that she is a wife."

An assenting murmur circulated around the table, blending in with the clinking sound of silverware tapping against plates.

"Unless of course…" the goddess in gold countered, a catty smile lifting the corners of her round lips as she reached for a salver of elaborately stacked macarons.

Without warning, Haden leaned forward in his seat, and in a flash, the tray was sitting before us, leaving the goddess with her hands still outstretched, holding nothing but open air. Indifferently, Haden plucked a red macron from the platter. I watched as he examined it, a sharp, viperous air about him as he leveled a testing look at the goddess in gold.

"Go on," Haden encouraged, a silent dare behind each of his words as he offered me the macaron.

Tentatively, I took it, uncertain of what to do. The goddess wavered for only a second before decidedly lifting her nose in the air.

"Unless, of course, Her Highness already knows what is to be expected, and that is why she and your Lordship are so eager to skip out on such a hallowed marital rite. My sweet sister forgets that she and I were not given the same allowance as our half-sister. We were not allowed to run away and live with some god of our choosing for half a year before taking ill," the fair-haired goddess persisted, her tone accusatory and laced with disdain.

A furor of curious hearsay chased the goddess's remark, spreading around the table like wildfire. Again, I could say nothing. I could only look down at my plate and attempt to weather the worst of their nosy stares with what I hoped was a look of imperiousness. I had no proof to put their prattle to rest. No clear memory to distinguish whether I was as lily white as I had believed myself to be or if maybe I had once been some scarlet-tinted rose, bright and in bloom. I supposed it mattered little now.

Beside me, a noticeable muscle twitched along the King of the Dead's jaw as he reclined back in his chair.

"Careful, Eileithyia. Slandering the name of a queen can have dire consequences, even for princesses such as yourself," Haden warned, his dark eyes issuing silent, wreckful, promises to all of the seated Olympians bold enough to side with the goddess in gold.

They immediately fell quiet, their scandalous chatter ebbing into a fearful silence as they all scrambled to fix their attention elsewhere. Hertha and her scornful daughter were the only ones sitting up straight in their seats, not a flicker of regret to lessen their wicked beauty.

With a sigh, Zane also rose from his seat.

"Enough. All of you!" he scolded, his voice suddenly thunderous and devoid of all drunkenness.

Angrily, he dabbed at the sides of his mouth with a napkin and shook his head disapprovingly at his wife and daughters. "If they wish to have their wedding night elsewhere, they are well within their right to leave this instant. I will not have members of my own house badger them into staying or making such lewd insinuations!"

The playful blue gleam in Hertha's eyes vanished, and for a moment, a menacing look of spite overtook her features. She was fast to disguise all looks of contempt from her face, though, gathering her queenly composure as if nothing had ever been said to sour her mood.

"Lewd," she repeated, a wide smile uplifting her crimson lips. "Oh, I assure you, husband, there was nothing off-color in my suggestions. I merely meant to pass along some suitable advice. Is that not what you asked of us? Of me specifically? To play nice with those who do not merit the right to clean up after my peacocks. You cannot deny that which is barefaced. Your Persephone is not as she was before. It's absurd to go about and pretend otherwise. As for the comments made by your *lawful* daughters, you should be happy with Heidi for wanting to uphold tradition, despite you giving neither her nor Elise a choice in their own marriages."

"I said, enough!" Zane growled.

Tension crackled in the air like heat lightning as the King of the Gods glared daggers at his wife. No one dared to speak a word or move a muscle as the two stared one another down. Hertha didn't appear perturbed in the slightest. In fact, she bore a sated expression as she settled in her chair, not unlike a grandmaster who had just declared checkmate against their opponent, or a spider who had successfully entangled another arachnid within its web.

Mercifully, the spell of hostile silence ended when Haden decided to stand up from his chair and abandon his place at the table. I watched as he made his way behind me, his hands gliding across the top of my chair before coming to rest atop my naked shoulders.

"I appreciate your hospitality, adelphós, and your house's concern for my wife," he smiled, his calloused fingers massaging careless circles into my exposed skin.

I bit back a quiet gasp and fought to keep my breaths even. I didn't want to give my father's court any more reason to talk, to wonder or speculate, but I knew I was failing miserably. Just the light brush of his fingertips, lazily drifting across the nape of my neck, had my heart hammering inside my chest, threatening to beat its way out. Suddenly I was clay beneath his touch—molten glass waiting to be shaped into something more, something new.

"I hope you can overlook my outburst," he continued. "I should not have allowed myself to be goaded into behaving so…impertinently. Nonetheless, I will not have my or my wife's honor so noisily questioned. Any disrespect shown to my queen is disrespect shown to me."

"Think nothing of it," Zane spoke, plopping back down in his chair, a drunken smile settling on his face once more as he brought a goblet to his lips. "And rest assured," he swallowed and continued, "those reckless enough to talk low of you in my realm shall be justly reprimanded." His eyes landed on his daughter dressed in gold, who was now white with worry.

"Your youngest daughter, Hebe, raised a very convincing assertion, one I am glad she decided to voice. In my eagerness to have my queen all to myself, I did not stop to consider just how cruel it would be of me to deny Demeter the tradition of readying her daughter for bed one last time. I do hope you will consider allowing us to stay one more night in Olympus. The Underworld will not be receiving any visitors during the extent of our honeymoon, and I feel it would be in the best interest of my wife to have this final moment with her mother," Haden said, one of his hands wandering up to play with my hair.

Zane nodded, giving his beard a thoughtful stroke.

"Of course! Feel free to take your leave whenever."

Haden glanced back at me, his dark stare wandering down to scrutinize the remaining amount of food left on my plate. Having nibbled on as much as my nerves would allow, I tossed my silk napkin aside and shoved the plate away in a silent gesture of readiness. He offered me his hand and I took it, rising tiredly. As nervous as I was to begin my journey toward the bridal chambers, I was ready to be out of my heavy gown, to take off my delicate shoes, and be blessedly freed from this constricting corset. Before I could utter a word, Mom was up and out of her seat, her arms outstretched to me.

"I'll take her," she said, her navy eyes darting to meet Haden's. "Give me forty-five minutes or so, and I'll have her ready."

He stared at her, suspension burning bright in his russet eyes as he held my hand in his, his grip on my fingers growing tighter as if he were wary of leaving me alone with her again and couldn't decide whether he should trust her or not.

"It's alright," I whispered, stepping to the side to catch his gaze. "I promise."

Something in my voice must have convinced him because he finally nodded his head and released my hand. I drifted toward Mom, who draped a warm arm around my shoulders. She guided me toward the leafy archway, and we turned away from the pleasure garden, taking one step after another, the long ends of our gowns trailing in the grass behind us as we began our ascent back to the palace. All the while I kept looking over my shoulder, stealing fleeting glances among the flowery hedges and statues, my eyes searching for Haden before finally landing on him standing beside my chair like a beautiful phantom, flickers of candlelight dancing against his shadowed face as he watched me go.

CHAPTER 30
THE BRIDAL CHAMBERS

By the time we reached the palace, darkness had overtaken Olympus. Crickets chirped all around us and a brilliant silver moon hung above, illuminating our way across the shadowy colonnade. Exhausted, I trailed behind Mom, following her to one of the nearest wrought-iron doors. Tiredly, she rapped her fist against the entrance, and I allowed myself a moment to slouch as we waited.

If I had thought myself ready to be out of my bridal attire before, I was desperate to be out of it now. The arches of my feet were throbbing, and the sheer lace of my sleeves did little to keep out the mountain chill. Just as I was about to bend down and free my feet from their satin shoes, the door swung open, and a rift of warm, inviting light spilled out onto the turning bridge, revealing the figure of an old, doe-eyed satyress.

She bent into a prim curtsy and opened the door wider for us to enter.

"My goddesses," she greeted. "Please, come in."

I offered the old maid a wearied smile and stepped across the threshold with Mom beside me. Immediately, warmth returned to my chilled extremities, and a sense of refined coziness flooded my senses, tempting me to wander further inside the chamber. Like all of the other lavish Olympian rooms I had visited, this part of the palace seemed just as extravagant. It was circular in design, tower-like and lofty, with a ring of sizable windows setting off the walls. A giant fireplace crackled ahead of us, and a few tufted winged chairs bordered a middle-sized divan. Curiously, I peered about the space. This was definitely some kind of parlor by the looks of it. The chamber had several gilt bookshelves and a few comfy-looking window nooks. Above us, a lifted ceiling loomed, and a golden chandelier twinkled. I grimaced when I spotted a spiraling staircase, leading to some unknown upper floor. Other than the door we had just walked through, there appeared to be no other entryways on this level, no noticeable corridors or open archways. Oh, how I hoped that meant the maid only intended to lead us up those stairs and not down some labyrinthine hallways, or through any cleverly disguised secret doors before seeing us safely to the bridal chambers. I did not know how much more walking my poor feet could take for the night.

"Will there be anything else I can get for my goddesses?" the satyress politely asked, her large, cervine-like eyes shifting between Mom and me.

I felt my shoulders slump with relief at the maid's confirming question. *Thank heavens!* This *was* the bridal chambers, then. I wouldn't have to walk any further. Well, not any further than up a few dozen steps or so, and then I would finally be free to let my hair down and undress and… My heart stopped, only to relaunch at a breakneck pace. *This was the bridal chambers.* I was here. I was really about to share a bed with my new husband.

All feelings of calm, of sleepy warmth and quiet, vanished. In its place rose a wave of dizzying panic. I hadn't the slightest clue what to do with myself. I was out of my depth here, embarrassingly so. *Would Haden be angry with me if I asked him for some time? Did I even want time?*

Flashes of our impassioned throne room kiss swept across my mind like a fiery stirring of glowing, hot embers. I had to waive the urge to lift my fingers to my mouth, to retrace where his lips had so fiercely claimed mine. It had been so easy in that moment to forget we were essentially strangers. My heart knew him. My body, so starved for his touch, recognized him. It was only when his lips broke from mine that reality had callously seeped in, and I was rudely reminded that time had not stood still, not for us or anyone. It never had. My memories were still closed off. If something similar were to happen tonight…if we both did choose to *act* a little further, would I have the self restraint to pull away? *Should I?*

Fearful, vicious thoughts muddied my line of reasoning, forcing me to recall my mother's dour warnings. *Gods do not love as mortals do.* Would things be different after tonight? If I let him have my body would the fire in his eyes gradually lessen? Would I, as damaged as I was, still hold his interest?

I tried to pare the fear away, reminding myself that whatever that bond was between us, that deep-rooted tie twining my heart to his, it had been grounded on something far more sturdy than just desire. If I closed my eyes, I could feel it…that very palpable, very ancient connection, burning with a sense of love so devoted, so bright, I felt certain it could never be extinguished. Even now, miles away from him, its vehemence thrummed beneath my skin like a bolt of electricity, chiming in my blood like a bell. There was no reason to be afraid, to fear waking up alone beneath our marital sheets. He loved me, truly. I was not just some long-awaited conquest to be notched upon his bedpost and then discarded. I was his wife, his queen. We were fated.

Maybe it would help, another part of me mused. Maybe, just maybe, being with him tonight would evoke some kind of memory, and I wouldn't even need to seek the assistance of this goddess of memory. All I had to do was be brave and surrender myself to him entirely.

The longer I sorted through my thoughts, questioning hypothetical theories and imagining different scenarios in my head, the more I could feel my cheeks growing uncomfortably pink. I hastened to think of something else. Anything else. This was definitely not an evening I had come prepared for. Mom smiled at the maid and shook her head.

"No, Maya, that will be all. Thank you."

The satyress nodded and then pointed toward a system of tiny bells hanging on the wall.

"Very well. Should you or Lord Hades need anything throughout the night, don't hesitate to give those bells over there a nice tug. Another maid or I will be happy to assist her highness, no matter the hour. The bath and your sleeping quarters are upstairs. You will find that everything has been thoroughly made ready, and all of your belongings have been transferred from your rooms to the wardrobe."

My belongings? I blanched, remembering all of the colorful bags Avril had brought inside the cottage with her. How could I have forgotten my fashion-loving sister had ladened herself with the job of revamping my closet? I could only imagine what she selected for me to wear tonight.

I managed to give the maid a nervous smile, and I bobbed my head in mindful understanding.

"Of course. Thank you for all your help."

Maya dipped into a final curtsy and then bade us each a good night. I watched as she spun on her hoofed heel and hobbled out the door, leaving both Mom and me behind.

CHAPTER 31
A FINAL TRUCE

A disconcerting sense of silence hung between the two of us. It was evident neither of us wanted to broach the topic at hand.

"So," I said, looking around the room. "Have you ever been to the bridal chambers before?"

A half-amused, half-grievous expression settled across my mother's pretty face. Slowly, she drifted toward the staircase, her fingers lightly skimming across the lacquered banister as she gave the room a quiet look-over.

"Yes, actually," she answered, a ghost of a smile tugging at the corners of her lips. "Your grandmother, Rhea, the nature Titaness who created me, who sculpted all of us, she had very little to do with her children after the war. To her kin, she was a doom-bringer. To the Olympians, she became a forlorn reminder of our darker days. Rather than be a dowager Queen to a new generation of immortals, she sought her own hidden banishment. In her absence, your aunt Hazel took on something of a motherly role for the five of us. She had always been the one who wiped away our tears during the war, who gave us our scoldings, and ensured we each felt loved. Unlike me, though, Hazel actually held steadfast in her decision to be a virgin goddess, so it fell on me to prepare Hertha the night she and Zane decided to lace threads."

I listened to Mom's tale with giddy interest. Hardly ever did she share with me stories of her past. Begging her for facts about her childhood, like where she had grown up, what had been her favorite stuffed animal, things I had once thought to be safe and within reason of asking, had invariably been met with the same short, difficult-to-catch responses. Like rooting for information about my father, I eventually caught the hint that she would never give me the answers I longed to hear, so I stopped asking altogether. Now, I understood why she so vehemently avoided each of my curious inquiries. She couldn't very well tell me that she had had no childhood or that she and four other immortal children like her had been swallowed whole by a monster without blowing her cover and sounding like a total nut job.

Never in a million years would I have imagined myself here, alone in a room with her, openly discussing my absent Titan grandmother without lies or evasive comebacks—just the bare truth. Each of us open and at ease for the first time in a very long time–she, a radiant goddess of the harvest, and I, a newlywed immortal Queen with amnesia. A faint smile quirked at the edges of my lips at the concept. *What a pair we made.*

"Is she still alive?" I wondered aloud. "You said she was a nature titaness, and I overheard Daniel say something about how several of the lesser worshiped nature deities faded with the land during the storm."

Mom shrugged her shoulders, trying and failing to look unbothered. The ends of her carmine gown rustled as she motioned up the steps.

"Nobody knows for certain. I have not seen her since the day you were born."

"She was present for my birth?" Shock careened through me as I trailed along after her, the noisy *tap, tap, tap,* of my shoes bouncing off the marble steps as we went.

"I think so. If not her, then one of her familiars."

I raised a curious brow in my mother's direction. "One of her what?" I faltered. "Gods can have familiars? I thought those were more like early Puritan cryptids. "

A sort of chuckle escaped from Mom."No, there is no such thing as cryptids. Any unexplainable sightings in the sky or unidentified monsters caught on tape by a handful of spooked mortals are usually just Creatures humans have forgotten the names of. The familiars we claim have no demonic ties whatsoever. In fact, most familiars are just regular animals that some of us can influence. Generally, we tend to choose beasts that strike well with our personalities. Your father, for example, chose the eagle because they are known for both their beauty and dauntlessness. In the old days, some of us would use these animals as spies or assassins, while others would sometimes choose to take on the image of their familiars and travel about the realms unnoticed."

"And that's what you think Rhea did? You think she showed up to my birth as an animal or maybe sent a pet so that she might watch over us through a familiar's eyes?"

The confusion in my voice was more than evident. I struggled to fathom how she—how *I*— had the power to shapeshift into any animal under the sun. I was even more interested to hear about my birthday. When I had asked her before, back when I had believed I was just an average, mortal girl, to tell me more about myself as a baby, she hadn't been *entirely* as reserved in her responses as she had been when talking about herself or my father. She told me I had been a quiet baby, born late in the afternoon, right around sunset, and I had come out with a head full of ginger hair. Like any Mom, she surprised me with birthday cakes every year, always homemade and overloaded with too many candles. The social security card I had never thought to question stated I was born on March 19, 1999. Now, I was curious to find my wallet. If I picked up the slip of paper, would it reveal itself actually to be a leaf, or would it simply disappear in a crackle of sparks now that the gig was up?

Mom breathed a weary sigh as if she couldn't quite decide whether she wanted to carry on with this conversation or retreat back into that acquainted, secretive silence she had hidden behind for years. I didn't push the topic any further. I had grown used to recognizing the signs of her restructuring her walls, and I knew when I had hit my quota of questions. I quietly resumed my walking, listening to our footfalls until she decidedly chose to continue her story.

"When I fled from Olympus, I was heavily pregnant. I had no plan, no thoughts of what I might do if I were to give birth before the healers had anticipated. All I knew for certain was that I had come to love you, this little flutter that lived beneath my ribs with a ferocity so great it startled me. I knew I would do anything to keep you safe, to see you thrive and blossom. I was willing to run to the ends of the earth if it meant I could keep you out of harm's way, so I made it my mission to see us into the human lands where I thought if perhaps we kept our heads down, we could live in peace. I traveled on my own across the mountains, through the darkest parts of the forests, and over restless waters. And then, one afternoon, in between your father's kingdom and the Realm of Man, I was struck with a pain so great I could barely walk more than a few paces before crumpling to the forest floor."

She paused, and I realized we were now standing atop the tower's second story. I had been so engrossed in Mom's words I hadn't realized just how fast we had climbed the stairs.

"The pain lasted for hours," she continued. "Even as a goddess with an immortal body, I was frightened. As a girl, I had heard tales about horrible, excruciating curses the Titans used to wield against one another. Ones so dark, so sadistic, that once cast, they held the power to suspend both a mother and her child in an endless state of labor."

Soundlessly, I listened to Mom go on as she guided us down a small sconce-lit hallway, my blood going cold at the thought of living through such excruciating pain with no end in sight.

"The older I became, the less I believed in such primordial writs until Hertha and Zane welcomed a daughter who could ease the throes of birth with just a simple touch. Hertha was fast to manipulate the poor child, persuading young Elise to use her conceptive gifts against the mortal women Zeus impregnated throughout the years, causing them to either lose the babes in their wombs far too soon or have the women themselves die from ensuing sepsis. Their bodies are not like ours. They cannot exist in such a torturous state of limbo without their blood turning to poison in their veins. For the first time, I was terrified of my immortality. I was scared of potentially becoming something like Prometheus. I did not want to turn into this stricken, undying thing, never able to succumb to any illness or blood loss like the mortals to free me from the torment."

Finally, we stopped walking, and I noticed two very tall ivory doors. One was stationed on my left, while the other was fixed on my right. Both faced one another from across the hallway, each inlaid with gold and engraved with decorative floral and cherub carvings atop their lintels. I watched Mom reach out and grasp the door on the right's bedecked knob. With a twist of the handle, the door glided open, and the overwhelming whiff of roses and vanilla assaulted my nostrils. Beyond, I recognized the alluring design of a white and gold bedroom. She turned her attention toward the other door, and I watched as she repeated the process, shoving open the door and revealing the enormous outline of a golden washroom illuminated with the flickering, idyllic light of over a dozen burning candles.

"So Rhea's familiar protected us from Elise?" I asked, my thoughts drifting back toward the beautiful fair-haired goddess I had met at the banquet, who shared mine and my father's eyes but her mother's sharp pension for cruelty.

Once again, Mom shrugged her shoulders, a slight smile rising to her lips.

"I wish I knew. A part of me would like to think so. I remember badly wanting someone's hand to hold that night. I did not want to admit whose hand I ached for, though. After everything she put us through, how could I? How could I find myself needing her support? But for reasons unknown to me, I did, and when I finally acknowledged it was my mother's hand I wanted, a lioness appeared from the brush. As you can imagine, the presence of this animal did little to ease my nerves. There was no way of knowing whether this big cat had been sent to harm us by Hertha, just as she had sent the serpents to strike the demi-god infant she could not stop from being born, or if it was just some ordinary beast who had caught the scent of so much ichor on the wind. The lioness made no attempts to harm me, though. She simply sat in the grass. One big paw crossed over the other as she watched me scream and writhe among the leaves. When you finally sprung from me, flushed and crying, and the last agonized groan left my lips, the lioness rose from her place beneath the trees, dragged her giant tongue across my sweaty brow, and left. When I awoke the next day, half-naked and with you asleep on my chest, I remembered that lions had always been Rhea's favorite animal."

I was silent for a spell, marveling at the otherworldly details of my birth. I had always known my mother to be highly independent and resolute. I hadn't expected her to be brave-the-wilderness-while pregnant-strong, though. *That should show you how much she loves you, how far she has always been willing to go to keep you safe,* some small part of me interjected. I already knew it was that part of me that was desperate to forgive her entirely and forget all lingering feelings of anger and betrayal. Love had made us both abrupt, and I couldn't deny that.

"Mom, I..." I started to say, the urge to cry returning as I struggled to find the right words to tell her.

The recollection of what my father had so sternly commanded just the night before and what Haden had admitted at the reception sprung to the forefront of my mind. *You will be allowed four weeks to enjoy your time as a newlywed. The Underworld will not be receiving any visitors during the extent of our honeymoon. I feel it would be in the best interest of my wife to have this final moment with her mother.*

I would be apart from Mom for a month. *A month!* That was longer than we had ever been apart in centuries. So many things could happen in a month. I couldn't leave without letting her know how I was feeling.

"I am sorry, Perrie," Mom interrupted, tears pooling in her navy eyes. "I shouldn't have snuck away with you. I shouldn't have lied to you for all those years. I am so, so sorry."

"Mom," I said again, my tone light as I tried to calm her down.

"I understand if you hate me. You're well within your right never to speak–to ever want to see me again after all of this. If that is what you want, I'll respect your wishes. As much as it will kill me, I'll leave you be. What I did… I know it is unforgivable, but please try and remember that I love you. I've always loved you, and should you ever need me…"

"Mom," I repeated, this time louder. "I forgive you."

"I don't see how you can, after what I did… The suffering I have caused you… All of your memories." Mom wept, covering her face with her hands.

"You didn't know that would happen," I softly reminded her, gently lowering her hands from her face and brushing away all her tears. "I made mistakes, too, and *I* am just as sorry. We both could have done things differently."

I felt Mom's arms wrap around me, pulling me into a tight embrace. I hugged her back just as fiercely, willing my arms to ascertain my words, to prove to her that I was willing to wipe the slate clean and begin anew. I loved her too much to keep a wedge between us, and I would miss her terribly. She hadn't even left my side yet, and I was already worried about her being all alone. Maybe I could coax Avril into checking up on her here and there just to ensure all is well. Although I was sure the goddess of love's colorful personality would wear fast on my mother's patience, I knew it would put my jumbled mind at ease. I didn't like the thought of her returning to Saint Simons by herself with those vile harpies still on the loose.

After some time, she pulled away from me, sniffling, and offered me a light, unbelieving smile that was teeming with love.

"You've always been too good for me, my little fawn," she spoke, one of her hands lifting to fuss over my ornery fringe.

Before I could open my lips to protest, I felt her arm hooking through mine.

"Come on," she sighed. "We need to get you ready."

She walked us toward the golden bathroom and positioned me in the chamber's center. Ahead of me, I could see our reflections in a full-length mirror framed in decorative gold laurel leaves, as well as other parts of the washroom. Altogether, this bath wasn't too different from the one I had used this morning. It was enormous, decorated regally in shades of medallion-gold and ivory. It had a giant glass shower in one corner of the room, with a furl of eucalyptus dangling from its head. A gigantic-sunken tub occupied another part of the chamber, its decorative faucet shaped like a swan. Across from the tub, a shelf was filled with all sorts of crystal bottles and fancily folded towels.

"Tonight," Mom began, carefully removing all the flora clips from my hair and dropping them into a tiny container she had summoned atop the washroom counter, "is not a night I thought I'd ever have to prepare you for."

My cheeks immediately reddened, and once again, I wished I could turn invisible.

"Mom, you really don't have to. I'm an entomology student, remember? I think I have a decent enough idea about nature to understand…*this*."

Mom grinned and continued her task of freeing the barrettes from my hair.

"Well, then, like any good naturalist, you should know that you have absolutely nothing to fear." She spoke confidently, spinning me about to see if she had gotten all the blooms from my hair and then steadying me once she was sure my hair was without any more ornamentation. "Tonight's happenings are quite instinctive, especially between two gods with a fated tether like yours and Haden's. Use that connection to your advantage, and do your best to keep calm. Worrying can make things…difficult."

I found myself smiling, both a bit amused and appreciative of her decision to phrase this very awkward conversation through scholarly analogies rather than some other way. It made the air between us a little less uncomfortable.

"You also need to be made aware of something else," she continued, her fingers undoing each of the ivory buttons running down the back of my gown.

Quizzically, I met her gaze in the glass and shifted from foot to foot, my nerves bristling in response to her statement.

"Okay," I said, worrying at my bottom lip.

"I told you once that the women in our family had very irregular cycles."

"I remember," I nodded, feeling the fabric around my torso begin to loosen and a drift of blessed air grazing at my spine.

I reached to hold the front of my gown in place while she turned her focus to my corset next, mercifully unlacing each of the lapping ribbons until I could feel my repressed breaths moving more freely through my lungs and the constraining tightness around my abdomen vanishing.

"I was not entirely truthful with you. The menstrual courses of a goddess are drastically different from that of a mortal. It is usual for our kind to expect their menses quarterly rather than once every month, and it is not uncommon for our cycles to be much lighter than that of a human woman's. Consequently, most goddesses cannot conceive as easily as the mortals, having shorter phases of fertility. Being a nature goddess, however, puts you in a precarious position. We embody life itself, making deities such as ourselves, by nature, more fertile."

I felt myself stiffen, alarm bells ringing in my head at the realization that not only was I a bashful, new bride, inexperienced and nervous to begin this fresh chapter of my life, but wholly susceptible. Surely there must be some way to abate my nature, some kind of godly contraceptive that could be used to prevent pregnancy.

Thoughts of Circe and the bargain I had struck to fuel the drachma magic darkened my thoughts, reminding me I was no better than any storybook maid, quick to offer up their firstborn in order to acquire some sort of fast-working enchantment, only to find themselves deeply distraught after the fact, and unwilling to part with their child. I knew the price I had paid was steep, but I had not expected to find myself worrying about its demand so soon.

Magical deals aside, I was not ready for that kind of undertaking. I barely knew myself. There were so many things I wanted to experience first, so much I ached to know. I longed to reclaim every millisecond of my life before, to discover all there is to discover, and atone for all of the stolen moments spent apart from Haden.

"Is there anything that can be done?" I asked. "To prevent, um…"

I glanced down at my stomach, one hand drifting to rest just below my navel, and then back up at Mom. *Maybe there wasn't.* Maybe our gifts over gravidity were simply *too* powerful to control, and that is how I came to be. Afterall, there was an entire hall filled with the tragic portraits of misbegotten babies. Seeming to sense the directions of my thoughts, Mom let out a little laugh.

"Yes, there is," she assured. "Several, actually. I was just, well, wild in my younger days and quite forgetful to use any of them. Your maids will bring you a special tonic in the morning. It is important that you drink all of this mixture as soon as possible if you do not wish to become pregnant."

"A tonic. Right. Sounds easy enough," I reasoned, watching Mom walk across the room to investigate inside a small closet.

After several moments of noisy searching, Mom reemerged from the closet carrying a large, striped box. I recognized it immediately as the one that had held my gown. She set the box next to the container holding my barrettes and dusted her hands on her hips.

"I assume you will want a shower before bed," she supposed, her navy eyes scanning up and down the length of my dress, scrutinizing all its elegant tufts of pink tulle and white lace as if she were calculating just how she might go about wrangling it back inside its encasement.

I nodded, eager to shuck off my shoes and step out of my dress. My hair still smelled heavily of the pomegranate and lemon verbena shampoo Euphemia had so thoroughly massaged into my scalp, and the fragrant aroma of freesia had yet to leave my skin. Nonetheless, I longed for a shower. I felt as if I were coated in a fine layer of sweat. From noon to night I had danced, and now all I wanted to do was scrub my face and freshen up.

With a flick of her wrist, Mom magically started up the shower. She turned her attention back to me and smiled.

"Go on then," she encouraged, giving my forehead a light peck before waving me toward the running shower. "You don't have much time until your groom comes knocking. I'll put away your gown and see you bright and early."

"Promise?" I muttered, uncertainty making me feel small as I tugged off each of my shoes. I knew I sounded childish, but for some odd reason, I was terrified. What if I overslept? What if I missed telling her bye before setting off on my honeymoon?

"I promise," Mom swore, craftily plucking my dangling shoes from my hands and motioning for the door.

I waited until I knew for certain she was gone before climbing out of my gown and wiggling the rest of the way out of my undergarments. Hastily, I placed both articles of clothing inside the striped box, pulled my hair up into a bun, and then hurried through the humid clouds of steam and into the running water.

CHAPTER 32
ALONE AT LAST

The anxious *thump-thump-thump* of my heart pounding resounded within my ears, mingling with the gentle splattering of the shower as I stood beneath the shower head, letting the scalding water wash away all the soap I had lathered onto my skin. I took several deep breaths, trying and failing to banish the nerves swarming within me like an angry hoard of wasps. The room was quiet now that Mom had gone, leaving me trapped with my thoughts.

"Relax," I said to myself. "Everything is going to be alright. You're just getting ready for bed."

I loosed another breath, and made an effort to pretend I was back at the cottage, following the same nightly routine as always. I was in the shower, washing away the day's grime and soon I would be…

I had meant to think of a book. Reading myself to sleep was a comforting ritual, something I had done time and time again before drifting off, but for the life of me I couldn't visualize a paperback. No, in its place was Haden. Alone, waiting for me in the darkened chambers of our marital suite. The memory of his lips on mine and the feel of his hands around my waist had my blood running hotter than the water.

Shaking myself free from those thoughts, I switched off the shower and nudged open the foggy glass door. With little grace, I sped from the shower, scrambling toward the bathroom sink with a towel haphazardly wrapped around my middle. I wiped at the condensation on the mirror, only to find a fretful-looking reflection of myself staring back at me.

A part of me had hoped that a shower would help bolster my self-esteem.

I had wanted to freshen up, to make myself feel softer and more feminine. Now, I was beginning to wish I had just climbed into bed as I was. The soaps I had found inside the shower were nothing like the ones Euphemia had poured into my bath this morning. These were overpowering in their fragrance. Pungent and a little too sweet-scented around my pulse points. I had twisted my hair up in a loose knot, knowing I had little time to fool with my thick tresses. Sighing, I promptly began to take inventory of all the items sitting atop the counter, glancing over a small decanter of hand soap and a lovely gold comb.

True to Mom's word, I noticed that my gown, as well as my shoes and the collection of floral barrettes, were all gone, presumably neatly packed away who knows where. A small sprout of concern rose in their absence. I hoped wherever she had put them, they were not someplace they might get lost. "You don't have time to worry about that!" I chided, urging myself to stop standing about and get to work.

I began to scout the counter top for a toothbrush. When my search proved fruitless, I panickedly rifled through the many washroom drawers, finding fancy perfumes, embroidered washcloths, and creams. Just when I was losing hope, a flash of turquoise caught my eye, and I let out an allayed breath as a toothbrush magically appeared, materializing within one of the compartments with a green, unlabeled tube next to it. I picked up the toothbrush, piled it high with what smelled like spearmint toothpaste from the tube, and started brushing my teeth. Once finished with that, I set to work on freeing my hair. It glided down my shoulders in a mess of ginger waves. Grimacing, I lifted the heavy comb up to my head and tenderly began to run the golden teeth through my hair, working loose the worst of the tangles and smoothing out my wayward curls before placing the comb back down. I knew there was no chance of me getting my tresses to spiral anywhere near similar to the way Avril and all the other goddesses who had recently taken to styling my hair had, so I settled on just running my fingers through the rest of my hair, twisting a few strands here and there. *At least it will look like you made some kind of attempt*, I huffily thought.

Not allowing myself to take another glimpse at my reflection, fearing it might prompt a panic attack, I tightened my hold on my towel and padded across the hallway. The foyer seemed darker than before, set alight only with dim sconces, and the air felt a little bit draftier after my time spent in the humid washroom. I quickened my steps, unwilling to admit that being alone in the tower made me feel jumpy. Stepping inside the bedroom, I was surprised to find a scattering of red as far as the eye could see. Bright, cerise rose petals littered the marble floor and the ginormous bed. I froze, my heartbeat rocketing at the sight—no wonder the room smelled so strongly of roses. My eyes settled on the bed, and I fought the urge to nervously gnaw at my bottom lip. *White.* The lacey duvet and all its many pillows were so pristinely white. Remembrances of history lessons, of the ancient practice of hanging bed sheets from balconies, came to mind, and I had to take several deep breaths to quell my rising anxiety. *Did they expect me to carry on that tradition...to prove our consummation before all of Olympus?* We were, in a sense, royals. I was now the wife of an immortal king. Even with our never-ending lifespans, was creating an heir to the realm still that vital to the gods?

I walked past the bed and over to a big, baroque-style armoire. Like everything else in the room, the armoire was a shade of ivory. Three rectangular mirrors adorned its wooden surface, the largest of the three overlooking the bed. Golden handles were fastened to the panels of the mirrors. I grabbed for the handle attached to the middle mirror and pulled back the door. Inside, row after row of expensive-looking night clothes hung, each one more gossamer and see-through than the last. I blushed a furious shade of scarlet at all the silk and lace. *This was worse than the corset. The towel I was wearing now covered more than any of this!*

"Avril," I grumbled, letting out a low number of curses as I flipped through the assortment of chemises and cami tops, hoping that perhaps my eyes were playing tricks on me and I had simply overlooked a nice pair of regular pajama pants.

Spotting a hanging clock on the wall and realizing I had spent far too long fretting over what to wear, I reluctantly snatched a purple negligee from its hanger and hurriedly stooped down to collect a pair of matching, lacey unmentionables from a bottom drawer. I refused to look at myself in any of the mirrors as I pulled both on, closing the armoire behind me. I had tried to pick the most conservative nightgown I could find, but even it left little to the imagination. The dress was, however, longer than most of the nighties hanging in the closet, just barely grazing the tips of my toes. Looking down, I could tell its delicate fabric was as sheer as a lilac mist. The straps were thin and lacey, plummeting down to meet a deep V-shaped neckline that left far too much of my breasts on display. Only a light pattern of filigree flowers prevented the gown from being entirely see-through. Self-consciously, I lifted my arms and crossed them over my chest, drifting back toward the bed and listening to the silence of the night.

I was ready. Or, at least as ready as I would ever be, washed and dressed with a handful of seconds to spare. *What should I do now? How should I wait?* My gaze flicked in the direction of a bench positioned at the foot of the bed. *Should I sit there?* I glanced back down at my sheer nightgown, at all its flowery lace, and promptly opted against doing that. *What if Haden was tired and had no intention of becoming intimate tonight?* Seeing me sitting at the foot of our marital bed, scantily clad and waiting surely didn't paint the image of someone wanting to maybe just talk. The last thing I wanted was to make him feel pressured or uncomfortable. The steady sound of footsteps approaching broke me from my thoughts. Frantically, I decided to bolt for the bed and tear back the blankets, tossing rose petals every which way as I dove beneath the silky sheets. I blew out several of the burning candles sitting on top of our nightstands, choosing to leave only a few lit. Perhaps having him see me like this, in near darkness and less exposed, would make things easier for the both of us.

With bated breath, I waited for Haden to enter the room, my back facing away from the door as I lay buried beneath the covers. After a tortuous expanse of time, the door creaked open, and the smell of smoke and cedar drifted in. I listened to his steps, surprised to find just how quiet they were. *Had he taken off his shoes?*

"Are you asleep, ánthos?" Haden asked, his voice low and sensual.

I shifted beneath the covers, sitting up just enough so that he might see me.

"No," I answered, feeling his fiery-brown eyes slowly assess me.

Gone, I noticed, was his dark dress suit. In its place, he wore a set of inky black night clothes. Drops of water still clung to his russet curls, indicating that he, too, must have decided upon taking a bath. He made no attempts to join me in the bed. He simply stood at the end of the golden foot board with his arms crossed behind his back, one dark brow quirked in curiosity.

"Are you cold?"

I shook my head, my grip on the blankets vice-like.

"Then why are you bundled up?"

My eyes darted in the direction of the armoire. He followed my gaze, and I blushed.

"It's Avril," I blurted.

"Avril?" he repeated, his dark brows knitting together in confusion.

"Yes, I mean, no. S-she bought me all of these really expensive clothes for our honeymoon, and they're all very stunning, but…"

I stopped talking, hating the way my voice was suddenly shaking. *I sounded like a stammering idiot.* Embarrassed, I tore my gaze from his and stared instead at the wall. This wasn't how I had imagined this evening unfolding.

"But?" Haden prompted, refusing to let me go quiet.

I sighed and sat up a little straighter in the bed, letting some of the blankets fall away.

"The night clothes… They're a little over-the-top, and I didn't want to–"

"Persephone," Haden interrupted, his low voice taking on a more serious note as he said my old name. "Come here."

I hesitated for only a moment before ultimately pushing aside the blankets and slipping out of the giant bed. The cold marble floor bit at the soles of my feet as I moved across the darkened room to meet my husband. I stopped inches from him, my eyes curiously traveling up to study his expression.

He was quiet and still, almost statuesque, as he slowly drank in the sight of me, the embers in his eyes darkening as he took in every little detail.

"You have nothing to fear from me," he finally said, his tone stern, ensuring.

I watched as he lifted one arm, his movements deliberately slow as he captured the side of my face with his hand. I shivered against his touch, feeling a sense of blooming heat begin to wash over me as he lightly stroked his thumb against the curvature of my cheek.

"I will not force you to lie with me, not tonight or any other night. Do you understand?"

Unable to look away from him, I nodded.

"If you wish for me to sleep elsewhere, I shall," he continued, his umber gaze drifting down to linger on my lips. "You need only ask."

"N-no, I don't want that," I answered, my body on impulse drawing nearer to him.

"What *do* you want?"

Considerately, he withdrew his hand from my face, and I found myself missing his caress.

What did I want to do? I glanced back at the bed longingly. It had been so lovely to lie down, even for just a few seconds. The mattress had felt like laying atop a cloud, and I was beyond tired. I did not want to go to sleep yet, though. I doubted I'd even be able to if I tried. My mind was far too restless, and my nerves were still running wild. I peered about the room, searching for somewhere we might rest until I was too fatigued to think straight, and spotted an arched set of wrought-iron balcony doors.

"You called me ánthos," I stated, timorously crossing my arms once more over my chest. "What does that mean?"

Haden flashed me a puckish smile. "So, you have decided upon asking questions."

"You did promise me answers."

He chuckled and stepped back a few paces, his hands lowering to his waist to undo the fastenings of a black robe. Languidly, he shrugged the garment off and offered it to me.

"Very well. I will answer your questions, but only after you put this on. You look positively perturbed wearing that."

With one arm, I reached out and took the robe, feeling heat pool in my cheeks once again.

"Thanks. I will have to have a serious chat with Avril in the morning. I hope she kept most of the receipts from wherever she got these outfits. I don't generally wear stuff like this," I admitted, sliding one arm after the other into each of the giant sleeves.

The robe was loose on my womanly frame, nice and soft as I tugged it closer around myself. Blessedly, it hid the worst of the sheerness, covering my body in a swathe of black, prompting me to relax and drop my arms from around my breasts.

"Tomorrow, we can buy you an entirely new wardrobe if you'd like," Haden offered, returning my attention to him. "Although you should feel no shame in wearing gowns such as these. You are beautiful."

I blushed an even deeper shade of red and drifted toward the balcony doors, readying myself to adventure back out into the crisp mountain air by cinching the sash to Haden's robe tight around my waist.

"Bribes and flattery will get you nowhere, sir," I teased, nervously cracking open one of the balcony doors. "I was assured answers, and I will not be so easily dissuaded from getting them."

Haden's smirk deepened as he followed me out into the starry night.

CHAPTER 33
IN THE BEGINNING

To my surprise, the balcony attached to our room was smaller, cozier than I'd expected. Vines of fuchsia bleeding hearts dripped from a marble awning, and two cushioned chairs sat on the stone landing, overlooking an expanse of dark, wooded mountainside. A tiny table rested between the two chairs, just the right size for a mug of something hot, or perhaps a book or two. I smiled contentedly as I sat down in one of the chairs. *Finally, somewhere a little less garnished. This spot would do perfectly.* Haden lingered by the door frame for a few seconds before gliding toward the seat beside me.

He spoke first. "Ánthos means flower in Greek."

"Flower," I repeated, leaning back against the cool chair cushions.

"Yes. It was a nickname I gave you. I used to call you *my flower*."

"Tell me more," I prompted, wiggling in my seat until I was reasonably comfortable. "I want to know everything."

"Everything," Haden repeated, his tone light. "That's a broad topic. One I'm not sure I will be able to cover in one night."

I tossed him a peeved look, and he only grinned.

"Tell me more about yourself then. I want to know more about you, about the balls, and the Underworld. Tell me about us. I want to hear about the night we first met, about how we fell in love."

Haden sank into his chair, resting his arms atop the armrests.

"I imagine Demeter has probably already told you how we came to be."

"I have somewhat of an understanding," I confessed. "But she and I... We didn't really talk about any of this. Not until Avril spontaneously showed up and pulled the rug out from underneath our feet, forcing Mom to tell me a little bit of the truth."

Haden gave a low chuckle at my response and shook his head.

"Yes, Aphrodite has a knack for doing that. She's as much a goddess of chaos as she is of love. As for your mother, I can't entirely blame her. Our origins aren't a pretty tale to tell."

He settled further into his seat, the humor in his eyes fading as he seemed to be sifting through his thoughts.

"I am not a very interesting god, I'm afraid. I have lived a rather sedentary life for many centuries. I have fathered no children, bore the humans no ill will, and taken only one goddess to wife. Before that, I recall very little. I know that I lived in the country for a time with a Titaness I had thought of as my mother. Occasionally she would take me out for walks throughout the gardens and would sing me cradle songs at night. I remember she had hair as black as a raven's feathers and eyes the color of storm clouds."

"She sounds lovely," I said softly.

Haden nodded his agreement.

"She was," he mused. "It is not in a Titan's nature to be compassionate. In their culture, forming attachments is an infallible way to prove yourself weak. Rarely did Titans marry for love. All couplings were based purely on who could produce the most powerful offspring. Mothers were encouraged to do only what was necessary to keep the child alive after birth. The fact that she showed me any tenderness at all is a taboo within itself that would have made her a pariah in her own peoples' eyes, had they discovered me sooner."

"How did you and she get separated?" I wondered.

Haden gave a sad smile, and his eyes seemed to darken with regret.

"Like all godlings, I was prone to getting into mischief. As a child, I knew nothing of the prophecy that drove Cronus to commit such enormities. I wasn't aware that my very existence was a secret. I knew only that Rhea allowed me to explore the gardens on special occasions, always under her supervision. Never was I permitted to go anywhere on my own, and for a year or two, I thought nothing of it. The older I got, though, the more curious I became. One day, while she was away, I snuck past my nursemaid and fled out to play in the olive groves. Not paying attention to where I was going, I ran headfirst into a stranger who turned out to be a high-ranking officer in Cronus's guard. Being fiercely loyal to the Titan King, he took me with him to Mount Othrys, where Cronus held court. Immortal children were a rarity in those days. For reasons unknown, the Titans were going through a mass recession in births, so to find me frolicking about in the royal groves, unattended, and dressed like a little prince was not something that could go without being reported. It didn't help that I bore a striking resemblance to the warlord himself, either."

"You look like Cronus?" I said, disbelief coloring my words.

My dark god was beautiful, shadowy, and ethereal, like a dense forest cast in moonlight. Cronus was a monster, hideous and cruel. Not a single image in any of the books Avril had shown me illustrated him in a pleasant light. Haden let out an amused snort at my reaction.

"What? Did you think he and all of his ilk would be hideous?"

Embarrassed, I smiled and shrugged my shoulders.

"I don't know what I imagined. A race of Goya-like giants, maybe. Or something like the modern day devil, all atrocious horns and red skin."

"You're not entirely wrong," he acknowledged. "Some are indeed monstrous. There were the Hundred-Handed with their hundred arms and fifty heads, and Typhon the Terrible, who fathered a legion of Creatures with his snake-like wife, Echidna. Others, though, could be striking and change their shape as easily as we do."

I felt myself growing wide-eyed with interest at the mention of all these new, terrifying-sounding immortals. The urge to ask him about each of these horrible Titans was nearly maddening. Nonetheless, I managed to keep quiet, knowing he'd never be able to answer all of my original questions if I flooded him with more. *Those would just have to be questions for later*, I assured myself, watching Haden exhale.

"As much as I would like for Cronus to be red-skinned and cloven-footed, his countenance bears more in common with the humans and us than those in his lineage who share bloodlines with Creatures. When Rhea made me, she made me in his image. We share the same hair, he and I, the same nose and mouth. In the right light, one could certainly mistake me for being his blood son. Cronus himself was nearly fooled. The mere sight of me was enough to send him into a blind rage. I remember being surprised when he lashed out at the guard who delivered me to him for not finding me sooner and then having to cover my ears as he bellowed for him to get up and find Rhea at once. When she arrived, I had to watch as he tortured her. She pleaded with him to listen to her, to look at me, and he would know I was not of his bloodline, but his fury deafened him to reason. He would not heed her words."

A deep-rooted sorrow carved its way inside my chest as I pictured my dark god as a child. I imagined him small, teary-eyed and frightened, standing before a vicious Titan king. Without thinking, I placed a comforting hand on Haden's forearm. The contact rattled us both, and I was catapulted back into remembering where we were. *Alone. Together. Right outside our bridal chambers.* Shyly, I snatched my hand back, and Haden cleared his throat.

"Eventually, he grew tired of hearing his wife's screams and turned his anger toward me. I'll never forget how his eyes looked that day. Black as coals and filled with a lacerating kind of hatred, the sort that paralyzes you. I knew then; I had never felt true fear—not up until that moment. I fully expected him to kill me, to snap me in half like a twig, but he didn't. It wasn't until he had me by the neck that he realized Rhea had been telling the truth. I did not bear the markings of a true Titan child. I was far too short, even for a boy. I lacked the height of a Titan. My canines were also duller and less extended in comparison to the elongated teeth of his kind. Neither did I have the glowing irises of a Titan. Not sure what to make of me, he tossed me aside, where Rhea, bruised and bloody, drug herself over to shield my small body with hers. She begged him to spare me, not to destroy her precious new creation. He honored her wishes only partially. Instead of ending my life then and there, he did something far worse."

A roiling sense of unease settled within my gut as I remembered how the rest of the story went. My dark god and all the others had been eaten alive, left to wait inside the bottom of a monster king's belly for eighteen years before finally being set free. The thought was frightening. It certainly made my skin crawl and caused bile to rise in the back of my throat.

"W-what happened after that?" I asked, curious to know how he and Mom had survived for so long, living in Cronus's stomach.

"After that? Well, I figured out the truth."

"The truth?" I repeated, perplexed.

Haden smiled again, although there was no humor behind the expression this time.

"Yes, I discovered I had not been eaten but tricked. You see, Cronus possesses a perilous kind of power, one that cloaks reality and manipulates the principles of time around you. The last thing I saw before being cast into darkness was Cronus transforming himself into a giant, plucking me off the ground, and swallowing me whole. For several decades, I believed I had been eaten alive. It wasn't until I was joined by others like me in my imprisonment, others like Hera, that I gathered we were living in an entirely different prison than the one I had come to know."

"What did Hertha do to change your mind?" I prodded, intrigued at the mention of my aunt. Not much had been written about the fairest Olympian sister before her time as queen, nor did any of the books I had skimmed through mention her role during the Titanomachy.

"Hera's greatest gift is her ability to slip into minds. She broke Cronus's illusion with one of her own and changed the scenery of our hellscape, uncovering that none of us had ever truly been trapped within the belly of a Titan but locked inside our own heads. It wasn't very long after that that we were soon freed by Zeus, who did, as it happens, poison Cronus by slipping a toxic draft into his drink. The poison was fast acting and caused the Titan to lose his grip on the glamour, keeping us all unconscious. When we awoke, all five of us pledged our loyalty to the god who had saved us and followed him with our mother back to Mount Olympus, where we would later build this very palace."

Habitually, I toyed with the ends of my hair, feeling equal parts startled and amazed at all the new knowledge I had just learned. The picture books Avril had shown me couldn't have been more wrong. So much of the truth behind our family legacy had been lost, diminished to mere legend. What else was I mistaken about? What other great truths had lost their credibility to time?

"What did you do next?" I questioned, eager to hear him tell me more. "How did you become King of the Dead?"

Quietly, Haden rose from his chair, and for a horrified second, I thought he was contemplating spending the night somewhere else. I had pushed him too far, and he was leaving. I had forgotten to word my questions gently, and now my fear of being left alone in our marital bed wasn't appearing as farfetched as I had convinced myself it was. *I had to do something, say something. I didn't want him to leave.*

CHAPTER 34

WAR TALES AND CONFESSIONS

Hastily, I sprung up from my chair, not caring that part of his inky robe had slid down one of my shoulders in my hurry to stop him from going, leaving more of me exposed than I would have cared for.

"Haden..." I stammered. "I didn't mean to...I..."

The rueful sentence I had thought of saying next died on my lips. Haden hadn't stood up to leave. *No.* He was undoing each of the midnight buttons along his shirt. My heart stalled inside my chest, only to double its beat, pounding faster and faster until I felt certain Haden could hear it from across the balcony. Try as I might, I couldn't look away from his fingers, from the parting black fabric, revealing glimpses of smooth olive skin and chiseled muscle beneath.

Our eyes locked, and suddenly I felt breathless. That pull to touch him, to be closer, and let the sparks around us collide and catch fire was back and it was stronger than before. *Hungrier.* A part of me yearned to listen to its demands, to go to him, to press my lips against his and tangle my fingers in his hair, answers be damned. I could always ask him these same questions again tomorrow. Or the next day. It didn't matter. We had forever, didn't we?

From the way Haden's eyes had darkened, it wasn't hard to decipher that he was feeling that same draw, prompting him to take me in his arms, to kiss me just as he had in the throne room. Restively, I waited to see what would happen next. Would we let the sway of the tether guide us through the flames, or would we carry on as we had been? A husband and a wife trying to relearn one another after so many lifetimes apart?

Haden was the first to look away, ultimately bringing the sparks around us to a gradual halt. I tried not to feel too disappointed or relieved, choosing instead to observe the downward trek of his fingers as he pulled back more of his shirt to reveal an awful, raised scar. The mark was long, winding up his ribcage and bending across his chest like a jagged, silver river. I gasped and clasped a hand over my mouth, fighting back the urge to cry.

"How did you get that?" I asked, a troubled edge to my voice.

To see such a lurid scar on my husband had my emotions reeling. I wanted to hug him, to take him in my arms, and thank whatever force had chosen to watch over him during such a contest, while another, more innate part of me was livid. I could barely keep my hands from shaking. I wanted to ruin whatever had done this to him.

"In the early days of the rebellion, times were difficult. We had scant rations and no weaponry, with very few allies to aid us in our minor skirmishes against the Titan foot soldiers. None of us had acquired proper dominion over our gifts yet, and Rhea could only teach us so much. It was clear to all that if we did not find any sympathizers soon, we would lose the war, so Zeus split us up. He sent your mother and Hestia to the East to make friends with the Titaness Themis and her two sons, and he consigned Poseidon and me to Mount Enta to free the Cyclopes being kept prisoner underground, which proved to be rather simple, thanks to my skills in shadow summoning."

Amazed, I watched as Haden conjured a small furl of shadow, rolling the misty patch between his knuckles like one might a coin before snapping it away.

"Like the others, we proved successful in our mission. We stole away with all three of the one-eyed brothers and persuaded them to join us in our fight against the Titans. We had nearly made it back to Olympus when a horde of Typhon's children ambushed us in the foothills. It was a close fight, one I'm not sure the six of us would have won had your father not arrived with reinforcements. I got this scar during that battle from the poison-tipped claws of a chimera."

I eyed the scar again, my thoughts wandering back to that pivotal day in the village, where I had had my own close encounter with a flock of Creatures. I could still feel the abrasive burn of the pavement gashing at my knees and the savage sting of the monstress's talons raking down my shoulders. I knew the attack had left me pretty banged up. I had felt it in my muscles, in the way my tattered shirt had become sticky with blood, and yet, when I had seen myself in Avril's mirror, my back had appeared no different than when I had first woken up that morning. Not even a scratch remained to show where the harpy had grazed me.

"You're fretting." Haden grinned, an amused glint sparking in his dark eyes as he redid each of the buttons along his shirt.

"Hmm? No, I'm not. What makes you think that?" I denied, a bashful smile toying at the corners of my mouth.

He gestured toward my forehead and then down at my lips.

"I had seen you rapt in thought countless times," Haden offered, "Each time, you would scrunch your brows and bite at your bottom lip, much like how you were doing moments ago."

His response struck something inside me. It was shocking to hear him speak of me from before, to hear more about myself, this goddess who was as familiar yet mysterious to me as my own shadow.

"Earlier in the week, I was attacked by a harpy," I said, modestly readjusting the fallen sleeve of Haden's robe around myself.

A muscle in the god of the dead's jaw twitched as he calmly stood and listened to me speak.

"One of them, their leader, gave me a pretty bad slash across my shoulder."

Haden met my gaze with a seething, black-hearted look that seemed to promise slow, excruciating violence.

"I know," he admitted, his voice as frigid as ice. "I have sent the Erinyes to search for the flock that marked you. They will make certain their crimes against you are justly punished."

A shiver that had nothing to do with the cool night air capered down my spine as my mind began to imagine what sort of creatures the Erinyes must be to capture and punish a harpy, and then my musings fell back to my husband. My dark, avenging husband who, in that instant, seemed far more terrifying than any Creature could hope to be. He had no qualms about threatening an Olympian princess just for speaking poorly of me and had been more than willing to throw the world into chaos when he believed me to be faded. *Was there anything he wasn't willing to do, any monstrosities he wouldn't commit?*

I swallowed and lowered myself back into the balcony chair, already knowing the answer to that thought. *No.* Nothing would be too much, just as there could never be a price too steep for me to pay for him. I patted my shoulder and then motioned toward Haden's torso.

"How come I don't have a scar like yours? Why did my wound heal when yours did not?"

"Because different primordial beings inflicted them." Haden reasoned. "In our world, there is such a thing as Lesser and Greater Creatures. Had it been any other monster, I would have healed in seconds, but the Chimera is an old beast, hailing from an even older primordial bloodline. This scar will remain for as long as I walk this earth. The species of harpy that attacked you are not nearly as ancient. Whoever sent them after you did not wish to have you killed or gravely injured; otherwise, they would have sent a much nastier beast to find you."

"Wait... We can be killed?" I uttered, a shoot of worry blossoming inside me.

"Yes, ánthos," Haden answered, a grim expression settling across his features. "There are many ways a god can be slain. Fading is one way. Having our eternal threads severed is another. Then, there is death by a higher power. Just as man can murder man, a god can kill another god. It is not an easy feat, but it can be done. You need not worry about fading, though. No immortal has been sentenced to death since Zeus came into power. We did not even take the life of Cronus, and there has been nothing but peace throughout all four realms for centuries."

Shock jolted through me, filling me with a sense of disbelief so strong it felt like I had been struck by one of my father's lightning bolts. I couldn't shake the aghast look on my face as I processed Haden's words. *Cronus was still alive?* I contemplated bobbing my head to the side. Perhaps I had gotten water in my ears from the shower and misheard him. There was no way my father or the council would allow such an evil entity like Cronus to remain alive. It defied all common sense.

"You mean Cronus is alive? Why did none of you fight to have him executed? After everything he put you through, it makes no sense."

Haden shrugged his shoulders and leaned against the balcony railing, his fingers reaching out to toy with one of the many bleeding hearts.

"I assure you, it wasn't an easy decision to make. The six of us were little more than children during our succession. We had much to consider after the war. After decades of ceaseless fighting, we finally emerged victorious, only to inherit a kingdom of ash and rubble. It took another ten years to resow the forests... to make the realms sustainable again. Then we had to create new laws and determine how to rule. None of us wanted to start the world anew with any Titan practices, so Zeus' first suggestion was to form a council where all our voices would be heard. We had seen firsthand what destruction could befall the kingdoms should only one deity govern over all. Never again would the realms answer to one immortal king, but to three. These kings, we decided, would be equal in power and would rule over their own territories within the immortal world. I won my title by chance. Poseidon, Zeus, and I drew straws resembling each of the realms. Whoever drew the longest straw would be King of the Heavens, the second to longest would become ruler of the seas, and whoever drew the shortest would be King of the Underworld. Once it was settled who would be ruling where, we summoned our newfound council for a final meeting to discuss what should become of Cronus. In the end, the six of us agreed that death would be too gracious of an end for our father, so we took it upon ourselves to imprison him and all those still loyal to him in Tartarus, where he and his court remain to this day, trapped within an inescapable prison."

I loosed a breath. The petrifying fears of someday having everything ripped away from me, of losing my family to a malefic Titan king dwindled to harmless flecks of ash. We were safe. Cronus, while still alive, was not a threat. Somehow, he was imprisoned, locked away with no hopes of ever breaking free.

"After that, we all went our separate ways, and Zeus ordained the others. He named your mother goddess of the fields and Hestia goddess of the hearth, and they left to care for those who needed their blessings in the Mortal Lands. Both he and Poseidon then took it upon themselves to find wives. Of course, your father chose Hera to be his queen. Poseidon married the daughter of an old sea lord, and I left to rule the Underworld alone."

"What is it like, the Underworld?" I softly implored.

CHAPTER 35

IN ANOTHER LIFE

A mesmerizing smile lit up the God of the Dead's face, one filled with great pride and passion.

"Imagine wildflowers as far as the eye can see, in fields as green as emeralds. And then envision shores as black as obsidian and forests teeming with life. There are mountains and valleys, and five magnificent rivers that run throughout our kingdom. The Isle of Elysium is where those pure of heart go to spend their eternity, and the Asphodel Meadows is where those souls not quite ready to move on may live and wait for their loved ones to meet them in the afterlife. There is also Tartarus, but you needn't worry about that region. It is far from our castle, and only I will go there until your memories are restored."

I nodded, feeling a furl of excitement and relief blossoming inside me. My new home sounded beautiful, nothing like the nightmarish landscape I had feared it might be, with only lakes of fire and brimstone to liven the darkness.

"So there is sunlight in the Underworld?" I wondered. "Seasons?"

Haden's smile broadened. "There is light, but not from the sun. The light that illuminates our sky comes from crystals hanging from the cavern roof. As for the seasons, we have those too, just not like the ones you're used to."

Intrigued, I drifted over beside him and stood beneath the clusters of pink vines.

"Why did you wait so long to choose a bride for yourself? Surely, it must have been lonely away from the others."

"For a while, it was lonely…but I needed that space to myself. I would not have made a good husband then. I was a different god. Angrier. We each had our own ways of coping after the war. Zeus had his affairs. Your mother had her work in the mortal lands. Hera had all of her gowns and pretty trinkets to fuss over. All I had was spite. It enraged me that my brothers and sisters could live within these palace walls so frivolously as if the war had never happened while I still struggled to forget the faces of the lesser beings brave enough to help us who had been cut down by forces much stronger than they. In truth, their capriciousness and self-indulgent ways still wear on my nerves, but I have found ways to better manage my emotions and put the past behind me. I channeled all that temper into rebuilding my realm and making my lands perfect for all of the departed spirits coming to stay in my kingdom. I began to love the Underworld so much that I rarely wished to leave and visit the world above. There was always work to be done…souls to attend to. What felt like a few months spent away from the others to me turned out to be entire millenniums. This behavior led me to develop quite the reputation of being a dark recluse. When I finally did return to Mount Olympus, there were faces I had never seen before," Haden said, his eyes finding mine in the dark.

"Hera had given birth to five children in my absence, the eldest being two sons, one a brutish god of war, another a clever god of fire smiths. They were both in love with a new goddess said to have been found on the island of Cypress. She herself had a son who bore an uncanny resemblance to Ares. The rest were all products of my brother's countless affairs—a pair of immortal twins to drive the sun and moon chariots across the sky, a goddess gifted with wisdom beyond her years, a mischievous messenger god with sandals enchanted to fly as fast as the four winds. And then there was you."

My heart thumped hard against my ribs as he spoke as if I alone were the reason behind everything good and happy in the universe. The chills I had felt from earlier reappeared, spreading across my skin in fields of tiny goosebumps. I rubbed at my arms and dared myself to hold his gaze, to peer deeper into his burning eyes.

"When I had left, Demeter had sworn herself a virgin goddess, never to be touched or bound to another by marriage. As you can imagine, it was bewildering to return and find her holding a daughter's hand."

His lips lifted into a wry smile, and he motioned to my hair.

"Your hair was as bright as fire. It glowed like Apollo's chariot. You wore this awful green gown with little blush flowers decorating the skirt, certainly some flounced frock Aphrodite had tailored for you. Your skin was as fair as porcelain, and your lips were as pink as rose petals. It was your eyes, though, that enchanted me. Those emerald-blue eyes…so bright and innocent. They were lovelier than any gem in my kingdom, brighter than any treasure. They drove me to abandon my indifference, to venture out and discover your name."

Unexpectedly, a hearty laugh left his lips, and just the sound of it brought me immense joy. I knew instantly I'd give anything to hear him laugh like that again.

"You weren't like the others. You were quiet. Reserved. You seemed just as out of place as me when surrounded by so much gold and intemperance."

I let out a little laugh of my own at his response and tried not to imagine how amateurish I must have appeared today before all the others with my fumbling feet and less-than-perfect posture. I certainly had been out of my element. Knowing I had never been good at soirees gave me comfort. Nervous to ask my next question, I moistened my lips and took a deep breath, doing my best to shrug off my uneasiness.

"Was that the moment you fell in love with me? Why did the storytellers paint you as my, um, abductor rather than as my lover?" I awkwardly asked, trying the romantic, starry-eyed word on for size and regretting it immediately. *Lover? Had we even been lovers? Why did I have to choose that word? On tonight of all nights!*

An amused expression flitted across Haden's face as if he could read my flustered thoughts, and I instantly felt my cheeks go hot in response. Something that seemed almost predatory sparked within his eyes…something that struck me as a silent, titillating answer. *Yes.* He had known my body once, just as he knew my mannerisms. The thought bathed my insides in the sweetest of flames and made my heart flutter. I gulped and did my best to fight off such desirous thoughts. *Answers! I wanted answers.*

Across from me, he seemed to be searching for the right words to answer my questions while also reminiscing. The longer he took to respond, the antsier I began to feel. *What could be running through his head?* Finally, the hunger in his gaze lessened, and he seemed to sober up.

"Yes, I believe it was. It was the first time I felt our tether. I watched you from afar for hours that night, behind pillars and through the crowded bodies separating us. I made it my undertaking to discover more about you. I needed to know your name and where you had come from, so I asked around the ballroom. Word travels fast in Olympus. I discovered that you were the product of a scandalous affair, that your mother and Hera had fallen out because of it, and no one had seen you in your father's court for eighteen years.

I learned it was *your* claiming day we were celebrating and that you had a throng of suitors hopelessly grappling for your hand in marriage. It was widely understood that Demeter planned to enlist you to the virginal Cult of Gaia, and if you would like for me to be entirely truthful, I was searching for something to hate about you."

The booming, frantic beats of my heart slammed to an abrupt stop in my chest, and the smile that had settled on my lips fell. All at once, I could feel the butterflies in my stomach dropping dead. The dazzling, romantic, love-at-first-sight vision my mind's eye had painted became a little less rosy and more drab around the edges. I suddenly felt incredibly foolish.

"Why?" I asked, trying and failing to mask the hurt leaching through in my voice.

Haden shrugged his shoulders.

"You were too beautiful for the likes of me. Whispers of your kind heartedness and creative mind froze me in my tracks. I did not want to ruin you, to rob you of your flowers and sunlight. I thought a god like me would do nothing but blacken your lively spirit, and I did not want that for you. I presumed you would be better suited in the land of the living and that pursuing you would only be a waste of my time anyway. Why try to woo a goddess sworn to maidenhood or steal you away from the arms of another who could potentially give you the eternity you deserved? I figured if perhaps I could find something to hate about you, it would make rejecting our tether easier, and I could let you go."

He ran a hand along the balcony railing, his fingers finding mine.

"At some point during the night, you managed to slip away from your mother. You were desperate to be free from the crowds, to feel the soil beneath your bare feet, so you fled to the gardens. Like the selfish monster I am, I followed you out, unable to resist at least hearing your voice."

He paused, his mood once again seeming to shift into that darkened state.

"About halfway through the maze, I realized I was not the only god who had chosen to follow you from the palace. Drunk off his ass, Hermes thought confessing his love for you would be a clever idea. You tried to let him down easily, but he would not take no for an answer. He grew more persistent in his pleas for you to marry him, and when he took hold of your arms, something inside me snapped. I stepped out from behind the hedges and demanded that he release you immediately and for him to get out of my sight. The idiot had enough sense to listen and fled from the gardens."

"That's why you hate Holland…" I muttered, feeling even sicker. No wonder his presence made me feel so uncomfortable and sad. Whatever friendship he and I had shared in the past must have been ruined that night.

"Hate is far too gentle a word," Haden said, grimacing. "Were he not a son of Zeus, I would have seen him quartered and cursed."

"And how did I react to meeting you?"

"You thanked me for my help and tried to excuse Hermes' behavior. Even after nearly being violated, you were insistent that he had just had too much to drink and that he was a good god who meant you no real harm."

His thumb rubbed an idle pattern against mine.

"I told you that he was a pig and that if you were wise, you would trust no Olympian. You made some sharp remarks about shouldn't that mean you shouldn't trust my word either, which led to us staying out in the garden and talking late into the night. You weren't afraid of me, which I found highly interesting. When your mother finally found us, she was furious. She immediately dismissed the idea of me ever courting you and told me I was never to call on you again. I reassured her I had no intentions of courtship, and she dragged you away. That next day, you sought me out and forbade me from staying away from you. You said that you saw no reason why we could not be friends if neither of us were interested in marriage. Against all my better judgment, I agreed and swore to see you in six months' time."

"And just like that, you came back?"

"I couldn't help myself," Haden said. "Every autumn, I would tell myself this was it, my final trek. I would leave you to decide your own fate, but the thought of you haunted my every waking thought. I couldn't bear to think of you in the arms of another. I knew I needed to let you go. We were burning through borrowed time, but I couldn't bring myself to stay away from you. With every stolen moment shared between the two of us, I could feel myself falling more and more in love with you. We carried on our little dalliance for three years, from the first orange leaf to the very last Olympian frost. Despite my growing feelings for you, I never pushed for more than companionship. When the day finally came that you told me you had an important decision to make, I felt like I couldn't breathe. I decided then I had to leave. I had been foolish to carry on this little game, and now it was time to move on. Just as I was readying myself to go back to the Underworld, you found me in the stables and confessed to me that you no longer wished to see me go, that you loved me and desired for me to take you back with me to the Underworld...so I did just that. I took you with me."

A bright smile upturned the corners of my lips, and a sense of deep, venerating love swept throughout my body, rattling awake slumbering memories that had been hidden deep within the brambles of my mind for centuries. Suddenly it all made sense—all of those dreams of running through golden fields of wheat with my dark god, playfully hiding behind trees, and spending afternoons with a book in my grasp and my head in his lap... Those had been during his visits to Olympus.

If I closed my eyes for long enough, I could still feel the ticklish blades of pasture grazing against the tips of my fingers. I could recall our laughter and see the bright flicker of fireflies glowing in the humid night air, the crisp scent of snowdrops and conifers as sweet as the one's in my waking life. I opened my eyes and found Haden staring at me with what appeared to be a fleeting look of hope.

"We left a note for Zeus, thinking he would tell Demeter, but he was unable to do so. Unbeknownst to us, Minthe, an old paramour of mine, had snuck into the castle and destroyed it before he ever had the opportunity of reading it. Not knowing what became of you, your mother fell into a deep depression. The first few months weren't that bad. It was barely noticeable, and then you began to show odd symptoms. It started with you wearing extra layers. Then, you became a little more fatigued, growing tired early in the day. I thought nothing of it. I assumed you were still adjusting to life in the Underworld. The land can be colder in certain regions, and time moves differently in each realm. Then, a staggering number of dead began to come off the ferry—more and more victims of starvation. I again dismissed it as nothing to take concern over. Mankind is a frail race. I figured it must have been because of some great war, or maybe a greedy king was charging too much for resources again. It wasn't until you fell ill, unable to eat or drink or keep yourself warm, that I began to worry. Awful shivers plagued you at all hours, and you seemed in excruciating pain. During one of Hermes' trips escorting the lost souls off Charon's boat, he asked if I had seen you and explained what was happening in the other realms. You overheard our conversation and decided you had to go back to Olympus. You told me no one else could reason with your mother, and I knew it to be true."

Memories of my other dreams, of those filled with horrible howling winds and frigid spikes of ice, began seeping into my mind. I was reminded of my vision in the Hall of Portraits. The world above had seemed so barren, so lifeless, and without color. I could remember how achingly tired I had felt in Haden's arms, how the blood in my veins had felt like frozen slush in my dreams. That same mask of agony Haden had worn in the throne room returned, storming across his features and making him appear like a dark, despairing angel.

"I did not want you to leave. I feared you would never return to me if I let you go, but I could not bear to see you beside yourself with so much guilt, and I did not wish to see you grow any sicker."

"So you let me go."

Haden met my gaze with a pained expression sharp enough to crack my heart in two.

"I had planned on escorting you back to Olympus the following morning, but you left in the dead of night. I suppose you thought you were doing me a kindness."

The two of us were quiet as I let his words seep in. I met his wounded gaze and felt tears filling my eyes. *What could I say? How could I fix what I had done?* There were no words capable of restoring lost time, of fixing an already broken heart. I swallowed back the lump in my throat and faced my husband.

"I'm sorry." I wept, tears sliding down my cheeks. No matter how valiantly I tried, I couldn't hold back the tears. Centuries of sealed-off emotions were seeping through the cracks of my broken mind, surging from me like a glacial torrent. I had never been so disgusted with myself.

"I-I didn't want to leave. I wanted to find my way back to you. Believe me when I say if there had been a-any other way, if I could have done anything differently, I-I would have."

I tore my gaze from him, angry that I couldn't get the words out without crying. Soon, my entire body was shaking from the intensity of my sobs. I could barely breathe. All I could feel was guilt. Sharp, rib-splitting guilt. I had hurt him—my greatest love. I had betrayed his trust—he who had known so little of happiness and love before me.

"Ánthos," Haden softly spoke, his voice like a flare calling me back to myself. "There is no need for you to apologize. What you did was selfless."

In two steps, he was there, cradling my face in his hands. With the pads of his thumbs he wiped away my falling tears.

"Had you not returned when you did, humanity would have surely ended, and all of Olympus would have faded in its wake. You saved the lives of billions."

He leaned forward and pressed his forehead against mine, causing my uneven breaths to settle.

"You didn't deserve that, though." I whimpered, shaking my head in upset. "I wanted to choose you, but I couldn't, and you never got to know that before I–"

Haden pulled me closer to him, his hands dropping from my cheeks to find themselves lost in my hair.

"Shh," he soothed. "None of that matters now."

"But it does," I argued. "I was gone for so long, Haden. I have only been awake for eight years now, and every second spent away from you has been excruciating for me. I can't imagine how painful this has been for you…not knowing whether I was alive or dead, and now that I'm back, this is what you get."

I pulled back from his grasp and gestured at myself in contempt.

"I am broken. A fragmented version of the goddess you fell in love with. I wear her face and possess her heart but I am not who you were expecting."

"I was expecting no one," he professed, a stern expression spreading across his face. "Do you know how many search parties Zeus organized for you throughout the years? How many I attended in hopes of finding you, only to return to the Underworld alone? I expected no one. Any hope I had of finding you in this life vanished ages ago. I aspired to have my thread cut by the Fates…to fade away into whatever oblivion you had. That was the only way I hoped to find you again. Seeing your face in that throne room, untouched by time and just as beautiful as the day I lost you, was everything I had pleaded would happen for over two thousand years. It matters little to me that your memory is clouded. Shards of broken pottery can be made whole again. If I nick myself in the process, so be it. We shall overcome this together."

I opened my mouth to protest but quickly found the words catching in my throat as Haden swept me up in his arms. He carried me bridal-style to the balcony doors and walked us back into our heated room.

"It is late," he spoke out, his voice a deep rumble against my side as he drew me nearer. "You should sleep. I will answer whatever other questions you have in the morning."

I wanted to argue. There was so much I still yearned to ask, but I kept quiet, unable to deny my climbing exhaustion. With great gentleness, Haden deposited me onto the giant bed, and I laid back against the pillows, my ginger curls fanning around me as I did so. My heart leapt inside my chest as I held his gaze.

"Where do you plan on sleeping?" I wondered.

A faint smile upturned the side of my dark god's lips as he lifted the strewn blankets and cast them over my body.

"Where do you want me to sleep?"

I eyed the other side of the bed that had yet to be touched and then looked back at him.

"I think this bed is big enough for the two of us should you decide to spend the rest of the night here with me."

"Then I shall sleep here."

I nodded my head in acceptance, and nervously scooted over. Haden strode around to the other side of the bed, blowing out each of the burning candles as he went. Bit by bit, darkness swallowed the room, and the lingering smell of smoke blended with the heady scent of roses until there wasn't a single ember left to illuminate the chamber.

Anxiously, I stared up at the bedroom ceiling and nipped at my bottom lip as I waited for him to join me in bed. The chamber was quiet. Still. Only the familiar hush of bed sheets being rearranged, and the sudden dip of the mattress indicated that my husband was still in the room with me at all.

"Good night, Persephone," Haden spoke into the darkness, his voice close and yet seemingly far away.

"Good night," I responded, turning on my side and eventually drifting off into sleep.

CHAPTER 36

POMEGRANATES AND GRAND DEPARTURES

"You've made up your mind then? There's no talking you out of this."
The hurt in his voice was unbearable. It wounded me to hear it, like a knife to the heart. Pityingly, I stretched out my hand, hoping to touch him, to beckon him back into my arms, but he was too fast. In an instant, my dark god was rising, throwing back the crimson blankets of our bed and cradling his head in his hands. A slip of space existed between us now as he sat on the edge of the bed. Such a trifling little sweep of distance, and yet, it somehow felt ever-growing, like a winding, monstrous ravine, or an invisible line etched in the sand, sundering us apart. *I hated it.*

I stared at his bare back and then at the empty spot where he had just been lying, unshed tears gathering in my eyes. I tried my best to swallow back the lump inside my throat, to summon forth a front of assurance. *I had to do this.* This was a discussion we could no longer avoid.

"Hades," I rasped, seeking his attention.

When he didn't look back at me, I willed myself to sit up, to make the trek across the mattress toward him. Pain seized my lungs, but I ignored it, mustering the strength to go on. I crawled across the bed with gritted teeth, spurning the ache in my withered muscles. Another wave of pain lanced through my lungs, growing sharper and sharper with every breath. I bit back a whimper and continued to drag myself onward, all but collapsing against him once I had made it to the edge of the bed. He was so warm it burned my frigid skin to touch him.

I pressed my forehead against his strong shoulder blades, my chest heaving from what should have been such a simple task. I stilled myself, giving my tired lungs a moment to rest before speaking.

"There...is...no other way."

A wave of lightheadedness rushed over me and darkness rimmed the edges of my vision. *I would not black out.* I squeezed my eyes shut. *I. Would. Not.*

Warm fingers curled around my forearm, pulling me from my determined thoughts.

"You're wrong," he lowly asserted.

I shook my head, not strong enough to raise my voice, to wield my words against his like I had done so many times before. It was all I could do to keep from crying out in frustration.

"Hades, I must. The earth is dying. Humanity is dying...I'm–"

"Don't you dare say it," he growled, whipping around to face me. "You are an Olympian. Ichor flows in your veins."

He held my arm up to my face, and I stared at the frigid, blue veins running up from my wrist. Mere days ago, I had been fair-skinned, with color in my cheeks and a brightness in my eyes. Now, I was ghostly pale—hollow-cheeked and cold to the touch, snowy streaks of white appearing in my once glossy curls.

"Whatever this is...it may yet be curable. We haven't exhausted every alternative. There is still much Hecate hasn't tried. You don't have to go. This is your home. You are my queen."

"Hades," I said again. "You know if I could...I would stay."

"But you won't. You have given up."

He released my arm and I took his face in my hands, gently stroking his bearded cheeks.

"I have a duty to the Realm of Man. Just as you, my love, are responsible for our subjects here. I cannot turn my back on them and let all life perish on Earth. I will not."

With a deep sigh, he rested his forehead against mine. He covered one of my small hands with his and held my fingers close, lightly gripping them as if he believed with enough effort, he could draw me into himself and hide me away from all those who sought to separate us. I wished he could, wished that our love could be enough to set right all the wrongs in the world.

"You know as good as I that Demeter will never be persuaded to give us her blessing. She will not let you return to the Underworld if you leave."

I peered up at him through my lashes and did my best to smile in defiance of the sorrow burrowing itself deep inside my chest, demanding that I cry senselessly and cling to him for all I was worth. I didn't want to go. He was right. *This was my home.* I belonged here with him, deep beneath the earth, amongst the shadows and misty dark, just as much as I belonged beside my mother, in every flowery meadow and quiet wooded glen. I could be a goddess of two realms. *I would be.*

"We will find a way. *I will* find my way back to you."

"How?" he demanded.

"I…"

I couldn't get the words out. They were stolen from me, taken alongside my breath as I was overwhelmed in a fit of coughing. A troubled look darkened Haden's features. He pulled away from me and gently lowered me back down against my pillows, pulling the blankets up over me as if I were an ailing child.

"We are done talking about this. You need to rest."

"Hades…no…I'm…"

More rib-splitting coughs wracked my body, wresting me silent.

"Rest," he said again, his tone unyielding. "I'll have Genevra bring you another ambrosia draft."

He swept a fading red lock behind my ear and I clung to his arms, trying to speak with my eyes as my coughing finally descended into quiet rasps. *No. Hades, please. We have to talk about this. I've rested enough!* He ignored my silent pleas, seemingly set in his decision, and stepped away from my reach. Angrily, I watched as he dressed and strode toward the door. He paused at the threshold and turned his attention back to me.

"I will be back," he promised, and then he was gone, shutting the door behind him.

I longed to scream myself mute, to kick and fume until I was red in the face, but I could not. I could do nothing. I was stuck in this bed. Confined to this room, too weak to even say more than a few words before being gagged by my own traitorous body. Wearily, I stared up at the red canopy above me and finally let myself cry. I wept and wept until my eyes were nearly swollen shut, and all I could do was hiccup my heartache out into the lonely room. Just as I was about to drift into a fitful sleep, the familiar sound of the chamber doors creaking open pierced the quiet. Using both of my elbows, I propped myself up, expecting to find my shadowy handmaiden. To my surprise, it was Haden who drifted into the room. In his grasp he was holding something round.

"I have a proposal for our predicament."

There was a slight dip in the mattress from his weight as he came to sit beside me. Weakly I shifted beneath the covers to make room for him. With loving fingers, he caressed the side of my face.

"I have no intention of losing you, Persephone. Not to your mother or this illness. You are mine, and I am yours. I will not go on without you. If I do as you wish, and I let you go, you must do something for me in return."

"Anything," I whispered.

From his cloak he pulled forth the round object, revealing a single, red pomegranate. Promptly, I caught on to his plan and felt a wide smile spreading across my lips. *How could I have not thought of this before? The food of the dead was our solution, our answered prayer!*

"Bind yourself to me, Persephone. Swear yourself to the realm."

From a furl of shadow, a glint of something silver materialized within my dark god's grasp. A pointed dagger. With the sharpened blade Hades cut into the fruit, exposing the seed-filled entrails of the pomegranate. He offered me a slice and with shaking, eager hands I took it, meeting his dark stare.

"You are mine and I am yours," I repeated, and then I brought the slice to my lips and bit down.

Tartness filled the inside of my mouth. I could feel the pomegranate's dark red juices gliding down my arms in sticky rivulets. It dribbled down my chin, and seeped through the white fabric of my nightgown, staining the material a deep shade of maroon. I couldn't find it in me to care. I was too overcome with delight. *We had done it. All was about to be right.* I swallowed seed after seed, and then all at once, like the burning of film, all the surrounding imagery around me began to crackle and fade, giving way to a blinding scene of white.

***

A warm, glare of light roused me from my sleep, prompting me to open my eyes. I could feel the sun's heat dancing upon my skin as I lazily stretched my arms, a drowsy yawn drifting past my lips. Outside the birds were chirping, and the sour tang of pomegranates still lingered on my tongue as I slowly came to.

It had all been a dream. Not a single wintry strand of hair shown in my ginger curls as I sat up and caught sight of myself in a trio of shining mirrors. Gone were my hollowed cheeks and thistle blue lips. I was the same as I had been the night before, just as freckle-faced and soft-bodied as ever.

Groggily, I let out a relieved sigh and grappled to gather my bearings. This was not my lofty upstairs bedroom. Nor was it the baroque-green suite I had found myself in yesterday. Sunlight poured in from a set of balcony doors, illuminating a gilded room scattered with rose petals. The sheets around me were not a rich, blood-red, but a pristine shade of white, and I was wrapped in a silky black robe. Memories of the night before filled my mind, and my heart launched into a nervous canter. I was in the bridal chambers. Last night had been my wedding night. *Haden...he...*

"Good morning," a husky voice greeted.

I turned and discovered my husband perched at the foot of the bed. He was just as he had been in my dream, devastatingly beautiful, with eyes so dark a shade of brown I felt certain I could lose myself in their depths. Only his hair was different now, an inch or so shorter, and more modernly cut. There was also a waning sense of weariness in his features that hadn't been there before, as if he hadn't soundly slept in eons. Regret picked at me as I studied his face. *I had caused that. I had been his nightly apparition, just as he had been mine.*

"Good morning," I said back, taking notice of his tousled, chocolate curls and dark pajamas.

A stirring of something like joy hustled beneath my ribs, causing my lips to lift into a bashful smile. *He had actually stayed.* After years of wishing, of ceaselessly pining for the chance to wake up beside him, here he was. *Alive. Breathing. Only an arm's length away.* My moment of bliss was short-lived, though, soon eclipsed by another, more worrisome thought, as it occurred to me he had been the first to wake.

My dreams were not soft-hued, whimsical, things, born of fanciful imaginings. They were vicious stirrings...devastating memories that left me tossing and turning all throughout the night. *What if I had woken him up? What if I had said something in my sleep to disturb him?* Guiltily, I met my husband's gaze once more. "Did I wake you?"

An immediate flash of something like sympathy softened my dark god's intent features.

"No," he reassured, rising from the bed. "I have always been somewhat of an early riser."

He turned away from me and I watched him stride across the room.

"Oh," I acknowledged, a slight smile returning to brighten my face. "Me too, although not by choice, I suppose."

"Not by choice?"

There was an edge of amusement in his voice. Even with his back turned to me, I could tell he was smiling, but there was also a touch of something else in his tone. A shred of displeasure that led me to believe his brow had furrowed in heedful curiosity.

"The Flower Patch opens at eight," I hurried to explain. "I am head cashier and flower arranger. I also do all the maintenance and upkeep of the shop. It's just me and Mom, and she handles all of the finances and other stuff, like plant care."

Haden made a thoughtful noise, the crossness in his shoulders waning by a smidgen.

"Well, rest assured you shall have no such obligations in the Underworld. The mornings will be yours to do with as you please. Not a single desire of yours will go unmet."

"I don't think I'll know what to do with myself," I admitted, nervously swiping my bangs out of the way of my eyes. I had never *not* had some sort of chore laid out for me to complete. In this life I had only ever been the mousy shopkeeper. *Who even was I beyond that? How would I go about finding myself in the Underworld?*

With curious eyes I watched him stop before a dresser, his hand reaching out to grab something off its surface. *A cup? No, a glass vial.*

"I have no doubts you'll come into your own rather expeditiously. You had no problems before."

Haden's gaze met mine and for a moment all I could see in his eyes was a storm of memories. Silence filled the room, neither of us quite certain what to say next. Eventually, he cleared his throat, and shifted his attention to the vial.

"This is for you," he said. "A maidservant brought it by this morning with an invitation to breakfast."

He offered me the vial and I accepted it, muttering a shy thank you before turning my attention to the item in my hands. It was a tiny thing, no bigger than a flask of perfume, made out of what appeared to be cut crystal and glass. A silky, blush ribbon was tied around its tear-shaped stopper, with a small bit of folded parchment dangling from the end. I examined the bottle, holding it up to the light just to watch the dianthus-pink liquid swirl and shine within. It was a pretty mixture, warm and alluring.

I unfolded the wheaten-colored note, detaching it from the dainty ribbon. I didn't recognize the hurried long-hand of whomever had penned the note. It reminded me of the efficient script of a doctor, written in a stunning rosette-tinted ink.

For best results drink as soon as possible. Can be blended with food or mixed with beverages. Take daily to prevent pregnancy.

Heat flared in my cheeks as I read the bottle's message once and then twice. The tonic Mom had mentioned to me last night, this was it. Quickly, I scrambled to discard the vial, clumsily shoving it into one of the deep pockets of Haden's robe to worry about later. If my husband noticed, he mercifully said nothing, nor did he seem inclined to ask what was within the vial. Whether the reason being because he already suspected it's contents, or he was simply allowing me my privacy I could not say. All the same, I was grateful for his patient silence. Rarely did Mom allow me such separateness. This would take some getting used to.

"So," I said, doing my best to appear put-together. "We've been invited to breakfast?"

A puckish smile tugged at the corners of Haden's lips.

"Yes," he answered. "Although, I'm afraid the kitchens may be serving crustless sandwiches in lieu of eggs and toast now."

Surprised, I peered at the lacquered clock quietly ticking across the room, its golden shorthand resting on the numeral eleven.

"Did I really sleep that late?" I wondered, shooting up from my sitting position and stumbling out of bed.

I had known I was tired, but I seemingly hadn't registered to what extent. Normally, I was up with the sun, dressed, and ready to begin my day. Sleeping in until noon was an oddity for me, although I supposed I could blame it on adrenal fatigue and maybe even supernatural jet lag. The past couple of days had been more than a little hectic. Portal travel certainly hadn't been the greatest experience. Despite Avril's hearty vote of confidence the night before, I was definitely not looking forward to doing it again. Maybe if I was lucky, Haden *would* opt for a less overwhelming form of travel. If such a thing even existed. Hertha's snide suggestion of a carriage drawn by flying horses didn't seem all that cozy either.

He shrugged his shoulders, his expression still one of amusement.

"It seems you needed it. I couldn't be bothered to wake you, either."

He took several leisurely steps forward until he was standing before me. Lightly he fingered a piece of my hair, an overwhelming look of awe burning bright in his eyes as he watched the sun play through my copper waves.

"I haven't had the favor of seeing your hair this wild in centuries."

Another searing blush crept across my face, and for a moment I forgot how to speak.

I often detested my wayward curls, doing all I could to brush them into compliance, but today, beneath his gaze… I was beginning to wonder if perhaps I had been wrong in judging them so harshly. Never had I seen anyone seem so completely and utterly bewitched by just my hair. The way he was staring at me had my heart stalling in my chest. He missed nothing. He drank me in like wine. Slow and luxuriating, careful not to rush, as if he were determined to commit this moment to memory. I couldn't help but to let my gaze linger as well.

He was so tall. Taller then I'd even realized before. I barely came to his chest. I had to remind myself to breathe as I felt the tether between us crackling to life. *Lunch. You need to get ready for lunch*, I thought to myself, but I couldn't seem to remember how to move. My feet remained rooted in place, my thoughts askew.

What would it feel like, I wondered, to have his hands fully fisted in my hair...to feel the entirety of his body pressed against mine? Goosebumps sprung to the surface of my skin, and a restless, catching heat wavered in my lower abdomen, spreading across the rest of my body like a fever.

"It needs a hairbrush," I contended, shaking myself free from the tether's influence. "I should go get ready."

With a nervous smile, I backed away from Haden and scurried out of the bedroom door before I could be persuaded to do anything I might regret. I staggered into the hallway and promptly bolted myself inside the bathroom, my chest heaving. I took a few steadying breaths and approached the sink, turning on the golden faucet. A jet of water shot out and I splashed my face several times, letting the cold spray douse the fire in my veins before finally turning off the running sink and drifting over to the bath. I sat on the lip of the tub and exhaled, shakily running my fingers through my hair. What a dangerous thing our tether was becoming...tempestuous and wild. It drove me to think rather uncharacteristic thoughts. Thoughts I had no clue what to do with. The temptation to surrender myself to its demands was compelling, but not nearly as strong as my fear of doing something wrong. All prior knowledge, if any, of being intimate had vanished with the rest of my memories. I was self-conscious and even worse, mortifyingly self-denying.

I had never had the opportunity to date before. Mom was as puritanical as they came, and no one had ever managed to catch my eye within our small, southern isle. I had willfully kept my heart reserved, blind to any admiring eyes. Even when Haden had existed only as a drawing within the pages of my secret journal, I think some ancient part of me had always been saving myself for him, this mysterious god who visited me in my dreams.

My gaze shifted to my reflection, to the copper-haired goddess before me, dressed in a lacey gown of purple, a black robe hanging from her shoulders like a dark, contrasting cape. Curiously, I rose from the lip of the tub and trailed my fingers down to toy with the fastened sash around my waist, tugging just so until a little bit more of my physique could be seen in the laurel-leaf mirror. Through the sheerness of my gown I noticed my breasts, round and magnolia-white, like two lace-covered bells. Lower down, I could catch glimpses of my stomach, untoned and rubenesque. I knew if I were to turn just a little, I would find dimpled skin along my upper thighs, and old, silvery stretch marks. This was the body I knew. The body I had seen time and time again. What if I looked different now than I did before? Could I be skinnier…more plump? Did my body still pique his interest?

He wouldn't look at you so idolizing if he didn't find you pretty, some sensible part of me chided. *He also called you beautiful yesterday. Multiple times!*

My thoughts drifted back to the night before, to our moment out on the balcony. He had felt the tether between us. I knew he had. I could feel the yearning in his blood as clearly as if it were my own, and yet there had been a rippling of reluctance in him too. The opportunity to kiss me–to do much more than that–had presented itself, and he, while equally enticed, seemed to be holding himself back. *Why?* Was he just trying to be chivalrous, or could it be for the same reasons as me? Was he afraid I wasn't attracted to him anymore? No, that couldn't be it. Anyone with eyes could see I was more than a little mesmerized by him. *Perhaps he simply did not want to touch me until my memories were fully restored.* A pang of hurt bore through my chest at the thought. There was no guarantee even this Mnemosyne would be able to fix everything. Whatever concourses she and I would have together in the near-future would all be merely efforts, not sureties.

The feel of something hard jabbed against my hip, pulling me from my troubled thoughts. I fished inside Haden's robe pocket and retrieved the glass vial, its liquid sparkling fuchsia in the sunlight. I debated opening the bottle and chugging it, and then decided against it. There was no need to take the draft now. Nothing had happened last night, and the note hadn't come with a best by date. I would save it.

Inhaling, I wandered back over to the sink to actually get ready. Determined to shake all feelings of bleakness from my mind, I picked up the heavy comb and drug it through my hair, and then rummaged around one of the drawers for something to tie it back. Like the toothpaste from last night, at first glance I found nothing, and then, like magic, an assortment of colorful hair ties appeared next, as if my very thoughts had conjured them into being.

I stared at them, momentarily befuddled, and then finally picked a claret-colored band from the pile, pulling my hair up into a loose ponytail. Once satisfied with my appearance, I wended my way over to the closet Mom had vanished into last night. I eyed the golden doors distrustfully, thinking back on the wardrobe in the bedchambers and its abundance of sheer lace and lingerie. *What would I find in here?* I loosened the rest of the sash of Haden's robe from around my waist and flung open the doors. I was met with a burst of color. All around me, articles of clothing hung from satin hangers. I looked over a beryl green romper with puffed sleeves, and then a flowery, yellow, mini dress. A selection of jeans caught my eye, and I let out a relieved sigh at the appearance of multiple simple tees and frilled skirts. Thank the gods Avril hadn't gotten carried away selecting my day-to-day wear. I settled on a pleated periwinkle blouse and a pair of cuffed capri pants, tugging them on and then jumping into a set of white slip-ons. On my way out of the closet, I snatched a brown satchel bag off a peg and shoved the vial inside, draping Haden's robe across my other arm as I sauntered toward the washroom door, ready to make my grand departure from Olympus.

CHAPTER 37
THE LUNCHEON

Stepping back into our chambers, I was surprised to find the room completely rearranged. The disheveled white sheets of our bed were aptly tucked back into place, and all of the vermilion-red rose petals were gone, leaving behind only a luxuriantly polished floor. The wide array of candles that had been scattered about the room, left to burn for most of the night, had also vanished, replaced with new pillars of untouched wax.

It was as if we had never set foot inside the intimately designed boudoir, I thought to myself. Everything was perfect, organized and situated just so that it could almost pass for an entirely different room in the daylight. A maid must have crept in while we were away, I figured. Or, perhaps the room was as magical as everything else in the palace, enchanted to clean up after its newly-wed guests. I could only wonder as my gaze drifted from all the furnishings to linger on my dark god.

He was standing before the balcony doors, now fully dressed in an arrangement of modern clothes one wouldn't suspect the Lord of Souls to wear. A pair of black denim jeans had taken the place of his sleek pajama bottoms, and a simple button-down shirt as dark as pitch covered his torso. Two shiny black boots peeked from underneath his pants hem, and he seemed to be wrestling with a pair of silver cufflinks. Gently, I shut the door behind me and padded across the room, tossing Haden's robe onto the giant bed.

"Here," I offered, bashfully making my way across the room toward him.. "Let me."

With nervous fingers, I took his arm in my hand, and he offered me one of the cuff links. I grabbed it, studying the heavy bit of metal for a moment before guiding it through each of the sleeve openings. The emblem of a ferocious three-headed canine stared back at me from his unfastened sleeves, each of their mouths open in a daunting, fanged growl.

"What sort of Creature is this?" I asked softly, recognizing the wide forehead and powerful jaws of something reminiscent of a wolf, but much larger and far more terrifying.

"Hm?" Haden hummed, his attention seeming to return from some far off place. Some place like the past, I imagined, where the freckled hands he had been so studiously watching were mine, but also someone else's. Someone who was not so shy to reach out and touch him, to bask in the blazing heat of our tether. "Oh, that is Cerberus. He is the guardian of our kingdom, and the sigil of our realm."

Cerberus. I pondered over the name, trying to remember where I had heard it before, and then recalled hearing Avril briefly mention it to Mom, right before the ceremony.

"He certainly looks intimidating."

A light chuckle resounded from my dark god.

"He's an oversized lap dog. There are butterflies more ferocious than Cerberus. You used to weave him collars made entirely of blossoms, and he would sit at his post, looking every bit a flowery menace."

I quirked an incredulous brow in Haden's direction, amazed that I had ever been brave enough to go near such a fearsome-looking beast, and cracked a half smile.

"So this Cerberus, is he just a guard dog of yours, or also a pet?"

A sliver of excitement shot through me at the thought of having an animal of my own to love and pamper, even if it were a giant, preternatural wolf. Mom had never been a fan of keeping indoor pets. She had always said, *Animals are naturally inclined to be wild, Perrie. It's cruel to shackle them with collars, and take them away from the outside world.* Having some inkling of how a canary must feel, never to know anything beyond the snug bars of a cage, I had dropped the subject, thinking to myself that perhaps she was right. A small, fenced-in life paled in comparison to the wild, open beyond. Funny how in the blink of an eye, all of that was about to change. I was no longer living within the same safe enclosure. I was free, moments away from facing the wide unknown for myself.

"He is a member of *our* household," Haden replied, drawing me from my thoughts. "Just as much a companion of yours as he is mine. He will obey whatever command you give him, and guard you with his life. He does, however, have a penchant for table scraps, and will try his hardest to woo you for your supper. You mustn't give in to his begging, no matter how heart-rending his expression."

"You seem to be speaking from experience." I smiled, peeking up at him from beneath my lashes for only a heartbeat before returning my gaze to his sleeves.

"Yes," Haden sighed, a slight smirk tugging at the corners of his lips. "I have only ever known two beings I could deny nothing: one, being Cerberus, and the other, you."

A furious blush reddened my cheeks at the sound of his low, rather serious response. It was enough to make my toes curl, to muddle my thoughts and set my pulse to hurtling. I doubled down on straightening his cufflinks, pretending to be totally absorbed in my work.

"You've had him for a long time then?" I carried on, interested to hear more.

"Since the war. He was just a pup then. I found him living in the remnants of a destroyed den. His mother and the rest of his kin had been slain, their bodies buried beneath a pile of caved-in rocks. Only he remained, a survivor amongst the ruin. I did not have it in me to leave him, this little beast of the wood who reminded me so much of myself, a youth forced to live in a world on fire. In a lot of ways, we grew up together, he and I. I have, thus, allowed a few bad habits of his to go unpunished."

Another genuine smile danced across my lips upon hearing my husband go on to talk about this supernatural hound. *His* hound. There was such warmth in his voice, so abundant a sense of love, that I couldn't help but find myself growing even more enamored by him. I liked this softer side of this immortal king who greatly cared for his kingdom and was ardent about his dog.

"Speaking of meals, you must be starving," Haden suddenly said, robbing me of the chance to ask him any further questions.

"Oh, um…" I blinked, and then took a few awkward steps back, putting a respectable amount of distance between us once more now that I was done fixing his sleeves. Somehow I had forgotten we were meant to be leaving. I had been so engrossed in his tale, in hearing him speak, I had forgotten we had a schedule to keep. With a half grin I shrugged my shoulders.

"I could eat. Maybe just a bite or two, though. I honestly haven't been all that hungry lately."

Haden nodded his head in quiet understanding.

"You've been through a lot. I can imagine food has been the last thing on your mind. We can always grab something in Rome if you'd prefer."

An apologetic look leached at the humor shining in his brown eyes, and I could tell just by his change in posture that he was blaming himself for any anxiety felt on my part. I opened my lips to speak, to assure him that he was not entirely to blame for my lack of an appetite, but with a smile that didn't quite meet his eyes he filled the silence drifting between us.

"It will not always be like this."

Ever so gently, he took both of my hands in his, and his serious gaze caught mine, pinning me in place.

"I will do all that I can to reacquaint you with a sense of normalcy, to make you feel safe with me, Persephone."

"I do feel safe," I responded, my thumb rubbing against his in that same abating pattern as the one he had brushed against mine last night.

It was the truth. In spite of it all, it was with him I felt the most at ease. Rationally, I knew I shouldn't. We were little more than strangers now, and yet there was no roiling sense of unease begging me to run, to flee, to put as much distance between himself and I as possible. If anything, I felt quite the opposite. I wanted to be closer–needed to be.

A brief flash of something like relief brightened his eyes, and for a moment I thought he might kiss me. His gaze lingered on my lips and my breath hitched. I angled my head closer and waited, my heart leaping with anticipation. He drew back and cleared his throat, and I did my best to convince myself that I wasn't actually disconcerted.

"I can barely bring myself to partake of much at present, either. It would seem I have forgotten just how…"

He paused, his lips curling into that familiar, puckish grin I was beginning to notice he donned only when he felt like saying something particularly devilish.

"…*sweet* Olympian meals are in comparison to the fare of our kingdom."

Memories of last night's banquet flashed before my eyes. There had been so many plates set before us, each dish more plentiful and exquisitely served than the last. I could hardly remember what all I had and hadn't sampled. From what I could recall, none of it had tasted horrible. The sauteed broccoli I had tried tasted like finely prepared broccoli, and the red macron I had nibbled on had both a sweet and sour taste, like sugar mixed with raspberries. Not a single bite of anything had struck me as bad.

"Is the food of the dead really all that much different than the food served here?" I tried to imagine what sort of meals I would soon find myself dining on in the Underworld.

An amused glint sparked in his eyes, and he leveled that mischievous grin in my direction.

"You'll come to find that almost all things are done in reflection of the realm in which you are in. Olympus is renowned for its superfluousness. Therefore everything, right down to how much salt is sprinkled over a dish is done in abundance. In the Underworld, things are done a bit differently. In spite of being the richest of the three immortal kings, I am a god of simple tastes. I do not find myself requiring such excess all the time, nor do I find it necessary to make every little orifice of my kingdom a spectacle."

He released my hands and offered me his arm. I took it, following him across the room and toward the embellished white door of our chambers.

"I look forward to returning home then," I truthfully admitted, giving all the gold leaf furnishings and glittering baubles that adorned our chambers one last look over before stepping across the threshold and out into the hallway.

My father's kingdom was breathtaking. There was no denying that. Nothing in the mortal world compared to it, and yet, I had found no true solace here, within these castle walls. That same stifling feeling I had felt at Saint Simons dwelled in the brickwork. It sparkled in the crystal chandeliers, and showed itself in the many shining suits of armor. Olympus was a cage. A much larger, beautifully designed one, but a cage nonetheless. I had never been meant to stay here, to live such a fanciful life. Some place else beckoned to me, and I was ready to finally return, to step foot upon its shores.

***

It didn't take very long for Haden and I to descend the many tower steps. Hand in hand, we drifted past the cozy parlor of last night and out into the bright outdoors. Birds chirped from the boughs of fir trees and stumpy looking oaks, and a slight alpine wind drifted through the ivory columns of the colonnade, fluttering through my hair as we made our way through the winding passageway. After some time of peaceful walking we came upon a large arched door frame. Two glass doors, trimmed in whirls of royal gold, stood before us.

Through the glass I could just make out the silhouette of my father, sitting and laughing at the head of a large table. Other gods sat scattered around him, and to his right I noticed the limber shape of my mother, her hands steepled and her lips drawn into a slight smile as she listened to the commotion around her. Beside her, Avril laughed as well, her attention fixed onto her son, who had his arm draped around Prilla's shoulders. A rosy blush colored his cheeks, prompting me to believe he must have been the subject of their hearty discussion. Across from him, Daniel was slumped in his chair, looking rather green around the gills, and still dressed in last night's attire, clearly nursing a hangover by the looks of it, but amused all the same to be there. They all seemed so happy, so content in one another's company. It caused my chest to ache. I had dreamt of this, wanted so badly to be a part of a family like that. Bit by bit the fear I had felt for Mom lessened, dwindling down into a faint flurry of concern. It felt like a weight being lifted from my shoulders. She would be fine. Whether she realized it or not, she still had friends here. She didn't have to be alone. I could trust her to be alright without me.

In the next breath, the scene before me was changing, the atmosphere of the luncheon shifting into something else as Haden reached forward and grabbed one of the door handles. He pulled the gilded door open and gestured for me to step ahead of him. I did as he suggested, and walked across the threshold. The space I entered next was grand. All around the paneled walls were colored an exquisite shade of yellow, and a scent tickled my nose, that of freshly prepared bread and something else, something that smelled heavily of butter and herbs. Large, floor-to-ceiling windows illuminated the enormous dining room, filling the space with welcoming beams of light. Like the doors, the long table seating both of my parents and the others was made almost entirely out of glass, save for its golden claw-footed legs. Everyone stopped their jesting, the rhythmic clatter of their silverware going quiet as they shifted their attention to me. My heart leapt inside my throat, and I offered each of the gods a bashful smile as I fumbled to find the right words to say. *Would good morning suffice, or good evening?* Before I had the chance to stitch together something, two warm hands were resting atop my shoulders, pulling me into a blend of cedar and smoke. I relaxed my tense posture, feeling an unexplainable sense of calm sweeping across me, as I allowed myself to recline against Haden's chest.

"Apologies for our late arrival, adelphoi. It would seem Eos's light slipped past us this morning."

A wide grin upturned my father's lips, and a seemingly pleased twinkle shined in his cyan eyes as he titled his goblet back and took several jaunty gulps.

"Bah, no need for apologies," he declared, waving his hands about dismissively. "Not even Nyx herself could have wrested me from the arms of my yineka when I was newly married. It is a wondrous spell, the honeymoon."

He took another deep swallow of his drink. "Enjoy it. Drunken yourself on its sweetness, for it is fleeting."

I watched as his gaze shifted in the direction of the empty chair positioned at the far end of the table. A momentary look of something akin to self-reproach darkened my father's jolly features as he studied the untouched place setting, and then, as fast as the passing of a cloud blotting out the sun, the expression vanished from his face. He smiled at us once more and sat down his glass.

"Shall I call for one of the kitchen boys? Would either of you like a slice of squash galette before leaving for the City of Seven Hills? It's quite good, if I might say so myself. Almost as good as if the goddess of harvest herself had grown it," Zane boasted, earning a small, appreciative smile from Mom, her navy eyes lifting from her plate to meet mine from across the room.

Through her worried gaze, I could easily decipher her thoughts. *Are you alright? Is there anything I can do for you? Are you hungry? Did you get enough rest?* I shot her a reassuring smile, hoping to put her panicked mind at ease, and the concern in her stare seemed to lessen by a smidge, her body visibly relaxing in her chair. Beside her, Avril tossed Mom a cheeky look, a told-you-so smirk brightening her face as she took dainty, lady-like sips from a porcelain teacup.

"Thank you for the offer, adelphoi, but I am afraid we must decline. I arranged for Charon to meet us exactly at high noon in Lazio."

"Very well," Zane conceded, setting aside a silk napkin and scooting his chair back from the table. "Do tell Mother hello for me if you see her. Rumor has it she likes to frequent the Roman Forum in the summer."

He rose from the table and drifted over toward us.

"Of course," Haden responded. "Although I have my doubts we will see her."

"As do I, but one can hope."

Roughly, he clasped one hand on Haden's shoulder in brotherly farewell.

"Now, I must be off. I have a meeting with Cheiron. He mentioned something about having some news regarding those Harpies. I will keep in touch."

He turned away from us, his gaze flitting in the direction of my cinnamon-haired sister.

"Avril, my sweet, I trust that you can see your sister off?"

"Of course, Daddy." Avril beamed, standing up from her place at the table.

Zane nodded his head contentedly and bid us all adieu one last time, giving my hand a light peck before exiting through the glass doors.

There was a short spell of quiet shared between the seven of us, and then in a flash of purple and pink Avril was there, pulling me into a joyous hug.

"I take it the two of you had a good night?" she asked, a mischievous light sparkling in her ocean eyes as she stepped back to read my face.

"Yes," I blushed. "It was very…" I paused, looking down at my shoes as I searched for the right word. "Enlightening."

"Oh, I'm sure it was." Daniel grinned, looking my husband up and down with a flirtatious expression that had a mild spike of jealousy blooming in the pit of my stomach. Haden, however, seemed oblivious to the god of wine's presence. His dark regard was set only on my smiling sister, a handsome glower settling across his features.

"She hated the night clothes," he said, drawing Avril's attention upon him.

Contemptuously, she placed both hands on her hips, not a trace of intimidation in her stance.

"But they looked ravishing on her, I have no doubt. I picked only the most complimentary pieces."

"I will be buying her new ones."

Avril harrumphed in response, as if she couldn't believe what she were hearing, and tossed a lock of her auburn hair behind her shoulder.

"Go right ahead, darling. Just know, I will not be taking any of them back." She turned her pretty gaze back on me and smiled sweetly. "They were a gift. Besides, you might find yourself taking a liking to them after some time."

She gave me a scandalous wink and then spun on her heel, gesturing for us to follow her through an arched threshold.

"Come along then. Let's get you two to Rome."

CHAPTER 38
THE ROOM OF PIER GLASS

Heart in my throat, I trailed behind the goddess of love, a titillating sense of nervousness nipping at my fingertips as we glided from space to space, past astonishing works of palace art and down sunlit hallways.

I didn't allow my eyes a second to wander, to linger over anything but the swaying, cinnamon locks of my sister's hair. I was determined not to lose track of her, to allow myself even a moment to fall behind. We were so close … so nearly there to setting out on our own. Every footfall was an overture, a prelude. The farther we drifted from the dining room, the closer we were to the honeymoon, to beginning our new life. I was equal parts terrified and eager, restless and inspirited to get to this portal.

What would it be like, I wondered. Would the cobble-stoned streets of Rome smell as I had always imagined… of pastries, and cigarettes, and ocean brine? What would we see? Would returning there, to this ancient city so beloved by the gods, bring life to more buried memories? I hoped so. I hoped with a ferocity so wanting it almost hurt.

The distinct feeling of having Haden's fingers interlaced with mine, warm and close, had me wanting to quicken my pace, to hurry us along. I couldn't explain it, but some silly, overwrought part of me was fearful. More than once I had to fight the nagging urge to glance over my shoulder, to tug him closer and grip his hand tighter in mine. What if something stopped us from getting there? What if some monster like the Harpy flew in through the windows and snatched me up last second, or the ground beneath our feet suddenly burst open and swallowed us all whole? What if, what if, what if.

I was being irrational. Around me was an entire group of very powerful, very primeval, gods. Surely any well-trained assailant would know better than to try anything now...and yet, it was hard to dismiss such thoughts. Especially when I knew there were forces out there that wanted to keep us apart, some god or Creature determined to see me dethroned and barred from the Underworld. Not knowing when they would strike next, if they would strike at all, horrified me. I was afraid of making a reckless mistake, of losing my dark god once more by letting myself become too at ease.

If we could just make it to the portal and back into the Realm of Man, all would be fine, I reassured myself. I would be able to breathe a little easier, knowing we had made it through one big hurdle without anything bad happening, and...and I really was being ridiculous. Thinking the portal could rid us of those dangers was as nonsensical a theory as burrowing yourself beneath your blankets in the hopes of duping the boogie man into thinking you'd vanished. It was, after all, in the human realm where the flock had found me. Nowhere but the Underworld was truly safe, and I would be there soon enough. In the meantime, I just needed to relax.

Restlessly, I did my best to suck in a few deep breaths, hoping to appear more composed on the outside than I truly felt on the inside. So very soon it would be just the two of us, with an entire month at our disposal to do with what we desired. I urged myself instead to think of those thirty days. Visions of intimate walks on Italian beaches, of candle-lit dinners, and days spent together sharing the same space filled my mind, causing my ears to burn and a slight flush to color my cheeks. Haden and I had only been around each other for a little less than forty-eight hours and I had already had to lock myself inside a bathroom to hide from the dizzying force of our tether. It wavered between us now, heady and alive, like an invisible sputtering spark waiting to catch flame. How much longer would I be able to evade its sway before giving in and losing myself to its siren song? How much longer could he? Once off Olympian soil would we truly begin to act as a newlywed couple? My heart pounded even wilder in my chest at the thought.

"I quite enjoyed staying at the Belmond Hotel Cipriana," Avril said happily, talking to whom in our little group of seven I wasn't quite so sure. She had been chattering off and on for several minutes now, and I had been too engrossed in my own thoughts to comprehend much of what she had been saying to the group.

"Henry and I had a wondrous time there on our one-millennium anniversary. Oh, and you really must take her to the AquaFlor Firenze, Haden! For a human establishment, it's really quite nice."

"Why in the Ourea would they want to go make perfume on their honeymoon, Aphrodite? I would expect a goddess of your disposition to suggest somewhere more, oh, I don't know, erotic," Daniel retorted.

"And what would you know of sensual places to visit? Last time I checked you have yet to find your fated match."

Daniel snorted and gave Avril a rather impish look, like that of a little brother delighting in the aggravation of an older sibling. "Be that as it may, I have sampled enough of married life to understand the honeymoon should be spent doing wickedly amusing activities with one another, not something humans would take their grandmothers to do."

Avril opened her mouth, a fiery comeback ready to spring forth from her lips just as Prilla bashfully tuned in, "We enjoyed the Saturnia in Tuscany." She leaned in closer to Cam and rested her curly-brown head atop his shoulder. "The water nymphs there treated us to the best ambrosia-glazed salt water taffy."

"Now that could be fun," Daniel grinned, flashing Haden and I a devilish smirk. "Hot springs are always entertaining, and if you truly want anyone's opinion on what to do on a honeymoon, it would be theirs." The god of wine made a gagging sound and gestured behind us to the young couple. "Believe it or not, Eros and Psyche have only been living in Olympus for little more than a decade now. They just recently returned from their very own honeymoon."

Perplexed, I turned back to study the spouses strolling behind us.

"But the two of you have been together for hundreds of years, haven't you?"

A brilliant smile illuminated the goddess of soul's face and a contented gleam shone in Cam's eyes.

"We have been, yes," he answered, bringing Prilla's hand to his lips.

"Then how… Why would you need…"

"Time works differently for us, darling," Avril responded. "For those of us who are lucky enough to be fated, the vehemence of the tether can be–"

"Nothing short of obnoxious for the rest of us who have to be within your vicinity," Daniel cut in. "Most fated immortals choose to take some time away from Olympus to let the bond run its course, and then return when they are able to think about more than their koinonos."

"A-and how long is that, usually?" I asked, a wave of heat tinging my cheeks once again.

My question was met by an unknowing silence.

"It's different for everyone," Avril finally acknowledged.

Daniel nodded his head in agreement. "Cam and Prilla are still as besotted as two teenagers, and don't even get me started on her." Dramatically, the god of wine waved his hand in the direction of my sister. "You'd think she and Hephaestus just laced threads by the way they carry on. I don't think they can be in the same room for more than a second without touching, and as for you two… Well, let's just say the tension in the room won't be so thick you could slice it with a knife once you're gone."

The fading pink in my cheeks returned, flaring in heated waves of red. Embarrassedly, I tucked a strand of hair behind my ear with my free hand, and dared a glance in my husband's direction to see what he made of all the conversation. His face was a guise of steely indifference. He appeared as if he cared very little about what the other gods were saying. His eyes, though… They told a very different story. A myriad of emotions seemed to be warring in his dark pupils, burning bright like two fiery coals. He was afraid, I realized. Maybe just as much as I was. Suddenly it dawned on me just how tight his grip was, how close his body was to mine, as if he too were waiting for a thief to run off with our happiness. I wondered if he'd taken his gaze off of me once.

With great empathy I gave his hand a brief squeeze, lightly brushing my thumb across his, tracing on his skin our secret language. *I'm here. I'm scared, too.*

"The tether is a beautiful thing," Mom interjected, breaking her silence after quite some while of quiet walking. "It is a sacred bond. Be proud you are among the few who get to experience it, Perrie."

She shot Daniel a disproving glower and he only smiled, amused.

"Am I wrong, though?"

"Always," Avril teased, stopping before a beautiful, bronze mirror.

She cleared her throat and glanced into the floor-length glass, her lovely reflection staring back at her as she said, "Patefio."

Much like in the Hall of Portraits, resplendent beams of golden light burst from around the mirror's edges, and a silvery rippling appeared across the mirror's glassy surface, like a stone being cast into a lake. The glow brightened, growing brighter and brighter until standing before us was nothing more than a gaping, arched entryway. Wafts of cold air drifted out into the hallway, pimpling my skin, and the smell of lichen and damp masonry filled the air. Beyond, a dimly lit chamber waited, and I could hear the distant howling of the wind echoing inside the chamber. This doorway was not like the others. Something as ancient and as powerful as the goblet, as the dagger resided here. It lived in the very mountain this palace was built on. This was the true heart of Olympus, the source of its power.

Confident as ever, Avril sashayed inside the room. The others soon trailed after her, leaving only myself, Haden, and Mom behind. I stared at the archway and gulped.

"Are you ready?" Haden whispered, his lips dangerously close to the shell of my ear.

A shiver scampered down my spine as I studied the archway's stonework, the sound of the wind still ominously humming in my ears. I curled my fingers tighter around his and nodded my head.

"Y-yes."

Together, the two of us crossed the threshold and Mom followed behind us, the open entrance to the chamber magically sealing itself shut once we were all inside, leaving only a mirror in its place. Inside, I was surprised to find how rugged the space was. I had grown used to seeing lavish centerpieces and chandeliers dripping with diamonds. This part of Olympus was like no other.

Above us loomed a cavern-like ceiling, its rocky surface not so unlike that of the cold, hewn floor beneath our feet. Stone sconces in the form of eagles were mounted on the walls, their taloned feet gripping lit torches. Not a single piece of furniture occupied the space. A collection of all-encompassing mirrors encircled the walls, their glass surfaces ebbing and flowing with vibrant swirls of magic. It was breathtaking and frightening. So many colors danced before my eyes, each a different shade and more vivid than any I had ever seen in the mortal world, many I didn't even have the name for.

The longer I peered into the mirrors, the more the room seemed to crackle with tiny sparks of electricity. Before I knew it, I felt myself moving. I was walking hand in hand with Haden, heading toward one of the many mirrors. We stopped before one that was positioned in the center of the room, the stone figure of a god half covered by a gathering of clouds and holding a lightning bolt in his hand decorating the top of the pier glass. A flash of something blue, something that looked like an ocean flickered within, and then quickly morphed into something else: a craggy jut of land, then a city filled with twinkling lights. Again and again the images changed. I saw orchards of olive trees, and fields of orchids, and the timeless outline of the columned Colosseum. I was staring at Rome. This was our portal.

I tore my attention away from the pier glass to find everyone staring at us. Cam and Prilla were the first to rush ahead and hug us each.

"Be safe," Prilla muttered into my hair, hugging me close and then stepping away.

"And don't forget to bring us back some of those taffies," Cam grinned, hugging me just as constrictingly tight as the first time we met at the rental house.

From across the room Daniel flashed us a mischievous smile, not bothering to venture from his spot.

"Whatever you do, don't waste your time making perfumes," he winked, earning an offended scoff from Avril.

She waltzed toward us with tears in her ocean eyes and a dazzling smile on her beautiful face.

"Don't make me wait another millennium before coming to visit me again!" She sniffled, adjusting my hair and kissing both of my cheeks. "And you." She pointed a manicured finger in Haden's direction. "Don't be a stick in the mud."

A ghost of a grin tugged at the corner of Haden's lips, and he inclined his head in what I presumed to be a gesture of goodwill.

A smile of my own overtook my face and I shook my head in agreeance. "I'll do my best not to keep you waiting too long."

She gave us one last knowing smile and then wended her way across the room to stand beside her son.

Mom was the last to step forward. She was, of course, crying, which only caused the lump in my throat to grow. Quickly, she brushed away her tears and gathered me into a tight hug. I hugged her back, bone breakingly tight, the familiar smell of her honeysuckle perfume lingering between us. Even though I knew I'd see her again, and that she would be alright on her own, it felt wrong leaving her here. She was the first to break away from our embrace, trailing her fingers through my hair and kissing the top of my head. She smiled at me tenderly, and gently wiped away the tears sliding down my cheeks.

"I'll see you in a month, my little fawn," she promised. "Be safe, call me if you need anything, and remember that I'll love you always. No matter what."

"I love you too, Mom. You be safe."

The sudden touch of Haden's fingers gliding down the nape of my neck had me starting. I turned back to look at him.

"It is time," he said softly, "The portal is ready."

I nodded in understanding and furiously rubbed the heels of my hands into my eyes to try and stop my crying. What an attractive bride I must be, all red eyed and puffy faced. He ushered me toward the portal where a street made of cobblestone appeared in the glass. Colorful buildings lined the street there and baskets of flowers were hanging from the windows. It was beautiful, everything I'd imagined it might be.

"Together," Haden whispered, walking us forward, his arm snaking protectively around my waist.

I looked again at the portal, at the shimmering shape of Italian cypress trees and the long-forgotten ruins bleached white from the sun, and felt an odd stirring within my chest. A warm feeling came over me, one that blossomed through the spinous thorns that spiraled around the memories I could not yet reach, and pierced through the furling black shadows that darkened my mind. *Hope.* It was hope that gave me courage to be here, that had driven me to journey across worlds and race against time. It was the voice inside me now, that shining, incandescent beam of light that promised me everything would be alright. *I could do this.* As long as I believed, nothing was impossible.

"Together," I repeated, squeezing my eyes shut as we stepped through the glass, vanishing into a tempest of whirling wind, jumbled sound, and electric color.

www.ingramcontent.com/pod-product-compliance
Lightning Source LLC
LaVergne TN
LVHW021809060526
838201LV00058B/3296